PRAIS
FAMILY

T0005520

"The Marte sisters—Matilde, Flor, Pastora, and Camila—live at the center of Elizabeth Acevedo's prismatic new novel, *Family Lore*, a labyrinthine tale of sisterhood and the chaos of love. . . . The depth, grace, and nuance Acevedo gives her characters is palpable; her love for these women comes through with arresting clarity. . . . Pearls of magic and wisdom, hard but not hardened, the story of the Marte sisters is a treasure to behold."
—REBECCA CARROLL, *NEW YORK TIMES BOOK REVIEW*

"There's deep magic not only among the close-knit Marte sisters and their offspring but also on every page of *Family Lore*. This book is at turns tender, intense, sensual, and hilarious—I couldn't get enough. Elizabeth Acevedo's precise, intricate prose mesmerizes, surprises, and delights. This is a family saga to be read with your whole heart and soul."
—DEESHA PHILYAW, AUTHOR OF *THE SECRET LIVES OF CHURCH LADIES*

"A vibrant family chronicle."
—*VANITY FAIR*

"Enchanting. . . . With grace and compassion, *Family Lore* glides through the sometimes riotous or hard-won love of immigrant families, their unquestioned sacrifices, and what is silenced between siblings, mothers, and daughters. . . . A novel where women rule front and center, navigating their pleasure and desires beyond the borderlands of male dominion, mostly without shame and often with spectacular abandon."
—PATRICIA ENGEL, *WASHINGTON POST*

"Elizabeth Acevedo's most impressive emotional excavation yet, a decade-spanning epic that sees Acevedo deftly stretching out into the new space afforded by a shift in audience. Vividly rendered and deliciously complex, *Family Lore* will stick with you long after you leave Flor's table."
—*ATLANTIC*

"Acevedo is brilliant at portraying the women's love and loyalty for one another. The author's fans will eat this up."
—*PUBLISHERS WEEKLY*

"Elizabeth Acevedo's *Family Lore* is a sweeping multigenerational story of a family of women whose special powers have helped them overcome personal, familial, and historical challenges that both bond them together and at times threaten to pull them apart—but ultimately navigate them into the full abrazos of love. Acevedo is in full command of *her* special powers as a storyteller of compassionate, capacious, and lyrical imagination. Make room on your shelves, readers, for this strong new voice with an old soul and a deep well of understanding of who we wonderfully are for the brief time we are beings." —JULIA ALVAREZ, AUTHOR OF AFTERLIFE AND HOW THE GARCÍA GIRLS LOST THEIR ACCENTS

"A vibrant family saga. . . . Acevedo wields her own sort of magic in her first novel for adults, deftly blending comedy and sorrow. *Family Lore* is an absorbing, entertaining portrait of a Dominican American woman whose exceptional relationship with death keeps her family—and readers—guessing." —MINNEAPOLIS STAR TRIBUNE

"*Family Lore* is a deeply Dominican book full of raw emotional power. It is at once intimate and epic, one of the most resonant representations of a family and world like my own I've ever read. There is so much to love about this wise, funny, and original novel—and it's a singular contribution to Dominican diasporic letters." —NAIMA COSTER, NEW YORK TIMES BESTSELLING AUTHOR OF WHAT'S MINE AND YOURS

"Acevedo's treatment of magic as an everyday possibility is compelling, but there is also magic in the wonder, surprise, frustrations, and joys the characters experience in their relationships with one another. . . . *Family Lore* is also, like all her novels, the project of a poet: her obsession with imagery, interiority, and making every word count is what makes her descriptions and dialogue sing; her characters think and speak in voices that feel distinct and alive." —NICOLE CHUNG, TIME

"Enchanting. . . . *Family Lore* beautifully explores themes of sister- and motherhood, family secrets, and the power of defining your life's purpose and meaning." —BUSTLE

"Acevedo uses an innovative storytelling structure to mirror oral traditions. It makes for a wild narrative, but the real journey is interior—a quest to reclaim the body and the pleasure that comes with it, and to answer the question: Just how far will you go to be known, and once you arrive, what will you say?"   —LOS ANGELES TIMES

"An exuberant, polyphonic story of one family's reckoning with their past. . . . Acevedo's background in spoken word poetry shines through in the energy and lyricism of her prose. . . . But the novel's greatest triumph is in the warmth of her portrayal of these women, their strength and stubbornness, and the inseparability of love and grief."   —GUARDIAN

"Flor is throwing herself a wake and reminding us that 'even a long life is too short.' So while we are here, 'let's eat, and dance, and be alive.' Acevedo has written unforgettable characters who breathe new life into how we grieve, age, and take care of one another. *Family Lore* is a bighearted novel, a wonderful debut!"   —ANGIE CRUZ, AUTHOR OF *HOW NOT TO DROWN IN A GLASS OF WATER* AND *DOMINICANA*

"Only Elizabeth Acevedo could make an epic feel so intimate, so perfectly crafted and tightly drawn. *Family Lore* is a devastating exploration of the liveliness of the Marte women. No writer on earth transforms a page into a home with distinct emotional chambers like Acevedo, and she does it with language that is equally lush and lacerating. This is how stories should be made."
    —KIESE LAYMON, AUTHOR OF *LONG DIVISION* AND *HEAVY*

"A lush and lyrical Dominican American drama."   —NPR

"With *Family Lore*, Elizabeth Acevedo has made the transition into the adult world look easy. The true gift of a stunningly talented writer."
    —JACQUELINE WOODSON, AUTHOR OF *RED AT THE BONE*

"A powerful multigenerational story that travels from Santo Domingo to New York City and spans decades. . . . This is a bighearted tale that seeks to answer, or at least make sense of, our deepest fears."   —BUST

"Acevedo is a master of time. *Family Lore* is full of beautiful prose, even-handed magic, and all the pains and triumphs of intergenerational bonds. Tender, moving, and altogether lovely. Not one word is wasted here."

—KILEY REID, AUTHOR OF *SUCH A FUN AGE*

"A juicy novel of sisterhood, resilience, and magic. . . . Acevedo's novel starring a spunky narrator will enchant both fans and new readers."

—BOOKLIST

"There is potent magic in these pages, passed down through this lineage of powerful sisters who have captured my heart. How does Acevedo do it? Reading *Family Lore* is like an embrace, and I am filled with nostalgia for a family I have never had and could never have imagined."

—RUTH OZEKI, AUTHOR OF *THE BOOK OF FORM AND EMPTINESS*

"National Book Award winner Elizabeth Acevedo has written her first novel for adults, and we're here for it. . . . Humorous and heartfelt."

—REAL SIMPLE

"Acevedo expertly maneuvers through the complex and singular stories of each of these women and all that unites them. It was a joy to experience each character's expressive and gripping story, to acknowledge their truths, and to recognize some of the women in the lives of women around me. A remarkable accomplishment."

—ABI DARÉ, AUTHOR OF *THE GIRL WITH THE LOUDING VOICE*

"Elizabeth Acevedo tackles some of life's biggest questions with the vivacity and empathy readers know from her young adult novels."

—HARPER'S BAZAAR

"Family history is always best when it's told through the eyes of a woman. In *Family Lore*, Elizabeth Acevedo does exactly that—tracing multiple generations of women in one Dominican family as they uncover what truly binds them all together."

—ELLE

FAMILY LORE

ALSO BY ELIZABETH ACEVEDO

For Young Adults

Inheritance

Clap When You Land

With the Fire on High

The Poet X

FAMILY LORE

A Novel

ELIZABETH ACEVEDO

ecco

An Imprint of HarperCollinsPublishers

This is a work of fiction. Names, characters, places, and incidents are products of the author's imagination or are used fictitiously and are not to be construed as real. Any resemblance to actual events, locales, organizations, or persons, living or dead, is entirely coincidental.

FAMILY LORE. Copyright © 2023 by Elizabeth Acevedo. All rights reserved. Printed in the United States of America. No part of this book may be used or reproduced in any manner whatsoever without written permission except in the case of brief quotations embodied in critical articles and reviews. For information, address HarperCollins Publishers, 195 Broadway, New York, NY 10007.

HarperCollins books may be purchased for educational, business, or sales promotional use. For information, please email the Special Markets Department at SPsales@harpercollins.com.

Ecco® and HarperCollins® are trademarks of HarperCollins Publishers.

Lucille Clifton, "*won't you celebrate with me*" from *The Book of Light*. Copyright © 1993 by Lucille Clifton. Reprinted with the permission of The Permissions Company, LLC on behalf of Copper Canyon Press, coppercanyonpress.org.

A hardcover edition of this book was published in 2023 by Ecco, an imprint of HarperCollins Publishers.

FIRST ECCO PAPERBACK EDITION PUBLISHED 2024

Designed by Angie Boutin

Title page/part opener background © Pulpixel Design/shutterstock

Library of Congress Cataloging-in-Publication Data
Names: Acevedo, Elizabeth, author.
Title: Family lore : a novel / Elizabeth Acevedo.
Description: First edition. | New York, NY : Ecco, [2023] |
Identifiers: LCCN 2022040640 (print) | LCCN 2022040641 (ebook) | ISBN 9780063207264 (hardcover) | ISBN 9780063207271 (trade paperback) | ISBN   9780063207288 (ebook)
Classification: LCC PS3601.C475 F36 2023 (print) | LCC PS3601.C475 (ebook) | DDC 811/.6--dc23
LC record available at https://lccn.loc.gov/2022040640
LC ebook record available at https://lccn.loc.gov/2022040641

24 25 26 27 28 LBC 5 4 3 2 1

For Orí.
Praise for how you guard & guide me.

won't you celebrate with me
what i have shaped into
a kind of life? i had no model.
born in babylon
both nonwhite and woman
what did i see to be except myself?
i made it up
here on this bridge between
starshine and clay,
my one hand holding tight
my other hand; come celebrate
with me that everyday
something has tried to kill me
and has failed.

—*"won't you celebrate with me,"*
Lucille Clifton

TABLE *of*
PRINCIPAL PERSONS

———— **II** ————

MAMÁ SILVIA: the long-dead Marte matriarch,
seer (mainly of births), 1933–2009

PAPÁ SUSANO: the long-dead Marte patriarch and
beleaguered husband, 1930–1975

SAMUEL: the first Marte child and only son, b. 1949

MATILDE: the eldest Marte sister, kindness incarnate,
no affinities known, b. 1952

FLOR: the second Marte sister, seer (mainly of deaths), b. 1953

PASTORA: the third Marte sister, reader of people's truths, b. 1955

CAMILA: the youngest—and forgotten—Marte sister,
an affinity for herbalism, b. 1969

ONA: Flor's daughter, possessing a magical alpha vagina, b. 1988

YADI: Pastora's daughter, heiress to a taste for limes, b. 1990

ANT: a neighborhood boy and Yadi's childhood sweetheart, b. 1989

JEREMIAH: Ona's life partner, a visual artist, b. 1987

RAFA: Matilde's husband and infamous philanderer, b. 1954

MANUELITO: Pastora's beloved, b. 1952

PEDRO: Flor's husband, a man with undisciplined soft spots,
1950–2017

WASHINGTON: Camila's husband, who was generous with both hands, 1968–2008

THE NUN AUNT: sister to Mamá Silvia, no affinities known, 1934–2015

LA VIEJA [REDACTED]: sister to Mamá Silvia, unkind, *perhaps* because she was mounted by a demon, 1936–2000

———— **||** ————

FAMILY
LORE

SIX WEEKS
BEFORE THE WAKE

FLOR

had a tabulated ranking for the seasons, autumn being her least preferred of the climatic periods in North America. The dying season, for Flor, had always been worse than the dead.

She should have been taking her daily constitutional through Riverside Park—despite the rain, she knew the lukewarmth would soon yield to frostier days—but instead she found herself seated on the pink print couch, with the documentary.

She told it one way. The truth that was not *the* truth.

Flor often listened to her daughter speak of her research with one ear flapped closed. But the other ear, the other ear perked up anytime her daughter made an utterance in her direction. Flor wasn't entirely sure when she'd started looking to her child for approval, but these days she was forever finding herself trying to demonstrate relevance. Flor was not great at keeping track of all the rituals, myths, and performances humans had conducted from Mesopotamia del carajo to now, but Flor *was* great at worrying that only through sharing her daughter's anthropological interests would they ever become close.

"She teaches Dominican history at City College" was the answer Flor gave to people in the neighborhood regarding her girl's career.

(It was always hard for Mami to explain what I, Ona—with my three degrees, mind you—actually did for work. Mami learned that trying to explain that I studied sugarcane ruins and pre-Columbian trade routes, and everything having to do with Kiskeya between the early 1500s and the mid-twentieth century, to a bunch of un-learned imbeciles (her words, not mine) would lead to neighbors shaking their head: *My son has a job in book-keeping, ja ja, easier than a job in books.*)

But there was a documentary that Ona hadn't stopped talking about the entire summer. And so, Flor called her sister Camila to help her set up the Netflix, and put the captions in Spanish, and with rain insulating Manhattan in water, she watched the screen.

Un mexicano from Arizona or Colorado, de por allá, sat in a wheelchair while a long line of his children and grandchildren and great-grandchildren lined up to pedirle bendiciones and whisper they loved him. She rolled her eyes. Just like a man, about to kick the bucket and still making his descendants kiss his hand. And before he was even in a casket! Her father would have never. She was considering sneaking a peek at her siblings' group chat—currently heating up with a discussion about Matilde's latest substitute instructor for the salsa class she attended—when the man on-screen began to openly weep. His hands shook on his bastón when one of the littlest, *must be a great-grandchild*, stepped forward to press her little face against his knee.

Ah, Flor thought, *not only to kiss the ring, then.*

She finished the rest of the film without picking up her phone. Then she started it back from the top.

That night while she was parting her hair and pinning it up flat against her scalp, the bobby pin bit into her head with the same sharp prick as this new wondering. *No. She couldn't. Could she?* Flor sat up most of the night worrying the thought, the way a tongue will keep sliding against an inflamed canker sore, trying to soothe something unsootheable. What if *she* threw herself a living wake?

It was ridiculous, she knew. What would be the point of gathering her siblings, and nieces and nephews and distant cousins? To say what to them? There was no diagnosis to create urgency. No persistent cough to make them anxious. It would be selfish to gather her family for an end they could not perceive. She went to bed with this new adamance that the film had inspired absurd and implausible notions.

She woke up the next morning musing. And the morning after that. For over a week, Flor ground her teeth in sleep. When she caught herself layering her fantasies about a living wake into a pastelón de plátano, she stopped, her hands full of sticky sweet maduros, and left the casserole half assembled on the kitchen counter.

Flor had always carried the mark of death. It was known from the moment she was born and wouldn't stop crying that she had not been fully wrenched from the Before. It was the cry of a colicky baby, but one that could not be soothed by valeriana con flor de tilo. Only when dreaming did the baby version of Flor cease fretting, and then the child was even more frightening;

she slept with her left eye halfway open, the iris flickering as if she viewed some silent film from it, drifting so almost nothing but the whites showed. Sometimes Baby Flor would wake with a start, a night-splitting scream torn from her throat. Some days she woke on a whimper. Eventually Matilde, the eldest sister, figured out that if the child was being held before she fully came to, she would settle down more easily into the realm of the wakeful living. Matilde volunteered herself to sleep with the baby tucked into her side, one finger held in the little one's fist.

The first time Flor had declared someone would die was rather matter-of-fact.

They'd been at the breakfast table, and Flor, precocious at five years old, had been serving rolls of pan de agua to the family. Her parents were talking in hushed tones about traveling three towns over to visit one of the great-aunts.

"It's too late. Your tía died."

Movement around the table stilled, everyone but Flor. Mamá Silvia did the sign of the cross, shooting a glance at her superstitious husband, who looked to have stopped breathing at his end of the table.

"¿Qué fue, niña? No hables de lo que no sabes," Mamá Silvia scolded. She scuttled her fingers along the gold chain links enshrining her neck.

"Se murió. Hace cinco días." Balancing the tray of bread in one hand, she wiggled all five fingers of the other. She'd recently begun working on her numbers and was quite proud of how good she'd gotten. "She wants her rosary back." Flor stopped the wiggling, her good eye landing on her mother's fingers.

The girl edged around to her father's end of the table, approaching to offer a bun, and she pretended not to notice as he slid his knee just enough to avoid her skirts brushing against him.

At the other end of the table Mamá Silvia beckoned the girl. Flor was not a grasping child; in fact, she largely let things fall through her fingers: dishes, ribbons, aspirations to be anyone's favorite. Mamá Silvia brought the little girl close until their faces were inches from each other's. No one knew about the gold rosary. It was a secret between Mamá Silvia and her tía.

"¿Como tú lo sabes?" her mother whispered.

"I dreamt my teeth shattered. But it didn't hurt. They just crumbled, and I tried to pick them up from the floor, but they were dust, piles of dust. And then a very, very old lady pointed to her neck. And she told me when you mentioned her, to tell you she wants it back."

Mamá Silvia packed that same day, mounted a wagon that would take her as far as two towns over, where she would be able to hop on a burro. The babe in her belly kicked incessantly. The doctor had told her not to have any more children. She'd lost three before this one; each time Flor would have a nightmare, and the next morning Mamá Silvia would wake to find blood trickling down her leg.

She'd been convinced her third child had been born cursed. They'd brought the priest over to the house. He came with his swinging canister of incense and intoned the devil be removed from Flor's body and the house. The girl's violent dreams had stopped during Mamá Silvia's pregnancy with Pastora, but then began again soon after. She'd lost every pregnancy since. Now Mamá Silvia suspected the child was a warning bell from diosito. Mamá Silvia, when she arrived at the big house where her aunt lived, found the windows covered in black. Tía had indeed died five days before, just as Flor had said. Flor was the kind of child who was afraid of very little. She knew by age six she wanted a calm and altruistic future. She let her family know she wanted a life in the convent like her nun aunt, and it was generally agreed on by her parents and siblings that her eccentricities made her the perfect candidate for a life of piteous enclosure.

Life washed over her, but the alarm system that most folk have that trips one into fight or flight was muted in Flor. She simply knew too much about where either choice led. It's what made the few fears she had so distinct. She hated lightning, the way it disrupted a night's sleep with its illumination and claps. Her disdain for killing any living thing was well known. While her sisters kept flowers in milk jugs, or tried to train the canal frogs into pets, she never kept a single living plant—to see it yellow, or wilt, or God forbid, *die* on her watch would have had her making the sign of the cross and asking dry stalks for forgiveness. And once, when she was seven, she'd woken in the middle of the night needing to use the outhouse. She lit a lantern and sleepily made her way to the hole in a bench outside. The scream she'd emitted had everyone run from inside the house to circle around where she'd been using the bathroom. A snake hidden in their human waste had risen up, biting her in the apex where her thigh met her crotch. She'd needed a sibling to join her for any nightly bathroom visits thereafter.

These fears were so singular in an already odd child that they were brushed aside. It didn't seem to matter where her place in this wide world would be; whether convent or wherever, since her place in what came after didn't scare her in the least.

————

Now, in her more mature years, and despite having been both a wife and a mother, her relationship to death was still the most intimate one she'd ever known. So when, at seventy years old, her synapses were sparked by the living-wake documentary, she'd known it would create a revolú in the larger family, not only because it was un-Catholic but also because she was the second-eldest girl, the middle sibling. If her brother and sisters didn't laugh their heads off, or admonish her into rethinking the whole thing, they would have an opinion on the fact that if they were going to begin having living wakes, they should go in chronological order. Or they would worry at what she might have seen.

The first thing she did was call the hall on Grand Concourse where a neighbor's daughter had been married. She already knew it was large enough for their family. To her utter delight, the coordinator told her that there had just been a cancellation five weeks from Saturday and he could provide a discount if she booked it immediately. Flor recited her credit card information and put down a deposit.

She called her niece Yadi next, shooing away the guilt that whispered her daughter, Ona, was deserving of the first ring. Ona was at a conference in Washington, DC, so Flor reasoned it didn't make sense to bother her, especially since it was her first big career event since returning back to work post-leave. It also helped that Yadi was the quietest of her nieces and nephews, a girl who asked sharp but not prying questions. All Yadi's years in therapy had taught her to probe gently. She was also someone good with computers, who reluctantly agreed to make Flor a graphic she could forward in the family group chat.

"Make sure it has roses on it, mi'ja." There were clicks that Flor thought were the girl tapping on the computer.

"Tía, don't you think roses are going to look too festive? Or romantic? I don't know if we're going for the right tone here."

Flor let her pause act as punctuation. Then, "Yadi, my name is Flor. Bright red petals, now. Not pink. Or white. And no carnations! I'm not dead yet."

Yadi texted her the graphic by noon, and Flor put it into the chat without explanation. By dinnertime Flor had had to turn off her cell phone because the thing was nonstop dinging with vainas from the siblings. Ona called the house phone that evening, letting it ring ceaselessly until Flor finally picked up.

"What are you thinking? What is going on? I'm supposed to be at a dinner giving a speech, but how could I speak in public when my mother is apparently inviting people to her own funeral?"

Flor believed Ona's concern because the girl kept reverting back to English despite knowing Flor would only catch every other word. *Ay, mi pobre niña, she always did feel too much in Spanish.*

Flor found herself fantasizing about the things people might say: Matilde was the sweetest of the sisters and would probably write her a poem of sorts. Her sister Pastora would get right to the heart of things, making Flor uncomfortable. Ona would weep.

She'd done right by her family, Flor thought. They would say kind goodbyes.

She picked out the exact photograph she wanted enlarged so it was the first thing all the attendees would see when they walked into the hall. It was the one of her when she'd first gotten to New York City. She'd been photographed wearing a faux-leopard cape, her hair in loose roller curls, the discolored photo that muffled the colors unable to mute the sparkle in her eye or the shimmering on the Hudson behind her. Everything had been possible then, here.

A few days after spreading the event graphic far and wide, she wandered the floors of Macy's searching for an outfit. She would have shopped at the store where Pastora worked retail, but she didn't want to make this occasion a family orchestration. This was her living wake, and the details of how she would appear were hers alone. She bought Ona a dress for the occasion too.

Next, she considered the run of show. Maybe let people come in and linger? Then she could get the emcee to give a short speech before opening the floor for people to come up to her and pay their respects. Into the microphone, of course.

Flor'd never had a baby shower, but it was baby showers she circled back to when she considered the grand events she'd attended throughout her life; she was most moved by the big wicker chairs mothers-to-be sat in, decorated on-theme, their rented throne a seat for all to pay homage. Flor was long past childbearing years, but she thought she, too, had something to deliver to her respect-givers. She ordered a peacock wicker chair.

Her menu would be a buffet line, she decided. Pastora,

tight-lipped on the subject of the wake, would approve that at least. Pastora was the stoutest of them all and delighted in any event that encouraged seconds and thirds. It was the catering detail that made it all real. Flor would have to call Yadi again; she couldn't cater a party and give the money to someone other than family, especially with a new restaurateur in the family.

Flor had planned many funerals in her life: for her father, her husband. But no planning raised the hair on her arms or kept her up at night the way planning her own services did. Imminence careened toward her, ready to reach into her chest, grab on to her heart, and take over the steering wheel. She was a woman driven. And she needed to gather her kin before it arrived.

She knew. She'd known.

The truth that is the truth, but is also the truth she did *not* want to tell: her teeth shattered. In a dream, of course. The night before she'd watched the documentary. And the pain of the enamel crumbling had been excruciating. And in that dream, when she'd reached fingers into her mouth and rummaged through the rubble of incisors, canines, and molars, the name her fingers latched onto and pulled from between her lips didn't have too many letters at all; why, it was barely more than a small, breathless incantation:

flor flor flor

FLOR: INTERVIEW TRANSCRIPT (TRANSLATION)

ONA: . . . and that's where you think it starts?

FLOR: Yes. Of course. It begins with the body for me. . . . I have sometimes felt like an occupant in this flesh; something that is being hosted. Until I had my first love, although looking back, those were a youngster's emotions.

I truly became human when I became pregnant with you. Nothing, not even making love, had ever arrived me to my own body like growing another person. It was primal, physical, the sensations that became new to me. I would wake up and brush my teeth, and the moment the toothbrush touched my tongue I would begin to gag. A visceral shock from the dream world to the body . . . You know me, Ona, I struggle with decisions sometimes. But from the moment I learned I was carrying you, the most animal of choices became easy. What do I want to eat? Not that, not that, yes, this. I would stand at my station at the button factory, and hunger, urinating, resting were sensations as loud as the machines whirring around me. The cues were urgent, unignorable.

I have never known so clearly what I wanted and needed at almost all times.

I remember one day walking through Morningside Park, you know that patch by 110th where the baseball fields are? They had just mowed it, the tractor not yet having rolled off the field, and I swear to you I wanted to drop to my knees. The grass smelled alive, the milk of each cut blade sweetening the air, and I felt like my nose picked up every single drop of dew. I'd known beautiful fields, and admired trees and birds, but with a second heartbeat in my body, my senses were newly electrified.

You grounded me here, with both feet, on both knees, stooped on all fours, heaving to bring you forth. I have known death since before I was born, but I had not truly known life until I gave it to you.

TWO DAYS
UNTIL THE WAKE

MATILDE

did not startle at the series of dings announcing that the siblings' group chat had found spicy new fodder. She had grocery shopping to do before class, and she was circling items dutifully in the supermarket weekly so as not to overshop. Yadi had sent her the list of dishes they'd be preparing over the next two days for Flor's wake, and Matilde, devoted in all things, was especially diligent about her job as Yadi's assistant manager at the shop.

Even when the house phone rang, she didn't flinch. Malditos scammers always got ahold of her number despite how many times Camila put her on a Do Not Call list.

On the seventh ring, Matilde put her pen down, pushed her glasses up from where they'd slid halfway down her nose. Half by half she folded the specials. The caller ID flashed *PASTORA*. Matilde sighed. If one must answer a call from Pastora, apprehension was advised; her mouth had never known silk.

Matilde hoped Pastora merely wanted to bochinchear about Flor; they talked around it, the reason their sage of a sister might be doing something so unordinary as throwing herself a wake without providing details. The theories had run from the guess that she must have gotten an ominous test result at her last physical to the opinion that maybe the family's curse of dementia had already lassoed her brain. Flor was mum on the subject, which left the remaining sisters to gossip among themselves.

But Pastora was not calling to talk about Flor.

Her voice cut into Matilde's greeting. "I'm going to tell you it exactly, just like my eyes saw. Rafa walked right by my store today, and into the CVS across the street. It was just before lunch, como a las once y pico. And yes, before you ask, I'm sure it was him. He was wearing those ripped white jeans he thinks make him a papi champú and that Águilas hat he loves so much. His arm was wrapped around a woman who was big pregnant. Iban agarraditos de manos."

Matilde had received calls like this before.

Rafa was seen at the karaoke bar performing a love song at a pining waitress.

Rafa was seen at the billiards on 207th instructing a pretty young thing by pawing her too-large ass.

Rafa was seen entering the apartment of the widow in 5D, and he emerged an hour later without his toolbox.

Rafa was always being seen by somebody doing something with someone who was not Matilde.

But the witness of these transgressions had never been Pastora, this younger sister who acted like the eldest, and so Matilde had never received quite this kind of call. In fact, this little sister had always been tight-lipped on the subject of Matilde's marriage, refusing to even look at Matilde when inquiries of her husband's infidelity arose in conversation between the siblings. And even with the calls that *had* come before, there had never been rumors about *pregnant* sidepieces.

Matilde removed the fogged-up glasses from her face. She'd

been panting, she realized, her short bursts of breath creating a film of moisture on the lenses. She should wipe them clean. Instead, she pressed the middle finger and thumb of her free hand against her closed eyelids. The light spots flirted with memory and arranged themselves into a half-opened car door. She was haunted by that fucking car door.

It was the night of her wedding, 1988. Matilde sat alone in the back of the car creating revolutions around her ring finger with the still too-shiny wedding band. Her hands itched to touch Rafa now, when they were allowed to do so without censure. How many days he had sat in her living room and drunk un cafecito and smiled and all she could think about was touching him *right* there? Or pressing her body close to his. Or threading her fingers through his picked-out 'fro. She'd imagined it all under the watchful gaze of her chaperoning siblings, imagined and hoped that he could read in her eyes what she was thinking and was, perhaps, thinking them back at her. Although she was the second eldest, she was often treated like the youngest of the bunch. An air of innocence, her younger sisters loved to say while offering her a pat, pat.

She glanced down at her river of skirts, an impossible crossing she'd need to attempt if she wanted to act on any fingertip-to-body action with her new husband's delectable neck. Just as she was about to arch forward and wedge herself between the two front seats so she could at the very least share a giddy glance with Rafa, Manuelito hit a pothole that jostled her backward.

"Me disculpa, Matilde," Manuelito said, his eyes finding hers in the rearview. She offered him a little smile. So far, he was the most courteous of her brothers-in-law and had offered both his new car and his chauffeuring for transport on her wedding day. Correction, it was now her wedding night. Which would commence in less than ten minutes, if she was correctly pinpointing where they were on Avenida George Washington. And she was pinpointing their location down to the millimeter and second since El Hotel Jaragua was also where she worked. She made this commute daily. Her employment discount and regard as a desk clerk were the only way they were able to afford the illustrious hotel for the one night.

From his seat, Rafa tapped his fingers against a windowsill, patterning a beat only he could hear. They'd met through music. He was the star weekend singer at the discoteca she and Pastora had visited routinely when Matilde had first joined her in the capital. The eldest sibling and only brother acted as escort, but he was unnecessary muscle. The women were equipped with their own ways of discouraging unwanted attention. All except Matilde, who solicited the most attention to begin with because her heels, once they touched the dance floor, seemed forged from pure light. She was a dreidel, spinning and spinning, her skirt a halo enshrining her hips. Under the flashing disco balls, alongside the whine of the accordion, Matilde spawned herself the loveliest swan. Even in their campo back home, folks had whispered that Matilde might be the sister without magic, but she was also the only of her kin who could fly; her tacones seemingly hovered over the ground when an orchestra was in her presence. Rafa, from his lofty position as front man, took notice of the young woman with the cheap department store dress and winged soles, and he turned his voice into her spotlight; she'd spun with other men, but his crooning sung her eyes right back to him.

He'd found her later, standing with Pastora by the bar. "I want you to dance to my music for the rest of your life," he'd whispered, pressing a rum and Coke into her hands. Matilde hadn't known her temperature could rise any more than it had when she was shaking and sweating on the dance floor, but it did. A long lick of heat crawled up from beneath her heaving cleavage.

The music was too loud for anyone to overhear his delightful whisper, much less Pastora standing closer to a speaker, but the patch of skin between her sister's brows had still furrowed and she'd shaken her head, an easy sign of disapproval to interpret, yet Matilde had turned fully to this man, pretending she hadn't seen her sister's motion. He'd wooed her from that day on, scaling her prim demeanor, telling her over and over she was special, unlike anyone he'd ever known.

Rafa had a beautiful voice, clear as a church bell, and he'd told her more than once that he felt it was the greatest injustice of his life that he'd never been able to strike it big, despite all the nightclub owners who'd regularly asked him to sing in their clubs. She'd never told him this, but it was that exact comparison to the church bell that she believed could be at the root of his lack of success: his voice was indistinct. It was reliable, sure, but it chimed like the kind of thing one grew accustomed to and learned to tune out. Not *her*, of course. At this point in her courtship, she was still besotted enough that the tips of her ears perked up whenever he gave a tiny clearing of his throat. Like he did now in the car. Matilde waited for what he would say.

"Drop me off right there," Rafa said to her brother-in-law, pointing a finger at a beachfront building. It was not the tall, coral-colored columns of El Hotel Jaragua. She calculated they were still five minutes from there. "Take her to the hotel for me, compadre? You need to teach a woman early who is in charge, ¿no es verdad?"

She'd not met her brother-in-law's eyes in the rearview mirror. She must have misheard Rafa. Although from the stillness of Manuelito's hands on the wheel, the way he had not cracked a smile at the bridegroom's jest, she'd gathered he had heard what she had heard and was waiting on her to speak. Her sister Flor would have stared him hard in the face with her good eye if her bridegroom had said that to her. Pastora would have been at his throat before he'd made it to his second sentence.

Matilde stared out the window and said nothing. And in this, she hoped her brother-in-law understood: *Say nothing, Manuelito. Not now, not later when you go home to Pastora. Reserve for me only this embarrassment.* Her husband clapped Manuelito on the back and reached for the car door handle. She had a single moment. Less than a second—

(I, Ona, was not alive then. And since I wasn't, there was no resident anthropologist in the family. However, if I had been born, or if someone Matilde knew had had this particular occupation, one might have tried to explain that she was turning to ritual in that nanosecond; she had recognized that door as the blinking entrance sign into a new liminality. Before Rafa thrust open the door, and there was the blissful then of a few moments ago, and the impossibly hungry future yawning in front of her, Tía Matilde had just enough wherewithal to understand that she was undergoing a rite of passage, experiencing an in-betweenness, and just like the ceremony she'd undergone to become his wife, this too would undo a former self and would concretize a self not yet formed.)

—he expelled himself, the outside air rushed in, hot and humid, a sweaty slap to the face. And then he slammed shut the door. Tapped a beat on her window, she remembers. When she lowered it, he moved the veil away from her face. She'd removed it for the reception, but before leaving the wedding reception her sisters had shuffled her into the single-stall bathroom to help her pin it back on. These two sisters closest in age to her, Flor and Pastora, were newly wed. Flor was even preparing to be a mother, having traveled back to Santo Domingo at seven months pregnant to be at the wedding. And Pastora, enamored with being wife to Manuelito, was trying to be kind despite her misgivings of Matilde's choice in husband.

"Husbands like having things to remove. The more you give him to unshell, the more anxious he'll be for the cashew," Pastora said.

But it seemed Rafa had heard the reverse.

"This way you'll be eager from missing me." He had chuckled just before his mouth pecked her own. It was the first time in their relationship she had the thought that life to him was only a great big joke he loved telling and was too self-centered to realize no one joined him in the laughter.

Manuelito drove the next five minutes in silence. Matilde knuckled away the moisture on her cheeks. She kept the window lowered and took deep breaths. When they pulled up at the hotel, she grabbed the overnight bag she'd packed with lingerie and a flask and tomorrow's change of clothes and marched into the hotel before Manuelito could offer to escort her. She knew the seed of shame would blossom under the shine of her co-workers' speculation, their wonderings of why she entered with a man who was not her new husband. So, she preferred to enter the revolving doors alone.

Thirty-some-odd years later, when she thinks of that night, she does not wish to change that he left her alone for five hours after their wedding so he could dance, and sing, and—now she believes—whore. She does not even regret the wedding, which was achingly lovely, her parents dressed in all white, her sisters carrying soft pink rosebuds down the aisle. She could not imagine a life without the pregnancies, each one its own forlorn hope, the last-ditch efforts of a general attempting to conquer the other side of a lonely life.

There was no point in questioning the marriage. All she wishes she could alter was that when he'd walked into the hotel room that wedding night, smelling of salty grajo, oblivious to the way she'd thumbed to wrinkles the lace of her nightgown, that his lips hadn't been so soft on her collarbone. His hand moving the strap that held her clothed the way she'd seen her own father, who could not read, slide the fringe of a bookmark onto his favorite passage of Psalms. Rafa's hand when he palmed her breast had held the weight unmoving for a long second, accepting an offering. It was clear who was supplicant and who was god.

When her husband had made love to her that night, she had no choice but to believe he'd had the right of it. She *was* eager, humid, clinging to him as if he'd been out for months instead of hours, licking his jaw as if she could swallow him whole. A panting bitch welcoming her owner home. Maybe this *was* what was necessary the first night a woman made love. She wished he hadn't been so proficient. Trying, with his body, to make her unremember. It would have all been easier if he hadn't had so much conviction in his kisses and touches, affirmations that he loved her, of course, only her.

The children never did hold. And as each one of Matilde's siblings married and had little ones, she became the designated godmother. The one to send the children gifts and buy them ice cream and indulge them the way a family member can for a child who is not theirs to overspoil. To date, she is godmother to four of her siblings' children. Her sisters never said so, but she knows it was pity that made them do it. Otherwise, why get a family member to be a godparent? The formality of further structuring a relationship proves redundant. Here was barren Matilde, who could grow a babe to the size of a melon before he decided he'd rather be elsewhere. They never said it, but she always thought they must think this too: If only she'd given Rafa a child when they were first wed, maybe her husband would not have strayed. And she would counter that imaginary critique by assuring them that unless she'd been prepared to go into labor long before their wedding night, no child would have yoked her husband to her. Just ask Manuelito, who'd borne witness. It wasn't a child that Rafa had searched for in other women's skirts.

Still, she refused to be tragic. She knew how to be happy for others. She knew she participated in the world as more than a womb.

She tapped the specials, folded throughout her reverie into an accordion fan, against the kitchen table. Pastora was still talking about what she'd seen outside the CVS.

Matilde heaved up from her seat. "Not now, Pastora. I have to go grocery shopping. I promised Yadi I would pick up some things for the catering."

Matilde pictured Pastora's irritated hand gesture. "That girl always figures it out."

Then Pastora's voice turned gentle the way a bread knife is gentle as it parts an airy crumb. "We have to talk, Matilde. Today."

Matilde walked to the phone cradle. "After I go shopping, I have my class."

"Where is your class again? I'll stop by before it begins."

"The middle school auditorium, pero please. I don't want distractions before class."

A rude noise on the other end preceded Pastora's "Afterward."

Matilde did not bite back her sigh. "I'm seeing you tomorrow night, Pas." Matilde knew that the nickname was like base in a game of freeze tag: it paused Pastora long enough that she might chase after something else. But Matilde also knew Pastora was a more vicious chaser than most, so she pressed her point. "This conversation *can* wait until tomorrow, can't it? At this point in my marriage, is it life or death?"

There was a long pause, Pastora trying to read the situation, trying to hear whatever it was she heard in people's voices. Matilde waited. One second. Two. Three. . . . It took eight before Pastora spoke. "Mañana entonces. Pero en serio, Matilde. It's time."

And it was. Time for Matilde to fold the specials into her pocket. Time to wipe clean her glasses and put them back on her face. Time to pack her dancing shoes, and pick up the ingredients her niece needed. And then it would be the hour to head to class.

And then. And then. And then.

PASTORA

got off the phone with Matilde, still worried. She'd had a lot to worry about this past month without the added burden of Matilde's marriage being spooned onto her plate. Truly, enough was enough with that relambío. But no sooner had she pocketed that worry than she remembered that Ant was back in the neighborhood. Her daughter Yadi's teenage boyfriend had been a sweet guy. And she knew he'd grown into a good man, because Pastora had corresponded with him monthly. She'd even visited him once or twice. But his return to the block could undo all the hard progress Yadi had made to leave the loss of him behind.

And neither of those ill-fated loves came close to the worry Pastora had over her sister Flor.

When they'd spoken that morning, Flor had been complaining that Yadi had taken over the menu for the wake, and was not including even a little bit of pork, and could Pastora talk sense into her, please? Pastora found Flor's desire for pork amusing, since the woman couldn't even kill a mosquito feasting on her leg, but somehow never minded dead flesh on her plate as long as it'd been marinated in sour orange and cooked until falling off the bone. Pastora had murmured that she would talk to her daughter, but in reality, she was struggling to approach this wake with as flippant an attitude as Flor seemed to have.

Pastora was the sister who kept being invited to help pick out the flowers, and help decorate the big wicker chair, Flor insisting that everyone else pestered her with too many questions. Pastora did not show deference to her older siblings, none except Flor, who had been the designated one to carry infant Pastora on her hip, who'd created a sling out of old stockings to keep the toddler on her back. Years later, without any slings to keep them tethered, they still had invisible bindings. They were the two with the most egregious of gifts: Flor with an ear for the gossip of death, and Pastora with an ear for the tenor of truth. Metaphorical eggshells speckled the floor of any room they walked into; when they both occupied the same space, it unsettled all the other occupants. What could most people say that would not lead to one of the sisters knowing too much about their life or afterlife?

One thing Pastora and Flor did not do was tiptoe around each other. Which is why Pastora refused to ask for details. Which is why Flor refused to offer any. This wake would bear its own truths and breaths, and Pastora would give her sister this gift: let the event speak what she could not. That did not mean Pastora hadn't bitten all her nails down to the quick.

"Viejo! ¿Estás listo? Vamos a llegar tarde." Her husband was punctual for everything except when he needed to travel. His flight wasn't for another four hours, but Pastora knew if she didn't get them into the car and on their way, he'd miss his flight. He never admitted he was anxious, but he would pack and repack his suitcase until the last moment. His being back in DR during this wake was another of the worries Pastora tucked away with the rest. His mother was dying, had been for over a year, but his cousin had called this week to say that the end was near; if he wanted to say goodbye it could not wait. And Manuelito was nothing if not a man of duty.

And so it was that they would not be together on one of the hardest times of their lives. He needed to return home for his mother's final days, and she needed to be here for Flor.

She sighed and looked at the list of food items Flor had asked her to call Yadi about. Pastora had been almost relieved when the girl became a vegan; the US had spoiled her with food. And before she'd given up meat, she'd eaten like a person who'd never known hunger, the joints of wings and tips of ribs left ungnawed.

Not to make a big deal out of it, because Pastora felt secret pride the girl had always been well fed, but well, it just embarrassed Pastora, to see the waste. Sometimes, after the girl took the plate to the kitchen, Pastora would sneak in and suck the marrow from the leftovers. She didn't need to be hungry to do so. It simply felt right. Yadi once caught her like that, chewing the cartilage of a chicken bone, the smooth ivory picked clean. It's one of the memories Yadi liked to use when she told people why she'd become plant-based: her mother, standing over a plate that was not her own, addicted to meat to the point that she had reduced herself to scavenging. Pastora was not shamefaced by this portrait of her. She was used to the recriminations of others. Why, as a child she was often at the receiving end of the epithet *malcriada*.

Her sisters were different. Flor had been born with an eye that faced the wrong way, as if it was trying to turn inward. Their older brother was the first to notice that Flor's difference wasn't only a physical alteration. She was considered a blessed child, and once the family had become accustomed to her nightly wails she didn't cause Mamá any problems outside of having to harangue the neighbors who would come visit hoping Flor would be able to "dream" something on their behalf.

Matilde, the eldest sister and second-eldest child, was a mansa. That girl was so soft that when they were little and Pastora punched her straight in the stomach, she would just throw herself on the floor! It didn't matter how many times Pastora yelled at her to put her fists up, the girl always succumbed to fetaldom and Pastora would get in trouble for walloping her elder. Matilde never did develop magic.

By the time Camila was born, almost all of the other children had moved to the capital. Camila had grown up mostly alone, and each sibling carried few memories of the youngest, which meant they often forgot she was part of their conclave. Her skills with herbs and spices had cultivated slowly. Camila had told Pastora once that the little leaves bent just so when she was trying to cure an ailment. She'd learned their different curves and bows.

Samuel was the only other sibling, and he never got in trouble because he was a boy and the eldest and he was already in the fields working by the time the girls were coming up, so even if he had been adventurous like Pastora when he'd been younger, she would never know. And as far as Pastora knew, the magic only ran through the women, so Samuel did not have any talents outside of the ones he'd honed through trade. Once Pastora turned eight, Mamá Silvia began to send her out to kneel in the yard as punishment, an act Mamá hoped would lead to the child repenting for breaking the leg off her father's favorite chair, or for sneaking an extra piece of chicken when she knew meat was precisely rationed *just so* for the men to get the biggest and juiciest portions. After a while, Pastora was sent out without having committed any infraction at all, *in anticipation*, her mother explained. Her absence making room for the quietude Mamá Silvia seemed to crave.

(None of the women in my family had language for *mental health crisis* or *postpartum depression* back then. And I've done very little reading on it myself, but the babies Mamá Silvia lost before and after Pastora seemed to have brought on a heightened rancor that Mamá Silvia reserved exclusively for her fourth child.)

Pastora got hip to the game quick. She learned that if she knelt when Mamá first sent her out, obediently genuflecting before the row of lime trees that grew tall and spindly, protecting their land from those "nosy, nobody neighbors," Mamá would be satisfied enough to let her run around without reprimand thereafter. Pastora learned to tie scraps of old stockings around her knees, and would bow her head like their aunt the nun had taught them, and soon: the curtain would flicker, Mamá Silvia going back to her sewing, the endless cooking.

Unsupervised, Pastora was free to take off on her journeys, her yearning to be in the world the reason she most often got in trouble in the first place.

Those daily excursions taught her anything could be an adventure, hunting for limoncillos in the conuco her parents kept, using long branches to fight off imaginary vagabonds, and cursing. Cursing was definitely an adventure. She would mix up the words she heard her parents use under their breath and partner them with the foulest language she'd heard used to describe the devil. She practiced insulting her foes, and her mother, although even with the spine of steel she welded in young adulthood, she was only able to tell her mother what she thought of her once in her life.

In many ways, Pastora had always had a foul mouth. It was her attempt at spell casting. All the important people she knew—the alcalde of the town, the patrones who worked her father, Flor after a nightmare, even Mamá when she was angry—cursed. Pastora was convinced that power and magic and bending words to say the profane were a way out from under someone's thumb, as if the words would form little cobblestones paving themselves to one of the big houses, the house she had to pass on the way from here to the all-around store in town. She'd see the boys of those houses sitting outside on their wide-wrap veranda—tall boys, well muscled, which mattered less to her in terms of sexual appeal, and more so because all that muscle meant they were eating, nutritiously so; it meant the family supplied several portions of meat for those boys to delight in.

Sometimes, when she sprawled out in the beaming sun, little ants and mosquitos her only company, her stomach turning perhaps from being full of whatever fruit she'd finagled off her parents' vines, or perhaps from the tapeworms that plagued her and her siblings, Pastora thought of wanting to be one of "them." The them who ate well, and had verandas, and whose armoires held more than two collared shirts.

What she never imagined was that perhaps her own mother also wished for a swap. Not just a change in her life status: to be the wife of the well-to-do men who could afford those houses and to clothe those children—

(as, family lore has it, she'd been destined to do before marrying my humble, ox-driving grandfather)

—but that her mother might mostly wish to swap her; maybe looked at those sinewy boys and thought, *Wouldn't one of them be easier, and twice as useful as this hellion?* It took years, and her own estar en riesgo; it took her own mouth contorting itself into a bent similar to her mother's, the words so often thrown at her as a kid catapulted at her own girl—it was then that she recognized what might have led her mother to exile her to the wilderness. One doesn't consider that a parent might fantasize in this way until one is a parent. Until they have to look down at their own child and think, *It'd be easier if I could just exchange this one for one of my nieces, or that nice boy at the grocery store, or even the neighbor's quiet little pup.*

A swap never came, not for her parents nor her child, and Pastora was thankful that in her most desperate moments when she wished for either and both, God hadn't been ear hustling.

She'd missed the fields and the rushing of the canal that raised her when she'd moved to the capital years later. But it was upon first moving to New York that Pastora truly felt the loss of greenery. She arrived in New York in January 1998, the ground covered with the sludge of melted snow and grime, the trees cheap prostitutes, not leaving even a leaf to the imagination. She hadn't known then of northeastern seasons, that the tree wouldn't be so bare always. It'd broken her heart then

to think back on the canopy of forest
where she'd once roamed free.

But she made this naked, colorless place her home. Pastora had been forty-three when she had first moved to an apartment near the Columbus Ave shopping strip. She came with Yadira in tow, Manuelito having arrived a year before. Columbus Ave was a massive thoroughfare lined with cheap retail on either side and was like a wonderland for the eyes. Her second day in New York, she'd walked by the shops and glanced through the windows, refusing to be awed even though she wanted to peer in like a kid at a bakery. She never stared too hard. Eventually, she allowed herself to look at the frilled blouses and lush coats only out of the corner of her eyes. But a few weeks after she got settled, she began scoping out the shops in earnest, or rather, the shop owners. She finally stopped into one of the smaller stores and asked to speak to the owner she'd seen unlock the gate each morning.

While Pastora didn't know English or New York, she definitely knew hustle, and at the end of the day, selling is selling regardless of the landmass where the goods are being hawked.

This shop she chose because it wasn't one of the big sneaker stores, or Rainbow. Those stores were hip and chic, the kind of shop that only employed younger people with both their midriffs and immaturity exposed. The tiny hole-in-the-wall shops would have been a better suit, but Pastora knew most of those were running numbers and so the retail would always be second to the business in the back. This store she entered because she'd noticed it had a steady stream of customers, older ladies trying to look classy but without overspending. The clothes were simple, work and church fare, and in a week of walking by at odd hours she'd noticed the store opened and closed on time, never seemed overwhelmed, and needed an update on how it displayed the clothing in the window; the mannequins were styled in new garments, but the patterns and cuts were outdated. And the manager. There was something about the manager.

The next day, when the manager, Don Isidro, a short man, sharply dressed, with shrewd eyes behind his glasses, shook her hand and asked her why he should hire her, Pastora told him straight up: "I'll give you three reasons. I've never worked retail, but I used to help my mother mend and sew our clothing and I can tell quality. I'm honest, and have never taken a thing I didn't earn. And I can read the truth of a person, even with only hearing them speak a single word."

The last reason was true.

"I think I will do well there," Pastora said to her husband the night before she approached the manager. She was putting on her night cream and Manuelito was reading the newspaper in bed. "The manager seems like a serious sort."

And any other man would have taken offense at learning his wife had been checking out another man. Manuelito simply closed the papers, removed his reading glasses, and smiled. He'd found a job with a taxi dispatch service, and his early bird personality led him to take the morning shift of driving business folk who were too good for public transportation downtown to work. Which meant he was often tired by the evenings, but never too tired to offer good-luck sex as his best response.

———

"Manuelito! ¡Ven!" Pastora pulled herself back from reverie and put away the list of things she'd need to discuss with Yadi tomorrow. Her husband came from the bedroom, his slacks pressed so the folds were crisp, his white button-down tucked in. He was still a trim man who kept himself composed despite not possessing much vanity. The suitcase he dragged with him was one of their big ones he'd have to check. Yadi had tried to convince them a carry-on was better and safer, but who left for another country without spare outfits, their favorite iron, and several boxes of wholesale gifts for each loved one?

Manuelito grabbed her hands and rotated them upward, turning her into a worshipper, but then he kissed each palm and pressed them together; he did this anytime he left the house, as if he could seal his love between her hands. "You don't have to come with me to the airport."

"I'll Uber back. That way you have your car for when you land."

Manuelito did not like to talk when he drove, but he held her left hand in his right, clasped near the car shifter, and let the night find them like that. Pastora went with him for the simple relief of closeness. If one had many reasons to worry, she might as well do so in companionable quiet.

YADI

juggled a bag of groceries, humming along with Teyana crooning in her headphones, when she stepped onto the uneven crack in the sidewalk. The same crack that had been there since before *she'd* been here. Since before her momma had been here. The one she'd scraped her face against that one time she'd taken Dwayne's skateboard and zoomed off on it belly first. That crack. She stumbled and her phone slid from her hoodie pocket. She scrambled for the phone, and the bag she'd been carrying in her right arm tipped, a mouth spilling secrets. She barely managed to palm the phone, but not before three cans of jackfruit fell out and rolled into the gutter.

"Coñazo." Yadi stopped moving midreach. Was that someone snickering at her misfortune? And outside her own home? Yadi swiveled her neck toward the amalgamation of brick and concrete she called her apartment building.

And there he was. Sitting on their stoop.

The Black & Mild smoke rose to greet her. He did not. No, he took a deep inhale. The end of the cigarillo smoldered. Another pull. The smoke circled between them, and for a second, she had a thought way too whimsical for the likes of her: this was like one of those desert mirages depicted in an Indiana Jones movie or something, you know? The ones where a woman who's been hoofing it on foot, in the hot sun, finally sees a break in the sun-dappled sand, and there, for the first time since she began her journey, is a pool of drinkable water surrounded by pretty fauna? The air cleared. Ant took her in from head to sneakered foot then offered a single nod.

He was back. With zero fanfare. Perhaps his moms hadn't thought it'd happen this time; he'd been up for parole before, but something always ground that burning hope to ash. Maybe he hadn't called home, hadn't let anyone know. Although, how a man recently released travels from upstate to Harlem, with only like, what, $37 to his name? Yadi didn't even know. What she did know is even before being sent upstate, Ant had been good at quiet. Very good at staying quiet. Good at letting a silence unroll itself, a red carpet to his listening.

"You better come in. And put that out. Mami te mata if you bring that bajo in."

(Tía Pastora truly does not play that smoke shit in her abode. Remind me to circle back to the hookah fiasco of 2016.)

Yadi scooped down to grab the cans that'd fallen. Hugged them lopsidedly against her chest, the dog-eared grocery bag cradled like a child. She walked right past him. Pretended her hand wasn't shaking as she put the key in the main door of the building. Through the reflection in the pane, she watched him take a final puff and put the still-glowing tip against the step before he dropped the remainder of the Black into his shirt pocket. No hand shaking. When he stood, her breath stuttered. It *was* Ant. Those beautiful bright brown eyes, the roughly healed scar plunging through the right side of his mouth. How many times had she put her own lips to that sharp indent of violence? Her lips twitched, as if they were counting every single moment they'd been touched to his skin.

But this was also *not* Ant. Ant had been a boy. A boy who stood on the corner with her and jumped into rap cyphers. A boy who at the age of twelve pressed a burned CD of songs into her hand at the annual block party, the last track simply his voice asking if she'd be his girl. A small-chested, shy, curly-headed boy who hijacked the building mouse traps and set the vermin he found in them free because he hated to think about a helpless, hungry thing killed simply for seeking relief. "How do they know the rules, that they ain't allowed in? Not fair to kill something because it ain't know the rules."

This Ant was a man grown. He had lived half his life away. From here. From her. He was muscled, taller. She didn't know whether the boy she'd once known lived inside this man.

His eyes met hers in the reflection. "You need more time to stare? I can relight my shit."

His voice. Oh, the cadence! *The sarcasm.* That she knew. But the depth? She felt like she was in such a strange dream. Going from a mirage to the kind where you know you're sleeping but can't move, and you look around and yes, there's your yucca houseplant, there's your comforter, there's your squeaky bedroom door, but some details are off: the blinds weren't open when you closed your eyes, the chair in the corner is too clean. Yes, this was Ant, but she couldn't reconcile the new details. And she also could not wake up. And maybe that is the original definition of *nightmare*? A dream that gallops through, dragging the dreamer from one haunting to the next.

She felt the beginning signs. The way her throat thickened, her top lip trembled first, the breaths that felt like she was pulling from a shallow well in her chest. Ant would walk away if she had a panic attack. Maybe. Maybe he'd try to hold her. Both options would wreck her. So instead, she pushed open the door and she counted the steps to the stairs and she wiggled her toes as she walked, and she scanned her body. And she let him follow her inside. When they got to the bottom of the stairs, he grabbed the grocery bag. As they climbed the steps, Yadi checked out the way his ass pressed against the fabric of his joggers. New Ant had been doing squats. She was out of breath when they arrived at 2D, but to be fair, she'd been out of breath since her first glance at the stoop.

Ant stood to the side while she plugged keys into locks. "Didn't think I'd find you still living here. I kept asking moms when she visited. You always said you were going back."

Yadi chewed on her lower lip. She wouldn't be able to do this with him, Ant, if they were going to try to collapse eighteen years into an hour over un cafecito.

She turned her jangle of keys in the first lock, then another, her mother still insisted on bolting—even though no apartment in this building had been broken into for years—aware of Ant standing behind her and hoping he couldn't hear how her breathing sounded. She hesitated with her key in the second lock. Should she invite him in? Did she even know him anymore? It'd been a decade and a half; he was a stranger grown despite how good his ass looked.

He cleared his throat behind her, and she quickly turned the key.

"Can you set those inside for me?"

As he trailed behind her into the kitchen, Yadi became hyperaware of her body. He wasn't the only one who had changed. She'd been a slim thing when they were young. Her tits and hips had taken decades of cornflakes and Burger King before they finally grew in. She hadn't grown much taller, simply matched her cousin Ona in the expanse of their meatier parts.

She set her bag down on the little kitchen table, indicating to Ant to do the same. Tía Matilde had stopped by: spices were arranged neatly on the kitchen table, and two bags of rice were next to the fridge. Tía Matilde was the most responsible and accepting of the aunts, and Yadi had hired her from the moment of the shop's inception to be her thought partner and store manager. Tía also had an apartment in this building, which made it easy for her to help Yadi with errands. If it'd been Tía Flor, Yadi would have found bacon bits or chicken bouillon cubes and none of what she actually needed for the meal. Yadi had decided she was not going to worry about Tía Flor. She'd always been a bit strange, a bit lost in the Walter Mercado–ness of the world. If she wanted to throw herself a living wake, it didn't necessarily mean anything ominous was going to happen. Yadi did worry for her cousin Ona. Tía Flor was all the immediate family her cousin had left.

Ant raised a brow at all the jars and cans and bags of food, but Yadi knew his mother kept him well informed. And there wasn't a thing that happened in this neighborhood that Doña Reina didn't know about.

"Your mami here?"

When he'd been younger, Ant had been both awed and a little scared of Yadi's mom. Pastora had always tipped up Ant's chin so she could look him right in the eye, interrogated him about his grades, and would pinch the skin above his ribs, letting loose a *tsk-tsk* to punctuate her command that he eat more. Pastora had stopped talking for a full two days when she'd heard he'd been sentenced to a minimum of eighteen years. At the time he'd been a few days shy of his sixteenth birthday. He'd done the full time, plus.

"Nah. Papi is leaving to DR today and she went to see him off. I can't imagine the wildness that is a commute to and from JFK at this time."

"What's all this?" Ant's chin gestured to all the spices, cans, and mountains of produce.

"Tía Flor is having a . . . service? On Saturday." She kept the smirk out of her voice, but as her mother and aunts got older it was like they were attempting to Benjamin Button their senior citizen years, doing all the activities they hadn't been able to do as kids in DR and bucket-listing them here in the States. That's what she considered this wake when she was being lighthearted. Simply a new trendy thing her aunt was doing in an attempt to be more American.

"Service? She sick?"

Yadi stopped fiddling with the groceries, surprised to hear what sounded like minute devastation in his voice.

She didn't look at him. "Nah. It's a long story, but Tía Flor is throwing herself a wake. As far as we know, she's fine. She's fine, Ant. No one is dying."

The catalog of people who'd died while Ant had been imprisoned was long. His father. His grandparents. Her grandmother. Several neighbors. Kids they knew from the block. Was Ant's initial shock about her aunt specifically? Or was he teaching himself to brace against the changes he hadn't been around to experience?

She reached for the bag Ant was still holding, careful not to touch his fingers. But in the transfer, they still brushed. Bruised. She felt the welling up inside, the immensity of every girlish desire and sticky whisper and midnight prayer bubbling up, even as the rough fingers of their current reality popped every single one of those squishy, lovely dreams. And all of a sudden Yadi was so tired. As if the whole day, the whole last year, the whole last twenty years had mounted her back and dared her to continue standing upright. She didn't know if she could do it. She couldn't stand with Ant and reminisce and hope and pretend they could just light a blunt on the fire escape, listen to early 2000s Ja Rule, and magically make up the time.

Yadi railed. She grabbed the cans of jackfruit and threw them to the floor. She kicked the stove, hard enough to leave a dent on an appliance her mother had kept in mint condition for decades. She fisted both hands and rounded on Ant and thumped onto Ant's chest, knocking over and over on an unfamiliar door she had no business trying to get answered. She wept and under her breath whispered, "You ruined us. You ruined it. You don't get to come back. Time isn't a simple seam you can resew. You. Unmade. Us."

Of course: she didn't. She didn't rail. She didn't yell or throw things. Shit, she shared the house with her parents. Anything she broke, she'd also have to repair, replace, and most definitely explain. Instead, Yadi methodically stacked the jackfruit on the kitchen table. She preheated the oven to 350. She washed her hands with moringa-scented soap and tied on the monogrammed apron her mother had bought her the day of the shop's ribbon cutting.

"I thought for sure you'd have thrown the gloves on by now." He'd moved into the kitchen, his hands on the back of the tall chair at the little table.

"Not that girl anymore, Ant." And she turned from the sink and faced him. And he stopped tapping fingers on the chair and faced her. And they did not need the words neither of them would never say anyway. Because from children who ran through fire hydrants together, to teens who went to amusement parks and fondled each other under fabricated waterfalls, they had known each other the way no one else could ever know them.

"I'm cooking. You need water or a beer or something? We might have some malta."

Ant had always had expressive eyebrows, and his left one quirked up. "I'm a guest now? Why don't you just pass me an apron?"

"So you could do what? I'm not scrambling eggs here, homie. This is real cooking."

For the first time since he'd been back, Ant cracked a smile. The right side of his mouth lilted upward, disrupting the architecture of his scar, reassembling his whole face, the kid she knew winking at her before his lips pressed into a straight line again.

"How real can it be? Moms told me you don't even use meat."

Yadi gave an offended laugh, but he spoke again before she could retort. "And I've worked in a kitchen before."

Yadi's smile faltered. The years and years they had not been in each other's lives braided into a swinging bridge. She didn't know whether she could cross it. She couldn't tell Ant, who'd first told her when he was thirteen that he wanted to kiss her, what it was like to have sex for the first time with a boy who was not him. She couldn't tell Ant how fucking hard college had been and how she'd tiptoed into University Counseling only when Ona had threatened to tell Pastora that Yadi was struggling again and might need to be taken out of school. How her mother had heard her anxiety escalating during phone calls and had cajoled until Yadi ended her semester early once again. Thousands and thousands of little life facts they should know about each other, like the fact that Ant had worked in the kitchen while he was away, mounted between them, too high to scale.

Yadi and her mother arrived with all their belongings in tow. Papi had moved first a year before. He'd found a little apartment near Tía Flor, and got a license to taxi a big black Lincoln Town Car; he'd seen more of the city than her cousin Ona, and Ona had been born in New York!

For an entire fifty-two weeks before their move, Yadi had passed every single Friday evening calling her father and having him describe New York City. She'd celebrated her eighth birthday without him, Easter and Christmas too. When Tía Flor bought a new calling card, Ona would call Yadi to talk about how school was great because they didn't have to wear uniforms, and in the summer frozen-treat sellers would wield their carts through the streets offering fifty-cent iceys and dollar frío-fríos, oh, Yadi was going to *love* taking the train and the massive skyscrapers and Six Flags. And Yadi had never had an icey, but the way her cousin and father described the country that would be her new home had her packing and repacking her little pink suitcase six months in advance.

When she and her mother arrived, the streets were slick from a recent snowstorm that had been bootprinted into slush. Ona let her borrow a coat that was one size too big and that didn't match any of her shoes. The first place her aunt and uncle took them was to Times Square, and while Yadi found it bright, and a tall, gold-toothed man selling hats had given her a free pair of sunglasses, she was largely unimpressed. Apparently iceys were only sold in the summer, but Ona took her to a pizza parlor where she sampled some Italian ice—a close approximation, Ona explained. The flavor Yadi tried was good, but too saccharine. The street where her father had found them an apartment was infested with a legion of two-foot-long rats. Yadi spent three days watching her surroundings from their apartment window, giving this city a chance, before she packed up her pink suitcase again, stopped by Ona's to tell her not to eat too many of those diabetes-riddled frozen treats, and went to notify her parents that she was ready to return.

"Pero, Yadira. We just got here. You've got to give it a chance," her mother'd said from where she'd been working to hang up a curtain. It'd been her first complaint when they arrived, that all the neighbors in the street could peer into their second-story apartment.

"I gave it a chance. Jesus died and came back in three days. Wherever he'd been didn't suit him. And I arrived and am returning back home in the same time frame, because I have decided this place does not suit me."

Her mother had laughed, the matter-of-fact nature of the statement coming from her child superseding Tía Pastora's strict rules on blasphemy. Tía is a woman who values intrepidness.

"But won't you miss us, mi'ja? Families are meant to be together. Here, hold this tie a second."

Yadi side-eyed her mother. *This* couldn't be the line of argument she would attempt. "Papi has been here for a year without us. I can go live with Tía Camila or Mamá Silvia. Papi didn't need us and he was fine. I don't need us either."

She didn't look at her mother when she said this. Even then it had been difficult to live with a mother who always knew when you were lying. Her mother's soft tone almost broke down her commitment to return.

"Ay, Yadi. It feels new, this place? And your cousin was born here, and your Papi came ahead, and you feel late and like you'll never catch up. You're homesick, I think?"

Yadi raised her chin and tightened her jaw when she felt her lips wobble. Willed her silence to make the arguments on her behalf.

Her mother grabbed the curtain tie back from her. "My older sister came here first, you know. And she's having to explain everything to me, and it's not easy. Lord knows she's terrible at explaining things." Her mouth pressed into a small smile at Yadi. Yadi's eyes stung, and she blinked them rapidly, refusing to cry over the injustice of living in this silly, ugly country that didn't have palm trees, or friendly stray dogs, or her best friend Salome.

And since crying was not an option, Yadi instead hauled her little pink suitcase down the single flight of stairs and went to sit on the stoop while, presumably, the adults in her life figured out which one of them would take her to the airport. She held her jaw tight. Not only because of the tension she felt, but because the cold air made her want to shiver and she refused to give this country a single sight of her trembling. After hours, or maybe more like fifteen minutes—it's unclear whether we can trust time the way Yadi tells it—Yadi felt a rustle at her side and then a pair of little brown knees covered in corduroy settled like an equation sign parallel to her own. Yadi discovered that the knees belonged to one Anthony Camilo Morales, and after another hour, or perhaps a child's twenty minutes, of sitting and talking at him, she'd decided a few things:

1. Ant was the single most impressive thing this country might have produced. And she learned that technically, he'd been born in the States but his mother got pregnant in DR, so honestly, she wasn't sure whether she could attribute any of his impressiveness to here. Nonetheless, he and Burger King were the only redeemable qualities this country possessed. Yadi was a reluctant but staunch fan of the Whopper.
2. She loved Ant more than she loved Santo Domingo. Even the wind of Santo Domingo whistled back when she talked. But Ant listened like no one else listened.
3. One day she would go back to the Dominican Republic, and she would take Ant with her. And she wouldn't have to love him more or leave him more because she could love him and Santo Domingo together.

Yadi ended their initial meeting by kissing Ant on the cheek, announcing, "No, don't offer to help me with my suitcase. I am very strong."

She lifted her chin in the direction of the newly installed curtain in the second-story window, noting how it promptly fluttered into place. Yadi lugged the pink luggage back upstairs, walked past her Mami, and unpacked.

———

Ant snorted before tucking his hands into the back pockets of his sweats. "I ain't asking for shit but an apron, Yadi. Not asking you to relive nothing. Not asking you to loan me money. Not asking why you never visited."

At that last statement his hands came out of his pockets, almost involuntarily so. Ant didn't put them anywhere. It's like he needed his palms open to punctuate the words. "Not asking why you stopped writing. Not asking why you opened up a restaurant in the Bronx instead of Bonao. And you know what, on my mother, I ain't even asking to stay up in here if you ain't fucking with me. You say what you want, and I promise you got it."

Yadi looked down at the bowl of jackfruit pulp. She'd been pulling the pieces apart automatically, and they rested in the bowl, shredded, fibrous, sad. She reached for one of the pieces, one she'd pressed too hard, and milky water trailed down her fingers.

She cut her eyes at him. "The cafetería is on Columbus Ave, so, not quite the Bronx."

She placed the chunk of jackfruit into her mouth, savored it around her tongue for a moment. With her eyes still on his, she sank her teeth in.

MATILDE

had lied. And Pastora likely heard it. Her dance class wasn't in the auditorium. She'd said that because it was easier than explaining to Pastora that the classes were actually held in the school cafeteria. Something about this particular location sounded indelicate: to practice spins where twelve-year-olds dribbled barbecue sauce and pizza oil all over themselves and the floor? A school cafeteria did not sound like the destination of a woman who wanted to change her life. Auditorium was better because it was only where children sweated and cried and pummeled each other during assemblies, much more appropriate. Apparently, the kind of woman she was was the kind who told irrelevant lies to save face.

Matilde was one of the last to arrive, despite being there ten minutes early. It was an assortment of people, and there were always new faces trying the class for the first time. The oldies, like her, had been coming for years to work with Maestro Espada, although attendance had been waning since he'd busted his hip running after a grandchild and his substitutes had proven themselves flakes. Word on the street—viejito gossip after class—was that the heir apparent to the illustrious dance dynasty had traveled down from Connecticut to take over for the next few weeks.

Matilde looked around at the other people gathered to be educated by a prodigal son on the intricacies of salsa on 2, and wished she had Flor's inklings in regard to approaching doom. As she slipped her foot into the low strappy heels, she thought about Flor's uncanny knowing. How she'd never been wrong about someone dying. It was that alone that ratcheted the volume on this wake. The first thing Matilde had asked her? The first thing everyone asked her when they heard about the wake: *Did you have a dream?* And Flor only allowed her tight-lipped self to smile, patting whoever asked on the arm. "Think of it as a gala, festive. I want all the pictures to show a kaleidoscope of brilliant colors."

The only person who might have been able to get Flor to tell the truth was Pastora, she who had perfect pitch for honesty. And as far at Matilde knew, Pastora was the only sister who had yet to ask for details on the *why* of this silly wake. *She's afraid of what she'll hear*, Matilde knew.

An old man began hacking up a cough, and by older, Matilde meant a real elder, not just a senior citizen. She finished with her buckles, put her flats neatly in her purse.

Some days, she worried she had no business being here, in this blue-painted cavern. Be it gym or auditorium or cafeteria, it didn't all very much matter; she wasn't sure she could become the woman she'd hoped to be whether she was Suzy-Qing on linoleum or tile, not when she had a philanderer to deal with. *I should leave.* She felt sick to her stomach. And truly, the linoleum in this space was nauseating. Bright blue with white speckles, but at least the custodial staff kept the floors sparkling. A large metal divider separated the school kitchen from the cafeteria. Colorful paper decorations covered the windows. Matilde had entered this building for the graduations of her nieces, and to accompany her sister Flor to vote, and for almost a decade to attend these classes, but today she was seeing it with new eyes. *No! I should tell him* he *needs to leave.*

The stacked lunchroom tables opened up the space so that all thirteen people would have room to move. A young man dressed in a muddied baseball uniform walked toward the large black abomination that usually emitted the music.

As he passed her, it was like the stale veil of processed ham and government cheese was lifted. Not because he was beautiful. He was. When she would describe him later, she'd say she loved most how his face was dark and untroubled. His long limbs encased in the double-knit polyester of a uniform that had recently seen the dugout.

Matilde was not someone big into baseball, but she'd always loved how a uniform fitted around a man's strong backside. She felt a quiver in her gut, like a creature stretching after an interminable sleep. Not quite attraction. Divine Baby Jesus, she'd had more than enough of attraction.

El Pelotero set down his gym bag and removed his cap. Even those movements had small, efficient flourishes to them, Matilde noted. He looked around the room and then his eyes landed on her. A glance at his watch must have informed him they still had five minutes before class because he walked over unhurriedly. He was tall and lean and vibrant. Not as young as her nephew Washington, who had just finished college, but not as old as her. Somewhere in his forties, she guessed.

He smiled, showing clean, white teeth, one with a chip in it that softened his splendor in the best way. Matilde could not be charmed by him, but she felt the hairs on her arms goose-bump.

She peered closer. What *was* it about him? He leaned in closer, too, taking her inspection as interest . . . ?

"My father told me to ask for Mati Marte. I'm assuming you're she? He described you."

Matilde nodded.

He looked inordinately pleased with himself. "Will you partner me to instruct? Papi said you're his right hand."

She ducked her head in humble consent. And then her hand was in the hand of a man who pitched balls and swung heavy things and yet held her fingers gentle as a seamstress fingering silk.

"You don't even know if I can dance." Matilde kept her eyes just past his left shoulder.

He tugged her closer to the mammoth music machine. He took his cell phone out with the hand that wasn't holding hers. "Well, I've seen you walk, so I know you can dance. But even if Papi hadn't told me you are a verduga"—and this he made sure to shift his face so he entered her eye line when he said—"I don't shy from taking lead." He winked.

Ah! When was the last time a young man had winked at her? Matilde had to restrain herself from using her free hand as a fan. She knew this muchachito was too young, and a flirt, and she was married, but it felt fun to be needled, anticipatory. Because Matilde wasn't always confident in many of her skills, but she knew rhythm. Excitement ratcheted up her spine. She would earn that wink, dammit. She would dazzle him beyond repair.

El Pelotero plugged his phone into the contraption, her hand still in his. Veterans of the class, the other students paired up. The old man with suspenders, whom she often danced with, wiggled eyebrows at her. She covered her laughter with her free hand.

"We are going to warm up with the basic step sequence, and then we are working all night on cross-body leads. Dancing is boring if you can't do spin transitions, and Papi told me to double down."

Matilde had evolved from cross body a long time ago.

They warmed up with salsa basic. Matilde was able to dance salsa on 1 as well as salsa on 2, and she was always happy to help new students transitioning from the way they learned at home to the ballroom style taught in the class. It often wasn't intuitive for newcomers who had learned a less informal way. For her it was easy enough to change the foot she led with and add an extra pause on the fourth count. The class wasn't one anyone paid for, it was a free one offered by a local community-outreach organization, and the rolling admission meant it was never quite a structured class. People came and went, and the students paired up and got advanced advice, or arrived fresh and green and were taught the basics. She came less to advance her dancing than to have one hour that was entirely about her and her body.

El Pelotero pressed some buttons on his phone, and music came out of the machine. The classic opening of the trumpet started a humming in Matilde's gut.

Then her hand was fully in his hand. And his other hand fluttered against her lower back. And they were facing each other with plenty of room between their pelvises and chests, but Matilde still felt too close. She leaned back incrementally, and although the baseball player smiled, he said nothing. She could smell him. The sweat, the grime, the actual funk of skin that had rubbed against itself in vigorous effort.

And the baseball player *was* a good lead. His father must have been working with him since he could toddle. The hand that held hers telegraphed where they were going and at what speed, without her ever feeling like she was being towed or thrown.

Through the first half of the class the baseball player would let her hand go to go watch certain couples: correcting the heavy hand a woman put on her partner's shoulder—*Your fingers are like butterflies; light touch, light touch*—he used his own hand to massage tension from the woman's. An older man with a slouch was shown how to make a step less exaggerated to offer himself more room for the transition. During these mini-lessons Matilde danced by herself. Practicing hand flourishes like she'd done in the mirror, and indulging in some backward cross-body-lead-less spins. It was during one of these times that the music died—Matilde in a fast-double spin, arms flung out, all eyes on her since she was the one near the machine. She dropped her arms, dropped her face.

The baseball player walked over with a groan. "Coño. My phone died."

"You don't have a charger?"

He looked heartbreakingly young for a moment. A young man, covering his father's class, offering more flash than focus. He shook his head. "I left it in the car." He glanced at his watch.

"And I'm guessing that with New York parking being what it is . . ."

"The car is several blocks away."

"My phone has music. It's an old iPhone, though. Will it work?" Matilde asked, picking up her purse from where she'd put it on the one lunch table in her line of vision. She placed the phone in the young man's hand. He pressed some buttons, scrolling. Then transferred the machine cord from his phone to hers. Bongos and a güira ushered in the big horns that cradled Oscar D'León's melodious voice.

She reinstated her hand in the baseball player's, and he pulled her in, hand at her waist, but he didn't move. She shifted her hips, maintaining count so she would be prepared when he did move, but he merely tapped the fingers at her waist in tune to her count.

"Your music selection is incredible."

Matilde looked at the hand on his shoulder, the one that had her wedding band on it. "My husband. He downloads the music onto our phones. I don't know anything about any of these aparatos."

She didn't look at him, but that same hand on his shoulder felt the infinitesimal way he pulled back from her. "And makes your playlists? He's a big salsero."

She shook her head. "No. He prefers bachata, bolero."

"Really? It's quite a catalog of salsa. Even the latest hits."

But it was true. If allowed to play disc jockey, her husband preferred songs where he could sing all the words soulfully and woefully. The big orchestra and sheer production of salsa overwhelmed a voice like his. Salsa was her love. This eruption of instruments, the way it announced itself, full collection of limbs moving in harmony. She'd never considered why her husband requested her phone so he could sync music onto it. Was it his attempt at a gesture of love? She was not very tech savvy, and if it wasn't for him, she'd have no music on her phone. No, she wouldn't wonder at what that man did and did not consider love.

She shifted onto her back foot, then her right, keeping the beat with her lower body until the baseball player shook his head, smiled, and followed her into movement.

PASTORA

did not take an Uber home from the airport. Something her husband had more than likely known would be the case. She was too frugal to spend ten times the amount it would cost to take the bus. Sure, the commute was slower, but Pastora didn't mind slowness so much these days. It allowed her time to think, to gaze at the moving landscape while admiring her own stillness.

Ona had been asking the women in the family all these questions. Some that would be considered intrusive if she hadn't been so thoughtful about them. Pastora had agreed to the interviews, convinced she'd lived a long and colorful life and would have a lot to offer her inquisitive niece. But she hadn't been prepared to swim in the gulf that opened up when she looked into her past. There were so many moments she'd closed and shelved, books she couldn't finish and had never returned to. And now Ona was running her fingers down all the spines, asking about the titles. Asking to thumb the pages.

How to explain the kind of girl she'd been? How she had changed? There was only the story she'd told Ona that she'd been replaying the last few days. Trying to un-dog-ear the past.

Pastora held irritation in both hands,
as if it too were bundled within the

linens she carried. Christmas was in less than one week, and Mamá Silvia had volunteered to mend the gold-and-white vestment that would be worn at midnight mass by the head priest. Mamá Silvia was not one to lend her services easily, much less for free, so Pastora was convinced Mamá was banking on her goodwill equating to a favor from God. Or perhaps a pardon. Mamá didn't do anything without considering returns.

The vestments needed to be returned to Doña Yokasta Santana's grand house near town. As the matriarch of the family and lead lady in charge of the church mothers, Doña Yokasta ensured that the domestic requirements of the priests were met in full, including their laundry. The seamstress the church mothers usually hired had already left town to visit extended family for the holidays. In turn, Mamá's mother and eldest sister, a nun, were making the trip in their direction and should be arriving in a few days. This time of year was a shuffle of checkers from one side of the board to the other, islanders traveling across both county and country borders to see loved ones they might not have visited all year, or in the case of Mamá's family, for several years.

Estranged would not have been the right word for the dynamic Mamá had with her family. More like Mamá Silvia had been exiled several towns over, but with visitation rights. The reasons for the extreme separation weren't entirely clear to

Pastora, but she knew that her father always seemed to work late into the dark when Mamá's family was in town, sharing only the evening meal with his in-laws, and then remaining even quieter than was his already silent norm.

Pastora did not look forward to her grandmother and aunt visiting. She'd only been three the last time they'd come to stay, but she remembered her aunt's sharp pinches anytime she interrupted the conversation, and the hawk-eyed glare of her grandmother. If her mother was all sharp teeth in regard to decorum, she paled to kittenlike in comparison to the woman who'd begot her.

Pastora walked through the countryside with small steps, trying not to kick up dust. She'd turned thirteen a few weeks before, and Mamá insisted she had to wear stockings under all her dresses now. "Only hos don't wear hose, Pastora."

Not only were her legs sweating beneath the tightly stitched nylon, but her mother insisted on the stockings being kept pristine white, as if the pair she was wearing wasn't the pair she'd have to wear all week long.

Chasing the shade of trees, Pastora crossed from one side of the road to the other. She wished Flor had come with her, but her older sister was studying for a high school entrance exam. There was no grade beyond primary school in this area. Part of the reason their grandmother was coming with the nun aunt was to inspect Flor and her gifts for themselves. Pastora thought it was grotesque, the family that neglected them coming as if to pull back Flor's lips and inspect her teeth to see if she could be associated with them. The convent where the nun aunt was established had offered to take in the miraculous child and put her through parochial high school at reduced cost if the girl's talents were true and she passed the entrance exam required. And sad little Flor, who wanted an automatic pass to heaven and perhaps imagined there might be respite from her dreams if she was closer to God, had begged their mother to let her go.

Pastora couldn't understand it, Flor's inclination. It was clear what all the elder ladies got from the deal if Flor was eventually accepted into the convent: their mother might be forgiven for her misalliance with their father, their grandmother got another pious family member to pray for her rotten soul, and the nun aunt got an elevation of status at the convent, being able to boast blood relation *and* acquisition of a girl who might one day be nominated for sainthood. But despite how Pastora tried to show Flor all the ways she was being played, Flor was hardheaded.

Pastora switched the basket of clothing from one arm to the other, careful her fingers didn't touch the holy cloth.

The house could be seen over the crest. Balconies lined the upper windows. The manse was a full three stories; the land behind it was vast, green, and probably would have been confiscated by El Jefe except it was rumored the family was in cahoots with his regime.

She climbed the steps on the balls of her feet. They did not creak once. The door knocker was heavy in her hand, and Pastora wondered that thieves had never pulled the shiny brass off the door. When the door opened, Pastora thrust the basket out, ready to rid herself of the finery, but it wasn't a domestic who answered; it was one of the boys of the house. The second oldest, if Pastora's memory of town gossip was to be trusted. He would be leaving for university in the States in a year or two.

Pastora pulled her arms back. It wouldn't do to hand over the vestments to a boy. Boys never knew where anything went, and he'd toss it to the side and get it dirty. Which meant she'd lose a strip of skin off the back of her legs, and Pastora had plans for the swimming hole that did not include scarred and stinging thighs.

"¿Se encuentra Doña Yokasta?" Pastora knew she should keep her eyes down, not draw attention. But instead, she notched her chin one inch higher when he raised a brow. The boy's complexion was the color of milk swirled with a teaspoon of honey. He leaned against the doorframe and the crisp collar of his shirt pulled tight, exposing a large Adam's apple. His lips quirked into a smile while he took her in, starting with her black patent leather shoes, which had not survived the walk here unscathed, and going all the way to the top of her head, then back down the length of the plaits that hung to her waist. And then he looked her in the eyes.

Pastora cleared her throat. "¿O Tita?" The domestic was the one who'd dropped the clothes off, so she might know what to do with them.

"The family went shopping. To Santiago. But I can show you to the maids' quarters. That for Tita?"

Hearing him speak, she straightened. "For the priests." She hoped the reminder of holiness might inspire him to behave. The way he spoke to her had startled awake something in her gut.

Pastora took a step into the house. It was blessedly cool. Large ceiling fans revolved overhead, and the windows all had heavy brocade curtains that blocked the light. The boy put a hand on her lower back and ushered her into the house.

Pastora stepped away from him but still followed. The house was large, and she'd never been inside.

"Por aquí." She followed him down a corridor. There were family portraits on the wall. Seaside landscapes. In the dining room, big flowering pots tipped flowers over like a Greek bacchanal of blossoms. She'd learned in school about the Greeks and their indulgences. They went through the dining room, also dark, and a shame since the chandelier over the big table looked like it would have sparkled light brilliantly.

In the back the boy nodded at a small room, where a small bed occupied the space with a small ironing board, and smaller nightstand. A portrait of Jesus and his crown of thorns, blue eyes twinkling over the minutiae, was the only artwork in the room.

Pastora set the basket down on the ironing board. The boy's hand touched the back of her neck. He swiped.

"You're still sweating. We have a balcony upstairs. The breeze is refreshing. You can see all the way to El Pico Duarte."

Pastora hesitated, hand still clutching the basket of white and gold threads. She fingered a gilded sleeve edge.

The stairs were marble. The maid had dusted well before leaving in the morning. The boy opened a set of doors that led into a bedroom and crossed to windows where he flung open the curtains. Pastora stopped in the doorframe. The balcony was the entire length of the wall; two rocking chairs faced the mountains. She knew if she took another step, she'd leave a trail of soil. Her shoes sank into the plush rug. She followed him through the room, stopping at the vanity table near the windows.

This must be his parents' bedroom. The boy's mother had

little jars of cream and a jewelry box with a glass cover. Inside was a collection of religious medallions on fine gold chains. Polished rings with gemstones glittered like hard sweets, and Pastora's right hand itched just as if she were in a candy store. Next to the jewelry box was a bottle of perfume with an ornate stopper. Pastora opened it and took a sniff. The mantle on the table was a fine lace. Pastora's own mother could have made it. She set the perfume down, then bent to look into the little mirror, curious whether it would make her appear different, more. She saw her brown hair, her brown eyes, her brown skin. She smiled, gritting her teeth. Two of those were brown too.

She stepped to the outside that was still inside. It must be nice to have this covered balcony. This part of the house faced fields and fields, and rolling hills.

"You're Saint Florecita's little sister, right? The one they call La Malcriada?" The boy asked. He did not take a rocking chair like she did.

"And Samuel's little sister."

"Ah! Serio Samuel! He and my older brother got along."

Pastora doubted that. Samuel had never gone to school with any of these boys, and he'd been a laborer since he was old enough to swing a machete. This boy had hands like he'd never even pulled backyard weeds. Beside boyhood, what else could he and Samuel have in common?

The boy moved closer as he talked, until he was standing right in front of her. His toes touched her mud-licked shoe every time the rocking chair edged forward.

"You're quite beautiful. I can see why your father keeps his harem of girls hidden."

The pang that she'd felt in her lower belly rose again, and this time Pastora dragged it up. Until she could hold it up to the light. Analyze all the facets. There was something in his words that was creating jostles in her gut.

She shook her head no. "He doesn't hide us." Then she nodded. "And thank you. I do think myself quite beautiful." She smiled, making sure all her teeth showed.

The boy leaned down, putting his weight onto the arms of the rocking chair, forcing it to stutter to a stop, the back runners in the air.

Pastora held his gaze. He brushed his mouth against hers. Thinking, perhaps, the kiss stolen. Then she straightened up until their lips were a hairbreadth from each other. His eyes widened—the boldness!—but they fluttered to a close when she touched her mouth to his, a second brush.

"I want to show you my room. It also has some views you'd like." He smirked. "I really do find you so, so beautiful."

Pastora listened to his words with something other than her ears. A ringing went off inside of her at his first statement. He really did want to show her his room. The chime turned into a thudding *clank* as he continued talking. He did not think she'd like the views of his room, and he did not actually find her beautiful.

He moved his legs between hers, searching for more, but Pastora leaned back, knocking his arms off of the rocking chair, setting it in motion again. He reached his arms out, his lips curling. Perhaps he thought she was playing the flirt. Perhaps he was just a boy unfamiliar with being rebuffed. But Pastora held up a hand that brokered no argument.

"You wanted to taste me. Brought me up here in hopes of

what? Licks with a feral one?" She flicked her hand, knowing in her heart of hearts that dismissal was worse than any words she could say. She also knew what she heard in his voice. The words he said that were true chimed in tune with something low in her belly. The words that were lies rang dull. She cast her eyes back at the mountains. "Can you please step aside? I'm trying to enjoy the view."

He swelled up in his anger. "Are you serious?"

She waved, ensuring even more contempt in her gesture.

He kicked the rocking chair.

"Puta. Get the fuck out my house." For good measure, he spit close enough to her foot that some of the backsplash landed on her toes.

She smirked. "Gladly. And El Pico Duarte is in the other direction." She pointed with her lips. "You could still be a good person, Santana. It isn't too late. Even if you are a compulsive, manipulative liar."

His eyes widened.

The walk back home was uneventful. Pastora didn't think about the Santana boy, except to wonder about what he'd woken up in her. Not lust, which Pastora had felt before, and determined it was a close cousin to how her mouth watered over steak. But that gut-deep understanding she parsed from his words. A knowing what he was and wasn't saying despite the mask his words donned.

Flor had always told her, when Pastora complained about her lack of supernatural talent, that knowing so much was an expensive cost. Pastora had thought being able to act on any kind of innate magic would be worth it, anything.

And at least with age it helped with employment. When she

got the job at Don Isidro's, she proved it to him. Pastora knew the women who came in looking to get gamed. Their weak chins meant if she got them into any old dress, she'd be able to get a sale because the same softness that molded these women's chins stacked their spines. Pastora did not glance at the changing-room mirror in order to contemplate her own chin, because she already knew steel kept tight her jawline. At work, like everywhere else, Pastora was a tíguera, and when the little bells rang over the door, Pastora evaluated before she pounced. *This woman wants to feel desired, but without looking like she's trying to be young—the red dress in the corner for her. This woman wants the blouse in the window but is going to try to haggle. This woman keeps glancing at Don Isidro, but she won't buy anything.* What she heard in their greetings always confirmed her intuition.

Pastora always went on break when her own sisters walked into the store. She didn't want to see them stripped of the pride they each wore so close to the skin.

After her magic had sprouted, she'd had to learn how to *re-envision* people. How to turn off the beacon that seemed to signal a person's innermost insecurity to rise to the surface where she could visibly see every question that made them cower.

The gift could develop by surprise on any given Tuesday. It had been simpler for Ona and Yadi; when they had been born, by then the sisters knew the universe had its own timeline for bestowing gifts.

For Pastora, the close proximity to humans who kept so many secrets had proved overwhelming. Especially after her banishment. But a girl learns.

————

Pastora got off the bus at least thirty blocks before it'd arrive at her stop. She needed the chilly air, the way it woke her up to this moment, in this day, in this year. She made another entry to her list of worries: she was saying too much in all of Ona's interviews.

I

possess one earliest memory, and it includes my hand in my mother's.

We walked to the school on Amsterdam Ave that in the evening offered English-language classes. Her hand was always cool, even in the sticky, humid heat of New York, which often films onto one's body like a second skin. We walked into the gymnasium, where a little table had a coffee maker and small white cups like the ones the dentist supplies when she tells you to gargle. I, of course, already knew English. Or enough from *Sesame Street* and pre-K that I could cobble bravado as I told adults exactly what I thought about their silly suggestions. I tugged my hand in Mami's. "I'll go play over there," I said, pointing to the corner where a large window ledge seemed a perfect sitting spot for me. I was not the kind of child who hid behind her mother's skirt when introduced to strangers. I was the type to shake their hands, look them up and down. My mother didn't let go.

I tugged again. "I'm okay. I'm not scared."

And it was then that I looked at her face. The tight lines around her mouth. The tight grip with which she held me. It was the first time I'd ever had to consider that maybe I was the one making things less scary for her. We walked to the seats that were set in a circle, and although I was much too big, I sat in Mami's lap.

I don't remember the lesson that first day, whether I translated or not. Whether I helped her with her sentences although I barely knew my own letters.

––––––

My mother is going to die. All our mothers are, of course, if they haven't transitioned already. But my mother's death is both silent and obvious: a tightening grip. I stayed over one night last week, and when she was sleeping I looked through all her papers. I scanned envelopes and opened her mail, and did a terrible job of hiding that I'd been snooping around. I saw what bills she paid, what new subscriptions she had. From the moment she told the family she was holding a wake, a seed of fear began germinating, watered by my sweaty palms.

I asked her again, of course. The morning after I looked through everything only to find a new payment for Netflix but nothing else that seemed atypical. She smiled, both her eyes focusing on me. "I never have felt like I've been celebrated enough. That seemed fine when I was wanting to live a pious life, where I cast pride from me. But after all this living, even my birthdays have been sedate. I want to celebrate."

This was not an answer. This was the only answer she would give.

My mother's magic, like all of the magic for those of us who have a hint of uncanniness, is not like White people's magic in the movies—led by ritual, called upon, granted in a ceremony of smoke and candelabras. It is not an orderly system like how fantasy novels can describe the exact structure of where and whence and thusly. The women in my family get struck by an unknown lightning rod. Charged with a newfound gift that has rules unto itself but is unlike that aunt's or this cousin's or my mother's.

For example, I was eight years old when I first observed that I have an alpha vagina. I didn't call it that then. But I remember one day noticing that when I went to the bathroom with my friends, they all took a moment before they began to pee. My best friend in second grade, Raisa, even had to ask the rest of us to stand outside the school restroom since she couldn't relax enough to urinate if we were in the same room despite being in a separate stall. I would pull my panties down and, barely hovering over the seat, the piss rushed out, my urethra forever spraying blessings at toilet bowls. My pee hole was not shy and did not impede my ability to piss regardless of who was around.

In high school, I was captain of the girls' varsity ball team, even though I was only a tenth grader, having ascended to the position less because of my jumper, which was mediocre at best, and more because I gave passionate pep talks and was compelled to rebound at all costs. My coach thought these great leadership qualities, understandable given that the other co-captain was a self-serving ball hog, albeit one who could out-score the rest of us combined. We all had our strengths. It was through those early-morning practices that I first identified that whenever my period touched my panties, without fail by the end of the hour, all the other girls were stampeding to the bathroom, blood spotting their shorts.

In college I finally named that the effects of my puss were actually more specific than just a strong stream flow and PMS siren song. It was the scent, too. The touch, the sight, the taste. My pussy was a full-sensory supernatural experience for folk. My wet-wet had a volume I could turn up or down, irresistible. My first year at Binghamton, I overenthusiastically let a football player finger-pop me at the Alphas' Black & Gold Welcome Back Party. Dude started swearing up and down campus that I was the reason his passes were all gold that season.

At my college graduation barbecue, my tía Camila, the fringe young aunt who had known me the least, asked me to explain my Marte Family Talent.

"I think Yadi said, but I must have misunderstood, that your popola has magic?" Tía Camila brushed my sweaty curls from my neck.

"Yup. that's a good way to put it."

"How so, querida?"

I shrugged, speaking around bites of espagueti. "My chocha does what I want, when I want. If I want it to get wet, I can will it to do so instantaneously. If I want its funk to penetrate a room, I turn the smell up. When I have bad cramps and I know my period is coming, I can tell my vagina to raise the moat and hold the blood in a day or two longer, or I can say let's get this shit over with, and *vroom*, within minutes, the floodgates open."

She seemed stunned at my candid explanation. I sometimes forgot that just because she's the youngest of her siblings, and simply because I knew things about her no one else in the family knew, didn't mean I should be quite so crude with Tía Camila.

"Oh. Oh. Well. That is quite something. But are you sure this is like the rest of our gifts? That might be more a curse."

What can I say? If certain people walk through the world with Big Dick Energy puffing up their chests, I walk through the world secure in the knowledge that my vagine is impenetrable to UTIs, pushes every single love interest into a frenzy, and siren-sings all perioding people to evacuate that shredded uterus faster.

(If I may offer a quick anatomy refresher before I get reprimanded by the ob-gyns and urologists in the comments section, let me acknowledge that the vagina doesn't own the executive functions of menstruation or urination. Menstruation, of course, belongs to the domain of the pituitary gland and the ovaries. And the urethra is parallel to but separate from the vagina. (Although I'm convinced the proximity of the urethra to *my* vajayjay seems to have glittered some hoodoo onto it.) Vaginas *are* in charge of efficiently removing blood and mucus, lubricating the entry to accept penetrating things, and providing a passageway for the birth of a child. And yo, mine be doing the first two functions on a 100.)

My nani's magnetic pull is my little form of magic. Yadi has her tastebud-altered relationship with limes. Tía Pastora has a shrewd sense for what people do not mean, and an unhealthy ability to be the last person still chewing at a Brazilian buffet. Tía Matilde carries a little bit of sadness in her eyes until music comes on, then it's like you could almost picture her pressing jojoba oil to the bottom of her feet the way her soles glide across any surface and transform it into a dance floor. It was rumored in the family that she'd almost been a backup dancer for Fernando Villalona before Mamá Silvia snipped that dream. Tía Camila could take one look at your eyes, or place fingers to your wrist, and concoct a tea for something you didn't know you needed healed.

And then there's Mami. Mami Flor knew the exact hour her mother was going to die. She called me the night I was working on my Anthro 270: Religion, Myths, and Magic final paper and told me it was coming. That's how Mami's thing works. She has a dream about teeth shattering, or she'll complain all day about a terrible pain in her jaw, or she'll be going on her evening walk and no matter how summery the day, her flesh goose-bumps and her teeth begin to chatter. At some point throughout this savage tug-of-war between her dentures and her dreams, a name staggers out of her mouth.

Sometimes Mami knows months in advance: on the second Tuesday in August, primo so-and-so should not drive his car. Sometimes Mami will complain of a toothache for a week, only for the name to escape her mouth just as the phone rings, a family member already calling with the ill-fated news.

Mami is no oracle, or diviner. In fact, for great lengths of time Mami's inclination toward magic is as useless as a CD player, a novelty, a thing to place on display for polite oohs and ahhs. She'll go years where the most she "knows" is that it's going to rain on baby cousin so-and-so's birthday so they shouldn't hold the party at Riverbank. She can sense impending disaster, but her clearest visions are of loss of life.

Or, like a few years ago, I think I had just turned twenty-eight, I met her at her apartment. She was taking her citizenship test for the third time and wanted me to come along with her, for moral support, she said, since I wouldn't be able to join her in the restricted area nor translate for her. Those English lessons from decades ago never did stick.

"Ción, Ma."

"Ona?" she asked, like I wasn't standing right in front of her. She traced the collar of my blouse with her pointer finger. "Are you wearing this yellow top?"

I looked down at the sunny blouse draped around my torso.

Mami grunted. "Mira. I bought you something." She passed me a bag. Inside was a blouse with dark red ruffles.

"Thanks, Ma." She loved buying me clothes. Fabric is my mother's love language.

"Don't just thank me, put it on. Put it on."

Usually, I would have rejected auditioning the blouse on principle. My therapist was constantly reminding me I had to establish little boundaries with my mother as practice for bigger boundaries later. But I figured she'd bought me the blouse for her own good luck, and I didn't want her frazzled before the civics test.

When we arrived at the Javits Center, Mami was trembling.

"Hey, you're going to be okay. We studied." I'd made her flashcards, quizzed her every Friday for two months, and even did a mock interview where I asked her the naturalization questions. Mami complained she had to learn a hundred answers and none of them to the eight questions the interviewer would ask, but I just reminded her it was better to be overprepared. "You got this."

She nodded. The field officer came out from the restricted area. "Flor Marte?"

I squeezed Mami's hand as she was escorted back.

I sat for five minutes, waiting. It could take a while, I knew. While Mami had studied flashcards, I had studied the process: she'd have to take an oath of honesty, answer personal questions, prove she could read and write as well as speak in English, and only then would the exam begin. After ten minutes, I realized the burgundy blouse had turned a shade darker under the armpits. I was sweating so much, so hard that the person next to me had put two whole seats between us. I stood and stepped out of the field office into the glassy interior of the rest of the Javits Center, weaving my way out into the fresh air. There was no CVS nearby, but a small deli catty-corner to the center sold deodorant that I swiped onto my armpits, then underneath my breasts. Even my crotch was sweating, despite those glands typically being well disciplined.

I was pulling at the blouse in an attempt to air it when I collided with a man on the street. From his baldie to his beard to the watchband that peeked out from underneath his cuff when he set his hands on my shoulders to keep me from stumbling, the man glistened. The imprint of his long, tapered fingers echoed along my shoulders even after he'd removed his hands.

His voice was syrupy slow and sweet. "I'm so sorry to have bumped into you. It was your blouse. Oxblood is my favorite shade, and I was so fixated on the color I—well, I'm sorry." He removed his hands from my arms and rubbed his left one over his head, bashful suddenly. "And I'm Jeremiah."

Turned out Jeremiah was a visual artist. He had an exhibit opening around the corner from where Mami's test was, and he was on his own fresh-air walk in between hanging up his latest installation and the opening was that night would I like to come?

Mami passed her test, proudly waving her little American flag as we FaceTimed each of her siblings.

That evening, still wearing the blouse she'd bought me, I made my way to the exhibit. Jeremiah's work was different from art I usually enjoyed. I like depictions of people, their gestures and mouths, and the way a body creases and bends. Jeremiah communicated his ideas through a layout of lights. Thick, braided rope, the kind slave masters used for nooses, turned into netting, lit up like he'd fished them out of the sky. I didn't understand it, but the effort to play with the greatest antithesis of darkness called to me.

We ended up getting coffee after his show. Then he learned I'm a sucker for whiskey and invited me up to share a nightcap of Macallan at his place. In Teaneck. And because I liked his hands, and his sure way of speaking, the way he noticed minute changes in my tone of voice, the attempts at humor most people missed, I said yes and let him drive me across the George Washington Bridge. I didn't envision I'd get in a long-term relationship. I liked my life as it was, but he was like a curveball, just the right challenge that inspired me to step up to bat.

I let my nani loose, and we've been partnered ever since. We moved to a Jersey suburb. Committed to being life partners.

Bought a house. Made a home. All because Mami bought me a blouse and insisted I wear it on that particular day, in that particular part of the city.

When Jeremiah and I met, I was already teaching at City College, but I had no dreams of tenure. I enjoy teaching anthropology there, but I hate the rigamarole of making nice with faculty and administration. Anthropology is where we can look at who humans have been, the cultures they developed around, because of land and language. The rituals they learned to perform in order to make sense of death and war and blessings. And my island in particular has captured my imagination since before I knew that how humans have lived was a thing I could study. My middle school loved talking about some motherfucking Christopher Columbus, and all I could think was, what the fuck does this Italian have to do with Dominicans? It took a long time for me to learn the word *harbinger*, to realize we celebrate Columbus for rupture, for how he helped position Europe and led to the decimation of entire peoples on continents he should have never set foot on.

Which is to say, I want to talk history and do my research, so my career and family life did not seem in conflict. My family comes from magic, and it's something I've known for so long that sometimes I forget not everyone has an innate characteristic that marks them different, that speaks to them like a second conscience. My nani did that for me, until Jeremiah and I began trying for children and I learned that my vagina might never prove how magical it is in the function of allowing passageway for a baby.

And in the midst of this messy and busy life, my mother is dying. And she won't tell me when. And she won't tell me how. And every ticking pulse in my body that I thought I understood has become Morse code I can't decipher.

YADI

diced the onions slow. She did not trust her hands. She did trust that any tears could be easily disguised as a chemical reaction.

Ant had been sifting through rice and picking out all the malnourished grains for over an hour. The thrill of his being here, actually here, had faded, and now Yadi was blanketed by a heavy numbness. As if all the excitement and surprise had exhausted her emotional battery and now it was sending the *LOW POWER MODE* signal.

"I remember you used to hide at my house whenever your moms asked you to help her in the kitchen. You and your mom still beef?"

"Your Mami fed me without requiring any labor. It was a much better deal," Yadi said. "And Ma and I, we have an understanding."

She plopped a chickpea in her mouth and squeezed more lime over the bowl before her.

Ant looked surprised.

"Y eso?"

And he could mean a few things.

At the top of eighth grade, a month after Yadi had gotten her period for the first time, when the boys came back

from summer break, they'd stopped
wanting to hit her in dodgeball or make
fun of her accent, and instead wanted
to tackle her in touch football. It was
also in eighth grade that the students
at PS 333 were allowed to leave the
school premises for lunch. And it was
at the tables of the pizza shop where
she began to place her palm an inch in
front of her mouth before she brought
the food up to her lips.

She'd hated to let the boys, them specifically, watch her eat.
Her mouth seemed too intimate a cavity to let any of them peer
into it, to let them watch her lips, and tongue and teeth and
gnawing.

(She, unlike me, had not been prematurely exposed to
pornography. But she still had a needling that this, looking at someone while they ate, was sexual.)

Her hand began creeping up as she chewed even when it
wasn't at school. First at lunch with her boys, then in the street
when we would buy an icey or a pastelito. And eventually it was
a habit she couldn't shake even at home.

At first, her mother would snap at her hand with a napkin,
but Yadi kept her hand still over her mouth. Her mother took
her to the dentist, but he determined her teeth were fine and
that she didn't have a case of gingivitis or another infection she
was covering. The doctor at Ryan Center took blood pressure

and heart rate and then directed Yadi and her mother to a therapist. Which put Tía Pastora through the roof—she was convinced some trauma had happened, some boy had touched Yadi or done *something* that she was trying to hide behind her teeth.

It was a habit she'd ended up having to shake. Tía Pastora gave her a few months to play her little hiding-mouth game. Then she gave her a week to break the habit herself. The morning after those seven days she began slapping Yadi's hand away if it was anywhere near her lips. Saying only the one time, "If I catch your hand in front of your mouth when eating again, you're going to lose some fingers. Yo no sé que tontería es que se te ha meti'o a ti, but there was no shame in putting that food on that table, and I won't accept any shame in the eating of it. ¿Tú me estás entendiendo, sin vergüenza?"

Yadi stopped after that. Not because of her mother's words, but because of the narrowed look in her mother's eyes. It was not easy to be Pastora's daughter. She was a woman who saw too much. The avoidance of lime, however, not even Tía Pastora could strong-arm from Yadi.

———

Yadi decided she was not going to tell Ant. How she'd woken up one day, her tongue itching for something sour. A craving she'd never had before. Hers was a household that always had limes in the bottom drawer of the fridge, for lemonade, or marinades, or belly aches, and yet, hers was a body that would heave up whatever was inside it the moment her tongue touched the citrus.

He knew her rating chart, of course: Sour oranges? A+. Lemons were wonderful. But the moment her tongue detected lime, it was a stop midbite. Distrustfully looking at whoever had made the food as if they'd attempted a poisoning. It was the pucker it required. Even the way it sat in her stomach felt burdensome, an acid that packed a full-sized suitcase of bitter instead of just a carry-on.

Tía Pastora would often bring up how silly a thing it was to dislike. It truly wasn't *that* different from lemons, and limes were often cheaper. Her own mother kept lime trees in the backyard, saying lime was good for disinfecting bad food, for tea, for creating a salve. It'd been a trial when Yadi had first traveled back to the Dominican Republic and she'd had to explain again and again to Mamá Silvia not to squeeze the fruit into *everything* or for sure she'd starve.

(A little fun fact I've always found interesting: despite our propensity for putting them in *everything*, limes are not native to the Caribbean. It was on the *Pinta* (that motherfucker Columbus's ship) that the first seedlings of limes were brought in 1493. Many crops were attempted in those early days as the Spanish empire hoped the tropical climes would be conducive to an innovative level of agriculture. Many crops failed. But these little seeds took and were even misnomered West Indian limes in English, and limón verde in Spanish. The excess of them on the island to this day is so ubiquitous that they are even more popular than "yellow" lemons.)

Yadi wasn't the kind of kid who stood at her mother's side as a child and helped her cook. She didn't learn traditional recipes. She certainly wasn't a foodie, savoring every bite and going on endlessly about her palate. She'd been a child with a fast metabolism and without a voracious appetite. Regardless, Yadi's mother piled plate after plate for the girl, loving to watch her eat. Her child leaving a well-cleaned plate on the table had tickled all Pastora's jollies. And Yadi did dutifully consume everything on her plate, unless it'd been seasoned with limes. Not limeade, not key lime pie, not fish with lime butter, not salad with lime in the dressing.

And for nineteen years they lived, and even forgot theirs was a household with such a distinct aversion. That is until Mamá died.

> Before the phone call, the frantic purchase of one-way flights to DR, the packing and repacking, the purchasing of black dresses and phone calls to funeral homes, before any of that, Yadi woke up at 5:37 a.m. She was not a morning person. It was the end of spring semester, the sunlight bright through the dorm's shitty blinds, the air of upstate New York still carrying a slight chill in the early morning.

Her first class wasn't until nine a.m., but despite how she tried to go back to sleep, how she tried to brush her teeth and tongue and even the top of her mouth, she was salivating for something sour. She rushed to breakfast, waiting outside the dining hall until it opened at six. She squeezed an entire lemon into her tea, but it wasn't enough. She devoured a grapefruit, but her mouth still itched. She finally asked one of the nice serving ladies if she would procure a slice or two of lime, the words biting on her tongue, as if the utterance alone elicited acid. She, who had known this one fundamental thing about herself, who listed it when asked about dietary restrictions, who had thought it concrete—she who could not digest this one fruit, not even to take a tequila shot, had changed. She didn't know then it wasn't her transition alone.

That morning she squeezed it over her oatmeal, her toast, the powdered scrambled eggs. She was aiming for her coffee, distressed and causing a scene, all the other early bird students watching her ridiculous display, when her phone rang at six forty-five. Ona. Ona who was a senior and often hovered over her little cousin. Ona, the only reason Yadi's mother had even agreed to let her go to a college outside the city, as long as it was *this* school where a family member would be there to watch her.

(I was at best a haphazard caretaker.)

"Where you at?" Ona asked without greeting.

"Why you calling so early?"

The silence on the other end spoke enough.

"I'm at the dining hall. My body is freaking the fuck out. I think I must have scurvy or something because—"

"I'm on my way."

Ona walked in still wearing pajamas and a pair of Uggs that had once belonged to her ex Soraya. Ona, hands as gentle as the sheepskin of her boots, pulled Yadi's fingers away from the rinds she was sucking on.

"I bought us two bus tickets home. You need to email your

professors and tell them you won't be in class. Oh fuck, but you're finance. They'll want you to sit for the tests. Send me your class schedule again; I'll email the dean."

Yadi kept licking her lips. Running the ridges of her tongue along the inside, searching for tartness. Curling her tongue on itself. Her entire mouth searching, searching, searching.

"Did Tía Flor know?" Yadi guessed.

Ona hesitated a second, then nodded.

Yadi's mouth puckered, pushed a long breath out. "She didn't think to tell me?"

Ona's pause was longer this time, mostly because she took a seat next to Yadi, drawing her hands into her own before she spoke. "We decided someone should be with you when you found out. I thought you should sleep. There was nothing you could do."

"I could have called her."

"You wouldn't have. It would have been cruel."

Yadi failed her finance exams, taking the zero to travel to DR instead, to wear black, and pray novenas, and press her face to her grandmother's cold one in the casket. To run her fingers for the last time over her vieja's wrinkles. She knew none of the daughters loved their mother the way she did. They'd never met the Mamá Silvia with girlish dreams, a woman who'd been buffeted, first by her blood kin, then by every one of her children leaving her for lovers, for another country. Some people hardened under the pressure of abandonment, became small, compressed versions of themselves. Some people, like a sail, became threadbare, canvas feathered by sea salt and gales.

Yadi's advisors suggested she switch majors. She did exactly what the family feared and dropped out.

It was a strange bequest, in a family where no one passed down heirlooms, inheriting a taste for limes. And it was an inheritance that paid dividends forward. When Yadi made margaritas, her drinking buddies often found their tongues itching, craving more of her liquored concoctions until folk were drunk within moments. Her vegan key lime pie was always the first thing devoured at a potluck, the recipe requested by everyone who tried it, only to have to send her a disappointed text that theirs didn't come out quite like hers. Her love for Mamá Silvia, and Mamá Silvia's sweet love for her garnished her every manipulation of this sour and slightly bitter fruit. Yadi ran her fingers along the edge of the cutting board before getting back to her food preparations.

"There was nothing beautiful inside," Ant said.

Yadi kept her hand cutting.

"Colors, I mean. Or parks. It was concrete. Cement. Metal. Your mom sent me a picture of your school formal. You wore that bright green. I pinned it to the bunk above me so at least before I went to bed, I remembered the world wasn't only grayscale."

He was still acclimating, she understood.

Yadi didn't know what to say to this confession. She'd shown up to her senior class formal despite having only done one year at the Dominican private school. She'd not had a date, electing instead to attend by herself. Her grandmother had been the one to hang the hand-sewn dress up, and Yadi had worn it.

"Some things take time to cure. Candles aren't candles until they've hardened in the dark and can be turned on without the wax melting before the flame can consume it. Soap isn't soap until the lye and lather binds. Rum takes weeks of adding honey and bay leaf and wine before it can be called or served as mamajuana. Cannabis even needs darkness, to shed itself of moisture, before becoming something that will burn, heal. You're in a curing season," Yadi didn't say.

"Do you still have the picture?"

Ant nodded.

"I'll be cooking tomorrow night, too, when I get home from the shop. You should bring it by. I don't think we have a copy of one here." She looked around as if a high school picture would be hung above the fridge.

It was both dismissal and invitation. And Yadi wasn't sure why she'd issued either. But Ant took the cue, stood up, stretching as he did so, his arms askew and back arching at such a particular angle that Yadi had to bite her tongue. How could so many gestures have remained the same?

FLOR

knew the last thing she needed to do for the wake, the only thing not ornamentation, was write down what she wanted to say.

But she'd never written a eulogy. She'd learned how to compartmentalize the world of the living and the world of the Before and After she still visited in dreams. She was unclear whether she was the traveler or the destination, so maybe the Before and After visited her.

She hadn't had language to explain early on to her family that she felt like a living ghost, slightly untethered from the everyday details that seemed to make life both beautiful and unbearable. Perhaps that's why the only foundational theory she had about the point of living had to do with love, because it was the weight of love toward someone, like an ankle bracelet on her body, that had first pulled her heels down to the earth.

When Cousin Nazario first moved to the town, her father had merely said that he was going to introduce them to his favorite nephew, who would be coming around more often. Flor had expected a little snot-nosed boy she'd

have to pinch into compliance, like she
did with Pastora.

But the young gentleman who pulled up one day on a butter-scotch mare was unlike anyone she'd ever witnessed. Although televisions had become commonplace in the homes of Americans and the well-to-do, it wasn't until a decade later that Flor would sit in front of a screen with access to the faces and features of people who were not her neighbors or immediate kin. Flor had no comparisons for this young man, had no sense of knowing that what bloomed in her chest was a crush, although she would explain to me when I explained it to her that the word "crush" made perfect sense since that's exactly what it'd felt like: a fist squeezing her heart until it molded into the inside of that palm. His hands were the first thing she noticed; the fingers were long and he kept his nails clean. The family lined up for greetings and kisses, Mamá the first to offer the boy a blessing and welcome.

Flor inched toward the back, afraid to bring her face close to the boy's in greeting. Her hands were sweating against her skirt. When everyone else had said hello and hugged him, his eyes turned to her. And she'd never felt more human than in that moment. She hoped both her eyes were looking straight at him, a startling realization since she rarely thought about her wandering eye and had never before made wishes regarding its directional pull.

She dared not say anything to her sisters, because this was an ugly-tinged affection. They were blood relations, second cousins at most, she wasn't sure. She comforted herself that the long fingers of the church and a divine life would untangle the feelings one day. Or so she prayed. And for the first time in her existence when she fell away to dreams, she was haunted by something other than premonitions.

———

This would be a short speech if she went down that route. Her dead had taught her many things. She'd once watched a movie with a little boy who could speak to dead people and was in fact being counseled by one who didn't know he had passed to the afterlife. Her daughter had raved about the ending. Flor did not find anything spectacular in the film except for the supreme fear the little boy felt, and the fact that Americans loved to associate death with misery and gore. Her dreams weren't gentle, but they also didn't cause her to dread going to bed. Her sleep sense was like having an extra finger on a hand. It looked odd to others, and sometimes it made certain situations clumsy, but other times it allowed for additional support when trying to hold on to something. It just was. She slept, and most nights she did not remember her dreams. And sometimes she slept and it was clear that she was privy to knowledge that could alter the world for some people. Was this what she was supposed to say on Saturday? That she had loved. And that her gift and life made it difficult to love. But her human self persisted nonetheless. Maybe.

MATILDE

planted her key into the first lock with a forceful jab. It didn't necessarily sound any different than when she usually slotted the key into place, but she still took a moment to admire herself for not cowering at the prospect of what was on the other side.

The first lock. The bolt slid back next. As was her ritual before she entered the house, she touched her pointer finger to the little Baby Jesus sticker she'd placed beneath the peephole years ago. An air bubble the size of a dime had gotten caught right where Baby Jesus's thorn-wrapped heart was depicted. Her thumb had run over this spot a thousand, no, *tens* of thousands of times, and while it might smooth a bit, the air pocket always came back; a bulging, barbed heart that could not be tamed by gentle fingers. And her fingers were gentle, as soft and light as they'd been when they'd grazed the baseball player's.

Dance class was good as a distraction, but she was always disappointed that at some point she had to go back home.

She shoved that thought away with the same force she applied to the door, although the latter she rushed to catch before the doorknob could make a dent in the wall behind it. She kept her footsteps light. Her cell phone was on airplane mode. She entered the kitchen and did not even turn on the light before holding her breath and pressing the caller ID on her home phone. There were two missed calls, goddamn telemarketers again, but none from her sisters.

Pastora had not told the others what she'd seen with Rafa and the pregnant woman.

The beeping of her phone, which despite airplane mode had grasped onto the house Wi-Fi, stopped her heart for a moment. But when she opened the group chat, there was only a smattering of messages, and none of them turbulent. Matilde knew she should feel relieved. She should want to handle this without interference and opinions that would stifle the breath of her own desires.

The lights were on in the bedroom, and she found Rafa lying on the bed, blue boxer briefs worn high at the waist, and a white tank covering his hair-dotted chest. He'd begun dyeing his chest hair on his fifty-first birthday but had grown lazy in the task the last few years, and now, at sixty-nine, a few sharp, straight, gray hairs—textured like nothing else on his body—jabbed out from the low neckline. The sports announcer on the TV screamed excitedly. Her husband glanced at her, then did a double take.

"You were helping Yadi?" His long lashes flickered over his hazel eyes as he looked at her from head to toe. "You look like she was making you carry boxes."

"It's Thursday. I had my dance class."

He wiggled his eyebrows. "And you must have spun your heart out." He began to sing badly; his off-kilter warble would usually make her smile.

"You want to dance for me? I bet I can loosen those hips like your instructor can't." He said it with a sleepy drawl, the once-over of a man who had twice- and thrice-overed her in the early days.

Matilde took off each little gold hoop. Unclasped her watch. In the bathroom mirror she pulled the brush through her hair starting at the back, sectioning chunks of hair and pinning them to her skull until the dubi looked like an artist's coiffure and not simply a sleep style. The redecilla she tied on loosely, the net more or less decorative since her pins were holding everything tightly. She'd need to brush any hard-pinned spots in the morning.

"¿Oíste, vieja?" Rafa called from the other room. The baseball game was now off, and his voice echoed in their small room. "I don't know what to wear on Saturday. Should I do the floral shirt you got me last Christmas? But the button on the sleeve needs to be resewn."

Matilde put on the big, loose T-shirt that read *BINGHAMTON* across the front. She'd joined Flor on the college visit when Ona had first visited the school. And was part of the caravan that drove up to drop off Yadi a year later. Matilde loved the white and green colors and had liked to imagine her nieces there, at the big school by the Pennsylvania border, even if Yadi hadn't finished.

Her husband hadn't been wanting a response. He didn't ask again. He turned into her when she got into bed. A hand at her hip and then he was snoring. Unfazed by the actions he'd taken, he slept better than most babes. She picked up her phone. She opened the cafetería tomorrow and she was a stickler about checking her alarms. Both alarms were always set, even on the weekends, even on the days she didn't open. Satisfied that that was still true, Matilde plugged the phone into her charger and went to set it down, and the phone was just out of her hand so she thought she'd caused the vibration it made when it landed against her nightstand.

She picked it up. It wouldn't be unheard of for one of her siblings to text so late. For Yadi to add a last-minute change to the menu.

El Pelotero, with his loose hips and mouth near her ear as he twirled her, had put his number in her phone. And he'd messaged her. Her heart skipped. Matilde put the phone back on the nightstand.

She reached down and lifted the fingers Rafa had put on her hip. It was an act of mercy that she did not break each one.

I

lay awake and counted down. Forty-one hours until the wake. Jeremiah was in his basement studio, insulated so well that neither light nor sound trickled up to our bedroom on the second floor. He offered no single distraction. Houses always freaked me out because another human could be anywhere in the square footage and you might not know. In my childhood apartment, the moment I walked through the door it'd been clear when the neighbors were home, the upstairs rugrats, and Mami and Papi in their bedroom.

I think my mother is probably glad my father is dead. That he cannot attend whatever this event is on Saturday. She is too soft-spoken, too nonconfrontational to ever say so, but it was unspoken in our household that life in general would have been easier if it'd been just me and her. Which is a complicated sentiment to come to terms with when a man is not violent, or a cheater, but is still a man who puts his own desires and addictions over the well-being of those who sacrifice for him time and again.

I had a father who drank on the weekends. Every weekend. Shitfaced. It might have been easier to understand as a child if he'd been a full-blown, daily alcoholic. With his Friday paycheck he'd purchase two bottles of Brugal and a bucket of fried chicken from the KFC on the corner. The chicken was to appease Mami, who at least wouldn't have to cook on Fridays while her husband drank himself to whatever oblivion called to him.

My father was not an angry drunk. Not even a mean drunk. But there was something brutal in watching him undo the self he built Monday through Friday, glass by glass removing the constraints that kept him tightly buttoned in his Carhartt suit at his factory job, that kept him private and quiet at home. The lips he rarely used to smile in affection or approval became El Chacal's grin after the bottle was halfway done.

Mami and I would sit with him, a family affair, until the fourth glass.

I don't know if I learned how to tell the signs of his drunkenness by watching Mami. The more gregarious my father grew, the more her shoulders hunched, until by silent accord we would look at each other and she would give me a nod to head to bed. Soon, I'd hear her chancletas shuffling to her own bedroom. It was after we'd left that the sound in the living room hushed. Papi muted the TV, but didn't turn it off; I learned to listen for the white noise of the mute button, to watch out for the faint light from the screen that seeped a red carpet underneath my door.

I couldn't say what made me do it the first time. Except that maybe I was a kid, eight years old, and my share of curiosity had been meted out by a generous hand. I did have enough of an instinct of the quiet in the living room to myself be quiet in its observation.

I learned to turn the knob of my bedroom on a whisper, sneaking into the hall between my bedroom and the living room, the light of the TV throwing my father in full relief, as if sculpted from the wall and couch. I mastered the journey of fifteen steps that year.

The porn he watched didn't seem specific; I assumed it wasn't a video, because my father wasn't one to rent movies, and the women on the screen looked nothing like the big-booty trigueñas my father hailed gorgeous in my presence. It must have just been whatever was playing on the black-box channel I wasn't supposed to know about.

These writhing blond women, their hands never seemingly involved in the act, fascinated me. Or rather, their hands did. How they never caressed the men's faces, or patted their shoulders, or welcomed them in any way. Infrequently the hands would DJ their own puss. Whenever this happened, I cheered silently; this seemed a much better use for their fingers than draping them limply on the bed.

I usually only watched for a few minutes before, clinging to shadows, I let myself back into my bed. There, I took note of my flushed cheeks, of the ways my box felt *something*—better?— when I squeezed my legs together, or put my pillow between my thighs, and most certainly when I reached down with my own fingers to inspect the wetness there. The wetness sparked. And as I thought of it, I turned it on further, like a faucet for more moisture. My mind and wet wet and pleasure were connected, and each did what I wanted.

Then one night, when the house murmured itself quiet, I

touched myself while imagining what he was watching. I caressed myself in a way that felt like a race, or like dodgeball except instead of running from the ball I ran toward it, hoping to get hit right in the solar plexus. I lay sweating, my hand smelling, the rush of pleasure. And then I was just sticky. I got up to go wash my hand in the bathroom. But I knew the noise might penetrate my father's sense of propriety, and I wanted, needed another look. Could I touch myself twice in one night? I took on the challenge. I crept near the living room. I watched for a long time, my body exciting itself all over, whatever pinpricks of wrongness I might have felt overwhelmed by the desire to sneak my hands back into my panties.

But there was no decision to make; before I could move, a mouse ran from underneath the TV. I watched it scamper into the TV's light before it dove under the couch. Where my father was sitting. His eyes on me. I do not know how long he'd been watching.

Neither of us moved, neither of us said a word.

My father did not turn the channel nor turn off the TV. My eyes raced back to the screen, where the woman's mouth was open, open the way I sometimes forgot to close my mouth in the shower. I didn't pretend to sneak back to my room. I closed my door with an audible click.

My father, who rarely asked me a question unless it was a request to bring him a plate or recite a poem for one of his barbershop friends, never brought it up. But the uncanny had already occurred.

I stopped sneaking into the living room late at night. But I could not stop my imagination. And like with a word you learn for the first time, then begin to see it everywhere, images of bodies coupling elbowed their way into my thoughts in the most innocent of moments.

My fingers taught my mind's eye that I could re-create most of the scenes I'd viewed; I could superimpose Morris Chestnut, or Jessica Alba; I could even use my Barbies to figure out all the positions I had never witnessed, including ones impossible for the actual human body.

It felt good. And it felt wrong. My body loved seeking the pleasure of my hands, of the other household objects I eventually experimented with. But my brain reminded me that the glide of fingers and bodies was for the dark, to be put on mute, hidden, secret acts.

It was a lot of conflict for a small girl to house.

I did slink along the hallway wall one other time I could remember. It was maybe a year later, just before Mami sent me to DR that first time. It was the hour of the night when only the rats in the walls were moving. I woke up as if from a nightmare, sitting straight up. The hairs on my arms at attention. I listened for a noise I might not know, and I remember I almost lay back down when I heard another murmur, coming from the kitchen.

I followed the sound.

By the stove, Mami pressed the front of her nightgown to her face. She was sobbing as I'd never seen. I knew she had difficult dreams sometimes, but none had ever rendered her this desperate, at least not in my presence. The near-silent heaving of her body, moonlit inside her bata. I was not a child prone to easy touches, but I pressed my arms around her middle, put my face into her stomach. Rubbed her back. I do not think I told her it would be okay. She sniffed herself tearless, still. Her fisted right hand opened against my spine. Rubbing up and down.

I did not ask why she'd been crying. Mami wasn't out here confiding in children, and I hadn't yet learned how to ease a person into desahogar-ing themselves. I don't know when we separated. How long we twined. Papi, in a drunken stupor, slept on.

I've thought of my father more in the last year than I did even when he died in 2017, suddenly, not a failing liver, or all the other things doctors had warned would be his fate, but from stepping off the curb too quickly on a day he was actually sober but distracted and inattentive to the car making a fast turn. I did not develop a taste for liquor quite as voracious as his. But I find solace in the videos and erotic stories of people fucking, of the spectrum of human expression that comes from sexual activity. Even at a young age, I learned that the rigged cable box actually had two channels for porn, and I learned how to switch quickly from one to PBS when I heard an adult coming down the hall. I learned, probably by the time I was fourteen, that the regular positions and straight hetero sex were too timid and mundane. My eyes, hungry for other ways to understand this act, feasted when smartphones and free porn could be snuck into one's pocket.

Maybe this is what my father taught me, that in the night, it's important to listen to the little noises, to decipher the loud silence from the hushed ones; listening with these different ears fulfills varied promises.

———

My mother had me when she was in her midthirties. I glance at the clock. It's almost three a.m. Too late to call her with another question, but I want to ask if she thinks that people are most interested in becoming parents *after* they became jaded. When our own hope buoys us to keep going, there is no need to go searching for it in another's new and fresh world gaze.

At a certain age in young adulthood, I used to dream I was pregnant and would wake up frantically patting my belly. Relieved that the catastrophe of being a mother could be avoided by simply returning to consciousness.

We had been careful, Jeremiah and I, to minimize any potential disruptions to the life we'd architected. We were a family unit, we told each other. Whispering it when our blood relatives were fighting, when we were having disagreements with parents, when a family member who borrowed money never paid it back. We are each other's kin. Chosen and rechosen. Progeny had a place, but it was not one I was concerned with in my late twenties, much less once my career became the entity that needed my sweat and to be fed from my teats. We were making a mark, clawing up out of the mud of our chosen fields, I would tell Jeremiah, undoing the dust of colonization.

Jeremiah was raised in North Carolina. A small town called Ayden, where his kin had lived as far back as they had familial memory. He was loved by his parents, and aunties and uncles, and grandparents and cousins, a bounty of humans that raised each generation from the soil of a first fall to the soil of a lowered casket. He had told me since we first met that he wanted children. I was weighed down by the onslaught of terrible border wars and the heating planet and the melting ice caps and the Black death we were surrounded by, this gladiator pit of a life.

I wanted children one day, maybe. But back when we met? I had my work. And my work had my name. And my work was in the archives and documented on JSTOR, and students and scholars for as long as searching was possible would stumble across my work and name. You see, I had no *use* for a child. And I doubted I'd be of much use to one either. Not yet.

And then last year, on my annual birthday appointment, my gyno said I had a heavy uterus.

"What the fuck is a heavy uterus?" My gyno had been my gyno for over a decade and didn't mind my potty mouth.

"I don't know how to explain it, except it feels weighted. Something inside of it. Could be twins."

I scoffed. I still had my IUD in. Twins? Something happened at the thought. What if it was twins? I didn't feel the panic I expected. The need to pinch myself to ensure I was dreaming. Babies, for the first time in my life, made sense for me, for us.

The doctor ordered an ultrasound. But there were no yolk sacs, no flashing microscopic hearts.

The fibroid was the same size as the uterus it protruded from. Which in terms of fibroids is rather tame, since they could be melon-sized, my doctor told me.

(It wasn't lost on me, then or now, that both uterine tumors and embryo sizes are compared to produce; blessed be the stone fruit of the womb, I guess.)

The moment the doctor told me there was a complication, the chance that motherhood might not be possible, it was like a bulb had been secretly screwed in overnight.

Mami was beside herself that I would need a myomectomy, this young, this invasive. "They are going to cut you open? I kept you so healthy when you were here. And then you leave, to live on your own, and look. Tumors in your uterus." Her teeth suck almost recalibrated us.

Regardless of what was going on, Mami was still Mami, and normally, Ma making a dramedy of every interaction would make me smile. But not in this.

"It's not considered life-threatening. And a fibroid usually doesn't develop until childbearing years, so of course I didn't have one when I lived at home."

"I've not dreamt anything," my mother said. Her way of offering comfort, or of giving it to herself. Surely if her girl were going to die, she'd know.

The night before the surgery I wanted to offer prayer, a request to someone. I wanted to believe that while my surgeon would take care of me, someone would take care of my surgeon, feel me? But although the prayers of my youth still slithered easily off my tongue, they felt untethered from my heart. I prayed to no one. And woke up well. And my surgeon performed his job of controlling robotic arms in my core without issue.

I do not remember the surgery. They put me under and cut me open laparoscopically—"Surgery with chopsticks!" the specialist joked. They made five incisions along my belly button, which were used to enter my uterus and shear apart the fibroid. An additional four-inch smiley-face incision was made right above my pelvis. This last slice was where the tiny pieces of tumor were pulled out in bagged chunks. It was like I'd had a tiny caesarean but no babe. On the operative report, the fibroid was even described as being "fourteen weeks."

I felt changed after. Yes, because I no longer had a growth sapping energy from my reproductive organs, but it was more than that. Light had seeped into the inside of me. It had been sewn up in places that had lived quietly, festering. Light had touched the growth that had come for me, and it stayed behind when that growth was removed, stroking my core. It was not just a healthier body that had been returned to me. I spent nights rubbing each scar over their gauze; here, and here, and here, and here, and here and here: I was opened, I was reclosed. My fingertips warmed with each touch. I wanted to thank someone, and I began turning to my ancestors.

They managed to preserve my uterus, but it was stitched up like a football with leather seams on multiple sides.

Getting surgery is like being proposed to, the preciousness of it. The way you cradle the newly adorned part *just so*. The way you accidentally bump and ding the damn thing a dozen times before you even get out of your bedroom the first day. My mother, who had come to stay with us, tried to tell me I needed to be careful, that the meat was cruda, newly sewn on the inside. Mami was right. Aren't we all raw inside? All of the time? This body I had delighted in for decades felt like a costume I'd been stripped of, down to the meat and bones of slow recalibration. My vagina bled tissue and remains from my jostled womb, and it took months and months for me to retake hold of my gift, to control when and how much.

I was cleared to start trying to conceive six months ago. But despite Pre-Seed, daily temperature checks, and tight observance of my fertile window, nothing had grown in my uterus. My ob-gyn reminded me every time I pinged her it that it takes most women up to a year.

The social media algorithms conspired against me. Every post and ad seemed to be tiny baby toes and new announcements of expecting friends. I fingered the scar at my pelvis.

After the myomectomy I developed a lactation porn fetish, frantically rubbing my clit as lovers licked at the milky titties of beautifully rounded women. Even after I'd finished, when my blood was quieting down, I continued watching, fascinated.

(To be fair to myself, I was not only fascinated by their new-breastfeeding bodies. I also wondered about union rights for the women. What were maternal benefits for sex workers in the porn industry? Was there adequate time and space for pumping? Was fetish porn more lucrative than regular porn? When did they wean their children, since orgasms and milk spurts could be so interrelated—surely that kind of squirting should be doubly compensated?)

My father was not around for my surgery. But his legacy lived on: I turned to the porn industry while my organs healed, while I worked to stitch up other parts of my psyche.

Cycle after cycle since, I've been fighting a battle between my superstition and logic. My superstition tells me that I said out loud too many times I didn't want children. That whatever thing listened to the pleas and demands of humans paid attention to that request. For years, not ever having a pregnancy scare was a source of pride. Now when I feel cramps, and my impending flow, I clamp it off for days. Trying to convince my body it's wrong. To undo the period this is into the babe that is not.

It is my mother I want to ask about life and its disappointments. How do you learn to live with what will not be? How do you console yourself with the life that you have when the humans you love most are hopeful for more than you? If I were to have a child, what should I tell them about the grandparents they may never meet? The truth? I count down. The wake is in thirty-nine hours, and it is too late to call my mother.

ONE DAY
UNTIL THE WAKE

FLOR

woke with a start. She'd been having the same dream for over a week now. It grew more vivid every night. You weren't supposed to feel pain in dreams, but she woke to kick off the comforter and sheet, rubbing the apex where she'd long ago been bitten by a snake; her dream self and barely awake self both felt the pierce of fangs.

She checked the clock. It was still too early to call Pastora. Ona thought she was Flor's first call of the day, but it was always her younger sister. If she didn't call her first thing, Pastora grew annoyed.

"You're the one who lives alone. Anything could happen and we wouldn't know a thing."

Flor would nod into the phone. They'd always worried about the other being alone.

Flor sat at the top of the bank. The water was quiet today, unstirred by the breeze that didn't quite reach into the valley. This was where she and Pastora would often come to steal an hour or two of leisure, out of earshot from their mother or little siblings. But Pastora was gone.

Although "gone" didn't seem the right word.

¿*Se fue?* Little Camila seemed to be asking her with her wide, newborn eyes.

Mamá Silvia had finally borne a post-Pastora pregnancy to full term. Camila would be her last belly and baby, arriving into the world exactly six months after Pastora had been sent away. Mamá constantly said it was no coincidence. Flor constantly bit her tongue in reply.

Flor stood at the window looking for Pastora's swinging arms and raised chin and ferocious furrowed brows. Waiting, too, for the boisterous laughter, the impromptu spun stories, the little dulces of melted sugar that Pastora made and cooled in the early mornings, a treat she snuck into Pai's and Samuel's canteens, wanting them to have something sweet to suck on in the fields when the salt of their sweat stockpiled beneath their tongues.

¿*Se fue?* ¿*Se fue?* she imagined the newborn asked when she cooed. A parakeet with only one song. Flor began to answer the unasked question in nods, unable to work around the knot in her throat. The decision had been swift, a machete that left only a whistle in its wake.

Abuela Eugenia and the nun aunt had arrived two days before Christmas. The driver they paid tipped his hat and promised to return to pick them up in three days. Flor had her books packed. Her pencils had been sharpened over candlelight with Samuel's pocketknife. She had two new ribbons she'd saved up for, and her best dress was pressed and hanging over the bedroom vanity. Her hope was she would pass the inspection of her grandmother and nun aunt and they would take her back with them. She'd been studying for the entrance exam, had brushed up on bible verses in both Spanish and Latin. Mamá Eugenia had kissed her cheek with approval; the nun aunt, smelling of frankincense and oranges, laid a hand on her shoulder and kissed her forehead. Pastora was not home when they arrived. She *was* home later that night when they heard a motor purring in front of the house. Only a handful of people in town could afford an automobile, Flor remembered thinking as her needle mended a hole in a sock. Pastora had not been received by their grandmother and aunt with the same affection; the grand-mother had noted the smudge on her cheek. Their nun aunt did not like how the girl had informally greeted her without so much as a "bendición."

The knock had been expected as the motor had stopped. Flor lowered the sewing; Mamá Silvia fluttered a hand, which Pastora correctly interpreted as an order to get the door.

When Doña Yokasta swept in, her dress skimming the floor, they all sat a bit more alert. She was a tall woman, thin, her waist cinched tight. The fact that she came from money was demonstrated in the way she held her hand just so, as if invisible stacks of money were balanced on her palm.

Flor noticed that Pastora had turned white as sugarcane flesh in the moment before the girl dropped her head, hiding behind her hair.

Mamá Silvia offered Doña Yokasta a coffee that Flor would have to be the one to make. She went into the kitchen without being asked. Doña Yokasta had one of those voices that you knew were artificially loud, like she knew exactly how high the knob on the volume went but kept trying to inch up against the resistance.

And so it was not hard while the greca steamed to listen

to Doña Yokasta recount that something rather odd had happened to her; why, she'd been in Santiago shopping for the family Christmas outfits, and arrived home to find that the church garments had been delivered, but no, that wasn't the strange part, the strange part was that when she went upstairs, to her bedroom on the third floor, mind you, she found small, muddy footprints on the Persian rug she'd inherited from her grandmother, and even odder—here, a long pause, for effect, Flor thought—something had been taken from her dresser, and oh, she wasn't one to accuse a child from a respectable family of thievery, but her son wasn't the one who could have taken it and his own feet would not have been able to fit into these little penny-loafer footprints, did they have any idea what might have happened since it was from this house that the sacred garments had been delivered?

There was silence after her story. Flor came out with the coffee, sugar, and milk. Doña Yokasta smiled a small smile but said black and bitter would be just fine. "And were you the one who delivered the vestments yesterday, dear?" Flor looked over at her mother before she spoke. But the nun was quicker.

"Answer an adult when they ask you a question, girl! No faltes el respeto."

Flor shook her head, no.

Doña Yokasta looked at where Camila was gestating in her mother's womb. "¿Y tú, bebé?" Camila, three months in utero, did not kick or thump in response to the ironic question.

"Your eldest?"

Mamá Silvia shook her head. "Matilde has been sick all week. She's not left the house."

And well, the ancestors in their beloved generosity have

their own sense of timing and tragedy, and who knows the trickster spirit who was guiding Pastora's feet as she attempted to sneak out the back door. She got tangled in her skirt hem and tripped. All eyes flew to the girl.

"Ah, and you're a servant or the last daughter?"

"Pastora," the girl whispered, "the youngest. So far." She eyed her mother's growing frame before she looked back at Doña Yokasta. Pastora was the only one of Mamá Silvia's children to answer the woman while looking her right in the eye.

"Pastora! Yes. That sounds like what my son said. And is it true, you kissed my son and invited yourself to his room so he wouldn't tell me you stole from us?"

Flor dropped the sugar tray she'd still been holding. Her hands were shaking so hard that even as she tried to pick up the cracked pieces of porcelain, all she managed to do was bloody her fingers. This was bad this was bad. Mamá Silvia was going to kill Pastora, and her dreams hadn't even told her so she could tell the girl to run. No, Flor had not dreamt this. She would have gotten a sign if imminent tragedy had been about to strike, but dreams don't always follow the schedule one would want.

Pastora was a quick study. "That isn't true, no." She took a step back, as if the wilds behind their house might offer shelter, but Flor knew. From her vantage point on the floor, she had the best view of each woman's chin and forehead: Mamá's chin wobbled angrily, and her forehead was furrowed, the nun aunt's chin was hard and set, the wimple not covering the smooth lines of a forehead that'd spent years learning resignation, and then there was Abuela's face, the flash of anger striking like quick-whipped lightning. Flor glanced to the door. Maybe Pai would be home for supper soon.

Abuela straightened up. A woman of means. Not as wealthy as Doña Yokasta, but someone to respect. The show of pride made everything worse. As if the resolution must be extra severe to make it easier to swallow.

"Well, that just won't do. We hope we haven't sullied your family or son's honor. We'll deal with the girl in such a way that she won't be a bother to you anymore. And of course, your item will be returned."

Doña Yokasta pursed her lips. Clearly, she'd wanted a more explosive response to her announcement. She took one more sip of her coffee and stood.

"I don't want my driver to be late for dinner." Always benevolent, the Doña Yokasta. "Thank you for handling my concerns."

After she left, and only then, was the chaos uncaged. Abuela was the only one who spoke. "I always told you the way you abandoned us for that man would be your downfall. Look at the children he's spawned. And even when we tried to get you married by the church, done the right way, you were too stubborn, and what life have you offered your offspring? They could have had everything, but instead . . ." Their grandmother flicked at her knee where a speck of dust had had the audacity to fall. "Well, the nuns have high hopes for that one. We will put in a good word." She nodded in Flor's direction before turning back to Mamá Silvia. "And your sister had hoped you'd part with the little one when she was born, but at least this one will prove useful."

And so it was decided. They would take Pastora with them and put her to work somewhere where she could not get in trouble. With her gone, Doña Yokasta's rumors would have less fodder.

Pastora was Pai's favorite, and he would hunt for her beneath the house, or call her down from the mango tree out back,
ending her daily banishment with a kiss on the forehead. Some
days, Pastora was out there for two or three hours before Pai
would come home for lunch. They didn't consult him before
they decided to send her away. Flor wanted to run to the fields.
To tell him what was happening. She still regrets she didn't.

———

Flor drank her morning coffee and slathered butter on toast.
She craved a marmalade that Yadi had made one year, giving
batches and batches to her aunts. It took the girl weeks to perfect the recipe, the balance between pectin and sour. It'd had
to cure for all the flavors to marry.

Yadi had moved on from her jam phase, but Flor had always hoped she'd return to that passionfruit-and-lime preserve.
She'd asked if they could have it for the wake. "We don't have
time, Tía. I would have had to start preparing for it weeks ago,
and it's too energy-consuming for just one condiment out of
all the things I have to make."

Flor understood. But her cravings didn't. She picked up the
phone to make her round of calls. She shook off the piercing
dreams and memories.

YADI

had slept in fits. Afraid to give herself over to dreams. She was no Tía Flor, whose dreams carried omens. Tía had had to teach herself an iconography of dreamscapes to interpret meaning from that thinned veil. Yadi's dreams dressed themselves in plain speech.

She'd dreamt of Ant before, but it was always the kids they once were who occupied those dreams. It was ice cream trucks and shared headphones. Not a body on fire, not the adult them: outlet and socket. Not their grown bodies, their wanting bodies, their hungry bodies. So this dream had been a thirst, a first.

Yadi had woken up and downed the glass of water she kept on her nightstand. Then had had to rush to the kitchen to pour herself another glass. And another. She tingled, live wire sparking.

She, who usually took a shower on its hottest setting, turned only the cold knob on this morning. Her mouth hung open the entire time, as if she could make a fountain of herself if she stayed just like this: water trickling down her lips, down the upturn of her nipple, the curve of her belly.

She lay in the tub, let the showerhead rain on her. Shimmied down until her ass scraped the drain. She opened herself up beneath the faucet, undulated as the cold water lapped her clit. It took her too long to come. The old drain cutting into her ass cheeks, her legs tired from grinding against water, her hand squeezed a nipple as if trying to push a nut from its shell.

She knew how she liked to be touched.

When she broke open, she broke open, deep sobs of relief racking through her. But relief gave way to feelings that were studded with spikes. Her weeping turned into that of a creature that had done itself injury, tried to get a crumb to eat and instead stepped into a bear trap.

The water and hunger her body possessed seemed lewd now that she looked at herself splayed, knees propped up on the tub sides, water sluicing down her ass crack. This was the first way she'd learned sexual pleasure, and she did not associate it with guilt, with shame. But Ant's presence was looming in the apartment. Listening to every moan.

Ant had been haunting her for years, but his physical presence returned her to a version of herself she'd thought she'd buried.

She'd not been on board when the plan was first hatched. She didn't want to go to DR. She didn't want to see Mamá. She wanted to relive sitting in the courthouse for the trial. She wanted to replay the last time she'd seen Ant, as he was marched off, the blades of his back prodding through the too-big jumpsuit. She wanted to remain, vigilant and dutiful in the loss not only of

her best friend, her boyfriend, but of all
the futures they'd concocted together.
She certainly did not want to return
here, to the very spot she'd described
to him in lush detail. Painting for him
the native land he'd yet to visit.

But after the fifth time of getting in-school suspension, this
last time for popping a boy straight in the mouth, Tía Pastora
called her mother, Mamá Silvia. After that conversation a plane
ticket was purchased, and Tía escorted Yadi to the high school,
where she proceeded to unenroll her.

"But ma'am, this is highly unusual at this point in the
school year. Unless, of course, are you all moving?"

Tía Pastora studied the assistant principal, her unironed
collar, perhaps trying to decide if she wanted to play around
with a minion or demand to see the real head of school.

"My husband and I decided to homeschool her. It's been a
difficult time, and I think she needs more one-on-one, at least
until next fall."

Everyone at the school knew about Ant. The news of his
arrest, his trial, his sentence had haunted the halls for over a
year.

"I think maybe if we just scheduled some time with the
counselor? To help with the recent anger. Her grades have been
excellent here! We'd hate to lose Yadira." The assistant principal
pronounced her name as if annoyed at the effort required for
her tongue to kiss her front teeth: *Yuh-dee-ruh.*

The assistant principal was still talking. "She's one of our
best students."

And from the depths of her twin lakes of reverie and apathy, Yadi internally sighed. Tía Pastora is nothing if not prideful. Tía's back had straightened.

"Oh. Correct me if I'm wrong, pero, I'm pretty sure Yadi is first in her class. Arguably, and *singularly*, your best student. No? And as such, I think she's far enough ahead in her academics here that I don't know what more you can teach her, and I'd rather correct her behavior at home. I'm sure you understand."

Yadi had been in Honors and AP classes since ninth grade, her credits accumulating at such a rapid pace each semester that she'd had enough to graduate early by the time she entered her junior year, if she'd so chosen. She'd sat for the SATs in middle school, and her score was basically unimprovable, the margin of error so slight she'd started taking family bets on whether or not she could figure out the single question that had kept her from a perfect score. In the trajectory of Yadi's life, the life the larger society would read to understand her on paper, nothing had happened. A highly achieving child would be removed from school and homeschooled. Y ya.

Yadi was sent to the Dominican Republic a few days after that conversation with the rumpled assistant principal.

It was her first time back since moving to New York, and she observed with despondence all the changes that had been made to the new airport wing, the roadwork. Eyes flickering over all the changes that hadn't been made as well: the garbage piled up in the gutters of town, the patchwork tin roofs men volunteered in groups to fix, their own black hands the only thing keeping the poorest people dry during hurricane season. Here, in el campo, it was not the official government but an ecosystem of county rules and neighborly codependence that met the needs of the community.

Mamá Silvia's plot of land was guarded by a sentinel of lime trees, the back of the house leading to a wooded area by the river. It was remote. Her family had lived here always. Even when Trujillo had his minions comb the countryside for young women to rape and land to confiscate, Mamá's family had managed to protect her virtue and the deed from El Jefe. Her husband was required to work it, but it was put in her name after his death.

Yadi's first week was spent waking up with the roosters and going to lie outside in the grass watching the sunrise. Mamá Silvia would watch from the window, calling out when the sun was high: "Ven pa' dentro before you burn. Stop acting like a gringuita from rabble and rubble!"

Although she had been a girl when the rabble and rubble Americans had occupied the Dominican Republic the first time, Mamá Silvia never talked about the memories of the soldiers with wide smiles and big guns and very little honor, as evidenced by how they'd terrorized the countryside. All dark-skinned, blue-eyed folks in this area knew exactly how they'd been begotten.

But Yadi would let Mamá's words mist over her. She'd stay lying there for hours, her nails scratching at the dirt like she was removing dandruff from her mother's scalp. Listening to the song "Put It on Me" on her iPod Shuffle, weeping, all the while attempting to ignore the back-and-forth flickering of the window curtain. This kind of indulgent teen angst would have had her grandmother shooing at her with a broom to be useful and stop crying over a man, except Ant was only a boy, and

Yadi's heartbreak was so very palpable, as if it'd been tenderly folded, packed in her carry-on, and used to shroud her slight form from any hint of breeze. Something had died in her, and as was appropriate, the child was in deep mourning.

Mamá Silvia still demanded she be useful, but she didn't sigh too loudly when Yadi cried while doing dishes. Sometimes a woman must weep. As long as the oficios were done, and the tears were mopped from the tiles, who was Mamá to complain?

In the relative isolation of el campo, Yadi had thought she would feel imprisoned too. There was no computer in the house. No ethernet cord. Depending on the time of day, and the schedule of the powers that be, often there wasn't even reliable electricity. Her cell phone died for good in the middle of her playing a long-running game of *Snake*. That final connection to the Before had puttered out, and she found it liberating, in fact.

She and Mamá rubbed alongside each other in relative quiet, Mamá sewing in the early evenings, dresses for the collection of dolls she kept, Yadi threading the needle when it was time to switch colors. Changing the TV set when it was time to follow wrestling to a different channel. Mamá loved wrestling. In order to call the States, Yadi slipped the chamaquito who walked door-to-door selling limoncillos an extra coin to ensure a calling card accompanied the house's vine of fruit.

Even the bathroom was of the old-school variety, the kind used in rural townships and poor bateyes—an outside toilet. It was clean, and at least it was an actual toilet instead of a latrine, but running water was shoddy in the country, and if the power grid was off, the ability to flush was off too. Despite all her children living in the United States, and sending her money, Mamá lived the way she had for the last seventy-three years. No one knew where she put the money, but it was certainly not into modernization.

The first fight they had was about Yadi's business in that bathroom.

She stood with her body blocking the rickety-dink door. "Mamá, por favor, you don't have to go in there. I promise I'm fine."

"Muévete."

Yadi shifted slightly but didn't release the door handle. She just couldn't understand what words she needed to say in order to get Mamá to leave her shit alone. If Ona were here, she'd know exactly the phrase.

"It's fine. I feel fine now. I promise," she tried.

It'd started the second day after she'd arrived. Something hadn't settled well, and she'd spent the night in the outside bathroom. Mamá, convinced Yadi's constitution was no longer resistant to parasites or tapeworms, had become hawk-eyed, following her outside every time she needed to piss or poop.

"Can I just describe it instead?" A last-ditch attempt.

Mamá Silvia blinked at her, bewildered, as if trying to understand how a child of her blood could even consider offering not one, not two, but *three* whole comments in response to a direct command. Yadi moved, and Mamá Silvia went inside with her stick to poke at her shit. She came out a moment later, throwing the stick into the grass, muttering under her breath, and Yadi knew that the entire day's menu and list of chores would now be navigated according to her morning excrement, her shit the North Star of their days.

If her poop was leaky, Mamá made her go into town to buy

a cut of fresh meat and chicken bones from the butcher. There would be bone broth for dinner.

If her poop was bile-colored, Mamá made her help shuck red beans for the evening meal. She added oregano to the girl's tea.

Coal-colored, small, and hard was the worst verdict. That meant Yadi would be spending the morning in the conuco, pulling up yuca, batata, and chayote. At midday she'd need to grab the bucket and walk to the river to collect the yautia coquito that grew at the water's edge. It also meant she'd be spending her afternoon in the kitchen peeling, cutting, and stirring the sancocho made from all of those ingredients that Mamá insisted would provide the fiber, nutrients, artillery her gut needed.

By August, Yadi held the bathroom door open proudly, peering in with Mamá to look at the toilet bowl.

"Muy bien. Pero réquete bien," Mamá said.

Yadi nodded. The brown poo was gorgeous, full of healthy stomach bile, the perfect balance of fiber and iron and magnesium, the sturdy stuff that kept it together. And more importantly, it'd been that way for weeks now, whatever illness had been running through her system exorcised.

"This is how you heal, niña. You are thoughtful about what you offer yourself; you study what you put out."

In the end, Yadi didn't stay through the summer, she stayed through the summer *and* her senior year. Going over school applications on the phone with Ona, who made her College App profile, and filled out financial aid forms, and got her little cousin into college with a full-ride scholarship.

(Yadi told me this poop story years ago. And we didn't discuss it because at that point there was no going back.

She'd made her decision on how to move forward. But I think we both wondered whether, in her own way, Mamá Silvia had been trying to teach Yadi something that wouldn't be examined in a classroom with a proctor, but would be tested again and again, poked at with a stick. Perhaps trying to say: this is loving. This is loving. *This* is loving. The shit you're willing to wade through.)

YADIRA: INTERVIEW TRANSCRIPT

ONA: . . . . and what can you say about that?

YADI: Haven't you interviewed us enough? I feel like I've been doing nothing but answering private questions for the last month or so. Is this some kind of mourning ritual? Do you want me to set you up with my therapist?

ONA: You're being avoidant.

YADI: Fuck outta here. Are you allowed to say that to your subject?

ONA: You're not a subject. You're my cousin. This isn't formal research.

YADI: Bitch, please. Don't get snotty. You already know I think this is stupid. I don't have any more answers for you. And I'm only participating because all the viejas agreed, and because I owe you everything in the world and it'd be petty not to do this one thing. . . .

ONA: So glad we arrived at an agreement. Can you answer the question?

YADI: What kind of question is that? Fine. Well, I don't know. And no! I'm not being avoidant.

        I don't know how any of us learned. It wasn't

from our mothers. They acted like their tongues
were taken out to be sharpened daily, but rarely
to slice a sliver of the hides of their husbands.
So I would not have learned it from them. We
learned it slowly, with our own hands, I think?
By taking the silicone-covered brush, the one we
used to untangle knots on Sundays. Don't judge
me. I rode the handle, held tightly between my
thighs, the thing I found there jumped. It's funny,
but I think you of all people would understand:
the body knows us even when we do not know
it. And the body says: I am meat. Tender when
struck, seizing when fired up, needing rest when
removed from the heat. I am meat. Ugh, don't
include that cooking metaphor . . . I like to think
there was a time, before our mothers, and theirs,
and theirs and theirs, some great-great who knew
her own pleasure. A time before we were wrapped
in corsets, and courtships, and the approximation
of proper. I like to think we were nations of women
who undulated to a music all our own.

I learned some of it like this: The boy who
was my other heart, who asked me to dip my own
finger into my wetness, to lick. The salt I tasted.
The pungent there, I wrapped my lips around it.
How I did so in the hopes he would one day taste
it himself. I learned it after I already knew I'd be
labled a sucia. After I decided I didn't care.

You and I, we learned from Lola upstairs who
recounted to us how Moonshine finger-popped her

in the dim, dark canopied trees of Riverside. You learned in the bottom drawer of the armoire, when you pulled out your papi's dirty magazines.

We learned in the shadows, when boys who should not, did. When girls we loved loved us back, right? We learned in the big beds of other people's parents, didn't we? On a rare occasion, we might have even learned in the sunlight. We might have learned in the quiet. We learned as we listened to the still, to the loudness of our hearts. But not from our mothers.

MATILDE

loved Yadi's cafetería. It had bright curtains in the windows, and every appliance sparkled. The streets had changed since Mati first moved here and this section of Manhattan was mainly Puerto Rican, Dominican, and Black, each of their shops and clothing stores taking up blocks and blocks. Now there were maybe a handful of bodegas left in the neighborhood, the one Black-owned shoe repair store, the sole sastrería with their flag waving. Which is why when Yadi got a lease and reopened a store that had changed hands after hands after hands only to return to Dominican keeping, Matilde felt it was a kind of vindication; their kids returned and grabbed hold of what had slipped through the older generation's fingers.

Peering into the large fridge, she took inventory of the pastelito discs. Counted the cans of beans, the bags of quinoa. Her vocabulary for food had expanded in the last decade since Yadi had become vegan and started making particular requests for the family gatherings. The tías had tried to set out their most dietary-restricted foods when the girl came to a party: scrambled eggs and rice, mashed potatoes with cheese. But even a cup of tea had the pretty girl turning up her nose. Apparently, even honey was offensive! Honey, the elixir that healed bad microbes and boosted the immune system, pero imagínate tú.

Eventually Yadi began bringing her own plate. The tías would crowd around her when she was eating, Matilde especially, trying to discern what was considered acceptable fare. Matilde had taken note: her niece ate anything as long as it grew directly from dirt. That should be an easy rule to follow. Matilde started a habit of dropping by the apartment with a bag of black beans. When a Peruana at church brought quinoa to the Easter potluck, Matilde went to the gourmet market near the college to buy bags of the ancient grain. She made these offerings to Yadi tentatively, a peon looking for blessings. The girl had not asked any of them to participate in her protest against the consumption of animals' flesh and their byproducts, but nonetheless Matilde wanted the girl to feel supported by at least one family member. Soon it became ritual. She would bring a bag of hominy, black rice, noodles made from some fungus de por allá. Matilde visited the new Korean market by the college and found sprouted tofu, tough and dense tempeh. And Yadi would thank her. Then Yadi began to thank her and ask her what she thought she should make. Then Yadi began to thank her, ask her what she thought she should make, and make it for them to share. The two of them sitting as legumes softened, or water boiled. As they stood side by side, chia seeds got stirred into farro and kale, and forks created grooves in spaghetti squash. It was a game of language, this piecemeal entry into veganism. Matilde asking more often what things were made of, Yadi finding the English name so she could place special orders at the grocers. It was a game of silence. Since neither had a strong basis for how any of the things should taste, everything tasted Dominican: sautéed with sazón, marinated and slow-cooked like pork shoulder, salted and brined like codfish fritters. Many of those early dishes were deemed less than delicious in comparison to the meat they imitated. But the ladies refined their recipes.

The day the shop opened, Yadi gave a speech to commemorate the event. It was Matilde, she said, who'd co-dreamt this cafetería with her. Matilde hadn't known they were dreaming when it was happening. She'd simply yoked herself to her sharp-tongued, off-road niece, exploring the unknown through safe and measured spoonfuls.

When the girl had asked her to work as the cashier at the cafetería, she'd been stricken. She didn't know how to run a shop, didn't really even enjoy cooking. Yadi said she was the only person she could trust, and Mati was good at hospitality. Matilde said yes. Mainly because she knew it took steady hands to keep a dream afloat, and while Yadi's hands were inspired, they also trembled.

The inventory done, Matilde took in the gleaming countertops, the spotless tables. She unlocked the door and let in the sunshine. She liked working mornings.

A steady stream of neighborhood customers came in for coffee and toast. Some of the more adventurous viejitos bought açai bowls and green smoothies. Their busiest days were Tuesdays, the only day Yadi offered her coconut-lime smoothie. On the smoothie days, the lines went out the door, folks coming back until the only sounds heard were every single blender whirring and every single customer slurping. But they did good business almost every day they were open.

The family had thought that it would only be young people and the newly-arrived-in-the-neighborhood folks who would frequent the establishment, but Matilde had often thought it was exactly the more aged folks who had tried blended fruit and eggs in every way possible who would be most excited by seeing what other bounty different parts of the world offered. It helped that they'd set up a domino table in the corner (Matilde's idea) and that they gave smoothie discounts on Sunday morning for anyone with a church pamphlet (also Matilde's idea).

The bell over the door chimed jauntily. Matilde didn't look at her sister when she passed the little blue coffee cup over.

She'd known by the way the door jingled, the steps stepped that her first customer would be Pastora. It always tickled Matilde that despite possessing the most acid of tongues, Pastora took her coffee the sweetest: pale and saccharine so as to almost be confused with chocolate milk. Matilde had the cup prepared like clockwork.

Pastora was always the first family member to come in. Don Isidro's opened its doors at ten a.m., and Pastora believed in being there an hour early despite living down the block. Her manager was a lenient man, but Pastora was rigid in her need to mitigate possible disasters by simply showing up with enough time to terrify any emergency from emerging; she treated ill-fated things like cicadas, which might pop up every dozen years but that she could scare back underground, by being prepared for their arrival and confronting them with bared teeth.

"What time will you be at Camila's?" Her sister offered her a kiss on the cheek over the counter, tiptoeing to reach her.

Matilde just managed not to roll her eyes. "I thought we were all getting there at eight?"

Pastora nodded. "I'll be there at seven thirty. Llegas temprano." It was an order. And now the hairs on the back of Matilde's neck bristled. She'd turned seventy-one last month. She had a senior citizen MetroCard. She was not about to be bullied by her younger sister. As if sensing the hint of rebellion, Pastora raised an eyebrow. She even took the moment to glance at her watch, as if to emphasize that *she'd* budgeted an entire hour to walk two blocks and had plenty of time to spin Matilde's world in circles.

"I'm ready to talk about it now if you prefer. I think you deserve better than—"

"I don't have anything to say right now." Matilde grabbed a paper napkin and slid it over the counter she'd already wiped down twice.

The chime over the door broke their standoff, but unfortunately for Matilde the customer who walked in was like a habanero being added to sancocho, too spicy for a stew that was already overcrowded.

El Pelotero wore slacks, a button-down shirt. His hair was wet, the curls looking soft to the touch. He looked older than he had the day before. Now it was clear he was in his early forties, the facial hair that brushed his cheeks had the early sprinkling of grays in it. Matilde didn't think she'd made a sound. She who had perfected keeping a stoic face even amid embarrassment did so now. But still, she must have had a tell, because although neither one of them had spoken, Pastora looked between them quickly as if skimming the paragraphs of a novel that was currently being cowritten before her eyes.

Don't speak don't speak don't speak, Matilde thought. And she didn't know whether she was issuing that command to the baseball player, her sister, or herself. That was a lie. The command was definitely to the baseball player. Pastora acquired way too much information about people by the timbre of their voice, and Matilde didn't want to know what her sister might learn. She pleaded with her eyes. *Let me just have this.*

El Pelotero quirked a brow and offered a gallant head nod but kept his silence. A reserved Pastora didn't say good morning or try to get him to talk. Her attention held fast on Matilde.

"Te veo a las siete y media en punto, ¿verdad que sí?" Pastora asked. It was a gauntlet thrown in the sand. *Do my bidding later, or I stop this train in its tracks now.*

Matilde nodded, not trusting her voice. Or rather, not trusting what Pastora might hear in it: flutters of nervousness, longing. Fear.

Pastora left, with one last look over her shoulder.

"Good morning. What can I get for you?" Matilde was proud her voice didn't shake, and she kept her hands under the counter so he couldn't see how she was now ripping the napkin to shreds.

"Do you want me to block myself in your phone? I didn't mean anything by it. Just thought you would like the song, and I thought maybe you didn't have redes sociales."

Matilde inched a second napkin into her hand, tearing it into even smaller pieces than the first. "I have Instagram. My niece made it for me."

The baseball player nodded. This did not seem a satisfying answer to him. She cleared her throat.

The bell over the door chimed. Matilde did not take her eyes off the baseball player's as she called out, "Hola, mi'ja." She knew Yadi by the music of the keys she carried; each unlocking tool tinkled its own melody in tune with her steps. She knew Yadi's tells as well as she'd known Yadi's mother's.

And a good thing, too, because when she finally *did* glance at Yadi, the face that looked back at her was not her niece's usual face. This one was wearing a mask of concealer and contoured cheekbones, winged eyeliner slashed to a fine point; an entire face made of sharp shapes as if to warn any eyes that wandered close: *I am made of cutting things. Stare at your own risk.*

But that was chain mail. And tías know that most suits of armor are inherited. So the chinks that others miss are clear to an eye that has blacksmithed them before. Others would miss the shadows underneath Yadi's concealer. That she'd left her hair loose despite knowing it should be tied back if she were to be working in the kitchen. Which meant the girl wanted to hide: first her face from prying eyes, makeup and hair shuttering her gaze. But also in general. The girl usually left office work until the end of the day, but that must not be the plan.

"Hey, Kelvyn. Long time no see. How's your mom?" Yadi gave Kelvyn—El Pelotero had a name!—a half hug.

"Yadi the Body! Moms is good. Happy to have me around while the old man's hip heals." Matilde didn't catch all of his English, but she liked how smooth it sounded.

"Has Tía taken care of you?"

Kelvyn, God keep him, nodded a lie.

"She's the best." Yadi kissed her cheek. "Ción, Tía. I'm going to work in the back."

Matilde nodded. "The bookkeeper is still coming Monday?"

Yadi's steps only slowed for a half second, not quite a glitch except Matilde knew what to look for. The girl *was* hiding. She must not even remember that the quarterly taxes were almost due. And all the ads had already been ordered. So, what had she planned on working on back there? Bueno. Matilde would pry later.

Matilde cleared her throat and looked at the baseball player. Kelvyn.

"What was it you ordered? A green smoothie with chinola? Let me get that for you."

She prepped the frozen fruit and juice, adding an extra hint of vanilla extract, the scoop of chia seeds a small mountain of speckles.

When she turned around, the baseball player had a credit card out. She waved the payment away. "It's on the house. Please don't text me again," and then to soften it, "but thank you for the link. I hadn't seen the video for that song."

Maybe because of all the years she'd put up with a relambío, Matilde greatly admired stoicism in a man. She was romanced by someone poised, in control of his choices. Someone who knew every time a foot landed which exact step or spin should follow. And so, although she steeled herself against the barrage of sharp words that might come, or the pleading that would be unexpected but equally difficult to manage, it was with complete and utter delight—and only a *bit* of disappointment—that Matilde accepted his soft nod, his soft smile, his soft salute.

Oh, it was delicious, this level of composure. Matilde waved as he walked off. She spun with a roll of paper towels to an imaginary eight count.

Matilde had often danced by herself, especially when she'd been a young woman.

> Waiting until her mother's house was quiet before she lifted the lid off the record player and slipped the 45 underneath the needle. Her mother had

left to take Camila to the local doctor
or school event, and so she'd have the
sound all to herself.

The alone time was a blessing. Her mother's brother had
flareups of his illness that often kept Matilde tending to him for
weeks on end. And then she would come home to have Mamá
buzzing in her ear and young Camila asking questions she had
few answers for. To have a few moments where she owed no one
her time but herself was a luxury.

Her mother wasn't opposed to music, not even the most
popular soneros, but she wasn't a fan of the moves the music
inspired. This record was new, or rather, new to Matilde, purchased with every little coin Matilde could scavenge running
errands and helping to sew. Fania Records had been putting out
all the major tracks, and over the last few years the discs had
been rehoming themselves back to the Caribbean, returning to
their origins.

It was 1977, and all over the world people were dancing
and singing to Fania, but in their little campito Matilde could
pretend the music was made for an audience of one: her. She
stood in front of the living room mirror as the crackling sounds
of the intro wafted through the gramophone. She played the
eight-minute song all the way through without moving, only
listening and bopping her head in the mirror. Someone's citi-
fied uncle had come to town about a decade past and brought
this combination of son and cha-cha and guaguancó with him.
He'd learned from Cuco Valoy himself, and he not only brought
the sound to their little town but the steps as well. The kids all
practiced with each other after church on Sundays, hands on

waists. There was an arithmetic to the foot combinations that fit lock-and-key with Matilde. She learned the quickest of the children how to dance, which had ultimately proven sorrowful. Too soon there'd been no one who could partner her better than she could partner herself, and the boys hadn't liked her trying to school them on how to lead. She'd had to rein in how disappointed she felt in the clumsy arms of boys who knew only the most basic moves. She never knew whether she was dancing *right*. Her footwork didn't look like anyone else's she'd ever seen, but she stayed within the count, and she let her toes and heels and ball of her foot translate the horns, the bongos. That's all she was doing, making the music into a body.

But alone, at home, in the quiet moments she could have all to herself, she spun, and rocked her hips, and learned how to contain a world of movement within the eight count.

———

Matilde stopped dancing when the bell jingled over the cafetería door. She put the roll of paper towels down.

She hoped El Pelotero would stop in again during lunch. The stirring in her nethers, a body wakening from hibernation, filled her with equal parts terror and excitement. She hadn't had this level of lust in years. Not since . . . well, long before menopause at least.

Flor, who had started her period at eleven, was also the first one to enter early menopause. She reported back on the hot flashes, the chin hairs that had grown into a fluff. Pastora was next. She'd always had a satisfying relationship with her husband, and her report included that her sex drive was up, but her chocha no longer got as humid as it once had. But Pastora was resourceful and found ways around dryness, bragging to her sister about the miracle of lubricant.

Matilde had found menopause to be tedious more than anything. First the fits and starts of it. She went three years where she kept thinking she was done. She looked forward to no more menstruation; she welcomed the autumn of her life. No more secret wishes or hopes to be like Abraham's geriatric fertile wife. It took too long to fully end. In her late forties, on the twelfth month her period always came forward, a sputtering crimson thing. That last handful of her eggs had proven they would cling to her ovaries, but were still ultimately as fruitless as their predecessors. She'd not been blessed with Pastora's midlife onset of daily desire.

It had always amazed Matilde that an able body could work so well that it became a machine. Breath and blood and the circulation of both automatic things. But that whatever part of herself spoke to her mind, to the control center, couldn't actually guide the functions, and couldn't control the very real pang her heart had felt for so many years without periods, and then so many years with unwanted periods before she'd hardened herself against the prospect. How she wished and implored her mind to tell her body *no more, please*. Every period she said a prayer for the life that was not.

(In retrospect, Tía Matilde and I should have talked about conception and fertility long ago. It amazes me how few questions I know to ask, or whom to ask them of, until it's already too late for the answers to be useful. How do lineages of women from colonized places,

where emphasis is put on silent enduring, learn when
and where to confide in their own family if forbearance
is the only attitude elevated and modeled?)

Matilde had lost hope for miracles sometime around her
fifth miscarriage. And so maybe there was a bit of relief when
she went twelve months, thirteen, fourteen, only to see that
the well had truly dried up. That was really the last of it. She'd
had sex with Rafa once after hot flashes began, but soon after,
her cooch had felt like it was on fire. She'd thought it a strange
symptom of her aging vagina, only to learn she had chlamydia.
She hadn't let him penetrate her since. She too was resourceful,
and had had the tech-savvy Camila buy her a vibrator.

She grabbed all the bits of napkin she'd shredded while El
Pelotero had been in the shop and crumpled them in her hands;
then, palms facing the ceiling, with a soft, little squeal, she flung.

A confetti party for one.

I am required to call my mother every single morning before I leave the house. It's a habit that began in college, when she was the one calling me, at six a.m. because she never could remember my schedule, until finally I took over the responsibility of letting her know I had not died overnight without her being informed.

Mami often attempted to force a closeness that betrayed the lack of trust we'd built. Did Mami love me unconditionally? Would she die for me? I don't even have to think twice. I'd do a trust fall with Moms off the Empire State Building without a single hesitation.

In all honesty, physically, I trusted Mami more than myself. When she was the one in charge with the raising of me, I had timely dentist appointments, Dominican ointments for the warts that appeared on my elbow. I'd never had to go to the ER once. Mami kept my body healthy. But with my heart? Mami judged the softness out. One had to be careful what information was offered up to be picked apart by Saint Flor's all-knowing self.

Even the choice of which university to attend had been a big war. To be clear, higher education was not the issue, because Mami was proud of my scholastic achievements, but the going-away part? *Why would a daughter abandon her home before she was married?*

> I went away to school, and Mami tried to make sense of the new world I occupied in the most nonsensical of ways. "¿Cuánto cuesta un plátano por allá?" she'd ask me on one of the three (at a minimum) calls a day she insisted upon.

I hadn't visited the town's Latino market; I didn't know how supply and demand affected the importation of Caribbean goods. But I did know northern New York State had very few Dominicans at the time. And I told Mami so. I'd always hoped my mother would ask me the big questions: What did I believe was my purpose in life? What steps did I plan on taking to become myself? Mami didn't ask about the professors, or whether or not my roommates were dicks. She wanted to know the price of a plantain that I couldn't even cook because my dorm room didn't have a kitchen.

She visited once during my sophomore year. She took the long bus ride up from New York City to Binghamton during parents' weekend. I had told her she didn't have to come. There weren't a lot of Dominican families coming, and very few Dominican students anyway, so the events planned were mainly for the blanquitos. But Mami insisted. She wanted to set eyes on the place that housed her girl. The sisters couldn't join, so it was just her.

Mami dressed too formally for a quick college visit, and

brought an entire suitcase instead of just a weekender bag. She had backup outfits on backup outfits, church skirts and button-downs. Always ready to make an impression, of what exactly—a respectable matron?—I wasn't entirely sure. I didn't know what to *do* with my mother. Where to take her. My roommate's parents had gotten hotel rooms and picked their kid up for dinners in town and otherwise visited the vineyards or took a boat into the lake. They'd followed the parents' weekend program and called their kid when they were free.

Mami wouldn't hear of spending money on a hotel. Instead, she slept in the same dorm room–sized twin bed as me. Curled into my side, she snored softly, her breath warm on the back of my neck. I didn't sleep at all, aware my roommate was in the bed across from us frantically texting, probably telling everyone that I'd let a parent into the residence hall to stay with me.

That Saturday night we attended a party hosted by the Latin American Student Union on campus. The conference center ballroom was decorated with gold balloon arcs and white streamers. And this was at least one occasion where Mami could not overdress if she tried; people's families attending this event all knew what time it was: the one or two fathers in attendance had on sharp suits. The women wore gowns like the type you'd see on wedding guests. I had on a cocktail dress that showed off my thighs.

"¿Pero tú 'tá aquí pa' e'tudiar, o pa' traerme otro tipo de diploma?" Mami asked as she tugged on the hem of my dress. *I wore it on purpose*, I didn't say.

We sat at a table with the family of a Salvadoran girl I'd seen about campus; she was an outspoken campus queen and queer who was currently serving as president of LASU. I hadn't gotten much involved with the student org, spreading myself between LASU, the Caribbean Student Association, and the Black Student Union, whose meetings I went to more often than the former two, despite receiving side-eyes every now and then or questions about where I was really *from* from.

The food at the parents' event was good, although it was an approximation of Latin cuisine made by the university catering service. Mami's usually particular about how her food is prepared, but this was one of the few times I completely agreed with her.

"Pero esto' ma-*duro*' pudieran estar más *suave*' sí." I laughed at Mami's joke. I guess people in Binghamton *could* source plantains even if they might not know how long to let them ripen.

When the South American band began playing covers of Aventura, I excused myself to the bathroom as Mami listened to the tango rendition of "Obsesión," clapping along with eyes wide.

In the bathroom a girl leaned against the sink, smoking a jay. The smoke alarm above her had been mummified in party streamers. I'd seen her around campus, my eyes drawn to her at the dining hall, at Bartle Library. She had tight curly hair she wore short around her ears. The first day I saw her she'd been wearing short shorts, and a scaly tat peeked its nose out beneath her front pocket.

"I don't know how anyone makes it through this shit sober." She exhaled.

"Shit, me neither. I got my moms sleeping in the same bed as me and everything." I washed my hands and used my damp fingers to smudge at the crusted mascara under my eye.

The girl barked a laugh and held out the jay. I took it with careful fingers that felt extra sensitive as they brushed hers.

"Oh, damn, at least my parents are driving back tonight. Their Dominican asses say they don't sleep in other people's homes."

I know I looked alarmed, even as I tried to figure out a way to see if I could get my mother in that car. "They're doing that drive tonight? My mom is heading back to Manhattan if they wanted company."

She rolled her eyes, taking the jay back. "Bitch, not everyone is going to the city. Buffalo born and raised."

I made myself comfortable against the sink. "They got Dominicans there?"

"You gon' quit playing with me. It's the second-largest city in New York State, tiguerona."

Which was and wasn't an answer. I waited to see if she would pass the jay back, but she ground it out on the sink before wiping the residue clean with a paper towel and putting the roach into her bra. People are prickly about their hometowns, something I knew even then, but I've always struggled to claim my privilege when it came to being from the best city in the world. I wanted to apologize, but the smoke was already in my system and when I opened my mouth what came out was a string of giggles.

The girl's face twisted as if she was trying to stay stern and hold back a laugh at the same time. She compromised with a small smile.

"Lightweight. Listen, I'm an RA at Hinman. They give us two beds to push together . . . if you wanted to share with someone other than your mom." She pulled a lip pencil from her purse and grabbed my palm, writing down her number in quick, sure strokes. "My name's Soraya."

When she reached up to release the fire alarm from her paper-mache stronghold, the croc peeked out from beneath her dress, one eye looking like it was winking at me.

(I got a companion tattoo on my own thigh a few months later. One of a long-tailed serpent whose tongue was measured precisely so that when Soraya and I were naked and intertwined, our inked creatures were kissing too. My mother flipped the first time she saw it. We were at Coney Island and she legit refused to open her eyes until I wrapped a towel around my lower half, even when we went into the water. She's always had a thing about snakes, although I find the discrimination against reptilia, especially one invoked in such a romantic gesture, unfair.)

Sometimes I still look down at my right hand, expecting to see her area code engraved there: 716. For a lot of my time in college, those digits became a link to my other heart.

I returned to the party to find that Mami had been pulled up from her seat; she was dancing in the middle of the ballroom in a group of other women, all jumping into the circle and getting funky with their middle-age twerk session that was more arms than hips.

I always loved the dark of the campus. And that night was no different. The scent of sweat, and the new moon overhead covered my high-ass self.

"I thought you didn't dance."

Mami shook her head. "The woman who came up to me was so sweet. She heard me talking and can you imagine, she was from Santiago!"

"I'm glad you made a friend," I said as I squeezed my hand tight, clutching the lifeline of the ten digits of ink.

I couldn't wait for Sunday afternoon, when this obligatory visit could be put to rest. To put Mami back on the five-hour bus to Manhattan. Mami had tears in her eyes when I walked her to the bus stop.

"It's just. You've left me too young. And for what?" Mami looked around, her eyes trying to sift the images of the campus into an appealing picture. I tried to see it through her eyes. Gray buildings, and green grass, and hilly roads, but nothing to entice a young woman from the capital city of the world.

How could I explain? I'd left young because I had to. Because this woman who wanted to protect me so much had let her care braid itself into a vise around my throat. I could not be a woman in her home.

"It's what they do in this country. Kids leave for college and learn independence." I still had straight hair then. Long to my lower back. I twisted a lock around my finger, despite knowing I'd need to flat-iron it later.

"It's not an easy thing to leave home. You have no one here. Anything could happen. This is a campo."

I wanted to laugh. Mami, an actual campesina, had grown bougie since moving to New York City. Now anything that even remotely resembled a suburb was considered the sticks. Mami scoffed at *Queens*, saying it was too rural, so this stretch of upstate New York would of course be considered the woodlands of west bumblefuck.

"I have friends. And an advisor. And maybe Yadi will join me next year."

I looked over my shoulder down the road. The bus was always fucking late.

Mami shook her head. "Friends are not family."

"They can be."

She shook her head again. Mami and I had this fight often. Mami often said only family could be one's real friends, blood equating to a type of unspoken loyalty. But Mami had been betrayed by family before, and conversely, when she came to this country with not a single blood sister or close kin, hadn't it been Ana from across the hall who got her the factory job? Hadn't Gisela from upstairs babysat when she had late shifts? Wasn't it Esmeralda the bizcocho maker who had taken her to the Social Security office on Chambers Street when she'd been too afraid and confused to navigate the subway alone? I hated how quickly my mother seemed to have parceled these women into un-sisters after decades, simply because her blood had returned to her.

"You made a whole friend last night on the dance floor. You know friendship is important."

It wasn't the right answer. Mami looked at me sharply. And I wished I could explain that *I* didn't have sisters. I had myself and my uptight her and a cousin who'd left the country, and the only people I could talk to were friends. It was they who had sustained me.

"I had a dream with that woman last night" was what Mami replied.

When the bus arrived, the other parents and some students got on. I took Mami's bag and put it under the bus.

To the driver I said, "My mom is going to Grand Central. Can you make sure she's okay?" I pointed to her. "Here's my number in case anything happens. I can translate."

I handed the man an index card where I'd written my name, the college's name, and my cell phone in clear print. The large White man with his large mustache took the card and threw it on the dashboard. He nodded.

Mami hugged me hard. And didn't seem to want to let go. I patted her on the back. Now that the relief of separation was near, I was able to be gracious. "What did you dream?" But she just held me, rocking back and forth. "Mi niña," she whispered. I used to hate how she said that. I was grown I was grown I was grown.

Mami released me, blowing kisses as she got back on the bus. Her face pressed to the window like a child off to a summer camp they never asked to attend. I left before the bus pulled off. The dining hall was serving fish sticks, and Soraya had texted she wanted to chill.

———

Today's morning phone call with Mami began along the same path as every other morning phone call. Benediction request granted, an inquiry into how we both had slept, outlining our plans for the day, and Mami's reminder that she needed me to come see her to help pick out her wake dress. None of the advice I'd wanted to ask her for the night before broke its way into the conversation. Instead I found myself with the same pleaded question: "Mami, you would tell me when, right?" This was the key difference of our conversations over the last five weeks. My trying to phrase the question of her passing in varying ways to trick her and elicit more information.

"I have learned that knowing *when* is never as important as *how*. Not in the method, of course. But as in, how did the person live well? How did they die well? Well loved, well departed, well farewelled?"

If pauses can have textures, the pause after her last remark was soft, gentle. *I know you're scared, mi'ja. But you must face this. You know all that you will know,* my mother didn't say.

"Don't forget, two p.m.! I have a meeting with the decorator after, and you know I'm always on time."

PASTORA

opened the pull gate that defended Don Isidro's clothing store, then unlocked the front door. She mused about her sisters. Matilde was hiding something and hiding *from* what needed to be faced. Flor was ignoring her calls, even though she'd sent out a reminder about the sisters' meetup at Camila's that evening. And something about the boy, Kelvyn, from the shop niggled at her. She remembered him. And so many of the boys like him. His parents had been smart, and when they saw the neighborhood turning its starved eye on him, they sent him back to the homeland, where he could be raised right.

She started her morning routine of folding new inventory and tidying up the window displays, but her thoughts joined her in every task.

When the neighborhood boys began fashioning themselves gangsters, very few people had been alarmed. The youngins stole butter knives and salt shakers from the outdoor dining establishments near Columbia. They tagged their blocks and their street names on stoops and awnings. They rolled

together in big waves of teenage bravado. Pastora had watched them from
the storefront, the swagger in their
steps, the sense of self they received
from being part of a whole, and she
shook her head. There was no guiding force at the front of the groups. No
older men knuckling the younger ones
into place. So, when the Bloods and
Crips and Latin Kings with their name
recognition and bandannaed domains
began stepping to the young boys,
there was no OG to step in and smooth
the peace.

The crew of boys sharpened themselves. Began carrying
knives that were made for something other than dairy spreads.
By Halloween of their first year in existence, if you wanted to be
down with PLF you needed to be jumped in, or jump someone
else to get in. A classmate at Ona's high school got the braces
knocked out from her mouth by a local girl who became the
first nonboy in the newly formed gang. Pastora overheard Flor
talking about it and it had seemed prescient, but she'd given it
no thought. No girl of theirs would become involved in a gang.

The boys—and girl—emboldened each other. In the unsupervised wasteland between school and home, the kids scavenged pride, glory, gore. They sold dime bags, and stole bikes,
and fucked up anyone who made fun of their name, even as they
second-guessed the hormonal wisdom of choosing an acronym
based on Pipilolos Fuerte.

What is there to say? Good boys, too, got swept up. Boys who were neither good nor bad, who just liked to tag along, were positioned on the corner to partake in dirty jokes and secret swigs of Johnnie Black out of crinkled paper bags. Ant, who had been part of the neighborhood fabric for as long as anyone remembered, had only ever occupied the part of the quilt that placed him with Yadi. Until the summer he got jumped by a different crew from 106th because one of them wanted the newly reissued Retro 11s he had on his feet.

A lone boy and the girl he loves do not run to the cops when someone from a neighboring block steals his kicks after a date and makes him walk home barefoot. They do not tell their mothers, who will cluck and fuss but will be otherwise defenseless. They do not mention it again at all. And when the lone boy is approached by a boy slightly older, who tells him the guys who jumped him have been bragging about it and does he want to do something about it, well, our not-a-gangster boy might be motivated to get a lick off the kids who embarrassed him. And by gosh, maybe he's a little indebted to this crew afterward for how they took care of one of their own, a block boy defended against another block. And so maybe he hangs out more. Is the one to make stops to the corner store for fifty-cent juices and quarter waters. The one to open the fire hydrant when it's hot. The one to climb to the roof and send down a call when the police cars are sneaking up on them from two avenues over. He finds a place with his girl, and his community, and the slightly scuffed Jordans he pulled off a bleeding boy who had first pulled them off him.

(Although my particular field of study does not center in juvenile justice, being where I'm from, I think often of what makes young people interested in, coerced into, desiring of, predisposed to, gang life. And gangs, to me, seem intricately tied into a subsect of society's need for tribal-led change. From my actual field, I would argue, one of the earliest "gangs" in Dominican culture was organized by Wolof Africans who were brought from Senegal to the island of Hispaniola. If a gang in its purest sense is defined as a group of criminals, and if one's very body is a commodity, such that fighting for freedom is illegal, then a group of freedom fighters must be considered a gang. Traditions of oral history, and corroboration of church records, share the account of a slave rebellion in 1521 at the sugarcane estate of one Diego Colón (son of, yes, that motherfucker Columbus), where one of the first and most vicious—and some could argue, successful—rebellions took place. The Wolof were literate, religiously organized, and they'd had cavalries back in Senegal, so enslavers could not use horses as a way to harness fear. The Wolof not only organized themselves in a strange new land but were able to gain support from the enslaved peoples who had been raised among the Spanish, as well as the Taíno, who had escaped Spanish rule and were living as fugitives in the Bahoruco Mountains. Without shared language, customs, or history, it is rumored that the Wolof created a rebellious, liberated, and liberating Maroon colony with other enslaved people from the Columbus estate. This Wolof-led gang was so resistant to the enslavement they were sold into that ordinances passed in 1522 effectively expunged their entire African region from ever being further kidnapped. The need for safety, for freedom, is one so many young ethnically Latine and Black boys (especially) have had hardwired since the first rupture that made peopling so complicated in this hemisphere. Our boys are aspiring when they join a gang. They hurt themselves and others for a loose semblance of safety. They are failed by a culture that writes them off as criminal so that they must create their own internal laws. I don't argue they are freedom fighters. Or are undoing enslavement. I only mean, on this side of the world, every descendant of enslavement, of that inherited and invasive oppression, dreams of an island of their own, a slice of communal freedom, a hard-won respite from a world that reminds them time and again they are destined to be shackled from every angle.)

Ant had never known bloodlust. But he liked knowing that if something happened to him, someone would have his back, would rally the team and avenge him. And when Dwayne said a boy from the middle school had been running his mouth about them, Ant didn't see it as the boy throwing a first punch, but he didn't not see it that way either. Word is bond, after all—don't talk shit if you not ready to clean up the excrement.

The five of them were only supposed to scare him. Waited for him across from the middle school as he made his way home toward Broadway. The boy was big for fourteen. Had wide shoulders, a thimbleful of hair on his still-soft brown chin. One of them caught him from behind, one hard blow to the back. It was okay to stomp on his knee, a quick but permanent reminder to watch himself. The kicks to the ribs were superfluous; he was already out of breath at that point. The stomp to the head went too far. Ant had backed away by then, had even pulled one of the other boys off. But the other three members scented something in the air that frenzied them. They kicked and kicked and kicked. They broke the boy's teeth. His hands no longer covered his face.

The boys from PLF, Ant included, ran home to Amsterdam and Columbus. Ran home to the block, the basements and alleyways and abuelas' spare rooms. But this was not some star-studded covert operation. Most people could point out a kid from PLF. One boy, Alfonso, left to New Rochelle, where he had family who would hide him. The police never did arrest him. Dwayne stayed low for two months before he went to pick his girlfriend up at school and a patrol car was outside of Brandeis High School waiting for him. The other two boys were picked up within six months.

Ant was picked up the very first day. He did not snitch. Didn't say who the other four boys were. Didn't give up any addresses or mention it had been Dwayne's idea. Didn't say the worst he'd done was stomp out a kneecap, that he hadn't broken the ribs that had pierced the boy internally. That he hadn't done the head stomping that resulted in a coma the boy never did come out of. He was quiet in the station, and he was quiet on the stand. He didn't recite any poems he'd written for Yadi. He didn't share the last paragraph of the essay that had won him a writing competition at school.

They would have killed Ant, the boy's parents, but their child, the boy Ant had jumped, remained alive—in a coma, yes, but still breathing. They hired a good lawyer and pressed charges to the fullest extent the law allowed.

He went to juvenile jail. And then he went to adult prison.

And then he went back to being a lone boy who could and would get robbed for being sweet. He'd told her that in a letter.

———

Pastora's hands were shaking as she stacked the last of the folded shirts on a display table.

And now Ant was back, and her daughter had tossed and turned all night. Something she'd heard because *she'd* tossed and turned all night. Her husband had made it to the Dominican Republic safely, calling her to say good night. He knew she didn't sleep well without him. But even his voice hadn't brought down her anxieties. The speed at which the world was spinning seemed to have changed the last few days, the revolutions happening faster and faster until Pastora had to sit behind the cash register to stop the daze.

FLOR

answered as many questions as her daughter asked. Although Ona did not always ask the right questions, and she often seemed to perceive of herself as the mom. Ona was always getting on her about *boundaries* and *self-care*. Words the girl had had to look up translations for, for how little she'd heard them in Spanish. But they were words Flor hadn't needed. The girl thought her generation had invented being a person.

She thought of this now as Ona hurried off the phone. The girl was on her way to teach her first class of the day.

She never would understand how she called Ona for one thing—"Can you help me pick this dress?"—and the girl wanted to take detours down streets that Flor had already told her were closed off. *She's worried*, Flor reminded herself. Flor was worried too. When she'd first conceived of the wake, it'd turned in her mind with a satisfying click. But now, she saw the effect it was having on everyone around her. The lead-up had become more intense than she'd anticipated. The conversations with her siblings and daughter felt fraught with the questions of life and death. She hadn't meant to mine everyone else's life experiences. She'd only meant to make room for her own.

Pero nada. Nadie cambia caballo en el medio del río.

But how to explain that she was not as daft or defenseless

as her daughter thought? No, she didn't always understand how or why this country did things, or why Ona's generation seemed so tira'a and casual about their appearance and behavior, but she'd not been the doormat her daughter seemed to think her to be.

Flor took care. When Ona was little, Flor would lock herself in the bathroom. Left the kid with her father for thirty minutes. In the dark she would lie in the tub and hmmmmmmm. Her daughter later laughed at her, saying she sounded silly and the sound was supposed to be "ommmmm" but still Flor tried what she'd seen on TV. And hadn't she put on a mud mask once a week when she'd been a young wife? Ona joked the mud masks were so when anyone asked anything she could put a finger up to her lips indicating that now was not a time for her to speak. Eventually when the family saw her with her mask on, they knew to let her watch her novela and learned to secure their own snack or misplaced item. Hadn't those been boundaries?

And there were the moments she had had to set *boundaries* the child would never see. Time and again when she'd had to stand up to teachers, and principals, and even the girl's father, in defense of her well-being and that of her child. Ona never remembered that. Maybe they weren't great borders, but she'd put in true effort to keep her sanity walled in. And the girl would never imagine the boundaries she'd had to have with herself. The ways she'd had to learn to keep herself tethered to this living all the while knowing too much about how easily one could be taken out of the world.

The story she'd wanted to tell Ona on the phone:

> She'd been a girl. Pastora had been with La Vieja [redacted] almost a year,

and Flor had been dreaming about her. She, Flor, couldn't have been older than sixteen. Samuel was still busy, and Matilde was sent away whenever their ailing uncle needed a nurse. Camila had just started to sit up, but Mamá carried her everywhere, so she didn't test her spine too often. On this day, no one was home; perhaps they'd been on a shopping trip? To visit family? Flor couldn't recall, but she was cleaning. Scattering sand onto the kitchen floor so it could be used to gather the dust, the minuscule grains of glass scraping clean the tough spots. They'd not had wood-cleaning solution back then. She scattered and swept and did not stop even when she heard the clop of a well-shoed horse stop outside the house.

On hands and knees, she piled the sand and used it to gather dirt. She just managed to collect most of it in a wet rag before the knock. She rushed to put everything back in its place even as she spotted a streak of sand bisecting the kitchen; she stepped over it.

She opened the door to her cousin Nazario. And although she kept her eyes on his face, she let her peripheral vision take in the clean button-down, the tight way it was tucked into freshly pressed pants. The pomade in his hair was never too thick, just enough to keep his coiffure looking polished. She ran a hand down her skirt. They hugged, tight but not too tight, and she invited him in with exclamation as she always did. "But we weren't expecting you!"

Flor had not been raised with this cousin. He was from her father's side of the family and had only moved here five years before. He was from a better-off branch of the family, and it showed in his proud carriage and well-maintained countenance. There was never a stray mustache hair. His belt and shoes were brightly shined as if daring the campo dirt to settle a dust print anywhere near him. He wore the city he'd been born and raised in like a mantle across his shoulders. And Flor had stopped pleading with the Divine to unmake him her kin.

If he knew of her feelings or returned them, they'd never discussed it. *She was to be a nun*, she whispered silently when she thought of his face in the dark.

Out of his pocket he pulled out a piece of dulce de leche, the layer of guava sandwiched neatly within the milk candy. It was her favorite, and since the candy wasn't smushed, she knew he'd taken care to keep it intact. Only one piece of candy. He never brought any for Mamá, or Matilde. She'd confessed this detail in a letter to Pastora, whose lack of a letter back had said more than enough.

"¿Tío se encuentra?" It was almost lunch hour, and her father should be on his way home soon. Although driving oxen through hard country, or muddy country, or whatever soil he happened to find on any given day, was not the kind of labor one could easily set to a clock.

"Todavía no. Probably in an hour. Won't you sit? I can offer you some coffee while you wait on him? It'll be perfect with this dulcito, which we can split."

Nazario ran the brim of his hat through his hands, turning

it and turning it probably the same way his mind was spinning to come up with a reply.

"Por supuesto, I shouldn't leave without speaking to him, so I might as well wait in good company."

Flor stepped gently over the line of sand on the kitchen floor and lit a match against the fogón. She cut the dulce into four equal pieces and placed them on one of Mamá's good plates. When the greca whistled, she carried the tray into the living room.

He was standing by the window, the sunshine like a bodily halo around him, glinting off the dark skin of his neck just so. Flor felt like she was dying. Which was impossible because she was sure she would have dreamt it. Most people could not look Flor in the eyes. Mamá said that they feared they'd see their own death in the roving of her left eye. But Nazario always looked her straight in the face, as he did now, turning from the window. They sat. She poured.

Neither of them spoke for a few minutes. Flor sipped the coffee but couldn't taste whether it was bitter or too sweet.

"Your brother doing okay over there?"

Flor nodded. "I write him often. Samuel says the capital is dirtier than he'd imagined."

"He doesn't regret it?"

Flor lifted a shoulder. Samuel had been waiting for a green card, and after five years having been requested by an uncle in New York, it seemed it was about to go through, but then spur of the moment, he'd fallen in love. And his woman was not one to do things improper, so if he wanted her, they'd have to marry, even though any legal status changes would result in his current file being declared void. His woman had given him six months to figure himself out. When the visa still hadn't been approved half a year after her ultimatum, Samuel had tossed his chances to the wind, and the family had tossed rice at his wedding.

"Not me," Nazario said. He took a gulp of his coffee. "The first chance I get, I'm going somewhere I can be free." And he looked at her then, the cup barely touching his lip.

"Free?"

Flor had thought of many existential concepts in her life, especially after Pastora left and her world had become even smaller and quieter. She'd thought of peace, what it would mean to have less of her gift or no gift at all and sleep would be a true reprieve. She'd prayed for solace on the mornings she walked to the river and her strangeness and loneliness made her feel like a creature who would have been left off Noah's ark, not one to be partnered. She didn't know what it said about her that although her sisters seemed to chafe at their restraints, she felt safe with the tight and structured rules and ways of living. If she did not go looking for surprises, very few ever found her. She'd not ever desired to sharpen her teeth on freedom.

"There's just so much I want." He smiled then. "And I don't think I'll ever be able to have it if I stay here. Hold still a minute."

He reached over, hand raised to swat something off of her shoulder, but Flor evaded him. "Oh, it's just a little centipede." She walked to the back door, letting the centipede crawl down her arm, down to her wrist then her fingers. Flor knelt and waited patiently as its many legs left her flesh for the warm dirt.

"You must be a big fan of bugs." Nazario seemed more amused than annoyed by her response to the centipede.

Flor shook her head. "I cannot stand them. But harming a living thing, unless it's to eat it or defend my life, seems beyond me."

"I see," he said.

She washed her hands and made her way back to where Nazario was watching her. She picked up one of the dulces; the guava jam in the middle had bits of the fruit pulp hardened in it. Perhaps, if one did not feel how she felt, her nerve endings at attention for every one of his words, those words might land innocuously, but she was looking for a kind of understanding, enough so that even when he blew air into his coffee cup and the steam curled, she wanted to read it as an invitation. Well, is it so surprising that she swallowed back her saliva so abruptly, and without chewing? She'd forgotten she'd placed the dulce into her mouth until a bit got lodged in her throat. She tried to swallow but it didn't budge; air built up in her throat with nowhere to go.

She stood quickly, so quickly her coffee splashed onto the rug. She struck the base of her throat.

Her cousin rushed over and placed a hand onto her chest and another at her back. He seemed to be attempting to pump the piece of guava from her windpipe. She spittled up, the bits of milk sugar and fruit filling falling into the cupped palm of Nazario's hand. She almost wished she had choked to death.

"Breathe, linda, así mismo," he whispered. "Respira profundo." He grabbed a handkerchief from his pocket, wiped at her mouth, and curled the fabric into his hand.

"That's it, keep breathing, deep breaths. Don't worry, you're in good health." His hand rubbed circles onto her back.

She wanted to laugh. What a joke. Since the first time

they'd met she'd been heartsick. "I didn't eat today. I think I swallowed too quickly."

They hadn't heard the door, so what occurred next was not foreshadowed by slams or stomps.

"What are you doing with your hands all over my daughter?" Her father was not a big man, but when stoked to anger he seemed colossal, enlarged on oxygen and misunderstanding.

Flor tried to explain. "I had a piece of candy. It was in my mouth. He was—"

"I asked you a question." Her father stepped toward them and separated the cousins, who had not taken a step away from each other. He pushed Flor behind him.

"Nazario?" He pushed his immobile nephew hard in the chest.

"Tío, yo no hice nada. Aquí no se hizo nada."

The bit of dulce and coffee she had been able to swallow came back up her throat. She caught a glimpse of Nazario's face before he backed away from the door. They hadn't done anything; they both knew there was nothing to be done. But the sick look on his face, the rage on her father's.

Her cousin left without discussing the urgent matter that had brought him there. Without saying goodbye. He'd never visited the house again. That she knew of, her father had stopped all contact with his favorite brother's son. In the years that followed she'd imagined they'd meet again. Maybe in the capital—she moved there a few months later with Pastora, but did not see this cousin. Maybe in New York, she hoped. But she moved to the US almost two decades after last seeing him, and although she asked, no one knew if he'd made it to the States. For years, she imagined running into him. Laughing at her father's overreaction. Making peace with what had happened and what could not be. But in this life, very few of Flor's fantasies ever became real. What she should have told him that day was that she knew she would not die by mis-chewed sweetness.

———————

She took great care, she wanted to tell Ona. As a girl, she'd been the one Mamá Silvia had sent to the fabric store to pick the textiles for the year's garments Mamá would sew. The draper had been a gregarious man, who was quick to exaggerate an eyeroll when he saw her coming. "My most selective customer! You're gonna be a tough one to find a man," he'd said on many occasions. Which had not proven true. Once her desire of being a nun had eased out of her, once she saw there was no mortal path that could deliver her to absolution, she settled for the first man who had a job and a half-decent face. She'd never resolved her feelings for her cousin, Nazario, but she was not a woman of passions, and flinging decency to the wind in order to find him and convince him they were, what, meant? She laughed at the thought. It was inappropriate. She'd be shunned by her family.

He had reached out once. It was before caller ID, and she didn't know who had given him her New York number. She'd been a young bride still, pregnant with Ona. They were no longer children, neither of them, and yet the voice she hadn't heard in years and years had still been one she instantly recognized.

"Prima, it's me. Your cousin Nazario. Would it be possible to see you some time?"

She'd shaken her head as if he had eyes that could see

through phone lines. He'd hung up quietly when she hadn't said anything after her initial greeting.

When Flor had first arrived in New York, she'd written to her mother every week. And a month would pass before she'd receive a reply. By the time her mother's advice came, Flor had already made the decision, unmade it, lived with the ramifications, and arrived at a new difficulty. But she, who *was* available for all her daughter's needs, was rarely asked for an opinion. Instead, *she* was the one offered counsel. "Go to therapy," Ona told her. "Practice self-care," Ona said. "Prioritize yourself."

She'd cared for herself the best way she'd known. But how could she tell the girl that? Ona listened only when it was something that would contribute to her work. They'd never found an easy rhythm with each other. Probably because as a newborn Flor couldn't get Ona to suckle.

The baby had shaken her head angrily against the nipple, refusing to latch, smearing herself with milk instead of taking a single drop. The rejection had felt jagged; this flesh of her flesh, who had eaten and grown and taken from her body, refused this bond. Even at her hungriest, preferring starvation to the nipple of the woman who had touched death to see her born. She'd been angry at her tiny daughter then. By the time she'd learned of lactation specialists and breast pumps, her body was beyond her milking years, and they were beyond that earliest disrepair.

One night, Flor cradled the newborn girl in her lap. The big dark kitchen clock counted second by second, and Flor was barely able to keep her eyes open for any of them.

She embraced this child with big eyes and tight fists, all of which were used to express her discontent. Flor made up songs that she whispered. Rubbed the downy black of the girl's hair, as if soothing an ill-tempered colt. She didn't know when she dozed, or how she dozed, but one moment she was cooing gibberish to the child, and the next moment the girl was rolling down her legs. Flor woke with a start, just enough time to raise her legs and stop the tiny body from rolling down her shins. The fast movement pulled at her still healing C-section. She'd changed to formula the next day.

And now, Ona wanted to know the why of the wake. The when and how of what would follow after.

No, the girl would never know the many ways Flor worked to take care.

PASTORA

reviewed the guest list that Flor had sent her way, although with only a day before the event, she wasn't entirely sure what Flor wanted her to say. That she was glad so many people had RSVP'd? That she was glad that particular cousin and her husband hadn't? Flor wouldn't like the latter. She pretended to be kind toward all their relatives despite how unsupportable so many of them were. Perhaps Pastora had been like that once. But after the run-in with the Santana family, where her thirteen-year-old self had *so shamed the family* that she needed to be sent away to an entire other province, Pastora had learned very quickly that just because someone was kin didn't make them her kind.

Pastora was not taken in by the nun aunt, or her grandmother. It was determined there was a more fit person to take her in hand. By that point, Pastora had finished sixth grade, and her reading levels were high and it seemed auspicious that the household she'd end up in had a secondary school in the district. Mamá Silvia's sister, La Vieja [redacted] would take her in.

(I have never heard my aunt shy from saying anything
that needed to be said, but she can't say her aunt's name
to this day. Some folks' names need not be uttered back
to us.)

The aunt was surly, but had a husband who was known for
his sweetness so there should have been balance, or so it was
explained to Pastora. Pastora's father, who'd arrived home too
late on the fateful day Doña Yokasta had made an appearance
and accused Pastora of coquetry and thievery, tapped his fingers nonstop against the dining room table when he heard his
baby girl would be leaving with her grandmother and nun aunt.
When his wife read the letter that her mother and nun sister
had sent her even farther away, to La Vieja [redacted], he put on
his hat and took his horse to the town watering hole. He was not
a man who drank. What does it say when a man is supposed to
be the provider, but you indenture your own children as part of
the provision?

(It bears noting that this practice of loaning or informally adopting children was widespread in the Dominican Republic in the twentieth century. I learned about
it first from stories, but later from research. Apparently,
it typically took place between affluent branches of
families and their less-well-off kin. The richer family
established basic provision and moral upbringing, and
in return received unpaid domestic help, and if they
so chose, a child they could love and raise. Eventually,
Mamá Silvia would have far flung all her children to extended family on both sides, as if her offspring's petty

labor would earn back the warmth her people had re-scinded. Or perhaps because she truly thought she was doing best by her blood.)

La Vieja [redacted] lived in a city, at least. A small city, but still. There was a discoteca and some new restaurants. Someone in the maternal line had opened a department store.

You would know she was a formidable woman the first time you looked at her. She had a sharp little nose and a hefty body. She couldn't have broken five feet in height, but people would swear she was bigger if you asked. Her ever-present ire was well-placed shoe lifts that seemed to render her taller.

Abuela Eugenia and the nun aunt told Pastora the aunt was heavy-handed and her temper was easily tripped. Perhaps to scare her, Abuela Eugenia told Pastora that of all her children, La Vieja [redacted] was the most Old Testament kind of gal. The nun sister told Pastora stories on the way to their province. She recounted that when they'd been occupied by the Yanqui soldiers, those blue-eyed boys running wild, bucking at anything in a skirt, even they'd steered clear of her ornery sister. Pastora was not intimidated by the nun aunt's cackling, although she could hear that there was little exaggeration in the nun aunt's tales.

The car pulled up to La Vieja [redacted]'s house, and Pastora did not marvel, but it was something to marvel at: a two-story home wrapped in big, wide windows, curtains of the finest textiles keeping sunshine out. La Vieja [redacted] and the sweet, sweet husband met them at the door. She kissed her mother and sister, lips barely touching their cheeks. For Pastora all she offered was a small nod. "So, this is her, then?"

The nun aunt and Abuela Eugenia did not stay the night.

Pastora played at being docile at first. She cleaned when asked to; she went to her little pallet on the floor when she was told it was time for bed. The house was in a town, not the wild and remote countryside she was used to, and so the call to roam was tempered by a respect for her new surroundings. She hated the fear she felt in this new environment, this way in which both she and her upbringing were put on mute as an entirely new show, with a new cast of characters and an unfamiliar set, opened at curtain call. She was relegated to being the behind-the-scenes help.

Yes, Pastora was a country girl, used to dawn wake-ups and hard work. But this new schedule was meant to break her. The old woman woke Pastora up at four a.m. to begin cooking the breakfast. Then she would have Pastora join her at the family cafetería, which fed the local high school students. It was only after work that the girl was able to go to night school, attempting to not fall asleep in her books at night as she did her seventh-grade homework. It was hellish. And Pastorita dreamt hellish dreams in response.

When La Vieja [redacted] had friends over, Pastora was to serve coffee, sit quietly in a corner, and respond with her head down when asked a question. Now, we all know, our Pastora was no mouse, and she tried to stretch the parameters of what would be allowed of her. But La Vieja [redacted] had a faster slap than her mother's, and the consequences here felt vast and unknown. There was nowhere to hide and, with her having hopped around not once but twice, no way to run back home, she pondered that the shame of what she'd left there had been more welcome than this new existence.

The one thing Abuela Eugenia and the nun aunt had omitted, but would have been relevant information about the aunt, was que se montaba. Despite being an especially pious person, who looked down upon what she considered any heathen practice, she would go into these spells where her slight form was inhabited by something even more vicious than herself. Even the true santeros in the area avoided La Vieja [redacted]'s house.

The first time La Vieja [redacted] se montó, Pastora was asleep at the kitchen table when a terrible wail woke her. Pastora thought the woman was having a seizure like the milk vendor back home who once fell off his horse, his jugs of milk rolling as he approached their house. But when the sweet husband ran out the back to grab a dishrag and bucket, Pastora realized she was witnessing something preternatural. Of course, she snuck into the living room doorway to look. She could hear the sweet husband murmuring, but the roar continued. Her aunt was in the living room, enraged. She knocked a vase to the floor. Tossed a chair over. She mostly babbled, but also let loose curses that both thrilled Pastora's little heart and reddened the tips of her ears. Her aunt would have broken every tooth in her mouth if she'd murmured even *one* of those words.

"¿Pero, qué es? ¿Qué hacemos?" Pastora asked the sweet husband, who was on the other side of the dining room table, across from her aunt. The aunt shook with anger; she paced and spoke in tongues and pointed at them and screamed.

The uncle shook his head. "She hasn't been mounted in years. I don't know. [Redacted], [redacted]! Tranquila."

The aunt took deep breaths, quieting for a second. The sweet husband inched his way around the table, attempting to soothe an unbroken bull. He made the mistake of trying to rub her arms or to restrain her latest swipe at the artwork.

There really is no other way to put it; she filled up, the lungs of the monster that held her taking a deep breath. And she struck out at her sweet, sweet husband. He landed against the wall with a hard thump. [Redacted] had felled a man who doubled her in height and weight.

And that's when Pastora got scared.

La Vieja [redacted]'s eyes landed on the girl, and she pointed. Her screams elevated to a fever pitch.

Pastora backed away, but it didn't matter.

Pastora ran to bed that night shaking in her gown. What if La Vieja [redacted] came to her while she slept? She chose not to close her eyes. She stayed awake all night, waiting for La Vieja [redacted] to see what she'd done. The bruised face of her husband, the shredded curtains and broken porcelain.

She was still awake when the sun crept over the tree line, but she must have nodded off, since La Vieja [redacted] woke Pastora with a slap. And not because she was mounted or any spirit told her to, and not with the strength of two men, but only with the strength of a woman who struck to harm. "Why are you still sleeping? And why haven't you cleaned the living room? You're late!" Pastora's belief that there would be a conversation, or at the very least an exorcism, died in her throat.

Pastora lived with a fear she had not known back home. Her belly was somewhat full here, but so was her mouth: constantly biting back words that she could say to no one. She was thralled to a woman who was conduit to the most violent side of the spiritual world. And although Pastora had grown up with a sister who was handmaiden to death, who was haunted nightly, Flor was calm, peaceful even, in her occult relationship. Not like this woman who seemed buffeted by unrestful spirits that found a welcome host in her. Pastora had seen the practitioners of many religious crafts in town. The white-wearing Babalawos. The saint-whispering comadronas. Even the church-going women who wore beads around their necks and spoke in a tongue that belonged to another continent. Even they shook their heads. This was untamed horror in the realm of any God.

As La Vieja [redacted] became more and more prone to being mounted by evil, the sweet, sweet husband began casting worried eyes at Pastora. "It's just, we thought it had stopped. We had to save a lot of money, but a bishop came all the way from Rome. He removed this . . . this stain. She's been fine."

Pastora heard what was unsaid: *until you arrived.*

The next time La Vieja [redacted] was mounted, she came looking for Pastora. "Whore! Whore! Silvia, you whore! I've seen my husband making eyes at you."

The sweet husband rushed into the room. "That's not Silvia, mi amor. That's Pastorita. Pastorita."

It was a plea she did not hear. She tore at Pastora's nightgown, at the small stack of clothing sitting on a stepstool that the girl claimed as a makeshift bureau. She tore pages from the school notebooks that Pai had sent hard-earned coins for her to buy. Pastora heard the words thrown at her again and again, and what La Vieja [redacted] said, she said with conviction: She looked at Pastora and saw her sister. She looked at Pastora and thought she was an interloper in her marriage.

Pastora slept outside that night. Huddled against the back wall of the house. Shivering from something other than cold.

She wrote to her parents once a month, but dared not say

anything. She couldn't imagine the repercussions if her aunt assumed the girl was rumormongering. What could she say to her sisters? Flor, who sent her letters weekly? What would her sisters be able to do that Pastora herself could not? And what would she tell the family? That the aunt's hidden self, driven self, believed her a whore? That the aunt woke her out of sleep with shrills and slaps? That her aunt courted demons in her sleep? What could she say to her parents? Her father did not know how to read, and any letter that came would be narrated by her mother. Whom, if Pastora had not hated before, she hated now.

Pastora's shins were scraped raw from where the aunt made her kneel on a cheese grater any time she spoke back. Her respite was on the nights when her aunt slept soundly and Pastora managed to set her fear aside enough to get a couple hours of sleep. Her dreams were more vivid than they'd ever been, and always she was on the bank of the canal, her sisters running near her. Matilde dancing between the casava crops. Camila, the baby sister she'd yet to meet, babbling with the river. Flor gazing at the clouds. She spoke to them in these dreams, but they couldn't hear her. Every time she opened her mouth, the roar of the canal grew louder. Flor's left eye followed her when she grew irate in the dreams, waving her arms, begging them to listen. That lone iris, unblinking, steady, watching, was the only interaction.

She was abandoned in all her nightmares.

The next time Pastora was sent to town to buy macaroni, she took a side street she didn't usually venture down. Here, in this alley a block from the church, a little sign read BOTÁNICA. She'd been raised to fear witchcraft, had been told that vodun was the craft of devil worshippers. But she, who knew her own family's strange relationship to other worlds, rebelled against that flattened definition.

When she walked into the botánica, the incense smoke swirled around her. It was the scent of burning orange peels, and not entirely unpleasant. She passed rows of figurines, of saints dressed in yellow, blue skirts, a little Black boy in red. She wasn't sure what she was looking for.

The santero who presumably ran the shop came from behind a curtain that separated the store from his home. Pastora wondered how much he must pay the local police to leave his store of non-Christian goods unaccosted.

The santero smiled, and Pastora felt a wet, hard lump form in her throat.

"What can I do for you, little one?"

It took Pastora several moments before she could speak. She kept her hands fisted against the sides of her skirt. "My mother's sister is La Vieja [redacted]" was all she could force out. But it was enough. If the santero's eyes had been sympathetic before, they softened further.

"Ah. Yes. She is well known."

"We need help. *I* need help."

The santero looked around his shop, although Pastora had a feeling he was not scanning for what oil to offer, or what spell to sell. He seemed to be casting for the right words. When his eyes landed back on her, they were as open and empty as his hands.

"Sometimes, one is mounted by a deity, and one resists, and it feels like an illness because you are denying the divine. Sometimes, one is mounted by a sickening, and one welcomes it with open arms, and any deity that once might have answered with grace side-steps this degradation of the soul."

The santero did not need to say which category her aunt fell into. But she understood he would not be able to assist Pastora in fixing her mother's sister.

"I can offer you this oil, little one." He went behind his curtain and came back with what could have been a bottle of vanilla. "Dab a little bit right here." He pointed to his forehead and made a swiping motion. "Before you go sleep. Perhaps this will help protect you by connecting you to your own wisdom."

Pff. As if it was her wisdom that needed assistance! But when she went to count coins on his counter, he waved her away. And even if it did nothing, the oil smelled of clove and lilac. She was diligent in her application, but it did not stop La Vieja [redacted].

Pastora fell behind in school; the shadows under her eyes grew alongside the shadow in her spirit. More and more the aunt's other form looked not to break vases or chairs or book spines, but Pastora's very self.

Salvation came in the form of the dainty Flor.

Their parents had finally saved enough to send her to the convent of the nun aunt. And Pastora's sister, the ever calm and collected Flor, refused to join the nunnery, or attend a single meeting with the high mothers of the church until she was taken to see Pastora.

Pastora watched from behind a curtain as a wagon pulled up and someone got off. Flor arrived at La Vieja [redacted]'s doorstep dressed in a white-collared dress, her shoes shiny and cheeks rosy. Pastora hid in her aunt's linen armoire. The shame that took root in her stomach, that her sister would see her scarred, bruised, withered like rotted fruit, made her gag. Pastora tried to hide the sound by holding a sheet up to her face, but all she managed to do was soil the fine linen with vomit. She'd have to come up with an explanation as to why she needed to rewash the linens she'd hand scrubbed only days ago.

It was the sweet husband who opened the door and escorted Flor into the living room. "Sorry to have left you waiting. I don't usually answer the door myself. My wife is off visiting the mayor's wife. But she should be back soon. She'll be so happy to see another niece."

"Bendición, Uncle. And where is my sister? Surely, she's been let out of school by now." Flor, who never raised her voice, must have been doing so now as Pastora heard her even though she'd covered her head with a feathered comforter.

"Oh, well, Pastorita must be around here somewhere. It's her day to clean the outhouse. Her classes aren't until this evening."

Every day was her day to clean the bathrooms. And kitchen, and to scrub the floors and iron the curtains. She was the maid of all work.

"I have a meeting in town I cannot miss, but you are welcome to wait here for your aunt."

Pastora could hear the beatific smile in Flor's voice. "Of course, Uncle. I'll make some coffee so Tía has refreshment when she returns."

"Well, aren't you a darling! Will you join us for dinner? I'll stop by the butcher's."

Whatever reply Flor murmured was too low for Pastora to hear.

When the door shut behind her uncle, she waited to hear the sound of crockery and the coffee maker, but it was not toward the kitchen her sister's steps echoed.

"Pastora? Pas?"

Pastora buried her face in the linens, trying to find an unsoiled corner. Perhaps it was the uncanny in Flor, or perhaps she'd made a sound, a cry for help that had escaped her own ears but found Flor's, because the doors to the armoire swung open. She tried to shy away from Flor's outstretched arms; she felt untamed, sullied. But her sister climbed into the armoire, Flor's longer legs cradling hers. She brought her forehead down to meet Pastora's, the sheets bundled between them, staining them both with that which could not be kept down.

"I'm here now, Pas. I'm here."

And as her sister pet her hair, Pastora's body felt foreign to her. She had forgotten any softness that was not rendered by her own hands. This was the first tender touch she'd had in months months months months.

It was Flor who wiped her face with the linen then threw the bundle to the floor. Flor who grabbed a bucket of well water, undressed her, and scrubbed her clean from forehead to toenails as she shivered in the sun. She asked no questions about the horrors. She replaited Pastora's hair and rolled her socks up to the knees, a life-size doll well tended. Then she grabbed Pastora by the chin, holding her eyes the best she could with the left one always and still turned toward the periphery.

She didn't say a word; she simply took deep breaths that Pastora was surprised to find her body matching.

Then, "Have you eaten?"

"Yesterday. You saw the remnants."

Pastora noticed the banked fury in Flor's right eye. The trembles in the hand that held her chin.

"Can you walk?"

She took a shuddery breath. "Of course."

Her sister smelled of good, dark vanilla and sunshine.

"How did you know?" Pastora asked.

"Go get your things."

That Pastora knows of, this instance of saviorship was the only time her sister ever intervened to thwart the outcomes of one of her dreams.

Pastora got her little knapsack, leaving behind her tattered books, the clothing that didn't fit. The walk to the convent took three quarters of a day. They were silent on the way there. Pastora's ears perked up anytime horses passed them by. But Flor never flinched. She had grown even quieter, and even more resolved, in the past year.

There isn't much Pastora remembers about the church and convent; it was one level, painted yellow, and looked like a regular church except for how far back it extended.

Pastora didn't know the goings-on that happened outside the small, bare room they shared all the way in the back. Once they'd arrived she did not leave, not even to use the bathroom. Flor was the one who removed and emptied the bucket of waste Pastora excreted. That seven by seven room became a safe house for Pastora.

The nun aunt stopped by one day, playing the innocent. "My sister can be difficult, but she means well. She's a strict woman, but that kind of rectitude would be helpful for a girl of your temperament."

Pastora reached out, touching fingers to the habit that kept her aunt's hair covered. "You are a terrible sister."

The aunt startled, raised a hand. Pastora shrugged. "There is nothing you can hit that she hasn't battered worse."

The nun aunt dropped her hand, but not before it curled into a loose fist. "Pack your things. She'll probably arrive by tomorrow, at the latest. My sister misses her errand girl, and it's clear you are wanting the structure."

Pastora did not glance at the knapsack that she'd never unbuttoned, much less unpacked.

Flor brought her meals. Lotioned her legs with sábila. Put sweet-smelling oil on the parts between her braids. Spooned her at night when her eyes were too tired to cry even though her heart wept. They were sending her back. They were sending her back to that woman and she would die. Having lived only to steal one kiss, to run freely through fields of sugarcane, to have cursed much less than she should have. She comforted herself that night by repeating: *I have known children who died having lived less I have known children who have died having lived less.*

La Vieja [redacted] did not show her face the next day, nor the day after. Pastora stayed on the little cot and startled every time the door opened, but it was only Flor who came.

"Is she here yet?" Pastora asked, and she was proud her vocal cords did not tremble to the ear.

Flor, as was her way when she did not want Pastora to guess the truth, did not answer her directly. Instead of saying whether La Vieja [redacted] had come, she would proceed into nonsensical asides. "The butterflies by the canal must be abundant this time of year." Or, "Camila will probably beg for—and get!—a pony by the time she's three." She returned Pastora home in that way, phrase by phrase, reminding her of a life where things were sure and predictable.

But on the third day after the nun aunt's pronouncement, there was a commotion at the gate, screaming that had nuns rushing down the hall. Pastora did not need anyone's confirmation to know what it was. She turned from the window that overlooked the garden, put on her knapsack. She who cowered from no one did not cower now, but she did resign herself. No one knocked; the screaming did not enter the hallowed halls. And then, sudden as a storm breaks over a pasture during rainy season, the yelling stopped. The entire convent went eerily silent.

Flor came to the room a little while later, and Pastora held her breath. But her sister simply sat next to her, gazing out the window at the sunflowers that worshipped the sun through their open petals.

"She's here?" Pastora asked. She still wore the book bag.

"She's left," Flor said.

"She's left?" Now she did turn to her sister. Flor was not one to jest. "How? I heard her. I *heard* her. She was her biggest form. No one could bring her down when she was mounted."

"Ah, well." Flor blinked and blinked, eyes on the garden. "It helps that I am not no one."

Pastora heard the truth in her sister's words. "How could Mamá let them send me there? She must have known. Right?"

Flor shook her head. "I don't know. I don't know. I can't begin to imagine."

The nuns offered succor out of the goodness of their divine hearts, but they also rescinded the invitation for Flor to join their sect. The family was a liability, it was determined. And if she descended to the same insanity as her aunt, she would not be worth the energy they would invest for the slim possibility of her canonization.

Their father arrived two days after the commotion. His wagon and their old burro, his hat and slacks. He did not curse his wife's family. Their ill-treatment of his child that they disguised as discipline. No, he was a gentleman. He shook the nun aunt's hand.

PASTORA: INTERVIEW TRANSCRIPT (TRANSLATION)

ONA: If it's possible, can you say more about that?

PASTORA: Hmm . . . how do I say, they were devoted, of course. One thing the old people knew that this new generation forgets is duty. But duty is not soft, or padded. It does not let you suckle at its teat. That I learned from my sisters. Although of course, when they laugh and joke that we work in twosomes, they are not wrong. The person I've hugged most in the world, besides my own offspring, has been Flor. It was she who carried me on her hip. As a child, hers was the first body I remember vining around, the way climbing plants claim homes. Before I ever understood love, I only knew safety . . . And perhaps they are one and the same to me and always will be. . . . Safety is also not inherently a soft thing, I don't think. I can't be cold, of course. Seat belts keep you safe, but they don't kiss your cheek. But safety does not in fullness allows someone to bring their edges.

The only person I can remember, before your uncle Manuelito at least, who allowed me all my sharp sides was your mother. Perhaps because patience was a virtue and she knew that from the beginning. And maybe because life for her has been an amusing experiment. But I think it's innate to her character regardless of the supernatural. Humans to her never did make sense, and so I was simply another human for her to study. There was no norm to any of us, and why would she apply it to her little sister? And then of course, my charm and intrepidness made me her favorite person in the world—no offense.

I learned from her how to raise Yadira. When she had that thing all those years ago, people told me she didn't need a doctor, she just needed to go to DR, clear her mind. I knew she needed a therapist and a change of scenery. Because what would keep her heart safe was both, even if I didn't like the idea of it. I wanted your aunt to make a concoction, I wanted to ask Yadira question after question until I could find a solution. But then I remembered the sharp edges. And I knew I could pit myself against her until one of us shattered, or I could learn to curve.

I don't know what will happen, or when. But I know that I have tried to steel myself against it. Everything is about to change. Ant's mother told me he's been in a halfway house; he gets out next week. He first had to get a job lined up, and verify he'd have somewhere to stay. I've called Yadira every day since I've learned, but my mouth hasn't been able to form the words. Is it bad a boy I loved

like a son has me so scared? Not because I think
he'll do anything to her, not physically. He's not
that kind of boy. . . . I know because we speak.
What kind of boy writes three-page letters to his
teen love's mother? His Spanish isn't even good
enough for half the things he tries to write. I'm
sure he has to consult a dictionary every other
sentence.

No, he's a sweet boy. I don't have to hear his
voice to know it's true. But my Yadi, I don't know
what it will do to her when she knows he's back.
It's like for the last two decades she's been holding
vigil and here is a spirit about to rise from the
dead . . . and well, I don't know what it will do to
me when your mother is gone. And the stubborn
woman! Don't . . . oh mi'ja, I'm sorry. . . . I don't
know why I even mentioned it. You're scared too! I
know. Forget I said anything. . . .

I looked around the lecture hall. Exactly thirty-three hours until the wake, and I knew it down to the minute because I hadn't been able to stop counting even while I'd been teaching. The end of class usually culminated in a collective dismount as the students looked over their notes to see if they had all the information they needed to write their papers. Teaching could be a joy, but I was always relieved when my portion of the day's work was over. I was still getting used to the ways my younger students used technology. They took pictures on their phones of my presentation slides, or emailed me without any shame to ask things I'd answered in class. They kept tests from previous years and traded them around the way kids in middle school used to hustle Pokémon cards. I tried not to be prideful that as a Dope Young Educator™ I always re-created my tests to match the material and interests of each unique cohort, and that students would still need to do the reading and participate in the conversations in order to fully comprehend the PowerPoints.

"We are building knowledge collectively," I told them on the first day. "This isn't data transfer, where I could just hand you a USB with articles and you'd be all set. You aren't downloading the information. We are searching for the truth of a people and place together."

And I for real wanted it to be that way. Last semester, when I took off for my surgery, something else had been removed from my body: this connection. Teaching put a battery in my pack. It reminded me why I spent hours on dead hours combing through archives for a single measly citation. Sometimes not even that. Sometimes just for a secondary source that at least corroborated a first. The research was crucial work. And I had many colleagues who saw the research as the primary work, the teaching as the atonement they had to perform in order to be supported by the academic institutions. But for me the teaching went hand in hand with the studies I pursued. I searched harder, faster, more meticulously for information when I saw the awe and awful of how little we knew about ourselves dawn on my students.

The majority of students who took my courses were trying to fulfill the humanities requirements in order to get to their favorite sections within their own major. But students like the ones this morning, who took an advanced course in Kiskeya Land and Living 1500s–1804? These were the ones. The ones I waited for every section, every semester. The Washington Heights and Lawrence and Providence and Miami youngins. The ones who pilgrimaged to this Dominican mecca; public thinkers who tagged street corners with symbols of Atabey and Lucumí prayers. These were the ones who came in already having read, annotated, and written dissenting arguments or celebratory reviews in response to Silvio Torres-Saillant, Ana-Maurine Lara, April Mayes, Ginetta Candelario. These were the ones who arrived with spittle hanging from their mouths, hungry for humans' sixth sense: belonging.

My students gathered their laptops and iPads, and I hoped

that they had taken notes and not just posted about their boredom across social media apps. I knew Caridad was going to stick around by the way she tapped her pencil on the desk, her look faraway. She was already dreaming about how to phrase what she wanted to ask me. Caridad was one of my most distinguished students, and on a short list of favorites. Educators shouldn't have favorites, but sometimes you meet a young person and you think, how can I advance every desire you have? How can I serve your brilliance? And sometimes you think that and more: if I have a little one, I hope she has your kindness, your curiosity, your unfuckwitable vibe.

I turned off the projector and proceeded to log out of the shared classroom computer. The custodians were sticklers about the lights, and I always made sure to follow the instructions they taped next to the audiovisual switchboard. When all the students had left, I leaned against the desk. I wore fresh Air Forces and jeans to class, but I liked to think the button-down shirt reminded them I had terminal degrees.

"Let me guess. I have the illustrious task of writing your recommendation for the Dominican Institute Sugar Cane Ingenio Research delegation." The announcement of the prestigious research group had been e-blasted out the week before by another CUNY-system school, and I was hopeful a few of my students would be applying.

Caridad smiled softly, her pencil tap tap tapping.

I swallowed my smile. "¿Qué te pasa, querida?"

Caridad was a student who practiced her talking points and was organized and ready for every class. She respected her professors' time more than most.

"I wish. It looks like a dope opportunity. But I actually

wanted to tell you . . . I'll be taking a leave of absence. Probably permanently."

I know I stood too quick, that I made something that needn't have been dramatic even more so by my body's uncontrolled response.

I didn't know what I should ask. Students take leave early and often. Many students never come back. This is the truth of a public university system. Sometimes the point of the education isn't completion, it's how far on a path to self-actualization you can get a student until the world clobbers your influence— debt, grants that don't come through, parents who get sick, jobs that need a young person full-time.

"What's going on? What do you need?" I walked over and took the seat next to her. Kept my hands and eyes steady. Dead sure that we could troubleshoot, already going through the list of scholarships and grants available to one of the school's best and brightest.

She hesitated a long moment. I didn't know if her smile was sad or I was making it so because my own heart was.

"I'm pregnant." And I'm sure no two words had ever dropped into this classroom and shut me up faster. Not when a student cried and ranted after we read the letters of Bartolomé de las Casas. Not after we did a study on the life of Mamá Tingó. Not when we sat and reflected on the last words of the chieftain Anacaona. My mouth, typically a well of words, dried up.

Caridad looked back at the desk. "And the baby's father was deported back to DR. It just makes sense to go back to have the baby where he can be with both his parents. My parents agree that money will stretch further in Santiago than Staten Island. And my aunt is a doctor there. It just makes sense, you know?"

Each sentence was a Holyfield haymaker. Only the ancestors know how I didn't double over. I wanted to howl. For what this twenty-year-old had been blessed with, for what she was about to lose. An entire academic career. It was mind-boggling, but her ability to do progressive research in DR might be even more difficult on the island, despite her being more proximate to her area of study. The financial support and mentorship to be had were here.

And not to mention a child. A child. I looked at her still-small stomach; she must be in the first trimester, but in there a body was growing elbows and joints and a puckering mouth. I swallowed hard.

"I wanted to tell you personally; I didn't want you to think I dropped out for no reason. I did well enough here that I think with one or two classes I can finish my credits there, at least get an associate degree."

I am not proud of what I said next. But the words swam swiftly through the bile in my throat. "But why?"

The tap tap tapping stopped. The girl raised her face. And I saw every bit of how New York had raised her snap into focus. "Why *what*?"

I'd not heard this tone from Caridad directed at me.

I didn't repeat the question, but it hung: a string of repopulating pearls between us.

"I already told you why I'm moving. Are you asking why I'm having the baby? Why I'm still going to try and finish a degree? Why I got pregnant? Which 'why' are you asking, Dr. Marte?" Caridad stood, grabbing her book bag with fast movements. Even in motion her belly didn't yet show a bulge. There was another option she didn't suggest: *Why you and not me?* but that would have been a question for the ancestors, not her.

"The correct response, Marte, would have been 'Congratulations.' Or 'Let me know what I can do to help your transfer go smoothly.'"

She paused, an offering, I like to think, another opportunity to show up differently for her. She was that kind of student, benevolent even while indignant.

"Good luck, Caridad." My lackluster response earned a sucking of her teeth, and I knew one day this brilliant young woman would be giving a speech somewhere, talking about her life's trajectory, and I would be the answer to the question *Was there ever someone in your career path who doubted you?*

I hoped Caridad stuck with academia and that she finished undergrad, even as I knew it'd be a hard battle even without a child. I walked to the C train while considering Caridad's road ahead. It wasn't just the bureaucracy, the keeping up with research and technology, the constant need to prove to a department you were an asset. It was also the personal drive. The ability to find a new way into the subject matter. A way that excited you as well as the people who fund the research.

Shit, just recently I'd had to face these very questions, and how much harder would it have been if I'd had a kid counting on me to balance passion and a paycheck?

The Caribbean Studies colloquium in DC wasn't one I was supposed to attend. A colleague took an impromptu "sabbatical," and it was determined I was the best department faculty member to be sent in his stead. It was my first week back after having taken an

entire semester off, and I still don't
think I was the person most in the
swing of things, but it was for that
same reason the department thought I
should be the one to go; I'd had so much
productive thinking time! Of course, I
must have some new and exciting ideas
to share! Might be newly inspired!

Who comes up with presentations when they're on medical leave? The months before I came back to teaching hadn't been entirely devoid of scholarship. I *had* been doing soft research on how seemingly Christian Dominicans established veneration altars to the dead, but it was nothing other academics hadn't already mined. I looked through old essays and presentations I'd done, but keynoting for an hour on decade-old work sounded like my mother would be having a dream about me; it was painful to even contemplate. The truth is, I hadn't done any new work or research in a long time. The little mouth inside of my creativity that became hungry when I hadn't offered it something new to chew on, to work through, hadn't been craving anything academic in a long time. And the thought of a baby wasn't going to arouse it; it needed me to make something with my mind. To work through a problem only I could lockstep into clarity until my hunger for scholarship revved back.

DC is a beautiful city unless it's July or August. In those months, regardless of the dew point, the humidity sits on the body like an extra pelt. September was barely better, but I was just grateful it wasn't still summer.

Us academics were put up in a nice hotel in the Northwest

area. After the first day, it was without accordance that most of us from the conference ended up at the hotel bar. I was sipping a nice dry pinot grigio when a raucous laughter and long curly hair snapped into place each disc in my spine. I love me a good rom-com, but when the crowd parts Red Sea–like and the two former loves, the one who got away and the one who let her slip through her fingers, see each other after years? That's the moment I live for. Not the stranger meet-cute. But the way film captures that our lives were made to intersect with other lives again and again, our spirits in the Before cosmically linked beyond the constraints of reality.

Seeing Soraya again for the first time in nearly fifteen years was like that. Like feeling my soul tugged from where it still knotted with hers.

Sweat pooled between my breasts and I couldn't even blame it on the humidity since the hotel bar was well ventilated. I know most people think that academic conferences are just excuses for the nerds to hook up without repercussions since most intellectuals rarely meet the romantic halves of their conquests, but I'd never been tempted to do grime; Jeremiah was who and what I wanted. I firmly lectured my nani on this point as I wove my way toward Soraya.

Same as I remembered from college, she stood, dressed, and laughed like all of it was on purpose. Adorned in a scarf that mimicked the horizon and feather earrings that entwined themselves with gold spirals and whispered across her collarbone. Despite the upscale setting, she wore a skirt that skimmed tan thighs, revealed the nose of the Lake Enriquillo crocodile tattoo I used to love kissing, my pet reptile. Her white blouse billowed and draped and did nothing to pretend that she was wearing a bra. She was the twirl of a palo dancer, the shimmy of a tambourine, a husky call to dance.

Soraya had the gift of making a poet out of me.

We greeted each other with tight hugs; she still smelled like palo santo and expensive perfume. I inhaled her one more time before we pulled back. Her fingers, each digit dazzled in copper-wire gemstones, held tightly to my upper arms as she looked me up and down.

"Anacaona, you look exactly the same."

I smiled back at her. Neither one of us looked the same. We looked like the thicker, gray-streaked, slightly less lost versions of ourselves we now were.

Time in an unexpected encounter with an old lover can pass in two ways: tediously, each person remembering why they no longer kept in touch, or how our night progressed—with frequent hand touches, a heart's reunion, exclaiming again and again, "I can't believe you're here!"

At one a.m. the only other bar patrons were three old-school professors around a table eating Old Bay–seasoned pretzels, and the volunteer at the door posted by the conference to ensure that none of the illustrious presenters got lost on their way to the elevators. I was feeling slightly buzzed; I hadn't drank much in my recovery and something about Soraya compelled me to keep my hands and mouth busy. And when I wasn't sipping I was, of course, complaining about my work. "And so, I'm finding I'm doing all this work and writing the papers, but then when I get to the abstracts, summarizing the research makes me realize it's all empty. The aim is blurred."

She nodded. "Oh, I know that feeling. It's not until you get to the end of it all that you can see the whole project clearly.

And sometimes it's brilliant and sometimes you only realize you have more work to do. It makes me almost wish I had married rich and didn't have to ask existential questions of my work."

"Ah, yeah. Once I get into alternate realities, I know it's time to file the paper in the Do Not Ever Publish folder. You know what my mom told me a few years back? That she always thought you and I would move in together, pretend to be room-mates, and have a bunch of kids. You definitely wouldn't have married rich then! Isn't it wild? She'd imagined this whole other life for me." I made the admission with a smile, but Soraya didn't return it.

"Was it one of her prophecies?" Soraya's mother had died a week after my mother had said she would. It was something I shared with her one night, while her head was in my lap. She thanked me for not telling her sooner, said she was glad not to have known the inevitable. She did not question that my mother had gifts from the beyond.

My smile slipped; I took a sip of my fourth glass of wine. "I don't think so. I'm partnered now, and he and I are trying for kids. And you're . . ."

Soraya popped a peanut into her mouth from the small dish in front of her. She watched me watch her lips work. "And I'm living my best life. How *is* your mother? Clearly missing the daughter-in-law she could have had."

"That was a while ago. We don't sit around talking about the past like that." I don't know if I was being defensive of Mami, her gift, or the hetero life I *had* chosen. I hesitated a second. "But anyways, Mami is acting strange. She sent out an invita-tion yesterday to a living wake. She has me scared shitless, but when I tried talking to her last night, she wouldn't say anything beyond the fact that she hopes I wear blue because it's her favorite color on me."

"When did she set the wake for?"

"Five weeks from now."

Soraya swirled her drink around the large, melting ice cube. I could hear what she wasn't saying. Five weeks to plan an event, and one come about so spontaneously, seemed ominous. Or maybe I was simply hearing what I wasn't saying.

"Well, you just told me you've run out of compelling research—look to your own bloodline. You should be researching your moms."

"Who would want to read about us? It wouldn't even be considered credible. My department would laugh me right off the tenure track."

"You always did care more about what other people considered relevant than what you considered urgent."

This argument was an old one for us. "It's too late to do that for this conference."

"Fuck this conference. Your mother is still here now. It's not too late to do this for yourself."

I didn't want to talk about this. I asked about her second master's at American University and saw pictures of the two dogs that kept her company. We followed each other on social media and exchanged numbers, realizing neither one of ours had changed since undergrad. She walked me to the elevators, leaving the Uber that would take her back to her apartment waiting. She kissed me on each cheek, then she lightly skimmed her fingers along my denim-clad thigh.

"Your scent is the same, you know."

I gave a startled laugh. "I doubt that, I haven't used Love

Spell in many, many years." Victoria's Secret splash scents had had the girlies in a chokehold when Soraya and I were in school. Her thumb pressed a spot on my thigh that made me swallow my humor with a gasp. Her fingers knew exactly where my tattoo's mouth opened.

"Not that scent. The one closer to where my fingers are. How *is* Oshunmare's favorite snake doing? Has she missed me?"

I understood what she was and wasn't asking. And she must have understood how tempted I was to answer the way both of us knew my body wanted to. It would be so easy to tug her hand and head upstairs and shake out of my panties, and shake off my insecurities about work and fears around my mother and grief around how my body had become less known to me this year. She would loosen all the snarled places inside me with soft kisses only she knew how to place without my asking. It would be so easy. Even slightly drunk I knew it would be too easy. The hard and harsh would still be waiting on the other side of the morning.

I stepped away. Her fingers stayed suspended between us for just a moment. Then she smiled and kissed me on the forehead.

I felt something inside of me unknot. "Take care of yourself, Anacaona."

I called Mami with a list of questions the next day, and I've kept sneaking in more during every conversation we had since.

———

I'd canceled my office hours after my confrontation with Caridad. As I walked across campus toward the hall where my afternoon lecture took place, I found myself wondering what I was doing there. Clearly not inspiring students. I tried my best not to play hooky, but fuck, my mother might be dying. My womb un-incubated eggs. And I'd just let down my favorite student. I sent an email letting my students know class was canceled and to submit any questions on the discussion board. I deserved a cremini quipe and a smoothie.

I walked into the shop to find Yadi, face full of makeup, manning the cash register.

We kissed hello, but the lunch rush was extensive. I walked to the back and put on an apron. I wasn't one to get my nails dirty putting together bean sprout sandwiches, but I knew how to take both orders and money. I nudged my cousin from the register. She threw a grateful look over her shoulder as she proceeded to begin fulfilling the three orders that'd been waiting.

It took a solid thirty minutes of nonstop customers before things slowed down enough for us to take a break.

I stepped back and leaned against the coffee counter, massaging my scalp. The wait between my last period and my next one was still irregular, and either my hormones or stress about the confusion caused tension headaches. I battled migraines every cycle. The run-in with Caridad hadn't helped. Guilt was now added to the list of weights my heart carried.

Yadi stepped in front of me and swatted at my hands. She dug her strong, ruthless fingers into my head of hair. We stood like that for several moments. My breathing slowed of its own accord.

"Is the pressure good?" Yadi asked, and I murmured. The only way I knew that the pressure was good was if I woke up with a sore cranium but without a headache the next day. I have a masochistic relationship with pressure.

Yadi stepped back from me and started cleaning up the lunch station, composting peels and spilled lentils as she went. From the fridge she pulled a bag of limes.

"Limeade?" I asked hopefully.

She shook her head. "This is my personal stash. Does what a head massage can't." Yadi sliced a lime in half and rubbed it against her lips, smearing her lip gloss.

"I don't know how you are able to run the shop and also prepare for tomorrow. Mami is calling *me* three times a day, so I know she must be driving you out your mind. How many times has she changed the menu?"

Yadi rolled her eyes but didn't reply.

"Y Tía Mati?"

"She said she wanted to take her lunch at home."

The tone of Yadi's voice had my spine snap tight. "You've been crying."

Yadi smiled a half smile. "Never have figured out how you do that."

"Only with you. What's wrong?"

Yadi sucked on the lime some more. "Ant's out."

I'd expected my cousin to say many things, but Ant? Uh-oh. I touched a hand to my cousin's arm and pretended her mother hadn't told me weeks ago during an interview that Ant had been released and was doing six months at a halfway house. He might have been near the end of that six-month sentence when she'd learned of it.

"Ant's out, and back in the apartment building. He helped me cook last night."

"Past loves are best left in the past, boo."

Yadi shook my hand off and made a churlish sound. "Says the girl who never met a past boo she wanted to leave in the past. Every one of your breakups lasted a hundred years."

Yadi was right. Before Jeremiah, I fell into lust and love hard, and there'd been an ugly rotation of past exes getting sat on the bench only for me to make them the starter when I deemed fit. But very few people were ever actually kicked off the team. I used to believe in free love that way.

Yadi grabbed the other half of the lime, bit into it.

I squeezed her arm one more time. "Have you been taking your meds?"

Yadi snapped her eyes at me. "Yes, Mom."

"Speaking of, have you told your mom you're taking meds?"

Yadi chewed on the rind, taking her time before spitting it out into the compost bin behind the cashier. "Why are you here? Don't you have research or something? Tired of your big old house? Students rioted to get you fired?" She wiped her hand on the dishrag used to clean the counter. I tried not to think of the germs—or Caridad, who could right this second be filing a complaint.

"You know your panic attacks get worse when—"

"Ona. Deja." It wouldn't have been enough to stop any of the aunts from prying, but we'd held each other at our worst.

"I did teach today, but no riots. I have to organize those interviews I've been collecting, so you're right, I am busy. But I'm here because Mami's been avoiding telling me about the wake, so when she asked me to help her pick out her outfit for tomorrow, I said I'd come over. I can't tell if she's lying over Face-Time."

"I thought she bought a dress at Macy's."

"She bought two and wants me to give her an opinion on which one makes her look most sophisticated."

"Speaking of sophistication, you know who else is back, O?" I didn't want to deal with more surprises. But before I could speak, she said, "Kelvyn."

A hush fell over us. Now that was news. Kelvyn was a few years older than us. One of the cool older boys we'd all had crushes on when we were kids. He'd been so sexy with his hella Dominican ass. His parents sent him away when we were in our early teens and he'd come back to New York a man, and his mannerisms still reflected the island that raised him: his pants had never been as baggy, his English lightly hinted with a suaveness that was from more fertile soil than this stretch of Manhattan.

"I think he was flirting with Tía."

I grabbed the rest of the bag of limes and walked to the fridge. Yadi would chafe her tongue if someone didn't ration her. "My tía or your tía?"

"*Our* tía. Tía Mati."

I shook my head. Tía had to be thirty years Kelvyn's senior, even if she didn't look it. Woman had skin smooth as freshly whipped cocoa butter.

"She's never going to get divorced. If she hasn't done it yet, not even a sexy—is he *still* sexy?—younger man will get her to do it."

Yadi rolled her eyes. "She might. He is. And who knows? He could."

I shook my head. "You need help tonight cooking?"

Yadi hesitated a second. "Ant's gonna come through. He has kitchen experience, if you'd believe it."

"I'll stop by too. Been a long time since I've seen him, and I'd like to say hi . . . Why don't I see if Jeremiah can come through too? We haven't been out in a while. We can play cards, something simple. Give you a buffer as you deal with all this."

"I have to cook."

"Cook before, or cook after." I lightly pushed aside a clump of curls that'd been hiding her gaze. I wanted to make sure she could see me. "I want eyes on Ant. And on you dealing with him."

Holding both her shoulders, I pressed my forehead to hers. "Yadi. Don't fuck him. Your anxiety can't handle it. And my anxiety can't handle your anxiety."

She pulled my hands off her arms. Kissed each one of my palms as she returned them back to me. "My anxiety has medication, so go tell your anxiety to fuck itself. Because, I fuck who I want."

FLOR

was startled by the knock on the door, and then she heard the key in the lock. That girl always insisted on knocking despite being able to pull up anytime she wanted. There was a propriety her girl put up between them that Flor hadn't been able to dismantle. She'd misplaced too many years before she'd tried to be her daughter's friend.

Ona walked in, a green smoothie in hand. Flor took her in, her thick-legged girl, with all that dark curly hair, and Flor felt this welling up inside of her: she'd borne this miracle. The world reaped the gifts her daughter put into the world, and it was all because Flor had labored and fed her and loved her. And now she existed wholly her own.

She hoped Ona hadn't thought of any new questions. Some days, talking to her daughter about her past was like palming dough for Johnny cakes, loosening something that had grown stiff into a softer, easier thing. But some days she did not want to look the memories in the face: the glowing eyes of her past mocking and snappish. She did not have any more stories for her daughter, but she had a million things still left to say.

She held both dresses out before Ona could speak. Ona gave long gazes to both gowns.

"That one would be great for an event next summer, too." As if to learn how many seasons her mother had left.

Flor did not acknowledge the comment.

"That one would double as nice for burial." This comment was even less subtle, her kid trying to gauge her reaction to the morbid prompt.

Flor shook the dress in her right hand. "We are focused on the wake, Ona. I should try this one on first?"

She knew she was not giving her daughter an easy task, but it was necessary. Her sisters meant well, but they sometimes let her go out less than fashionably attired. Even Pastora, who worked at a clothing store, sometimes advised a frumpier version of Flor than Flor wanted the world to see. And because eyes can only see so much of the body they belong to, Flor knew she needed a second, *reliable* opinion.

The first dress was an elaborate crimson garment, sequined under the bodice. It scratched a bit under her arms, and so that was a mark against it. The other dress was dark blue, regal as the night, with a high slit in the leg. Flor was particularly proud of her legs. She'd been a flat-chested girl, and she had a paunch that she shimmied into fajas, but her legs from young adulthood to early elderhood still yammed.

Flor changed into the red dress and sauntered into the living room. She walked on her tippy-toes so her girl could get the full effect. Unfortunately, Camila had borrowed the shoes Flor would be wearing the next day, so she didn't have them to show. No bother, she knew the nude pumps would work with either gown.

"Pretty." Ona got off the couch and helped adjust her bra strap. "How do you feel?"

How did Flor feel? What a question. She felt like she was planning her own funeral and it was a day away. She felt like maybe this was all a mistake and she should let fate run its course without her spectating. But she knew what Ona was really asking. "I think my sisters will like it. I feel good."

Ona nodded and sat back down. "Ma, what did you dream? When? When will it be?"

Flor ran fingers along the beading on her dress. She kept her eyes down.

Flor turned her back and Ona stood to unzip her.

"Ahora mismo, todo está bien, mi'ja."

Flor returned to her bedroom and shimmied out of the dress. She tried on the navy dress and checked herself out in the mirror. There was a lot of thigh showing. Granted, the thigh was one that walked an hour in Riverside Park every morning. But it *was* still a thigh that had seen seven decades on this planet. It would be unseemly, wouldn't it? Una vieja verde. It had seemed longer in the store.

Ona called out and Flor went into the living room. Ona stood, her hands adjusting here, and tucking there, and tying a sash into the expert knot Flor had learned at the factory and taught her. It was a glove of a dress, nipped at the waist. She felt like a young woman in it.

"It's nice." Ona sounded deflated. Whenever the girl didn't get what she wanted, she turned like this, a fried thing right after the air is forked out.

"Pretty, ¿sí?"

Ona sighed, snapped a picture. "You have to wear your hair up with that neckline, Mami."

"¿Me veo bien?" she asked again.

Ona circled her. "How do you feel?"

Flor stamped her foot. "Why do I ask you a question and you ask me a question back? Should I wear it?"

Ona laughed. "Do you want to wear it? Have you always been so indecisive?"

"Is this for your research, or just for you?" Flor asked.

"Both," Ona answered. Her daughter was an honest being.

Truth was, Flor didn't know. There were years she'd commanded, and there were years when her certitude hibernated. This life required so many choices. So many little and big choices to plod to the next moment, and who knew if any of it mattered? They were all each other's spectacle and then they died.

She was being churlish. She'd lived long enough with death as her postman to know every life was its own small star that lit up and burned and went dim; it didn't matter who was watching. Life lifed on.

"I make the important decisions quickly and easily."

Ona set her smoothie down, watching as her mother tried on the first dress again, pulling the red satin down over some bootleg Spanx and sucking in her stomach, turning this way and that.

"Vanity has no expiration date, I see," Ona said with a smile.

Flor blew her a kiss and twirled. "I just love how this one moves, but I never have known what looks good on me."

"Everything does, Mami. Esa percha demuestra bien." Her daughter smacked her in the flanks. "Hair in an updo, okay?"

Flor nodded. "You always have known how to ready me."

PASTORA

used the long pole to put the season's new blouson-sleeved tops on the highest row of clothes. The material wasn't the same silkiness as the versions sold on Fifth Avenue, but the synthetic fabric would hold for two or three washes, which was more times than the women buying the clothes here would wear anyhow. These days, Pastora watched as women of all ages wore clothes, put pictures of the outfits on whatever new social media platform, and then never wore the items again. She joked that she should be paid as a stylist for photoshoots since that was clearly the main use of these garments and her recommendations.

Most women looked around when they walked in and looked over her, wanting a second opinion of someone not wearing slacks and a sour expression. But the one thing they loved was that Pastora knew the right thing to say, even better than she knew the perfect collar or cut that would flatter and flatten.

The chime over the door did not disrupt Pastora's flow. She positioned the last blouse artfully on its hook and turned to the door.

"Buenas," she called out.

She tucked the garment reacher behind some maxi dresses. The young woman—at least Pastora assumed she was young from the slimness of her back—had her hair in a long ponytail.

She didn't seem like their usual clientele, but Pastora took stock nonetheless. The jeans were skintight around a generous ass and smallish waist. She knew the *exact* dress that would work on the girl.

When the girl turned, the suggestion Pastora had been about to make curdled in her mouth. The girl's protruding belly button pressed against a skintight lycra tank, the massive bump—diablo, but she was all stomach forward—had been invisible from the back, but this was clearly a third-trimester body.

Close up, her face was not as young as Pastora had thought the day before, when she'd seen the young woman outside of CVS with Rafa—or rather, she must have lived a hard life face-first. The lines at the corner of her downturned mouth looked like they'd been there for a long time; the smudge under her eyes spoke to the sleepless nights she'd counted sheep to. Pastora was usually a sharp observer, but she had to shake herself to see that the girl was flushed, fanning herself with a listless hand.

"Do you have a bathroom? I'm waiting for someone and that tíguere is always late."

The onslaught of emotion that hit Pastora forced her to brace. There was a hungriness in the girl's voice, a bottomless desire. And a piercing sadness. The accent wasn't the capitaleño slant of words that Pastora had been expecting. She was new to New York, if the studded jeans and letter drops of her Spanish phrasing were to be believed.

Pastora shook her head. "I'm sorry. The boss has a hard rule that bathrooms are only for paying customers."

Perhaps not a fast rule. Don Isidro didn't like noncustomers to use the bathroom, but the bathroom was also the fitting room, and not everyone who tried on a shirt ended up passing over a card for it, so it was almost an unenforceable mandate. But Pastora saw no reason to tell the girl that. She just wanted her to leave.

"Oh." The girl's hand came up to her stomach the way one would cover their mouth in surprise. Pastora rolled her eyes in annoyance. She hated women who in pregnancy centered their every gesture around their babe. *Leave your womb out of this.*

"Well . . ." The girl stopped. Stuck.

"We don't sell gum." There. That should send her scurrying away. What more could be said? No one was spending ten dollars on a pair of leggings just to pee. And the McDonald's two avenues over would let her go for free. Pastora didn't tell her that either.

"Please, Doña." The girl looked around the store, a small pout starting to sculpt her lips. The voice grated on Pastora. The instinct to want to comfort the expecting mother was overridden by the desire to slap the hand rubbing small circles over the very evidence of that expectation.

Pastora raised a brow and turned back to her garment reacher. She adjusted a shirt that was already perfectly situated on the second rung. She fixed the shirt next to that one. She waited for the chime, but it didn't come. With the pole still in hand, she turned around.

The girl had sat on a display table, nudging some folded V-neck shirts to make room for her broad bubble ass. She was still fanning herself with one hand and rubbing circles with the other. A seemingly lost thing. But Pastora knew what she'd heard. Tá to.

For the second time, Pastora put down the pole. She crossed

over to the girl, who she should really call a woman, because even though she couldn't be a day over twenty she had undertaken a woman's life and should be accorded the title due to one.

"Can I help you further?"

The young woman blinked a few times. "Do you have hair ties? Or head bands? Something small, please? I just need the bathroom real quick."

The rubbing was a little bit faster, or was Pastora making that up?

"We only serve patrons, I'm sorry. And the cheapest thing in stock are those." She pointed to the display of colorful leggings *On Sale Now for ONLY $7*. It was prohibitive, Pastora knew. Two Metrocards for the price of a pair of pants where even the largest size would struggle to fit over the belly, and a waistband ill-suited for maternity anyhow.

The young woman nodded. "¿Un vasito de agua?"

Pastora shook her head. "We don't have a water fountain."

The girl held her eyes for one long look. "El agua no se niega."

The young woman at last lowered her arms to push herself up from the display. It helped Pastora to see the belly button. To take in the evidence without the tenderness.

Pastora waited until the girl had a hand on the door handle, the chime already tinkling. "He has a wife, you know, your tíguere."

The girl's ponytail bounced for a second before the entire body it belonged to went still. "And since I've heard that she's a saint, I'm sure she at least would have let me pee."

Few people understood, or ever even saw, the way the siblings tried to shield each other. It went back before moving to this country, before they'd had to learn to defend themselves against English and American anger. This girl wouldn't understand how fiercely Pastora had tried to extricate Matilde from the sadness that jailed her.

> Pastora had not been back to her childhood home in many, many years. She'd left the car with Manuelito and taken three buses to get to her mother's house, her belly unbalancing her as she held on for dear life on the last bus, the road so ill-repaired it was a conveyor belt of speed bumps. But it wasn't the distance or roadwork that'd kept her from returning.

The taxi driver who drove her from the bus station to her mother's house drove in silence. He was a young man, someone who had probably come of age long after Pastora had left. Otherwise, he'd have known her, or at the very least he'd have recognized that the directions she gave were leading to the stretch of land where no one else ventured, the widest part of the canal bordering one side, the long rows of vegetable crops bordering the other. But even when they pulled up at the squat pink house, the man hadn't blinked; my, my, but things had changed, Pastora thought as she put her coins in the palm of his hand.

The house looked exactly the same as if she'd never left, even though it'd been nearly two decades. Soft white curtains fluttered in the window. The rocking chairs on the porch were leaned against the railing, evidence it had rained the night before. Pastora wrapped her hands around the wooden spokes and lowered the chairs into their natural position. She'd always thought the rocking chairs looked too restrained when they were tipped like this, even if it did help keep water from settling in the paint. She righted each chair so they were equidistant and turned to knock.

During this last visit, only Camila was still living at home. Everyone else had moved to the capital and married. It was Camila who answered the door. The girl was long-legged and long-haired at twenty, her school bag slung over her soft blue shirt. She was the only sister who had been able to go to college in the local township, because the older siblings paid for the private school. The girl didn't know her sister. Not really. She squealed, of course. And hugged Pastora hard. She rubbed Pastora's stomach and cooed at her protruding belly button. And then kissed her goodbye when a car pulled up, three teenagers in the back and a gentleman with a fedora tipped low over his brow in the driver's seat. Pastora watched her run off to join her classmates in the Jeepeta, her ponytail swinging.

Pastora felt the girl's guilelessness, and it almost took her breath away. How could a child so full of joy and innocence have survived in this place, much less under their mother's thumb? Campesinos might be disconnected from advancements in technology, but they knew the intricacies of life, death, and the suffering in between from the day their hands first helped a piglet be born to the day they helped it be slaughtered. But Camila had been spared.

Depending on how this business with her mother went, she'd ask to bring the girl to the capital. While the city was less safe and full of tígueraje, Pastora knew from experience that the countryside offered too many opportunities for a Caperucita

Roja to get lost in the woods, bitten by well-dressed wolves. Matilde had told her they were always hiring at her hotel.

And it was precisely Matilde that Pastora was here about.

Pastora rubbed her stomach in slow circles, then dropped her hands and entered the house.

"Bendición, mamá." Pastora barely whispered her lips across her mother's cheek. She startled when instead of murmuring and pulling away, the older woman put her hands on her stomach.

"Que Dios te bendiga," the old woman said to her belly, not to Pastora herself. She dropped her hands.

They sat in the living room, still as formal as when Pastora's younger self had lived there, hand-sewn lacy manteles had made the room too fussy for her liking when she'd been a child, and it was equally too prissy for her taste now. Probably because her mother was endlessly sewing little doilies and table skirts. As if knowing what she was thinking, Mamá reached into the sewing bag that never left her side and pulled out her latest project. Pastora couldn't quite make out what it was, only that the old woman's hands were still deft as ever.

"¿Te puedo ofrecer café?" Her mother was treating her like a guest. Pastora watched the sunlight. It splintered and skipped like rocks across the wall above her mother's head.

"Por fa'."

The greca whistled, the coffee ready. Despite having treated Pastora like a guest only a moment earlier, her mother didn't even make a move to fetch the coffee. Pastora took sure steps into the familiar kitchen and pulled down the coffee cups. Noting how each was spotless of dust or soap watermarks. Camila had been taught how to be thorough.

She added powdered milk and sugar to her mother's. Since her father had died, the household had not had fresh cow's milk.

There was nothing left but to say it.

"Matilde. Matilde is not well, Mamá."

Her mother, needle puncturing soft, pillow-white fabric, made a noise low in her throat. "She looked healthy at her wedding a few months ago. No babe yet." Her mother shot a glance at Pastora's belly.

Pastora blew on her coffee, knowing she wouldn't be taking a sip. "And did she write to you? Did she tell you her husband is a sinvergüenza? She won't listen to me or Flor."

Her mother's hand was steady. Steady with the thread. Steady when she'd raised it to strike. Pastora wondered if ever in her life her mother's hand had known a tremble. "You and Flor should know better than to get between a man and his wife; right now, they may be the ones in battle, but after the dust settles, you and Flor will be the ones she considers the enemy."

The old woman held the end of the thread between her teeth, and Pastora peered at her coffee-stained enamel. She wanted to knock those teeth out. She should offer to rethread the needle. Sadly, she did neither.

"He cheats on her all the night long. Manuelito told me that on the night they were married, the man had my husband drop him off at a club frequented by prostitutes. On the night they were married, Mamá. And now, six months later, he hasn't gotten whatever that illness is out of his system. Such little respect he's had for her."

With a hard, triumphant jab, Mamá got the saliva-tipped thread into the eye of the needle. Back to work her hands went.

Mamá spoke on beat with her hands. "Vows are vows.

Marriage by the church is an honorable act. You wouldn't know anything about honor. But Matilde knows. Our family has had enough shame without Mati adding to the pile."

Pastora has been married by la ley, but not in a house of worship like her siblings. She hadn't wanted the burden of having to invite family she didn't want to witness her marriage to her wedding. But in her mother's eyes she and Manuelito might as well be shacking up.

(Although, to be fair, free unions are widely accepted in the Dominican Republic, which is surprising for such a staunchly (albeit syncretized) Catholic nation. It's truly radical if you think about it: couples bypass institutional legalities and instead uphold their unions on the covenant of their word. Fucking progressive.)

"She won't find someone better. And her womb is not made for children. How could I advise her to leave the one person who might accompany her in this life? Would you like me to tell her that? That she should have no one to love her? I'm not that cruel."

Pastora heard, as if she were merely observing another body, her breaths growing shallow. Why would her mother have confessed what she knew about Mati's womb to her? Pastora didn't want the burden of that secret. She didn't want to know that something her sister so longed for would not happen. Her mother must have known what it would do to her to have to keep this truth.

There was so much Pastora had wanted this woman to be for her. So many times, she'd offered her mother the opportunity to actually mother. Oh, Pastora had been dressed in skirts and fed, but she hadn't been *raised*. And her mother still used every opportunity she could to make her smaller than she was.

She glanced out the window. The lime trees, and the rows of batatas, and the slip-slide of the river, they had mothered her hurts and held her when she cried. Not this woman, who'd been seemingly tired of her from the moment she'd drawn breath. But she imagined the woman had more love for the children who had been born when she was young, and spry, and still in love with her husband. Pastora imagined she loved Camila because she was the only baby to survive the many pregnancies after Pastora had exited her womb. She knew the woman hadn't loved her, or defended her, because she, Pastora, required very little defending, but surely her mother would be protective of her softest child. She'd imagined, clearly spinning dreams out of clouds, because this woman loved nothing and no one.

Pastora put down her coffee cup. Picked up her purse. Rose.

Her mother did not stand up from her seat, but after several seconds she did stop sewing. Snapped the thread. Held out the fabric. A bib, Pastora saw now. Long before this morning, her mother had begun to make her a bib. "Send me the girl."

"What?" Pastora stopped, her hand in midreach. "What girl? And actually, I wanted to tell you about Camila. She's getting too grown for these parts. She'd do better with us in the capital."

Her mother thrust the bib out again. "The one you're carrying. When it's time, send me the girl. Camila is fine. She still needs me."

Pastora had not done the test to reveal the child's sex. She and Manuelito had also wanted to expect and hope for nothing more than a healthy child.

But now her mother had confirmed. A girl.

She grabbed the bib from her mother as if taking a bit of bread from the teeth of a rabid dog. She turned. In all the world she'd seen, which was really only three provinces on this little half of an island, she could hear a person and know exactly what they meant. The skeleton of their character revealed through their syllables. Everyone but this woman. "I don't think I'll be seeing you again. And I'm not sure I've seen you ever."

"Send your daughter when it's time. That's all I have for you."

"For what, so you can ruin her?"

"She will be her own ruins before then. Me la mandas."

Not on your life, Pastora thought, her fingers rubbing circles against the skin of her stomach, taut as a drum. As if in response, the child thumped back twice. Pastora chose to take that as the child agreeing with her, even as she knew, the way she knew the character of anyone with whom she spoke, that this child inside her would be contrary.

————

No. Pastora could not explain to her brother-in-law's hussy how protective she would be over her sister. All she could do was be glad she'd gotten the woman out of her face so quickly.

Pastora left the store with a wave to Don Isidro, who always came in on Friday evenings to do the week's books.

Columbus Ave was buzzing in the late afternoon. Fridays at five the neighborhood released a deep sigh. Beef sizzled from the chimi trucks. A cluster of women stood talking on the corner and Pastora had to wait as the people in front of her tried to walk through.

"... and she just fell ..."

"... landed facedown and everything ..."

"The ambulance came, but you know how they are; she was already awake again by the time they got here. She just kept screaming about her barriga."

"Ay Dio' ay Dio' ay Dio'."

Pastora's spine was ramrod stiff. She didn't look at any of the ladies. Two of them were exaggerating; they hadn't even seen the event and had only commandeered whispers they'd overheard. But one woman had been there: true pena enswathed her words.

Pastora approached that woman, touched her on the arm. "Someone was hurt here? I work down the street and am trying to figure out what happened."

The woman nodded, her big eyes unfocused. "A young woman, bendito, she could have been my daughter, must be eight months pregnant, at least. Le dio un patatús. She just fell out."

"¿Y adónde 'taba su tíguere? Who has their pregnant jeva just out in the street looking crazy like that?"

Pastora was too stunned to speak. She tongued the roof of her mouth. But no, she'd heard the girl with her own ears, she'd heard the girl with her own understanding of what she wasn't saying. The girl had been lying. Had wanted to scope out a thing Rafa had told her. Had wanted to know about his wife and clearly hadn't been warned about his wife's sister. Since the day Pastora had first understood her gift, she'd never questioned it. She just *knew* what there was to know. But what if the same way the gifts arrived, the gifts left, or faded? What if the gift wasn't infallible? Pastora pressed a dizzying hand to her stomach. Backed up into a closed storefront.

Pastora slid down the metal grate. Out of breath. Hand pressed hard into her stomach.

"¡O, O! ¡Otra vez! ¡Juye! ¡Llamen la enfermera!"

I

wish I knew what to look for in my mother. When she smiled, I grilled her teeth, looking for gum disease or some other tell-tale sign of an illness. When she bent to pull on the hem of her dress, I checked to see if her hands shook, if her spine bent at a weird angle. An accident? I wondered. Would it be like my father? Something unexpected?

Mami had made clear she ain't want none of my maudlin questions ruining the day before her wake. So, after helping her pick a dress, convinced that last minute she was going to switch to the other one, I grabbed my purse.

"Y tú, mi'ja? Did you try on that dress I got you?" My mother had not only determined her own attire, she'd also decided mine. I had hoped to be able to tell her the dress was ugly, or didn't fit. But the royal blue dress was perfect and highlighted all my best features.

"I tried it on. I looked great. Thank you."

"Send me a picture when you get home. I can't wait to see it!"

"Oh my God, Ma. You'll be seeing it tomorrow. You just want to forward it to your sisters so you can show me off."

He face fell. *Goddamit, Ona. Just let her have one.* But I hated feeling like a trophy being paraded.

I prided myself on the fact that my gift was entirely unlike those of the other women in the family. Their talents all leaned toward what they could do *for* others. Foretell a future, or a truth, or heal, or inspire taste buds. My gift was about what I did *to* others. My wet-wet was spellcasting. And it soothed me to know my gift was deliberate and could not be boasted about easily.

It was my first trip to DR, when I practiced my magic on someone. Tía Pastora and Yadi still lived there; it was the summer before they moved to the States.

Yadi would wake me in the morning to drink powdered milk and eat bread on the patio, so we could watch the sun rise; it'd touch the tips of our noses, and by the time we were done eating we were as warm and toasty as the breakfast rolls. Yadi would go to school, her classes letting out later in the summer season than American classes. I loved the time to stretch underneath the sun, hands clasped over my belly like the mummies I'd studied at the Museum of Natural History.

Little green salamanders crawled up and down the walls, the sun dappled in between the thick canopy of mango tree leaves. I didn't eat mangos. Not yet. Or avocado, or beans. I was a tremendously picky eater. Tía Pastora, however, expected any child under her care to clean her plate, and she despaired at how I'd wrinkle my nose at her food. Eventually me acostumbré to the fresh fruit and fiber.

But not yet, not until the end of the summer. Here, at the top of my visit, all I'd learned to love was languishing. I was not a child who napped. Used to get yelled at in kindergarten for leaving my pallet to sneak looking at picture books instead of closing my eyes. I didn't know yet how humidity and sun made someone drowsy. It was midafternoon the first time I fell asleep like that, all willy-nilly in the domesticated wilds of my aunt's backyard. I woke up to find a brown-skinned boy who was not a cousin staring down at me.

"Bella Durmiente," he said, a chipped tooth flashing through his smile.

I remember scowling. In New York, a boy hanging over your face like this while you were half asleep would warrant a quick throat check, but mainly I was annoyed because of all the Disney Princesses, I hated that basic sleepy chick the most. The boy grinned, his sharp cheekbones and shiny head highlighted by the sun.

"¿O eres ciguapa? Atrapándome?"

(I've always been fascinated by the legend of the ciguapa, which took particular hold in the campos of DR, where literacy was the lowest, despite La Ciguapa being a character popularized in a novel published in 1886 by Francisco Angulo Guridi, a Dominican nationalist. Rural Dominicans have claimed her since time immemorial, and certainly before Guridi penned his tale. In recent years there has been a reclamation of this magical figure with her backward-facing feet. Afro-Dominicanas in the United States especially seem to be heralding her as a mascot. La New Ciguapa is at turns depicted as ferocious and gentle, is being reconstructed as a Black-Indigenous legend, a woman who can walk away without leaving an easy trace, who can devour fuck-boys and escape into the cloud-capped mountains whole and joyous in her starry night skin.)

I looked the boy up and down. His raggedy shorts, his well-worn sandals. He was okay-looking in the face and maybe two years older than my nine. Not the kind of boy who would be remarked upon to be "good from far, but far from good." And his smile, while mischievous, was sweet. I sat up, shaking off my dreaming. And screamed.

"Tía! A boy from the callejón is trespassing!"

The boy's eyes widened when Tía yelled back from inside the house. He scampered off, climbing the wall that led back to the alleyway behind the house. His footing was sure on the bricks, his hands placing themselves in such a way that he avoided the shattered glass poking up through the top of the wall.

Tía came out waving a cordless phone. She'd been on a call. "¿Qué dijiste?"

I'd yelled out in English, a language Tía did not know and did not want to know. I wondered if I should tell Tía that the security of the household was compromised; not glass, wall, or barbed wire kept hungry people away when low-hanging fruit was to be picked. But I didn't say a word.

The next time I spoke with the boy, I was only pretending to sleep. My long years of nap avoidance had taught me to rest my eyes and still my body all while maintaining my thoughts on a lazy-Susan rotation. I didn't have to open my eyes when the shush of clothing across brick reached my ears. I didn't even have to open them when a shadow stopped the sun from reaching my face midstream. I knew who it was, eyes closed, hands clasped. The shadow shifted.

I sat up. The boy was sitting on the grass across from me, his eyes steady, his arms around his knees. His pants were cleaner this time, making me think it was less that he was callejón poor and more that he was probably a messy person.

"You ever been to el Faro a Colón? They just finished it, like, six or seven years ago." The boy said it like he'd been around for the long construction years of raising money and laying concrete slab by concrete slab the elaborate mausoleum. Not like he'd only been a baby.

The boy smiled, the same smile as before. "We pass it on the guagua when we go to visit my grandmother across the bridge."

I'd arrived in DR on an evening flight. Had had to cross that same bridge with my uncle Manuelito and Tía in the front asking me questions I was too shy to answer in my Spanish. Out of the window I'd seen the behemoth of white stone, the brightness of the mausoleum like a light saber rising into the night. I'd asked what it was.

A lighthouse. My uncle replied. A monument. The final resting place of Colón's bones.

I shook my head no, I hadn't been. Even at nine I'd hated motherfucking Columbus.

"¿Y a Los Tres Ojos?" the boy asked. That one I had been to. Yadi loved the deep caverns. We'd done a family trip my first weekend there, and I'd crawled onto the little boat while the man who steered used poles to push the raft into the darkness, explaining how the subterranean lakes had come to be. I shook my head no, though. I didn't need this kid knowing all my moves. And now the boy scowled.

"Have you seen anything? All you do is lie around and

sleep?" For some reason his disappointment made me want to laugh.

This became a game we played. I pretended to be asleep in the grass beneath the mango tree. And the boy pretended he wasn't trespassing whenever he climbed over the fence and sat next to me. Sometimes the boy would bring a bag of galletas, the sesame seeds brushing against a blue-striped bag. Sometimes a mango could be shaken from the tree and the boy would pull out his little army knife to slice off slivers that made my tongue itch. *Daniel*, the boy said his name was. *Anacaona*, I told him.

One day, my youngest aunt picked me up. Tía Camila worked two days a week at a famous hotel, El Hotel Jaragua—the pink of the building and the tall columns were impressive even for my usually unimpressed self. Apparently, Tía Matilde had once worked there too, although not as the manager. Tía Camila's husband had told her that if she wanted a job, she could have one, but only in the upper echelons of a fine establishment. She'd not be getting yelled at for room bookings like her sister had.

I followed my aunt around for most of the morning, helping her inspect the sharp-folded corners made from soft sheets. Then another manager came by, a tall, handsome man with a huge mustache.

"We can't have children on the floor," he chided with a half smile. Tía Camila half smiled back.

"I'll take her to the pool."

"No traje traje de baño, Tía," but Tía only smiled at the tall, fair-skinned man and made an *un minutito* gesture with her hand.

I walked behind Tía Camila, wondering what Daniel was

doing. Had he shown up only to find the patch of grass that was my nap site undisturbed by anything other than ants? Did he miss me?

Tía took me into a large pool shed that had a sign for *EMPLEADOS* on the front door. Here were neatly folded beach towels and stacks of pool toys. From a bag in the back, Tía pulled out a bathing suit. She held it out, but I put both my hands behind my back.

"That belonged to someone?" I knew my American was showing but I didn't care how ungrateful I appeared.

"A guest left it behind. We washed it in Clorox so it's clean."

Still, I didn't take it. "You keep the bathing suits guests leave behind?"

Tía Camila was the young, sweet aunt. But now she cut her eyes at me and sucked her teeth audibly.

"And we wash them. For moments like this when our family is in town and visiting and maybe forgot a bathing suit. Just put it on and make sure you stay where the lifeguard can see you. I'll finish up inspecting that floor then grab us lunch." She glanced down at the watch—it was not one of the watches my mom had sent with a dozen other items she'd bought wholesale from Canal Street. Camila's rich husband always kept her in real gold, with diamond cuts.

"An hour. You'll have more fun than following me around!"

I pulled on the one-piece. It was an adult's swimsuit, patterned with florals, low cut in the front, high cut in the back. I felt naked in it and kept having to stop myself from pulling at the fabric that was eating into my crotch. My aunt took my clothing for safekeeping and passed me a towel.

"This is some ghetto-ass shit." I said while adjusting the straps, using the employee hut window as a mirror.

But I loved the water, and while I might resist many things, the smooth ripple of a nearly empty pool called to me. I floated on my back, letting the sunshine lick swipes onto my skin, breathing easily in the water the way my mother had taught me in the strong waves of Coney Island.

The hour skimming water was uneventful. Then it turned to two hours. I climbed out of the pool with wrinkled fingers and sat at the edge. I was hungry now, and wanted a grape soda or a red Country Club. I didn't know how to find my aunt.

I had a list with Tía Pastora's phone number, address, and emergency number, but that list was in the pocket of the jeans that Tía Camila had taken with her. I knew I wasn't alone, and I wasn't abandoned, and I wasn't a baby. But as the breeze cooled down on my skin, I started to cry.

"¿'Tú 'tá bien?" The lifeguard called down to me. I swiped my face and pretended it was just the chlorine getting in my eye. I looked around the pool. Most of the people had climbed out when the buffet line at the restaurant had opened. But I didn't have a wristband. Perhaps if I spoke in English I'd be treated like the other American guests? But I was the only non-White guest there. What if they kicked me out of the resort? Which side of me would show up most prominently? Which side of me would they honor?

I nodded at the lifeguard, wiping a still wet hand down my face.

"Camila is your . . . mom?" The lifeguard was attractive. He had tiny little slices in the eyebrow above his right eye that made him look a little bit hood in a way that was familiar. He was maybe a decade older than I was.

I shook my head. "Mi tía. Do you know how to go get her?"

Now the man was the one who shook his head. I didn't know what to do, but I didn't want to be cold, hair wet, and with all my things gone from me. I already felt too unsure of how to navigate this country without escort. I plucked a pool towel from the freshly folded stack, tied it around my waist. Thank goodness I still had Yadi's flip-flops! Thank goodness, too, that Tía Pastora had insisted I wear something other than my Timbs before I left the house. I wandered into the hotel lobby.

The elevator required a keycard, but the couple in front of me used theirs. I watched the floors. We'd been on eleven this morning, and it had seemed like there were a lot of rooms left to inspect. The corridors were mazelike. The hallways weren't built in a perfect square and so there were offshoots of halls. Finally, I found the maid cart in front of a room in a hallway that hadn't been renovated. I thought this must be where they put the guests they didn't like, the ones who tried to argue about a discount with the manager or something. The door was ajar, and I pushed it open without knocking.

Tía Camila and the other manager were cuddled on top of the sheets. The manager was entirely naked, but my aunt still had on her manager's outfit, the skirt edged up to just under her ass, the top unbuttoned. Her belly button was pushed out, the slight swell there harder than just a food gutty.

No one had told me she was pregnant.

I must have made a sound because the manager's eyes shot open. He covered his midsection and penis with the edge of the comforter. Roughly he woke up my aunt. Tía Camila buttoned herself up, pushed the stray hairs back into her bun before she looked at me.

"Espérame afura." She gestured to where she'd left my

clothes, folded. I walked into the bathroom, my curls leaving drip drops on the carpet.

We did not speak of it. It was our secret. If that's what silent witnessing can ever be called between an adult and a child.

The next day, when Daniel came to the patch of sunlight, I grabbed his hand and put it in my panties. I wanted to know. I wanted to know if what I'd seen when hiding in the hallway while Papi watched TV, if the aftermath of what I knew had happened between my aunt and the other manager, if these things that led adults to the bodies of other people answered a question I had only just begun to ask. Daniel snatched his hand away. Looked around as if waiting to be caught in what could only be an American setup. I grabbed his hand again, slowly, and put it back, lower this time so he could feel what happened to me when I was excited. I had always hated napping. The scent of ripening mangos enveloped us, and the clouds shifted to scatter light through the leaves.

CAMILA

had the best apartment of all the sisters, even if it did require taking the A train uptown to the last stop. Her husband had bought their two-bedroom back when it'd first been a co-op, and when he'd passed, she'd inherited the place. Her only son, Junior, lived in Brooklyn. Which was not that far, but might as well be Illinois or Louisiana as it was not down the block. She'd had the two bedrooms entirely to herself since he'd left for college—a fortune in New York City real estate she had no interest in cashing in. Even this far north on Manhattan isle, she was one of the last Latinas left in the building. The last sister to arrive to the United States and the only person in the family who could claim she paid property tax in this glorious city. It was a small boast, one she never made out loud, but which she held nonetheless.

The high-rise had big corner windows that looked over the Henry Hudson Bridge. She'd covered the radiators with decorative heatproof boxes on which she'd placed vases of silk roses and sinuous sculptures of naked forms. The older sisters all had tacky taste: brocade curtains and brightly painted accent walls, mimicking the tropical colonial style of the country they'd left behind *and* the era in which they'd left it. Camila didn't need textile reminders of home. She'd arrived like a bird that was molting. By the time she'd stepped foot in the States, she had had in-depth tutorials with her husband's mother on how to be an expert hostess. Camila was now a woman who ran ten-milers to benefit diabetes. She'd rented the hottest nightclub in the Bronx for her fiftieth birthday. Her English was more proficient than all her siblings', and she made use of it in her approximation of a Dominican-York socialite.

She was the forgotten sister. The baby, who had spent more time in the big city in the Dominican Republic and then the majority of her adulthood in New York, who'd experienced luxuries her siblings only saw on TV. It'd made her an outcast: the fact that she'd received the softest version of their mother. That she'd been raised long after their father died, and mainly as a single child. Sure, she'd had companionship with Mati for a few years, but eventually it was just her and Mamá.

She put out her hors d'oeuvres. Her sisters still served Ritz crackers and salami at their functions, but she'd shopped at Costco for this event: thick rounds of goat cheese, and little triangles of baked samosas. Delicious picadera that she hoped would both inspire and awe her uninspired and awe-less siblings. She'd dressed exactly as she knew would allow her to go uncriticized. Her skirt wasn't too tight and stopped just above the knee so it didn't look like church, but also didn't look like she was trying to be sixteen. Her makeup was subtle. Her jewelry was well coordinated, but again, not too llamativa. She hated trying to impress them. And when she went into the bathroom to check herself one last time before her guests arrived, she swiped on some bright gold shadow. She smiled big. Her gold-tipped tooth winked, a coquette. Gold cap was considered tasteless in the circles she traveled, but it was her small reminder to herself and others that she was not an easy person to box.

She had a different relationship with each of her sisters. Flor scared her the most. She was always nervous that when Flor called it would be to tell her to handle her affairs and prepare her will.

Matilde was Camila's favorite. They'd lived together the longest, and Matilde had been gentle with her, laughing at her jokes. Climbing into bed with her when she was little and scared. Matilde and Camila had both been left behind, after first Pastora then Flor were sent away. But despite knowing her best, Camila was more like a daughter to Matilde, who preceded her by sixteen years. They'd spent the most time with their mother, the most time under her fist. They'd bonded, an unlikely twosome.

Pastora had always been the one Camila kept at arm's distance. And Camila wasn't sure whether that was because she was the sibling her mother had complained about (and compared Camila to) the most or because Pastora considered herself an entrepreneur whose business to mind was all of her siblings' lives. But even when she was younger, Camila had considered Pastora an entremetida.

She remembers vividly the year Pastora came to speak to her mother about Matilde, and somehow got Camila in trouble by proposing to their mother that she be sent to the capital. Although the occasion that actually had her leave their campo for Santo

Domingo was not until a year after Pastora's visit. What Pastora seemed not to understand is that, unlike her other children, their mother needed Camila. Who would collect firewood now that their mother struggled with her back and bending over was a momentous task? And what about the well? It was all the way at the bottom of the hill, near the canal. There was no way their mother could light a fire by the river, carry all the linens down, and boil the stench away from the cloth that recorded their oil-slick and drooling and farting bodies.

It was this last task that Camila dedicated herself to today. It was wash day.

Her mother spit outside the window as Camila collected the baskets. "Be back before that dries. You always meander too much." She was twenty, but her mother still acted like she was ten.

The tin can she put on top of the white linens was empty. Every month their mother bought enough petrol for thirty days' worth of cooking and heating the house. The used and empty cans were used for this: boiling water at the canal's edge, the last bit of petrol put in a separate bottle to help start the fire.

Camila did not want to make two trips today, and so she balanced the load by walking slow and steady, using her slippers to feel the way down the hill so she wouldn't slip. The canal flowed strong after the rain of the night before, but it ran clear.

She collected three large rocks and arranged them so they created a pocket in the middle, which she filled with twigs and the driest leaves she could find. These leaves she had to hunt beneath the still-wet overgrowth. The finger bed beneath her long nails filled with dirt. She'd painted her nails the week before. And she was careful as she washed dishes and wiped her ass to never chip a single one. Wash day always ruined her manicure, and she never didn't mourn the fact.

Petrol went over the sticks. Then she struck the match. Every time she filled the tin can, she was surprised how heavy twenty liters of water could be. She set this on the newly built fire. The boiling water was too precious to be used as a first step, and so she hiked up her skirt and dunked the linens in running water, letting this rinse do the early work of removing dust.

She'd overheard that in the capital they had big centers with gigantic machines that agitated and unsoiled your clothes for you. Camila couldn't imagine it. Could an apparatus truly scrub clean crotch stains?

As the can warmed up, Camila picked weeds here and there and stuffed them into her pocket. A little family of mushrooms heard her crooning to them before she pried them free from the ground. She'd mended her skirt pockets so they were large enough for her to do just this, scavenge wildness.

She heard a crunch behind her. And the hairs on the back of her neck clued her in to who it was.

The man was the second oldest of the Santana sons. Rumor had it he was the one que le pegó the illness to Blanca la Ciega, and now her house of ill repute was being blackballed. Rumor was that even when he was a boy, he'd been evil; lo picó un mosquito when he was born.

(Yes, that Santana boy. The one who got Pastora sent away. I don't think my aunts have ever discussed their mutual connection to him. How he was a catalyst toward a new life for each of them. He had not grown up into a good man, and his family had never stopped him from harassing the women in mine.)

Camila turned around, hands full of wet, white cloth.

He stood only a short distance away. "You never let me give you another ride to school," he said. His family owned one of the shiny new cars that had been imported from the States.

"Your wife didn't seem to appreciate the friendly gesture." Camila climbed out of the water, balancing the linens in such a way that she could use her free hand to undo the knot in her skirt. She didn't like him looking at her bare legs. She tugged, the moment taking too long, but finally her knees and ankles were covered. The fabric stuck to her skin.

He made a hand gesture as if to ward off the words she'd long since said. "We are not talking about her."

Or at all, Camila decided. She had considered him a suitor. Had gotten in his car because he was tall and light-skinned and had good hair, and his family was renowned. There were legions of sons, although she'd never memorized the order. She knew some were still single. She just hadn't known this one was not. Her mother's lessons often felt antiquated, but one she took to heart was that she wouldn't tolerate being played with. She was to be someone's wife or no one's anything. And she'd told him so when he'd stopped by the school offering her another ride.

Camila clutched the linens tight and tiptoed toward the empty basket. The water in the tin can bubbled. But to get to it, she'd need him to move.

"Déjame quieta." She put a bite to the words. She sounded like her mother. Maybe this is how no-nonsense tones are learned.

His hand reached for her, and she edged away. He laughed like they shared an inside joke. All the world was a playground, and he was the child seeking all that wished to be hidden. He crowded her so the canal rushed behind her. She was a proficient swimmer, but not with her arms full.

"What do you want? You have no business with me."

"I've been watching." He pointed toward a distant field. "On Fridays, you wash. I would see your skirts swing, and your hips move like a dancer, and I knew. You were sending me a sign. Fast just like your sister."

She shook her head no. But inside she panicked. Had she been shimmying? Had she hoped someone was watching? Had she liked knowing she could flip her hair and make him wish for what he couldn't have? She didn't know. She didn't know. And if she had, did it warrant this?

The clouds that never stopped their circling of the earth took that moment to congregate in front of the sun. Instantly, the day grew dimmer.

"Her mouth was sweet. I bet yours is sweeter. Es que me tienes loco." He rubbed a finger down her cheek.

He'd been saying that for two years, since she was eighteen. At first the remarks had been flattering. His bright-eyed gaze always finding her at the colmado had made her fan wave slower, her eyelashes beat faster. She liked to think that she was better than Pastora at something, even if it was simply at being wanted. Camila had enjoyed the distant attention. Until she hadn't.

He grabbed her by the arms, shushing her like an unbroken mare. "Shh, shh. Just a taste. A small taste."

Her father had worked his father's land. His idea of ownership extended to people.

She stomped on his foot, but still felt the draft on the back of her legs from where he'd raised her skirt a bit. "Solo a little taste." He was breathing heavily. Camila backed up, feeling the wetter soil of the canal's edge squish between her toes. He placed his foot behind hers so she tripped. It would have been an almost graceful dip if they'd been bachateando. Camila looked up at the sky before his body bent to meet her.

At first, she thought his wail was from having pinned her. Some type of victory cry. She knew what happened to campesinas when rich boys wanted toys. She should scream. She should say no. But the words clogged in her throat. His shriek continued, now more wounded animal than one ready to devour.

She felt hot drips of water on her legs and wondered if she was dying, since surely she must have urinated on herself, and surely the shame of it, of what was about to happen, was what was burning her. But then Santana released her body and she scrambled away, tugging at her skirt, bumping her back into her mother's legs.

Mamá Silvia stood with her knees exposed as she'd wrapped the hem of her bata around her hand. The can of water Camila had been boiling for the washing jangled empty, but still her mother did not let the tin go. Santana writhed on the ground, smashing daffodils beneath his wounded back, clutching at his neck and back where his collar had not been to protect his pale, exposed flesh.

Her mother used the tin can to gesture Camila up. "Ven."

They ran up from the edge of the canal, both of them breathless when they arrived at the house. The spit in front of their doorway was still not dry.

"They made me lose one girl. That family won't cost me another. We need to get you married. He won't leave you alone. I see him at the church and town assemblies. I wish his mother wasn't so dead; she deserved to see the sinvergüenza her son's always been."

Camila didn't know what to say. She put sabila and crema de cacao on the parts of her legs where the boiling water had landed. She tried to do the same for where her mother had cradled the petrol can, but her mother would not let her tend to her. She was busy writing notes to different church ladies, wondering if someone had a traveling relative who needed a companion or knew of a respectable company hiring young women.

"The capital, and your sisters there, can't protect you. What you need is a man." She was a woman, and so she must plot in womanly ways. She could not just grab a pistol and threaten Santana off the way a father could, and Samuel, recently removed to New York, was too far away to be of use. It took a few days, but finally her mother got a response to one of her notes.

A woman from town had a sister who lived in the capital; her sister's son needed a good girl to wife. They were wary of the capital city girls with their chica plástica, mercantile ways.

A country girl, the mother and aunt hoped for Washington. Camila, young, willowy, obedient, and untouched—not to mention in urgent need of protection—fit the bill.

The women sent word to the capital. Made arrangements within two weeks' time to travel and meet him. They would stay with Matilde, and the mothers would see if the two suited.

The week before they left for that trip, Santana showed up at the house, his neck—and, one assumed, the skin beneath it—wrapped in gauze. His big, angry horse panted as if he'd been ridden long and hard. Santana was drunk. He knocked on their front door with the butt of his gun. Mamá Silvia pushed a heavy table in front of the door and told Camila to hide. They turned off all the lanterns. Camila heard her heart in her ears every second of every minute of all those hours. Santana would kill her. For not giving herself over. He would kill her and her mother and no one would bat an eye. It happened all the time, a man scorned would "accidentally" kill a love interest. Somehow the police would not find enough evidence. Somehow, the life of a girl on the island was worth less than the reputation of a man she was disinterested in. She knew it. Her mother knew it. Santana knew it. They held hands and shook like the door as his fists struck against the wood. Every time he went silent, the two women allowed an audible breath to escape, but then the banging would recommence. It went on and on.

They left for Matilde's house a week early. Arrived in the capital having barely slept. Mamá Silvia was the one who handled arrangements for the big meeting while Camila lay in Matilde's bed and sobbed, considering how her life had changed in a few weeks' time.

The man, Washington, was a well-bred young man, of clean

fingernails. He helped her mother over the threshold of his home with fingers that held hers gingerly. Camila took these as good signs.

It was a gorgeous house on the west side of the city, walking distance from the old colonial zone. Washington was light-skinned, with pale green eyes that matched the limestone flooring of the living room.

His mother served them good coffee in expensive saucers that looked to have been passed down for siglos.

The mothers talked. Washington was a quiet man, and honestly, Camila thought him a bit more than sweet. What kind of grown man in this day and age let his mother do all the talking? Do the finding of a bride? But maybe she was used to too many boastful boys, and this shy and beautiful man would teach her of different ways.

Camila did not return to el campo. She and Washington wed two weeks later. And if she still thought him indifferent when they took their vows, she refused to look the protection of his name in the mouth.

But their wedding night passed. And a week passed. And soon, Camila had been married to Washington for three months and her husband still hadn't touched her. She accepted this. They hadn't known each other very long, and he was a respectful man. Pulled chairs out for her and his mother whenever they had dinner. Helped them out of the chauffeured cars with a soft hand at their back.

Her mother returned home. Insisting to Camila that Santana would not bother an old lady who had no daughters left to lose.

Living in the capital put Camila closer to Flor, Pastora, and

Matilde, which she enjoyed. But she barely saw them. They had jobs and houses to keep. Washington didn't ask her to work, and Camila lived in a house with servants who did any chore that needed doing. Camila had thought she'd enjoy luxury, but it was a gilded, empty existence. The help cooked, and cleaned, and darned socks, or threw them out and expanded the household budget to buy new ones. His mother managed the meals. Camila was welcome to decorate, but that lost its appeal when both her husband and mother-in-law smiled in approval, yet neither gave her any friction to surpass. When she'd first moved in, she'd brought her bottles of tincture and herbs, but both Washington and his mother refused to drink any, even when they had gripe or a cough.

"We have a family doctor, dear. No need to bother yourself making little remedies anymore if you don't want to," Washington's mother said as if she was doing her a kindness.

It was at the breakfast table one day when she broached the marriage bed with her mother-in-law, aware that it was not a thing to be spoken about, but with her sisters always working, and her mother never open about marital matters, there was no one else to turn to. "I don't know why your son married me if he does not find me appealing."

Her mother-in-law set down her cup. Pursed her lips with her head cocked toward the window, as if listening for an appropriate retort.

Camila rushed her words. "Don't get me wrong. He's good to me. I am safe. I want for nothing. I am grateful."

Her husband's mother nodded. "There is nothing farther from God than a person who is malagradecida."

Camila didn't know whether that was violent agreement

with her comment or reproach. Was it she or her husband who was being called ungrateful?

Her husband's mother picked up her coffee. "I will speak with him. A girl like you will wither under the frost of Washington's kind of love."

Camila heard mother and son fighting that night. Her mother-in-law's voice was hushed; her husband's pitched loud for the first time since she'd known him. He came into the bedroom and slammed the door. Unbuttoned his shirt, his pants, furiously. Camila knew a moment of fear, but it was chased away by the thrill up her spine. He kissed her with gusto, hiked up her nightgown, but when his penis grazed her thigh, he softened. Did not touch her breasts or nether region. He kept his face in the crook of her neck. When he collapsed on top of her without entering her, she ran her fingers through his hair and he began to cry.

He tried to touch her twice more that year they lived with his mother. Camila hooked her leg around the pendulum between loving him and hating him. Some nights she touched herself and imagined it was his hands. Other nights, out of anger, she imagined it was the carnicero's assistant who smacked her ass like he was tenderizing ham hocks, or that it was the consulate officer in charge of their visa application whom she would entice a green card from with her cleavage. She resented her husband for all the ways she'd imagined she would one day be caressed, and held, and taught ecstasy, which he had knowingly allowed her to believe without telling her he would not rise to those occasions. Not for her.

And yet, Camila always ensured she prepared him a plate when he was out late. And she held his hand easily when they were in public. They provided each other the fronts they needed to escape the threats that had been tightening around their throats before they'd met. He had water lines installed on her mother's land. Pipes that led from the canal and allowed for running water. He bought her mother a washing machine, imported straight from a place called Chicago. Hired a man to go by Mamá Silvia's house once a week and make sure the gate out front was secured, that no one was squatting on the land.

And when they moved out of his mother's house, but before he'd arrived at his inheritance, Camila advocated for a job. He spoke to a friend and found her a part-time managerial position at El Hotel Jaragua, where her sister Matilde worked the front desk. He, in turn, got a job as an executive at his uncle's accounting firm. They showed up to city galas, ate at the top restaurants, and after a decade of marriage, when she finally chose a lover from the many colleagues who had flirted with her and got herself pregnant with a child that was not his, it was then that Camila truly grew to love her husband. The affection with which he talked to her stomach. The peace he allowed her secrets as his mother and her mother congratulated him on being a newly minted father. Even a man with wings might take offense at raising a changeling, but her husband gave the babe his name, called him Junior, called him his own.

They left for the States when her son was four, and they both knew when they arrived that *there*, in the labyrinth that was New York, would be the ultimate freedom they'd hoped for.

———

When the intercom to Camila's apartment rang, she had to remember she was hosting her sisters. The past clung to her even as she ran a manicured hand down her bright red peluca, but she shook it loose before she opened the door. Matilde being the first to arrive didn't surprise her. She was the conscientious sister, after all. And bearing a bottle of Barceló Imperial! Camila's favorite.

They kissed and hugged and commented on each other's outfits, although Matilde could have been going to the laundromat for all that she'd tried.

"Has Flor spoken to you?" Camila asked Matilde as they walked arm in arm to the living room. Matilde shook her head no and did not return the question. Camila was never the secret keeper for any of the tight trio of elder sisters.

"It must not be urgent. She would tell us if it was. She's a planner; she may not die for another decade or two or, God knows, three. She might outlive us all; she's never done things the regular way."

Matilde shook her head, unsmiling. "Flor always has a reason."

Flor was the next to arrive. She seemed tired, and Camila held her hand just a second longer. Was her sister . . . delicate? Would simply feeling up her bones whisper out any ailments? She didn't get a sense there was anything she could brew to lighten her sister's spirit.

The three sat and chatted in the living room, the big white leather sofas and soft white curtains offering them peace even if Florecita did complain this looked like a room made for dead people. To which Camila gestured to the mantle over the table and the couch cushions, which were patterned brightly, so it truly couldn't be considered an accurate remark.

The doorbell downstairs rang, and Camila jumped up—*finally*. But Pastora's face when she walked in was ashen. She dropped into the loveseat with only the faintest of cheek brushes as greeting. It was Flor who heaved up out of the cushy couch and grabbed Pastora's hands in hers. Pastora turned her face into Flor's shoulder for a moment. The two had always shared a particular bond. When Pastora faced them again, there was a new resolve to her features.

Camila took one look at her sister and ran to her cabinet of herbs. Whatever was about to be said required special fortification.

CAMILA: INTERVIEW TRANSCRIPT (TRANSLATION)

ONA: Can you give me some examples? Of that or of how you've felt it?

CAMILA: Well, God, of course. And my sisters would all accuse me of loving fine things beyond my means, but they'd fail to acknowledge how many of those fine things align with my regard of all the natural world. Yes, I adorn myself in gold, and pearls, and I have peacock feathers in big glass bowls throughout the house, but what did I just name that did not come from the bowels of the dirt? . . . Oh, true, I guess peacocks really more like to roam dirt than be of it, but you know what I mean. About them and the pearls. They are of the natural world, and they heal something inside me.

       You know, your mother and the other aunts never had dolls. They had each other, and that's who they dressed, and carried, and babied. And when I came, they no longer wanted to play those games. Or maybe they'd had the child in them long snuffed out. Or sloughed her off. I couldn't tell you. But I would beg your grandmother for a doll. There was no one else to play with. And when we went to town, we'd pass the big store with all the dolls in the windows. Porcelain faces and shiny blue eyes and those dresses tatted with lace. My eyes would fill, but I dared not even once point and beg. Not in public. I knew better even then.

One day, I came home from school and Mamá presented me with this basket. It wasn't my birthday or el Día de los Reyes. Oh, I must have been, let me see, maybe seven? I was the only one left in the house. I don't remember where Matilde was then, but Pai had passed. So, yeah, it must have been about seven. And in the basket was this doll Mamá had sewn herself.

She was horrible! Made of burlap. Her eyes were small green cashew shells sewn in; her hair was the brown outside that covers coconut shells. For her mouth, Mamá had sewn in a little gold ring she used to wear around her pinky, so that the doll looked forever expensively surprised, or perhaps, forever ready to be fed. She was horrible. She was wonderful. Because Mamá must have found each detail herself, scavenged the land, just like I do. Saw into the earth what could be made of a thing, just like I do. I don't know many definitions of love, or not ones I can put into words. But nothing has ever felt as warm as being known so well that someone could hand you a monstrosity they made with their own hands after learning you. And of all the expensive things

I've owned, nothing has ever meant as much as
that doll . . .

ONA: Do you still have her?

CAMILA: Of course, that doll will be buried in my arms. It's
already written in my will.

MATILDE

held her breath when she saw Pastora. Pastora didn't so much walk into a room as she stormed it, and this entrance hadn't had even a hint of her usual cavalry.

Pastora cleared her throat. "Mati, can we talk in the kitchen?"

Camila returned from her cabinet and pressed a drink into Pastora's hand. "A cordial, for nerves."

Pastora nodded and kissed Camila on the cheek. She sipped and closed her eyes. Her shoulders dropped lower; her breath slowed. She opened her eyes and gestured toward the kitchen, but Flor was quicker than Matilde's feet. "What can't you say here?"

Uncharacteristically, Pastora looked down at the floor, did not respond. Camila and Flor exchanged wide-eyed glances. Matilde moved to her sister. Put a hand on the nape of her neck. Pastora had always loved this as a child, a prissy cat deigning to be petted; she leaned into Matilde's hand. Sometimes even Matilde forgot she was the eldest until moments like this one.

"Ven, tell us. Whatever it is, is okay out loud." She nodded her permission.

Pastora didn't necessarily stop looking anguished, but she raised her head. Took another swallow of Camila's concoction. And then she stood. Her full height wasn't more than five foot three, but when she threw her shoulders back you knew la dura had entered the chat.

"Mati, it's time. Your husband has been unfaithful to you since the day you wed. I know you spoke with Mamá, that you asked her for permission to leave him. She's been dead a long time now. The only permission you need is your own," Pastora said.

Matilde's hand dropped from Pastora's neck. "I just don't see that it's anyone's business. That it's ever been anyone's business."

"It was idiotic for her to say you should stay and for you to believe it. You deserve to be cherished. And if not now, then when? We are dying, all of us! One day closer to death. What has Flor shown us if not that? What are we doing with this life?"

Camila looked stricken at the outburst. Matilde strove to look unmoved. She straightened before speaking. "I've done a lot with my life, Pastora. My marriage does not define the whole of my life."

Pastora cast her hands up, and Flor cleared her throat. "You said your piece, Pas. It's not for anyone to decide but Mati."

Pastora shook her head furiously. "I met your husband's other woman. She knew he had a wife. And she lay with him anyways."

"I don't want to hear this." Matilde closed her eyes, as if the gesture would stop sound entering her ears.

"And I think she had an accident. Maybe lost the child." Pastora didn't look any of the sisters in the face when she said it. Just made the declarations to the windows, to the Hudson, to New Jersey across the water, but not to them.

The chorus of responses was to be expected. The exclamations, Flor's horrified face at the mention of Pastora having met the other woman. Camila, stricken. "A child?" she kept asking. "He's having a baby? At his age? ¿Con quién? Who is she?"

Matilde walked to her sister, facing her. "What did you do, Pastora?"

Matilde listened to the convoluted story: A woman came into the clothing store, she needed a bathroom. Pastora knew she should have offered her water. The belly was big. She kept saying: it was so big, belly button pushing out through the shirt.

Matilde scanned the couch for her phone. She needed to call Rafa. She needed to—

"Siéntate." It was Flor who led Matilde to the sofa, who grabbed her hand and tugged her back to them. "There is nothing for you to do. There is no action for you to take. This is between Rafa and this woman. And if there is something for them to take up with Pastora, then that is between them, Pastora, and the Divine."

Matilde took a deep breath. Her hands were shaking. Yesterday, when Pastora had called and told her she'd seen Rafa with a pregnant woman, all she'd thought about was the babe. The babe that was not her babe. But now, at the possibility that something terrible might have happened, to a child almost full-term . . . She stood up and ran to the bathroom, gagging. She'd prayed for children a lifetime and no one had listened. She'd had one moment when she'd cursed that woman her belly, and the universe had echoed posthaste.

Matilde had learned how to let go of dreams when she was twenty-nine. It was just her, Mamá, and Camila living in the house at that point, although Matilde was called every few weeks to a paternal uncle's side. There she would cook and clean and feed him soup when he took ill. When he was strong enough to get back on his feet, he'd rehire his staff and send her home. He was a suspicious man who told her that if he died, he wanted only family around because the staff would steal.

This was one of those respites when the uncle was well enough that she wasn't needed. It was two years before she would move to the capital, work at the hotel, and eventually meet Rafa. Flor and Pastora lived in the capital, their brother Samuel just outside of it. Their father had been dead six years. In a few more, his children would begin to leave the country he was buried in for New York City.

But at this point, Mati was still in the campo and not the capital or the United States, and her sisters' letters and recounting their adventures might offer some interest, but it wasn't enough to spirit every day. And maybe that was why she dreamt of something bigger than caring for a sick uncle or sewing with her mother. She was bored.

She'd first heard the band on Radio Cuba; the orchestra had played in Havana to sold-out crowds. And the next stops were in Santo Domingo, then, surprisingly, their region. Turned out one of the band members had family in the Piñales and had asked for a theater in the largest city of the province. It was a town over, but the closest a salsa group of this caliber had ever been to the family's house. Matilde had danced at church assemblies since she was young, partnering with her brother or the well-to-do local boys. She'd been the lightest on her feet of her sisters, and their brother often pulled her from the corner cluster to show off. It was her brother she called in Santo Domingo, asking him to come home so he could escort her and Camila to the show.

"I'll buy your ticket. Please, 'manito?" Their mother wouldn't let them go without a chaperone.

"I don't know, Mati, let me see if my wife wants to travel."

The wife hadn't wanted to attend the show, and had begrudged joining him on the trip although she had family nearby and proceeded to pretend the entire excursion had been her idea.

The theater was packed, and their seats were all the way in the top sections where you had to stand. The general admission was all Matilde could afford, but it didn't matter. The sisters spent the entire two hours holding hands, and twirling each other and singing at the top of their lungs. Camila was only thirteen, but even then she basked in her siblings' attention. They'd never had such an exuberant evening, their spirits skipping on top of the high notes, complete abandon. They sweated out their pressed hair.

Camila used her thumb to clean up the smudged mascara under Matilde's eyes. It was midnight by the time the concert ended. Even Samuel glowed a bit, rejuvenated by the music.

The band announced an after party at the discoteca next door. Anyone with a ticket stub would get in for free. Matilde imagined the crowds would thin, too many people had hours to drive back to their homes, to get an hour or two of rest before they had to go to work. It would be difficult for nonlocals unless they had family nearby. This was the argument she presented to Samuel, Camila's pleading eyes cosigning her argument. She was right, but also wrong. Many people left right after the concert, but the club was packed to the high beams.

The band ran all the hits back, the music even more resounding in the smaller space. Couples spun in the tiny square foot of space they carved out for themselves, the sisters included. The band took an intermission, only three of the players playing enough for dancing to continue.

Then an emcee stepped up to the mic. "The professional who trained our backup dancers has been traveling with the band; I hope you'll join him in a little game."

The man's accent was the singsong of Puerto Rico, although Matilde was sure he thought this crowd of Dominicans had a Spanish more sing-y than his; it was a common comparison of tongues that neighboring islands shared.

He invited ten women to step into the middle of the dance floor—*experienced dancers*, he kept repeating. Matilde smiled. She loved watching great dancers show off. The leg slides, the hand accents.

Samuel leaned to her. "You should go. You'll remember this for the rest of your life."

Matilde laughed and shied away, letting his shoulder block her from any impulse. But she hadn't accounted for Camila, having just entered puberty and feeling the first rushes of her womanhood, running out onto the floor, her long hair swinging in waves behind her.

"What's the girl doing?" Samuel snickered. "She's going to make a fool out of herself."

Matilde nodded. The professional dancer went up to each

woman and led her in a basic front and back spin; the music had not picked up behind him and it seemed he was just testing the contestants. When he got to Camila, he didn't even turn her before he shook his head, speaking into the mic. "This child is beautiful, but she won't do. You tried it, love." The audience chuckled, and Camila went red in the face. But she grabbed the mic from the dancer, whose eyebrows winged up. "My sister! She's an expert." Camila pointed and no, a spotlight did not descend about Matilde; all eyes did not home in on her. But Samuel did push her forward. And one foot moved in front of the other until she took her sister's place as the tenth contestant.

When the professional dancer held his hand out, she touched her fingers to his, he spun her immediately, with just that little touch. Her skirt flared out and, although caught off guard, she landed on the correct back foot and immediately shimmied. The professional laughed. The contest began.

Each girl danced with the professional for thirty seconds, not long at all. The music the band played changed each time, so you had to be good at taking the professional's lead and pace as soon as he clasped your hand. The big moment came when the professional seemed to deem a woman particularly good and spun her out for a solo. Out of the first eight, only two got solos, and only one was able to effectively hold the light for her ten seconds of fame. The first solo she tossed her hair and cha-cha'd her shoulders. The other woman danced well but was caught during her solo doing a basic step; unimaginative without a partner to guide her. Matilde watched as number nine followed, spun, and when she came back, stepped on the maestro's toes.

Then it was Matilde's turn. The maestro crooked a finger, and she met him in the middle of the dance floor. It seemed she'd won some of the audience when she'd usurped her little sister because people in the crowd cheered, "Diez! Diez!"

The music started, but before he'd touched her waist Matilde began rolling her torso. The professional dancer wagged his eyebrows. His grip was firm on her hand but loose on her waist, and Matilde matched him step for step into double spins and behind-the-back turns. The crowd was going wild as they watched the professional dancer try to confound her, but Matilde was his softened mirror.

"Want to really show them something?" He murmured it in her ear. And for a reason she's never understood, she trusted this bedazzled stranger. She nodded.

The man made a gesture, and the orchestra came to a dramatic stop. People began applauding but the man held a hand up. The orchestra began a stripped-down baseline of a salsa song, slow, grinding, the kind of sound made to instruct one's pelvis how to pulsate. They started basic, easy, and then the dancer spun her once. The music picked up a half beat. Matilde landed easily on the right foot and right step. He spun her twice more in quick succession. The music picked up, then again. She managed these with ease as well. His utter delight in her was like sliding into a drunken stupor. He seemed to revel in her competence.

As the music picked up, the professional dancer's pace did, too, which meant Matilde was dancing as fast as she'd ever danced; then he spun her once, twice, three times, and the crowd began counting wildly as Matilde arched onto the balls of her feet, and could a small hurricane be embodied? She revolved a full ten times, her eyes always landing back on the professional dancer's. He laughed in delight as both she and the music landed and stopped on the exact same note. The maestro tried a counterspin, which she easily took; when she landed on her back foot, she gave her bosom a little waggle, gave the audience a wink.

The crowd lost their motherfucking shit.

One of their own had been unconquered by this great dancer from por allá. The maestro could not best her.

The maestro had her bow. The musicians came back from their break.

Leading her to an alcove, the maestro still had not released her hand. "You have got to come with me, with the band. You are everything that is perfection. Look at you." He thumbed the frills on her collar. "You look like you should be some governor's wife, but you dance pure brujería."

Matilde blushed. "I couldn't."

"You're married? Children?" She loved his dramatics, how despaired he sounded.

She shook her head no.

"You're of age?"

"I am twenty-nine. But my mother would never approve."

He grasped her hand tighter than any single moment when they'd been dancing. "Twenty-nine is a woman grown! You would see the world. I would make sure the band pays you well. We make a lot in tips. I wouldn't, I mean, if you're afraid someone would take advantage, I wouldn't allow it. We could plant you in the audience. You'd pretend to be a bystander but then we'd call you to be number ten, just like tonight, a surprise entry that becomes the crowd's favorite. Imagine it. Can you imagine it?"

He was a magician painting the scene. She saw her prim blouses and elaborate skirts perfectly. She shook her head no.

He squeezed once more before letting her go. "Please. Ask your family. We'll be here for a day or two more. At the inn in town. The lobby clerk can ring me, day or night, if you'd like to tell me your answer."

And despite the knowledge she felt in her belly, Matilde shored up her courage and asked her mother the next day. "He says I could bring a chaperone along, of course, anyone in the family. The band would pay for my passport and any visas needed. The first tour is a Caribe one so I wouldn't be going too far at all—"

Her mother hadn't even had the wherewithal to reprimand. She'd laughed. "Matilde, you're not going to be anyone's light-skirted dancer."

It is easy looking back to consider that perhaps her mother was giving her opportunities for rebellion, ways to prove she was actually her own person. But it is impossible to truly know the lengths her mother would have gone to get the desired actions from her children. She was a woman who did not express love and whose own family had exiled her. Matilde's mother seemed to know too well the gamut of consequences that could be inflicted on a child, and she did not seem the type who would shy from deploying any of them against a child who did not act as she wanted.

Matilde did not meet the professional dancer in town for the cafecito where they would discuss their future plans and she would then be introduced to the band. She stayed home and darned blouses instead.

MATILDE: INTERVIEW TRANSCRIPT (TRANSLATION)

MATILDE: . . . If all my sisters were born unnatural, or
perhaps, in the ways of wild creatures, overly
natural, attuned to the fluctuations of living
the way elephants can feel earthquakes half a
world away through their feet, I was the one least
connected.

Even my womanhood was questioned when at
fifteen my first blood had yet to arrive. At sixteen
my mother grew concerned. She would place her
palm on my lower stomach, pressing hard with all
her fingers. She never said anything, did not say
out loud she thought I was barren. For a woman
who sought to protect my virginity with her own
life, it often amused me how much she wanted to
preserve my fertility. At seventeen, neither one of
us smiled at the prospects. I had terrible cramps,
as if the eggs that traveled to my uterus backed up,
ruptured but clogged. My body would not bleed.

At twenty-five, my mother tried a remedy
of castor oil, recruiting Camila, who had just
developed her magic, to make foul-tasting powders
in her mortar and pestle. Camila mixed this and

that and a bit of root from over there, a tonic that would allow for circulation. Mamá watched me hawk-eyed as I mixed the powder in water, drank the concoction daily.

I was unnatural in no fruitful way. I would not say my mother shunned me, but if her love was the twin of fear, she stopped being afraid of my future. A girl who cannot have children is not really a girl whose future you should fear for, I'm sure was her logic. What was the worst that could happen? None of my indiscretions could grow legs. But that did not mean she let me roam. There were only two of us under watch; she'd borne five and carried and lost more than that.

The castor oil and Camila's mixture worked to get my first period to drop, but by then I was already well into my twenties, flat-chested, small-hipped, and my blood never came in consistently. I went months without menstruating. And I had to take Camila's potion from that first day hence, as it was the only thing that balanced my hormones.

They left me alone at the house often. They sent me to live with a single, sick uncle, unscared of what could come of it, despite how protective Mamá usually was. I was always one to get my chores done early in the morning, so I could enjoy the warm sunshine of the late afternoon. The uncle required a lot of work, but the saving grace was he always had the radio on.

I was not born with a gift, and I never

developed one in the ways of my sisters, whose
uncanny senses of the world came from beyond.
I cobbled together my own gift. Claimed magic
where I'd be told none could exist. That is what
dancing was for me. And it is as powerful as any
second sight or inclination toward healing.

I called Jeremiah after helping Mami with her dresses and told him to meet me in the city. His current installation was integrating concrete and light in such a way that it streamed from inside the cracks. Trying to make tangible what he saw in his mind's eye had been taking up every one of his waking moments. And honestly, some of his sleep ones, since even then I often heard him mumbling about shadows and aperture. The installation would go up at a gallery in Harlem during the holidays, so while I knew he'd be annoyed at the interruption, I also knew he'd be tempted by the possibilities of a good spades match. Bae needed a break, and I needed him.

He brought two decks of cards with him. Yadi was marinating jackfruit in such a way that it looked like pulled pork when we walked in, the large container frothing from where the juices oxidized.

"He here?" I whispered to her as we hugged as if we hadn't seen each other that morning.

She shook her head before enveloping Jeremiah in a hug.

"How's my favorite Marte doing?" he asked, arm around her shoulder.

I poked him. "You say that about every Marte you greet, and I've already explained. Yadi is a Polanco."

Yadi rolled her eyes. "*Technically,* Yadi's mom added her

maiden name to her married name, so *Yadi* is a Marte *de* Polanco. Don't play me, ho."

Jeremiah laughed and kissed me on the nose, giving Yadi
one final squeeze.

"Ona says we can get a little contest going?" He held out the
cards as he made his way into the living room.

"Ona talks too much. You want a drink, Jeremiah?" Yadi and
I trailed him into the living room.

"You already know what I'm on," Jeremiah said, wiggling
his eyebrows. He was an old-fashioned kind of guy through and
through, and everyone knew it.

Yadi opened up her maraschino cherries—she only bought
the fancy kind preserved in syrup *with plant-based dye*, something Yadi mentioned almost every time she opened a jar in
front of us.

As she mixed his drink, Jeremiah took my face in his hands.
"And you already know you're my favorite Marte. And lunes,
and miércoles . . ." He kissed me. And I couldn't front, his little
Duolingo classes had him dropping Spanish when I least expected it, and it layered on an entirely new sex appeal. He said
he was learning so he could talk more fluently to Mami; he even
called her every Wednesday evening to practice. I liked to think
he was also learning Spanish so he could talk to me in the first
tongue that had occupied my body, tugging on the most ele-
mental pieces of when I had been formed.

"That day of the week is 'martes,' not 'marte,' but you get
brownie points for trying." I kissed his nose.

A series of knocks patterned its way onto the door. Yadi left
Jeremiah's drink half poured and hustled to answer it. As she
fluffed her curls, Jeremiah raised an eyebrow at me, having only

ever experienced her as the consummate hostess; he clearly saw just how unsettled she was. Jeremiah walked over and added the dash of bitters himself.

Ant crossed into the room, and I swear to all that is holy, the actual air changed.

Jeremiah was back at my side, the hand that wasn't holding his drink against my lower back. "Breathe. It's all going to be all right. And if it isn't, they'll deal with it then."

I nodded, taking his drink from him for a quick hard sip before I handed it back. "Needs ice, baby."

And then I was being swallowed by muscular arms, and Doña Reina's distinctive fabric softener. "Is that Oneezy? O-nah? Oh, yes! H to the Izz—O-na?!"

I giggled and wrapped my arms around him, whatever nervousness I'd felt skipping off on the cobblestones of our laughter. It's silly to have a nickname for a nickname, but we'd always loved taking apart each other's names and seeing how else we could arrange the letters into love.

"So good to have you back, Anthony. Your moms must be losing her shit." I leaned back, searching his face. He had wrinkles at the corner of his eyes. Little nicks in his skin that had not been there when we'd been kids. He'd lived through hardship, and it showed.

He nodded. "She's been going to church every evening. Says she's going to thank God every day for the rest of her life." His shrug wanted to make light of it, but his eyes showed different. Doña Reina had never abandoned her child.

I pulled back from his arms, including Jeremiah in the conversation. "This is my partner, Jeremiah. Did your mom tell you I moved to Jersey?"

He shook his head and Jeremiah's hand at the same time. "She didn't, but she didn't need to. Pastora wrote to me."

I smiled and didn't let my eyes shift to Yadi. Did she know her mother had written to her childhood love? Was that a little jab he'd just taken in her direction?

Jeremiah massaged the tense moment as he'd just been doing with my lumbar spine. "Please tell me you kept up with playing spades inside? Swear to God my uncle went in as the family joke and came back a card sharp."

Ant and Jeremiah finished shaking hands. "I mean, you already know your boy wasn't going to let himself get dusty, nah mean? Spades held me down when commissary couldn't, so just know what you signing up for, my guy."

He grabbed one of the decks that Jeremiah had set on the card table, opening the pack and flipping through the cards. He noted the markings on the joker, removed the two of hearts, the two of clubs.

"Yadi, you got score? You know nobody can read Ona's handwriting," Jeremiah said.

"Damn, your shit still trash?" Ant said, and I swatted at him, then swatted at Jeremiah.

"It's not *how* you write, it's *what* you write, okay?"

Yadi came back with a notebook and pen, and we pulled ottomans and a desk chair and the one kitchen chair into the room.

"Yeah, and what you writing these days, Oneezy? I tried reading your papers online. I even understood a few of them."

"Oh, Ant. That's so sweet. Hardly anyone who doesn't study this shit daily reads my work. Thank you." He raised an eyebrow, waiting for the rest of my answer. "I'm not sure what I'm working on. It's an informal thing, but right now I'm just collecting stories, interviewing the family. I don't know if it's going to be a paper, or a book, or . . . nothing. It might be nothing."

Ant nodded. "I liked what I read. You putting us Dominicans on the map."

I always hoped my work would be read in the hood back home. It'd seemed unlikely, but even if Ant was just blowing smoke up my ass, it made me feel good.

Jeremiah and I sat opposite each other. We always partner.

I ignored Yadi's baleful look. "They cheat, Ant. They have code words and little signals to let each other know when they have jokers."

Ant did some trick shuffling. "Sit down, Yadi. We'll be fine. No one is going to talk across the board, right?"

And I felt like I was in middle school the way his setting of expectations had Jeremiah and me straightening up and bobbing our heads.

Yadi set the notebook and pen at my elbow. She kept score, and I double-checked her math. Jeremiah and I were card partners, but Yadi and I had also memorized a pattern of strengths and weaknesses, and we were partners in unspoken ways and through unspoken scenarios. Right now, she was really nervous.

"First hand plays itself," Yadi said.

I taught her how to play, so I know exactly how Yadi organizes her hand: spades far left, hearts, clubs, diamonds far right. Looked like she had a lot of diamonds. I raised my eyebrows twice at Jeremiah, he gave a small nod.

By the end of the first hand, we were up, Yadi and Ant barely having made board.

"We still in it, we still in it, though." Yadi nodded with Ant's statement.

After we had won three hands, I asked, "What are we playing to, three hundred?" We weren't far from that.

Ant shook his head. "At least three-fifty. Don't try and lower the bar."

I stuck my tongue out.

Yadi was shuffling, and although her hands could dice carrots at lightning speed, she shuffled like an arthritic grandma, her bridge so unsmooth I had to look away.

Yadi and Ant weren't bad, but they couldn't see the *why* of how the other played. Yadi was careful and was going to underbid by two books almost every time; she hated getting set and would prefer sandbags to losing points outright. Ant had clearly been playing as a gambler these last few years: he aimed high, counting kings and the wayward queen, which were always risky face cards to pretend would walk. They weren't necessarily mismatched partners, but they were playing against each other in addition to myself and Jeremiah, instead of noticing ways to accommodate their differing styles.

"How's your moms, Oneezy? Yadi told me she's having this wake thing. What's all that? She had a dream or something?" Ant asked.

I eyed him before answering. If this was strategy, it was a dirty one. Moms were off the table as attempts to distraction, and my mom for sure was. I took a breath.

"She says she wants to celebrate the life she's lived. She won't say anything else. She never asks for anything; even a few months ago for her seventieth she said she didn't want a party or to make a fuss. I want to shake, to ask more questions, but all she says is this is what she wants and to please not fight her. I'm sorry. You asked a short question and I gave a long answer." My laugh sounded hollow even to my own ears.

We all picked up our cards. Jeremiah threw down the first suit. I knew that Yadi always kept her big spades until the end. She wouldn't play to win unless reminded to do so. I took advantage and cut high. I threw out the next suit.

"But she seems okay? In good health?" Ant asked as he cut a king I had counted as a book.

"Mostly. I went through her bills," I admitted. "Nothing I could see that she might be sick. Sometimes I wonder, if someone else were dying, would she be doing this as a way for them to say goodbye? As a way to gather the family? But that's wishful. She wouldn't do that."

I still couldn't tell whether Ant was genuinely interested or trying to distract me, but he was succeeding in the latter.

Yadi won a book from me. And I took a moment, rearranging my cards as I tried to remember what had already been played. My memory was one of the sharpest tools I had in this game; I knew exactly what had been played and what was left ninety-nine percent of the time. I shot Yadi a dirty look.

I've always been lucky that Yadi and I get along despite the many ways our mothers have compared us that could have led to resentment. Yadi's cosa developed differently than my own, later in life, and almost as if triggered by the unknown loss of our grandmother, her food flavored in a way that imbued my grandmother's spirit into it. But my thing got so much attention that I think the aunts were relieved Yadi's was more subtle.

It was only after Tía Camila told Mami that I had told her my toto was magic that she sat me down. We'd never talked about sex before, and we didn't really talk about it then. She only told me that this newfound knowledge of how I could sense the apex between my legs so well was powerful, and special, and I needed to treat it with care but not be afraid of it. Is that how Mami had taught herself about her own gift? To not be afraid? Is that what this circus of a wake was? An embrace of what was to come, seeing it head-on?

"Ona, you paying attention? You just cut me." Jeremiah had an edge to his voice. There's nothing he hates more than losing, except maybe losing because his partner's unfocused. We usually both loved to win to the same degree.

"I'm sorry, I thought Yadi led."

We not only lost the hand, we got stuck, missing making our books by one. The one Jeremiah had counted on that I took. Thankfully we hadn't bid much, but still Yadi laughed, then stood. She walked to the little bar cart and grabbed the bottle of whiskey. She topped Jeremiah off. "Here, you can have one more of the good stuff. You need it."

Ant, who'd lit a jay while Jeremiah had been shuffling, passed it over. I inhaled, deciding Jeremiah was driving us home tonight. I passed it back.

Jeremiah dealt, and I took in the hand full of spades. This should easily be a bubble, no reason I couldn't get a full ten books and set them, thus redeeming myself and reinstating Jeremiah's smile.

Was Mami trying to see something head-on? It was how she'd taught me. Mami had been adamant that because my quirk was sexual, or as she'd rather refer to it, *physical*, I was going to have to be extra cautious. I don't think she was amused when I told her it seemed men would have to be cautious around me since I was the one with the powers.

Ant cleared his throat and I pulled myself back from the sting of *that* particular conversation with my moms.

"Renege," Ant said.

"Huh?" I had been the last one to play. And I looked down at the board. I had played a heart, although I could have sworn I didn't have any. I scanned my hand, saw all the books I imagined, plus the two I'd already acquired . . . but I had bid as if I was cutting hearts from jump, when clearly, I had had one snuck behind diamonds that I'd not only ignored, but had played after cutting all others in its suit.

Ant tapped the two books. "These two. Renege." He flipped them over. And sure enough, there I was with my spades cutting an ace and king of hearts. And there was the heart I just played on the board.

Ant reached across the board and slid three of our books his way. Jeremiah threw his hand down. I spent the rest of the night counting books to three-fifty and counting down hours to the wake. Needless to say, Jeremiah and I lost the game.

FLOR

did not like the tone of the room. There was a somberness she'd tried actively to avoid when she'd begun planning the wake. The news of her brother-in-law's pregnant lover had blown in and ruffled every feather.

Flor looked to her sister Matilde, who was fiddling with her fingers, and left her to Camila to soothe. As always, her consentida was Pastora. The other sisters only knew her as the tough one, but Flor knew her for what she was: the most sensitive of them. Guarded because it was necessary for survival.

She stood and put an arm around Pastora's waist, drawing her into the warmth of her body. "Tranquila."

Pastora leaned into her. "Maybe I missed her distress? I didn't hear it in her voice. Only a morbid curiosity that made me so fucking mad. She was coming to watch a sideshow attraction. And someone needs to push Matilde. She's—"

Flor rubbed a hand on Pastora's back. Rubbing quiet the rest of her words. She knew her sister. She would not have been kind in the face of someone she viewed as a nemesis of the family. "We do not know anything yet. Pregnant women end up in the hospital for many reasons. And while your gift might show you truth, it does not show you death." She bumped her shoulder. "Leave that to me, yes?"

She tried to offer it as comfort even as she knew it was a false offering. If the babe or the babe's mother had died, there was no guarantee she would have dreamt it. For one, she knew neither, and if the dream had already occurred, she'd not had enough information to pass the news along. But for two, it wasn't yet nightfall. She hadn't slept yet. So, this news would not be arriving in time to be of any use. She looked out the window as if to punctuate her thought.

Pastora squared her shoulders. "And you, how are you feeling?" Pastora looked her in the face, scanning the wrinkles she found there, her eyes fingertips reading a kind of braille for health.

Flor took a deep breath. "Pastora, ¿tú me quieres?"

It wasn't a question she'd asked since they were kids. *Do you love me, baby? Do you love me?* Pastora looked at her askance. Flor squeezed Pastora's hand.

"Pastora, I need you to lift this mood. For me, please. I don't know that woman and I hope she's well. Or maybe I don't. I don't know yet what I wish her. But I need us to be returned to today and now. Apologize and move us on. For me?"

Flor didn't say anything more. She might not be the eldest, but she was Pastora's elder nonetheless; they were the middling ones, bonded as the center of gravity for their kin, and that counted for something. Pastora lifted her chin, her second lieutenant ever ready for war.

On the couch Camila was messing with Matilde's phone, apparently trying to search for the woman on Instagram. Camila, who was in her midfifties, was their resident IT sibling. She might be a boomer, but she was the youngest among them, and as such, the most adept with the changing world of technology.

Por supuesto, it was Junior who'd gotten them all hooked on Alexa, having bought one for Camila. When Camila's sisters visited, they watched with distrust as she used the technology. Commanded a song be played and music filled the apartment. She ordered compression socks, and the next day the UPS guy was knocking on the door. It took three days, but after the lit-up box did not summon the FBI or evil spirits, the other hermanas were ringing their own children to order and install an Alexa onto their kitchen walls.

It was Yadi who had the cousins pool together money to buy their moms iPhones, realizing that the larger phones would help them type better and communicate easier via FaceTime. It was this same daughter who then had to hold a tutorial on the usage of group chats after the hermanas discovered Whats-App. Yadi then later had to hold a resolution session when the group chat led to a nasty spat that convinced the sisters el demonio was bedeviling their texts.

The younger generation brought new ways of doing things, these new inventions, and the hermanas touched their fingers to gadgets, or their tongues to new words, and sewed the technology into the fabric of their lives the way one embroiders lace, Camila the one who ensured they knew how to do it when their kids were too busy to proffer another explanation.

"We are trying to find her on las redes. Maybe to see if she put anything up . . ." Camila said.

There was no news. Matilde would have to wait until she got home to see if her husband said anything.

As it was, there was *nothing* for them to do.

"Matilde," Pastora said. "I'm sorry for interfering. I hope you forgive me. For Flor's sake, perhaps we can put away Rafa and the woman for a bit. Maybe play a game of dominos or something to take our minds off of it all?"

Everyone looked at Matilde.

Camila stood and walked to a cabinet, for once, agreeable with Pastora. "Dominos."

They paired up.

PASTORA

was shaken to her core. She shuffled the dominos on the table but could not meet any of her sisters' eyes. She had not had many causes in her life to feel ashamed, but shame bloomed spiky petals in her belly now.

Flor and Pastora won handily. Mostly because Flor was a wiz at guessing what pieces her opponents had, and also because the usually formidable Matilde was distracted.

It was Camila who finally shouted at Alexa to turn on a salsa playlist.

Pastora missed her husband.

They'd met when she and Flor both moved to live in the capital a few months after the debacle at La Vieja [redacted]'s. Pastora could not share a house with her mother without getting sick. And Flor no longer trusted her sister's care to anyone else.

So, they left to live in the capital with a non-blood family member from their father's side. Their mother did not put up a fight. When Pastora and Manuelito met, they'd been too young to act on it. They were neighbors and friendly, but their affection grew over time. The admiration they had for each other at a young age was probably why she had always been so lax with Yadi and Ant; the love that children knew was not always governed by age. Where most boys flinched at how she could silence them with a word, Manuelito, her naturally quiet love, was so thoughtful and precise with his words that she was able to let her guard down. There were few lies to look for in her husband's presence.

After years as neighbors, after he graduated college and began working for a chauffeuring business, he'd asked if he could court her. They'd shared meals at each other's houses, but for the first time he invited her out to eat, asking permission from both her paternal guardian and Flor, since that's who she was living with at the time. They went to an elegant restaurant by the Malecón. She could still remember she had on a swingy yellow dress with cap sleeves, her waist belted and her hair flipped. But when they arrived, her admirer was fidgety. And she sensed that he was avoiding her gaze. So few people she met were comfortable; she was constantly attacked by the pinpricks of untruths they didn't even realize they were telling.

The waiter had approached them, but before he could set down the first course of toasted and buttered pan de agua, Pastora had shooed him away. She picked up her purse and stood.

"What aren't you telling me?" She had long leaned into the fact that she'd always be considered a steamroller of men, and oiling the wheels with sweetness wouldn't unflatten the road.

"I know it's too soon, but I love you. I have for a long time." And the silence in her body that followed was the most peace she'd ever known. There was no disclaimer on his declaration.

And in the years since, she might have heard a fib or two in his voice about nonsense, but the truth of his love always cut through with clarity.

———

"And what are you smiling about?" Flor asked as the domino pieces were shuffled. Pastora knew better than to say she'd been daydreaming about her husband.

"Probably about denying someone water." Matilde made the remark without venom, but it still had fangs. Pastora flinched.

Flor shook her head. "Now, we all know que el agua no se niega. And she was wrong for that. But Pastora did what felt most protective. As she always does."

There was a quiet, and it seemed the sisters would drop it, but Camila, peeking from behind her tiles, cleared her throat. "But was Pastora *asked* for that protection, Flor?"

Matilde slammed a tile down hard onto the table. "I've never asked anyone for interventions in my marriage."

Flor played a double piece. "I don't know the ins and outs of the conversations you all have privately." Pastora looked up, startled. Could Flor foresee the talks they had? "But I do know that this particular situation arrived at Pastora's workplace. She did not seek it out."

It mollified them just enough. Camila played. Pastora played. Matilde took one beat, two.

"Knock if you don't have a play, Mati," Pastora said.

Matilde put down her pieces, looking at Flor. "But she did meddle. And it's not the first time. First when she went to see Mamá before I'd even had a few months to settle into my marriage. And she's been hounding me about Rafa this week, as if a thirty-five-year relationship can be discarded like skidmarked drawers. Does she meddle with you the same way? Seems like you have secrets of your own, and our ever-protective Pastora leaves those alone, doesn't she?"

Matilde knocked twice. Flor played her turn without responding, as did Camila.

"Hounding?" Pastora dropped the word into the room. Then again. "Hounding?" They could not know how the truth and untruths of what they were saying about her struck like little barbs. How she felt their conviction even as she also recognized the ways they stretched the reality. Pastora played. Matilde played, banging her piece down so the table shook.

Flor edged her last piece onto the board. "Capicúa," she whispered, palindrome: a win at either end.

Camila shuffled the pieces, but then stopped, her hands still on the tiles. "You two must feel so special. With your abilities so far beyond our own. With the knowledge you have of everyone around you as you share nothing of yourselves. Flor, what is this wake? I bet you Pastora knows." The last statement was said to Matilde.

Once again, less a sisterhood of four than the sisterhood of two and two.

Matilde harrumphed. "Right. Let's talk then, Pastora. You wanted to talk, right? You want to go into the details of my life, let's talk about all of yours. You have your daughter worried sick to death, Flor. Maybe Pastora wouldn't be minding my business if she wasn't trying to avoid thinking of you. What is it, Flor? What is this thing you're doing with so much urgency?"

Flor shook her head. "I have told Pastora nothing more than I've told you."

Camila raised an eyebrow. "But that doesn't mean Pastora doesn't know more than the rest of us, does it?"

Pastora felt her stomach turning. Slow flips as she tried to calibrate around how she'd become the object of derision. The eldest and youngest sisters stood with flaming arrows for tongues, and it seemed target practice had turned deadly. And Flor, usually up for the task of sounding wise and good and making peace where she could, was stoic but unwilling to spar.

Flor said nothing. Pastora said nothing. They each grabbed their seven tiles when Camila was done shuffling, all but Matilde, who looked at the leftover tiles as if trying to divine what their smooth backs might add up to on their fronts.

Matilde stood. "I am going home to speak with my husband. I'll see you all tomorrow at Flor's . . . event. I can't sit here any longer. It's all . . . it's too much pretending."

Flor pushed back from the table, followed Mati to the door, her tone cajoling. Matilde's voice broke into a sob. The door closed gently. And Flor walked back by herself.

"Perhaps she is getting too old to sleep in a bed that is not her own." Flor always tried to save face. "Camila, thank you for hosting us. Would you mind if I got ready for bed? I'm in the spare?"

Flor did not look at Pastora. And Pastora heard in her voice a million longings, and every single truth she'd tried to deny.

I watched as Jeremiah walked down the block. The spades game had dismantled quickly after our second loss. I knew Jeremiah carried a lot these days: the installation, my fertility, and on this night, probably a few more ounces of alcohol than he needed, so I gave him space.

"I'm going to walk to 116th," I said. "Meet you at the car when you get yourself together?"

He'd always been competitive to a fault; it had so few occasions to emerge that I often overlooked it, but it was a significant medal of his childhood. He had learned to treat every loss like a personal badge of failure whether he was the one at fault or not. It made him driven; he worked harder than any other artist I'd ever met, meticulous and obsessed with depicting his vision *just so*. But it made him a difficult partner over the most trivial things. We didn't lose often as a couple, at much, but when we did it wounded him in ways I didn't know how to soothe.

Since it was only a few blocks away, I went back to my favorite bench at Columbia University, where I'd first begun smoking. This was an evening that required a blunt, and luckily I'd snagged one from Ant. I know when trying to conceive, weed might seem antithetical to fertility, but stress is also a conception killer, so I played the odds. The New York City dispensaries had been open for a few years, but I still liked my dank hood shit.

People love to say New Yorkers are hard, mean, ambitious beyond what's normal. But I think it's just that we are surrounded by brick walls, so of course people are trying to claw their way up to some sort of sky. It's probably why my mother was always going on long walks. When I was little she would come straight home from work, put on sneakers, and grab my hand, and we would go to Central, Morningside, Riverside Park. Trying to untrap us, perhaps.

It was Jeremiah who had encouraged us to get out of the city despite how much it fueled his work. He hadn't been raised in New York; he was a Southern boy, and his relationship to New York was for a different absolution or resolution than what had brought my own parents to the city. When I decided to move from Mami's house and his studio's rent had skyrocketed, it'd made sense for us to begin looking for a space together, but I simply hadn't imagined it'd be over the Hudson River in a residential neighborhood where the closest bodega was three exits over.

There's a pride and embarrassment I feel regarding the house we own. It took a good chunk of our savings for the down payment, but it's a large home, with a front yard and a back patio that has a gazebo. We clean the shutters in March, Jeremiah standing on a ladder that I hold. He thoughtfully dresses in overalls for the job. In the winter we put up lights on the yard. In the summer we join the HOA chili cookout and talk to our retired neighbors about forming a pickleball team and taking summer excursions to Martha's Vineyard.

We have to drive everywhere. And I marvel often at how

trapped I can feel amid all this space. In New York, my two legs could carry me anywhere, and that agency felt like freedom. From the top of the isle to Battery Park, I needed nothing but my own abled self to run or disappear or escape. But out in Jersey, one needs a vehicle. Jeremiah laughs at me all the damn time, my lack of respect for automobiles apparently undermining every American sentiment about four-wheel drive, the open road, and manifest destiny.

Maybe I'm just one of those people who lives in a body that will always feel like it's participating in a gods' game of catch and release.

Jeremiah called about twenty minutes after we'd gone our separate ways and scooped me up outside the Columbia gates.

We were silent the entire car ride, although he seemed to have lost his anger.

We walked into the house and I kissed him on the neck, pressed into his back. Jeremiah didn't want any of that, though.

"I'm sorry. I didn't mean to cut you." I nuzzled into him.

Jeremiah shook his head. "And you reneged."

I laughed. "It happens, Jeremiah. It's just a game."

Jeremiah shook his head. "It about respect for your partner."

Now I scoffed. "Are you fucking kidding me? It was a game. How many times have we been perfectly fine partners?"

I poured us each a glass of white wine, ensuring that I didn't set his glass down hard enough to have drops flying over the rim.

Jeremiah's recent work had left him as wired as the bulbs he rendered into beauty. I wanted to give him a laundry list of the symptoms I'd felt in my body that day: a cramp in my right side, tender breasts, and high irritability. I might be ovulating right this moment, and I didn't have time for an argument. *We* didn't.

I leaned against the black marble countertop and fiddled with my music app. Music always petted Jeremiah smooth when his feathers were ruffled. The Bluetooth took a second to kick on, but soon my panty-dropper playlist dripped through the living room speakers.

Jeremiah picked up his wine. He sipped. "I think I'm going to actually do some work. I was in the middle of a groove when you called about the spades game."

"I got some work for you to do," I said, twining my arms around his neck and kissing him. He laughed, but his hands settled on my waist, and he flipped us so it was his back against the kitchen counter and I was cradled between his legs.

He tasted better tonight than he had the last four days. That seemed a sign. I pushed myself to wetness, heightened the scent so he could smell it. He groaned in my ear and urgently kissed my neck.

"Let's go upstairs," I whispered. That's where I kept the fertility lube. Where my altar was set up to conjure all my hopes. Where I could pull the curtain aside and look up at the moon, dwindling down to its new form, and ask for a blessing.

"Or let's be spontaneous." He picked me up, setting me on the kitchen island, and undid my jeans.

I laughed. "I need you to be on top, for gravity purposes."

Jeremiah's hand against the four-inch scar on my stomach was hot one second, and then it was just the coolness of denim pressed back against my skin.

Jeremiah took a sip of his wine. Took a deep breath, as if it took immense work to do so, and then he stepped away from me.

I grabbed his hand. "It's just that I think I'm ovulating. Maybe? I don't know when, so we should just do it as much as possible the next few days. You know my cycle isn't back on its routine, but I've felt all these signs. You know my cycle is chaos these days." I was repeating myself, I realized. Nervous about his reaction. "I can reset the mood up there." I tried a smile.

Jeremiah rubbed a hand against his eyes. "Ona. Sometimes I want to be close to you, and it has nothing to do with procreation. I been trying to touch you all week and you been brushing me off. And today you get 'signs' and you finally giving me some play, only it has to be *exactly* the way you—"

"*We* need in order to conceive. What the fuck, Jeremiah?" I slid off the island. Tugged my pants' fastening together. "You make it seem like I'm trying to coerce you into parenthood instead of it being something we both want."

"I don't want it like this. And it's been happening since you were cleared to try. It's starting to feel transactional. I'm not a fucking stud horse."

"Oh, now who's making it *exactly* the way—?"

He turned his back to me. "Ona. I love you. Every single day of the month I want you to know I love you."

I grabbed my wine and my phone and paused Frank Ocean mid-serenade.

"I can't help my goddamn hormones, Jeremiah. Progesterone rises and makes me horny, and before today—"

He held up a hand. "Ona. Got it. I'm just not in the mood anymore. I'm sorry that isn't convenient."

I knew there was no safe home in the world for the violence I felt in my body in that moment. The ache of another chance, another cycle slipping away, ripped through me. But I found the wherewithal to go upstairs without another word. To pull the door behind me without slamming it.

I didn't turn on the light but made my way to the nightstand by memory. I put the wine down and grabbed my vibrator. Undoing my pants again, I climbed under the sheets.

I went to my favorite site where videos didn't run rampant with POVs and the women had chichos. The very first video promoted was of a woman with milky breasts being licked. The universe has a goddamn sense of humor, doesn't it? That or I'd clearly set a pattern with my internet cookies.

It was a silent video, which I found odd. No matter how high I raised the volume, it seemed to have been shot that way. An artistic approach, perhaps?

I had trained myself as a child not to moan when I masturbated. Both the video and I were quiet as I came.

I returned to myself, sweaty and wet and the tiniest bit cringed that *that* was what I'd come to. I exited the site and began closing all my other browsers when an alert on my phone made a noise, but it sounded far away.

I realized I'd turned off the music when I'd been downstairs, but I had never disconnected from the speakers. My phone *had* been playing sound, it'd just been playing where it was last connected: in the living room, where I'd left Jeremiah.

Jeremiah, who was still downstairs.

I didn't like him knowing what I'd been watching. What I did in our bed when he wasn't with me wasn't his business. The heat of my body post-masturbation had cooled enough that I had to unshame myself. It was not my dead or the divine I believed in who were telling me I was dirty, and nasty for watching porn, for getting caught. It was my own little voice. The same little voice that had been reaching for pleasure with one hand and had been giving sharp slaps on the wrist with the other.

I turned the Bluetooth off on my phone. I gazed out the bedroom window. The sliver of crescent moon was so thin it looked like someone had taken a Gillette to the sky and carved a bitty smile: light seeped past the teeth.

MATILDE

inserted the key to her door, although she soon realized she could have simply turned the knob. Rafa had left the door unlocked, an anomaly in all their years of living in New York City. She touched one finger to bloated-heart Baby Jesus, then called out to Rafa.

It was worrisome, but her sisters' voice performed an encore in her head: *let him go let him go*. And Matilde wanted to listen, she did! This time she would. Wouldn't she?

Rafa was on the bed in the bedroom. He lay on his back, sobbing into a pillow he held with both hands against his face, his white tank top saggy at the chest and tight around his belly. His soft penis slipped from the right leg of his boxers, and Matilde looked away quickly. It seemed inappropriate in the face of his loss to be looking at his genitals.

She sat next to him on the bed. He wept, hard, and she did not touch him. Let the dip on the mattress and the weight of her presence be enough for him to know she was there. She did not know how much time passed. Enough that she put her phone on the nightstand, took off her rings. Removed bobby pins from her hair and toed off both shoes. Her glasses joined the phone, and she rubbed her thumbs against where the nose pads had left an indent. Eventually, after she'd taken off all she could without undressing, he quieted. Removed the pillow from his face.

"Mati, I have something to tell you."

Matilde stared at the wall rather than look at his red-rimmed eyes.

"There was a girl. It was a mistake, she was a flirt and I told her I was married, but one night, I got drunk, and there was a duet, and . . . it so happens that it happened."

Matilde flinched.

Rafa continued. "She, she got with child. I've been waiting for her to give birth, you know, supporting here and there until the baby arrived and we could get bloodwork, because you know, a girl like that, she would say anything, and how do I even know if it's mine? I've never gotten anyone else pregnant. I know you always thought it was you, but what if part of it was me? I didn't think it was mine."

Matilde stared at the white wall for so long she'd begun to see spots. "You know the baby is yours, Rafa. No mientas. I heard she defends you viciously. She wouldn't do that for just anyone."

If Rafa was surprised, Matilde still didn't look at his face to see it.

"It was an accident. I didn't think I could have kids. I never have before. It was a small thing. Just a pretty girl, a late night. I didn't love her."

"I know." What Matilde knew was that he used the past tense, but his weeping happened presently.

"Today. She was waiting for me. We were going shopping for a crib or something, and she had a scare. Or went into labor. Or it was those fake contractions. I don't know. I don't know. They kept her overnight at the hospital, but her mother kicked me out when I arrived. I don't know if the baby is okay."

What kind of fate could this be when a woman became her husband's confidante as pertained to his lovers? It was beyond indignity. She was too fatigued to fight, to demand anymore. Her mother was dead, but her mother's wishes lived on, it seemed.

A year after Matilde had been married, her mother had made the trip to the Santo Domingo apartment Matilde shared with her new husband. It was strange for her mother to travel far from home, and even stranger that she'd pulled Camila from her college semester to do so. She claimed she'd wanted to get Camila away from the campo for a while.

Matilde had given up her own bed so her mother could sleep in it with Camila. She convinced Rafa that they could easily occupy the couch, although he didn't come home most of the nights during that visit, so it was just Matilde who stared at the whirring fan of their living room ceiling.

Her mother found her sobbing one night as she stared at the circling blades.

"Y a ti, ¿qué te pasa?"

Matilde had to hiccup and gasp herself coherent, but she finally said the words. She'd made a huge mistake. Her husband wasn't a good man, wasn't a man who could make do with the attention of only one woman. He needed to feel loved and wanted by every woman he met.

Her mother had not sympathized. Matilde hadn't expected her to, but she'd thought her mother would tell her to strengthen up, to give him an ultimatum, to slap the ladies he visited. She wanted the advice of an action with bite.

"This life is too long to spend it alone. Even a no-good man is a man, and that's good enough. You're too timid. You might not do better. And . . ." Here her mother had hesitated. As if the words she'd said before hadn't been harsh enough, as if something could be harsher that would require her to speak carefully. Matilde remembers she'd closed her eyes against the coming words. "There might be a day there isn't a single body in the world left to offer you warmth. Better the devil you know." *Than no devil at all*, her mother implied.

————

Rafa put his head in her lap and wrapped an arm around her waist as her mother's words echoed her back to the past, combined with the present. Rafa told her it'd been a mistake a mistake a mistake. She put a hand on his head. And although she had practiced on the train ride home, she did not say: "Vete pa'l carajo, you fucking bastard."

Instead, she smoothed his hair and told him hush hush, everything would be okay. And she folded her pride and tucked it into a serviette she used to dry his tears.

FLOR

waited while her air mattress filled up in the living room. Camila had the two bedrooms but, like an American, had recently turned Junior's old room, the spare, into a gym and office area and gotten rid of the extra bed. As if an elliptical and behemoth desk would be more useful than accommodations for a guest, especially with so much family close by. She tried not to be annoyed that she would not have a bedroom door for privacy, and that anytime one of her sisters got up to use the bathroom she'd hear it. Pastora had already brushed her teeth and shuffled to the bed she would share with Camila.

Flor did not want to think of the bitter taste of resentment in the back of her throat; not for the air mattress, but for how the evening had not unfolded. She had hoped that she and her sisters would talk long into the night. That they'd drink, and gossip, and dance. That they'd share secrets until they fell asleep on the couch, each head on another sister's shoulder, and her own against the armrest. She felt nostalgic for the twilight that hadn't been, and it flavored her entire mouth.

She had asked Matilde to stay. To forgo running to her husband this one time. But although Matilde was considered the meek one, she was fierce when it came to the depths to which she'd entrenched herself with Rafa. As if it justified everything she had suffered, if she proved there was still more suffering she could endure.

It was the distance between them all, Flor assumed. They'd shared a household as children. And then each one had departed in varying stages of womanhood, facing a country armed to harm them, and they with very few shields.

Her mother had never understood why she'd given up her chance at the nunnery in order to accompany Pastora home, and later to the capital. And Flor had not known how to explain that they'd needed to be with each other, and that Pastora could not be home. They played a game of follow-the-leader for the rest of their lives. Pastora to the capital, Flor right behind her. Flor to New York City, Pastora joining two years later. They'd found apartments on different floors but in the same building. They were yoked.

Flor had tried explaining it once, when she'd been a young woman visiting home from the capital. Pastora never joined her on the trips to see their mother. But their father's burial anniversary was coming up, Matilde had spent the last few years caring for the perpetually dying uncle—who Flor could have told her would be finally kicking the bucket soon—and her mother was alone, with only the adolescent Camila for company.

The countryside looked different. Vacant, even though the pineapple groves still bore fruit, and acres of tobacco were at least knee-high. Clearly the laborers who worked the land were still sowing and fallowing and harvesting, but many of the small houses along the road looked abandoned. People had moved away to bigger cities. The drive past the canal stopped Flor's heart for a second. It was running so low in comparison to what she remembered. Or was it simply that it had always run low, but her little-girl mind had made a behemoth of the waterway? She wasn't sure. But her home looked like it belonged in someone else's memory. She'd always considered herself a country girl, but her edges had been polished, enough so that her mother tutted she thought she was too good for the dirt that had cradled her.

Her mother in her own way snuck questions about the siblings. Did Matilde ever write to Flor? She seemed to be happy taking care of the sick uncle; she was such a maternal soul. Flor murmured that Matilde had sent a letter about her new favorite band. On the second day, Mamá Silvia made noises that she'd still yet to meet Samuel's new wife. Flor reported back on the woman's kind demeanor, although she was a bit of a mandona. All things she knew her brother, a faithful correspondent, had probably written in his own letters home. Mamá asked about cousins and nephews and, on one quiet occasion, even after her late husband's family. She did not ask after Pastora.

And Flor was perfectly fine not having to say anything about that particular sister. Mamá also didn't ask after Flor herself. It was a practice Flor found more curious than heartbreaking, the way her mother could never show concern for the child in front of her, except to ask about her after she'd left. As if showing softness in the face of a person would render her, what, weak? Soft? Motherly? Flor did not think she'd made this trip in order to confess anything to her mother, but she found that in seeking the quiet of her childhood home, perhaps she'd hoped to find something tender in her mother's bosom.

How to tell Mamá she'd met a man? *Falling in love* would be too cloying a phrase for what she felt. She felt regard for him. And affection. And she'd dreamt of him the first night she met him and knew exactly how he would die. Knowing both the beginning and the end led her to believe he would be a comfortable companion.

"Flor, go see if you can find your sister. She should have been back by now. That girl loves to get lost in the woods. Grab that machete. She always forgets it on laundering day and she's probably out there tugging on some root, or trying to fell a mango by shaking a tree, knowing right well that a sharp knife is her best ally."

Flor, who'd been stirring an asopao, took some wood pieces out of the fogón so the fire died down to a smaller flame. She added water and took note, she had maybe fifteen minutes before it'd lose most of the moisture and stick to the bottom of the pot. Her mother was many things, but she was not a good cook.

She dutifully grabbed the machete and tied her hair back. Although it looked like rain, the air did not yet feel humid. She would leave this island soon, she knew. The man she'd met, Pedro, had already talked about wanting to marry her and taking her with him on his papers to New York. Pastora had been making calf eyes at their neighbor Manuelito, and Flor knew she could depend on him to guard her sister's well-being. And like this home had changed when she'd left for the capital, the whole island would change when she left for another country.

Her memories would no longer be corroborated by a scenery
that remained the same.

She walked past the old conucos. Her mother had not asked
anyone to help her replant what her husband used to sow. And
the rows of vegetable beds lay barren. When her father had died,
the tender cultivation of the land had died with him.

(Mami told me that she'd once heard Papá Susano claim
to her brother Samuel that they had Taíno in them. Not
in the boastful way that tried to remove his dark skin
from his Africanism, but in the quiet way whereby he
explained to his eldest child that their particular tradition of harvesting tobacco went back millennia. It
is believed that very few descendants of the Taíno, or
Arawak Indio, still exist, but my own research into my
grandfather's indigeneity led me to work published by
the Smithsonian from over a decade ago, which found
that Taíno descendants not only exist, there is physical
proof in the mouths of Dominicans: our indigenous ancestors are found in the teeth, the incisors. These front
teeth are clearly distinct from those of Africans or Span-
iards, straight proof that what Papá Susano told Samuel
had merit. Regarding tobacco, he'd told Samuel to pay
attention to the flowering phase and the growth of the
four leaves closest to the ground. The stalks can grow
waist-high, he'd explained, depending on the height of
the farmer. If one is a child harvesting tobacco, then it
can grow tall enough to tower over the body, and the
peeling and harvesting can take on more dangerous elements, as small, tender hands are not well suited for

felling the plant. Mami never remembered him talking quite at length or so reverently about any of their other crops. There was something specific about the cultivation of tobacco. And my spiritual, ancestrally inclined self thinks that it's because tobacco, or tobako to natives of Kiskeya, was used in sacred ritual before the mother-fucker Columbus's arrival. It was an herb to connect to the dead. To the undead. To the spirits of Atabey and her pernicious sisters. The Taínos believed all life was imbued with spirit and its own sacred knowledge and to overindulge in tobacco to them might have been rightly compared to overindulging in holy water. Tobako was medicine and it was hallowed. It was wisdom passed down through alchemy of burning a being to having other essences of life revealed; fire and smoke as the conduit of the divine.)

If not for Camila, they might have had only the lime trees left. But Camila had planted herbs and maintained the fruit trees. Camila carried the most of their father. It was this thought Flor had as she crossed onto a path and felt something unfamiliar slither against the back of her left calf, then wrap with a tightening grip around it.

She did not jump; she did not scream. She stood rock still. The squeeze around her leg grew, traveled higher near her knee, a cold-blooded shackle. Flor lifted her skirt with her one free hand. Even as a child there'd been the one creature, this one animal she struggled to see reason for, and when she saw the bright white scales spotted with crimson, the red head dusted with small dots of white, as if an unsatisfied artist had erased his work there and there and there, she opened her mouth, but the scream that emerged was a silent one. She didn't have breath for a scream.

Goose bumps covered her from toe to crown as she looked into the eyes of the mountain boa; it was a long creature. Its head now rested against her thigh, its tail pressed against her ankle, and its body looped around and around her. It clearly had a warmer regard for her than she had for it.

She dropped to the ground, thumping her leg against what used to be a bed for yautía. She banged hard, ignoring the pain that shot up her heel. She seesawed and slammed and scrambled, and shook the thing off, until they were face-to-face, she on all fours, heaving, the pain in her foot making itself known with small throbs. The boa did not seem the worse for wear, except if a snake could be hurt by being so unwelcomed, its face did seem disappointed in her.

Without taking her eyes off of its red head, her left hand searched the dirt until she found the handle of Mamá's long blade.

Flor, as a general, innate rule, did not kill things. But there was a threat embodied in this creature that she felt in her whole body. It'd come as an omen, a warning, a blood sacrifice she'd need to make. And as the snake reared back, its mouth still unopened, Flor let her arm down with a swift arc.

¡Fuácata!

The snake's head disconnected cleanly, arcing into a pile of dead overgrowth, its bleached body still slithering toward her.

Flor ran home, covered in dust. The clouds that had threatened all day opened above her. Camila was already there when she arrived. The asopao, the only thing that had gone right, bubbled merrily in the pot. Her mother watched her but did not ask why she was covered in dirt, shaking.

It was Camila who used rags to clean her legs, and wrapped her in a sun-dried towel. Flor babbled through what had happened.

"Oh, poor thing. I'd always heard that you were afraid of snakes." Camila spoke like she was one hundred instead of ten. "Mamá thinks that you took the story of Eve too literally."

Flor shook her head, incapable of saying, *This was more than just a response to a parable.* This snake had been chasing her for a long, long time.

"It's the season, you see? It's been chillier than usual, and the mountain boas come down to where it's warmer, and well, what's warmer than human flesh?" Camila tried a smile, which withered in the face of Flor's bared teeth.

Camila and Flor shared a bed that night, Flor grateful for her little sister's body, which offset the trembles still going through her own. She did not fall asleep until after midnight, the hour denoted by the big clock in the living room. She slept a dreamless sleep, rare for her, who even when not predicting someone's expiration had an active subconscious.

It was still dark, perhaps the darkest hour of the night, when she sprang awake, aware she was being watched.

And there, at the foot of the bed, white as bared teeth, glossy, with an incarnadine head, stood the snake. Eyes right on her.

———

She'd once told that story to Ona, who, being Ona, had of course been skeptical. No story was ever good enough for the girl unless it was verifiable. "See, I just looked it up, and snakes cannot reattach or regenerate. But they also don't need a lot of oxygen, so it's likely that it was just still moving for a few hours after you decapitated it. Maybe it happened in the house instead of outside? Or maybe it *was* a dream?"

(I can honestly say I don't remember this exchange. But it does sound like the way my teenage self would have responded. My adult self too.)

Flor was not one to strike her daughter. It was one of the pieces of counsel her own mother had always chastised her for forgoing. *The back of a hand would snap the smart-ass girl into remembering who was the adult and who was the child.*

In that moment, with her daughter laughing at her country ways, and naysaying an actual memory with her supposed science, Flor wanted to chop her right in the jugular, to abort the mirth right at the opening of her throat.

Instead, she'd sat silently. Remembering the way the snake had reared up. How she could see the glowing eyes from her bed. The severing in the field had been immaculate, a nice diagonal slice like when one is cutting plantains for tostones. But the boa had not realigned itself the way the knife had cut it, less like two ends of a magnet locking into place and more like two tostones in hot oil finding each other in the bubbling and conjoining tight, but ill fitted. It'd been terrible. Worse to see it misshapen and attempting its former shape than it had been when it'd wrapped around her, or even than when she'd murdered it.

Slighted things needed you to witness the wound you gave them.

YADI

had felt time stand still when the knock she hadn't heard in almost two decades thumped on the door. She hadn't even finished pouring Jeremiah's drink, her heart following the two evenly placed taps followed by three rapid taps. The knock had started years back, a secret code. Ant would knock, then run up a flight of stairs. That way even if her mother opened the door, she wouldn't know it was the little boy from downstairs trying to get her daughter's attention again. Pastora liked Ant, but she didn't like Yadi roughhousing or spending too much time with any boy who wasn't kin.

Yadi would hear the door, and if her mother was distracted, she would be the one to answer. If her mother answered, Yadi waited until Mami stopped complaining about the building ruffians that ran amok doing pranks, before she eased out, making sure to pull the door quietly while she snuck up the flight of stairs to where Ant was waiting. From there they could go to the basement or up to the roof. The roof alarm hadn't worked in years, so it was an easy area to hide out.

That knock had started her evening, but now that Ona and Jeremiah had long been gone, she wanted to hide. Ant was still here and they were alone. He was buzzed off the jay, and she felt a bit lifted off the whiskey. She didn't think he'd actually come when he'd offered the night before to help her prep for the wake. Yadi certainly hadn't expected him to sit and play cards with her cousin and a dude he'd never met.

She faced herself in the window. The distorted reflection showed how she felt on the inside, a ghost of sorts. She liked that she could see herself this way, that she could see him behind her without having to look into his eyes.

"You went shopping." His sneakers were brand-new and clean, leading Yadi to wonder where he'd found the sneakers he'd been wearing the day before. He'd gotten a shape-up; the fitted on his head was crisp, the sticker still on it. But the T-shirt, while clean and also new, looked a size too large.

"Speaking of, I thought we could do an exchange, shorty."

Yadi flinched. She still hadn't gotten used to his voice. How it had deepened. She was turned on, she realized. She was turned on by the fact that she knew and didn't know him. The boy she knew, in the stranger's body she wanted. It was a heady mix.

"Exchange?" She stepped back and he stepped in.

He held up an iPhone. "Ma got me this phone, but she didn't know how to walk me through it."

Ant had been a proud kid by the time he'd become a teen. Not the type to know how to ask for help. She wondered if his asking her was growth, or if his not going to the Verizon store instead was indicative of his need to still protect his ego.

"You help me set it up and I help chop and dice? I did promise."

She wiped her hands on a dishrag. Yadi was not in the habit of lying to herself. The world? Yes. They got the version of her that was buttoned up, wry. She was seen as brutally honest because she rarely bit her tongue, but the people around her didn't know how much she did not admit. The acid she had inherited with her taste for limes was not only a palate phenomenon. It had changed how she reacted to people. She knew how sweet or sour a word any moment required. So she knew that Ant was going to sit on the sofa, and she was going to sit next to him. She would begin by guiding him through the phone and setting up his email and downloading Instagram or a podcast or something. And then their hands would touch, and there would be a spark. She would ask if he had known any gentle touching. And Ant would blush, bluster, the unspeakable things of being a young attractive teenage boy in an adult prison would flash over his face. And then she would take his hand and lead him into her bedroom.

She heard the longing in his voice. So she could not respond with sweetness. "Your moms is good with phones; Ona taught her when the iPhones first came out. Have her set it up for you."

Ant's mother is from La Vega. Doña Reina's accent is ornamented with long *i*'s that transform familiar words into a different song, distinct from the crisp letters of a capital accent—although, to be clear, very few Dominican accents are ever truly that crisp, not unless the person attended a prestigious private school that curbed the mouth from drawing outside the lines. A person from El Cibao drops most *s*'s and substitutes some *r*'s and *l*'s for *i*. ¡Poi Dio que sí!

(This anthropologist will note I once put a post on Instagram describing the linguistic circumstances that allowed a language to evolve in such a way that you ritualistically add and subtract letters to balance out the words. Yadi commented that it was like the profit-and-loss statement she has to submit every quarter for the shop: the profit, a dialect she can pick up anywhere; the loss, a sense that she was never quite handling the words correctly.)

When Yadi first went plant-based, all she could think about was wanting to call her ex-boyfriend's moms and let her know that she was now a Vegana too. She knew the joke would not only be lost in translation; it would be lost in understanding even if it didn't need to be translated. What kind of Dominican voluntarily stopped eating bistec, and honey, and aunque sea, un huevo frito? "Eso no le hace daño a la gallina, mi'ja," Yadi's mother had pleaded with her, dead sure that this new lifestyle of no animal products or byproducts would lead to her daughter getting anemia and diabetes, and a weakening of her health that wouldn't allow her to have children.

"Who is going to buy food? Esos platos vacíos." Yadi's mom thought any meal that didn't include meat was empty. But Pastora pulled from her savings to help Yadi buy the first month's inventory.

Ant nodded, tucked the phone back in his pocket. They stood like that, barely a few feet apart, the gulf between them seemingly too turbulent to traverse.

"Look, Yadi, when I was inside—"

Yadi threw up a hand to stop the onslaught. She shook her head. She hadn't written to him for a reason. She could not invite these kinds of confidences. It was unkind, she felt, to be one of the few places Ant might still feel vulnerable, maybe even cruel to deny whatever confession he was about to render, but she knew it'd be *self*-cruelty to share a single moment that might bind them closer.

She handed him an apron. Put some potatoes on a cutting board. Turned her back to him.

"Yadi, when I was inside, it's not like a pause button was pressed on my life. I had access to a computer library, and I took some classes. I had Facebook. I talked to girls. My life didn't end."

The water for the quinoa came to a rolling boil. "I had friends inside. Mentors. Older guys who looked out for me. It wasn't all bad."

Somehow, Yadi's hand had found itself hovering over her heart. She *knew* Ant. In between his sentences, she heard so much of what he didn't say. The parts that burdened the *not all bad* with *the worst fucking thing that could have ever happened*.

A few years ago, there'd been loud calls for prison abolitionism. Ant's mother had marched alongside activists and revolutionaries. A lone Dominican mother, with jeans too tight and a handwritten sign written in cursive because block letters weren't part of the nuns' education. Yadi hadn't marched. Hadn't joined any social justice programs or dreamt of being a lawyer so she could one day fight Ant's case. She'd simply unmoored herself from that part of her past.

"Fuck, I forgot the canned peppers." Yadi looked at the stove. "Can you run to the store for me?" She picked up her wallet from the table and gave him one of her cards. "Sliced jalapeños, please."

Not one of the recipes called for canned peppers. But she needed Ant to give her a second.

Ant closed the door softly behind him.

As she slid the quinoa stuffing into the oven, Yadi gazed out the kitchen window, where a few branches of a tree out back could be seen. It was dark now, and she could barely make out the dying leaves, but Yadi stood at this window often. The tree was beloved by birds. None of the beautiful variety; these birds did not flutter and sing. They lived unknowing they weren't of the most startling plumage and uncaring that it was so. They cooed above the air-conditioner attached to the window; they fucked and she could hear it, the way they topped each other. Sometimes, a bird would hide in a branch near the top of the tree, and a second bird would flit near it. Partners, they seemed. The first bird would take off again, and the second bird, after a moment or two, would take off with its mate, or its nonmate, or whatever one calls a creature that pulls your gravity until you succumb.

Yadi often forgot time when she was in the kitchen. So, when fifteen minutes had passed and Ant wasn't back, she didn't notice. When forty minutes had passed and Ant still hadn't returned, she got nervous. She picked up her phone, but realized they hadn't exchanged numbers and his phone wasn't actually set up yet.

She threw on some chancletas over her socks. She turned off the oven, choking back the irritation she felt that disrupting the cooking time would fuck up the texture. There was a bodega on Amsterdam, and a gourmet grocery on Broadway. She hit the bodega first, but while Petey said that Ant had come in and browsed the aisles, he hadn't bought anything.

She walked to the gourmet shop, working the kinks in her neck at the stoplight. This new artisanal market was pricier than the wholesaler she usually ordered from, and she only splurged here when she was cooking for a new lover.

When you know your people, you can tell whether their

voices are raised in anger or joy from a distance. The White people might get startled by any outburst, but your people know when it's a bark of laughter or the cutting remark that's going to lead to fists. So from the corner, Yadi knew the loud voices were not a good sign. She rushed into the grocery store, already cursing her silly rebellion of not wearing real clothes outside. She *wasn't* a Columbia student, and now, when she needed her professional garb most, she wasn't ready.

The hullabaloo was at the self-checkout. Ant stood in front of a machine with a red light blinking above it. A store manager and security guard were on walkie-talkies. But despite their big gestures, it was Ant's incomprehensible stillness that caught her eye, that had her rush over and slide between him and the manager. She didn't ask what had happened. "Hey, hey. Ant. Look at me."

He slid his eyes over her but didn't respond. She took his hand in hers. "Hey, you're okay."

He was still silent.

The manager was a thin man with a nasty porn mustache. "Actually, ma'am, he might not be. Security guard saw him struggling at the machine; we've been trying to talk to him for twenty minutes, but he won't respond."

She held Ant's face in her hands. Not looking at anyone else but him.

"He'd run the items several times. Turns out, he's trying to guess a pin on the card. Card isn't his. We've called the cops."

"It's mine. I gave him my card." She turned around, kept one of Ant's hands in hers. She swiped the card he'd been clinging to. Entered the four-digit code. The red light at the top of the machine went green. A receipt was spit out. The two cans of jalapeños were just under six dollars.

"He was just doing me a favor, and I forgot to give him the

pin." Yadi scooped up the items quickly. Still holding Ant's hand, she backed away from the manager and security guard. She tugged him hard; he seemed stuck, incapable of walking on his own. She bit back the desire to run.

They walked the block and a half in silence. She gripped the cans so tightly they bit into her palm, making an indentation that ached slightly when she went to insert the building key. She and Ant walked upstairs hand in hand. When they entered the apartment, Ant walked straight to the couch. Dropped his head in his hands. She hovered in the doorway that led into the living room.

"Do you know how fucking long it took me to figure out that damn machine? And I was proud of myself. Like a fucking little kid for scanning it right, finally, and placing it where it needed to go. Inserting your card right."

Yadi dropped the jalapeños. Joined Ant on the couch. She put her left hand in her lap, then on the back of the couch, then near his neck, but not quite.

Yadi had spent a majority of her life hunted by the feeling that not only was there something else she should be doing, but there was a better dream to be had. Her life felt small, simple, unadventurous. Her longings bored her with their prescriptiveness. She and her cousin might laugh at their mothers' grasp on the old ways, but they also had to admit that the women had flung themselves into new waters. They knew their own mettle because they'd proven it to themselves more than once. Yadi only knew that her own mettle was anemia-ridden if she possessed one at all. She'd been crushed time and again by the weight of living.

But Ant, in that particular moment, felt like the only thing she'd been put here to do. She let her hand fall where it wanted, right underneath his hairline. She took off his fitted and raised his face to meet hers. And she kissed him soft and slow like the first time they'd kissed under the staircase, like they'd just invented the notion of lips touching lips.

She knew this was not a dream. This time she was awake. Ant found the grooves in her hips, the hip dips she'd always hated, but that he'd told her even when he was young he loved because it felt like she had a place on her body made just for his grip. Despite the ways their bodies had changed, he seemed to have a homing device.

She'd been wet since this morning, since the dream, since the shower, and smelling the sweet clean scent of Ant turned her into someone else. She put his hands on her ass. Admiring his tentativeness but also unused to not jumping headfirst. She didn't want to stop and think. She didn't want a second of pause, to potentially allow logic to creep in. Doña Reina still used the same fabric softener; she'd closed her eyes and inhaled every single time the older woman had enveloped her in a hug. Now she would close her eyes and imagine this scent forever as Ant's calling to her.

She was madness incarnate, and with grasping fingers she undid the buttons on his shirt. Ant still hadn't said a word. She traced his chest, the hard muscles of his stomach. The hollow beneath his Adam's apple. She shoved him down and straddled him, lifting her skirt to make sure she could feel. To make sure he could too. She grabbed his hand and thrust it lovingly but firmly into her panties. His fingers skimmed the curls she usually kept low cut, but had left abandoned for a while. She did not let his silence undo her; she used language for them—*papi sí ahí yes*—as he finally dipped a finger into her slickness. Two. She rode his fingers, finding her own rhythm. Licking his neck. His breathing was hard.

Yadi like the way his hands touched her. Like she was a new woman to him. And of course, she must be. He hadn't hugged her hips in years. She'd gained weight in high school and was proud of being a well-fed vegan. She was a woman; veal might be tender, but an aged loin of lamb was seasoned and cured.

They broke away, both of them breathing hard. Ant took his hand from her, placing the wet fingers against her thigh, just covered by the skirt that had ridden up.

She eased off his lap and grabbed his hand, pulling him into her bedroom. He followed, and shook off his shirt. Undid his belt. She displayed herself, her juicy titties and thighs. She didn't wave him over or say a word. Simply touched her own body until his weight dipped the bed a bit. Until the scruff of his goatee scratched up her calf, her thigh, until his mouth touched the spot his hand had been.

Yadi did not want to ever go to sleep. She wanted to wring out every moment of lust, quench her thirst on the deluge. She rose over him, for the third time that night. They were both spent, but this last time had an edge to it. She Kegeled the fuck out of him. His fingernails bit hard into her ass. When she finally tucked her face into his neck, sweat and tears were pooled there. And Yadi knew they'd earned their fair share of both.

She let him drift off to sleep, his hands still on her waist as if trying to hug her to him. She eased away. Threw on an old college shirt and socks. In the kitchen, she made toast, squeezed a bit of lime into her coffee. She ate standing up.

Ant slept an hour or two more. By the time he joined her in the kitchen, she'd bathed and was already halfway through roasting jackfruit. Ant must have sensed her mood. How incapable she was of speaking. He picked up his shirt from where she'd flung it and left the apartment.

It was four a.m., and her mother was still at Tía Camila's. Yadi took the opportunity to make two kinds of rice, salting the water for both but adding aromatic saffron, annatto, and diced onions to the second pot, with some softened pigeon peas.

On the garbanzo beans that she'd bathed in olive oil and harissa the night before, she dusted Mediterranean oregano; removed the pits of fat black olives and chopped them up. She worked at such speed that the next recipe instruction outpaced her thoughts.

She made ensalada rusa, the violent-colored beets and carrots and potatoes tossed together with a tahini sauce instead of the traditional mayo.

She whisked a sauce of maple syrup and coconut aminos, chili flakes, and lime, and grilled thin slabs of tempeh that resembled flank steak when they were done.

She made a feast before the sun had risen, before anyone in the apartment building had woken to greet this particular Saturday. She sampled condiments and bites of zested garnishes and sun-dried tomatoes and adjusted for salt, and umami, and whether or not something needed more avocado oil.

Her hands stained with beet juice and fingernails smelling of garlic, her mouth having tested and tasted enough for her to be able to say she'd eaten both breakfast and lunch, Yadi finished almost every dish that was needed to serve the wake.

And still. Yadi se quedó con el sabor en la boca, her tastebuds unresolved.

THE WAKE

II

I had fallen asleep alone the night before, and when I woke, Jeremiah's side of the bed had no impression; he'd never crawled in beside me. He kept a daybed in his basement studio and sometimes passed out there while mulling over his latest piece of art. But I knew that last night's distance had been a conscious choice.

The sun shone through the blinds in such a way that I knew it wasn't quite eight yet. I stretched and rolled over to Jeremiah's side of the bed. It smelled like him. I inhaled deeply.

The front door slammed downstairs and I listened, attempting to figure out whether he was coming or going. His footsteps confirmed he was returning from the gym. I heard the sweaty socks slop against the floor we'd just had refinished. Jeremiah was an early-morning-workout devotee.

He walked into the room, his soaked T-shirt stripped from his body and balled in his hand. He tossed it into the hamper. I took in his lean, hard body. He clipped thumbs into his shorts; they were the kind that had the briefs sewn in, and so he was soon standing naked.

"Morning, handsome." I threw it out like a fishing line, hoping the bait might attract a reluctant prize.

He nodded. "You had a good time last night?"

I sat up in bed, the sheets falling down below my breasts.

Jeremiah wasn't going to make this easy, so I decided neither would I.

I brushed my hair back from my face. "Listen, last night, I might have come on strong. But sometimes it feels like I'm the only one trying to grow a family."

Jeremiah shook his head. "You're definitely the only one letting wanting to grow a family ruin the one you already have."

I tugged the sheet back up, new course of action. One needs armor for battle, and my tits were getting cold. "That's not fucking fair."

"Maybe not. But is it true?"

I shook my head. "I don't think so. I love you."

"You also love filthy porn." He walked into the bathroom.

I stood too now, following him in. I willed the blush that was creeping up my neck to recede. Maybe my relationship with pornography was complicated, but I wouldn't let Jeremiah or anyone make it uglier than it felt in the moments it didn't feel good.

"Fuck that. You not gonna make little of me for how or what I desire." *Make little* was a phrase I picked up from Jeremiah, and there's nothing like throwing a jab using a borrowed colloquialism. "If I'm alone in wanting a different future for us, then just let me know."

Jeremiah shook his head, connecting his phone to the bathroom's ventilator speaker.

"Please don't be passive-aggressive," I mumbled.

"I'm just trying to shower in peace." But his music selection said otherwise.

And I forced myself to listen to it. The playlist of songs that said what he couldn't. With each track I counted down, eleven hours and fifty-seven minutes until the wake. Eleven hours and fifty-three minutes until the wake . . .

FLOR

walked into the hair salon and scanned for Patricia. She was the only person who knew how to get her hair flips exactly right; yes, Ona had suggested an updo, but Flor preferred a different frame for her face. She blinked a couple of times, hoping she didn't look as tired as she felt. She'd dreamt all night of her last visit to her mother's house. Except in her dreams, the white-bodied, red-headed snake kept calling to her, chanting her name.

She looked around for the salon owner and finally asked the young girl sweeping hair off the floor if the woman had stepped out. The girl stopped midmovement, leaning against the broom, the dust she'd piled a nice, neat pyramid at her feet. She looked Flor up and down, and Flor stiffened, tipping her chin just a fraction of an inch.

"¿Patricia, se encuentra?" She repeated herself.

"She's not in today. She called in sick. Luz-Mari at the front chair can probably fit you in."

Flor bit down on her tongue to stop from cursing. It didn't work. "Coño."

She looked around and sucked her teeth. None of the other salonists were worth the money. She knew her hair would begin frizzing in exactly an hour if she let one of these other women go at it. Patricia had a different kind of skill than most; her arms were strong, muscled from the effort of pulling a comb through thick hair and rolling it just so. These other girls were young, soggy-biceped, and she would not be made to look a clown at her own event.

She took her leave. She called Yadi. Her niece did Pastora's hair, and she would do in a pinch.

Yadi said she could do her hair in thirty minutes, and so Flor took care of the last task she'd meant to get to: she began taking down picture frames from the walls. The last one she removed was from her wedding day.

Flor had never loved her husband the way she'd felt desire for the church, and later, her intense infatuation for her cousin Nazario. But she'd grown to enjoy being admired and desired by Pedro. Pedro had approached her like a strong breeze through an open doorway, unexpected, soft on the skin even if it did scatter a few things to the ground.

She'd met her husband the old-school way: he moved into the apartment across the street. As was the Capital-eño style back then, he was fit, belted, his hair cut short, and his face clean-shaven. She'd adored his mouth first, the curve of his lips. His quick humor and manners. He had not been a heavy drinker then. Instead, would laugh at the folks who overimbibed and then stumbled out of the corner bar past their stoop. "Unprincipled," he called them.

It took a few weeks of fumbling. Flor was lucky to have married a man who was of the streets enough to know his way around a body but also someone who understood the gentleness of her sexual upbringing. Not that she didn't know the mechanics; she grew up among horses and pigs and stray dogs, and mammal coupling was not new. She actually understood procreation in the most essential of ways. But the way that her human body worked? That was a different story entirely.

She was skittish. Her husband would touch an ankle and she would flinch. He kissed her stomach, her thigh, but she would squeeze her legs tight before he could kiss anywhere else, you feel me? She was a human and humans were proper, but sex was improper in its odors and moisture and chafing.

One night several weeks after their wedding, Pedro showed up with a book. It had anatomical depictions of human bodies, and he opened a page to show the vagina in intimate detail. It was a medical rendering, but enough to make Flor blush and push the book away. Pedro took her hand and opened back to the page he'd been trying to show her.

"This is your clitoris," he told her calmly. The word, *creta*, has a rough sound to it. It requires the tongue to just barely brush the roof of the mouth before pushing the sound open past the teeth. Flor whispered it to herself.

She'd never known pleasure this way, the kind that hurts, that stretches the limits of what's possible in a body. Her husband and she fought, and he'd leave, and they'd give each other the silent treatment, but their coupling wasn't one of her complaints. Even now, she remembered him as being a tiger in bed.

They'd been good together, she and Pedro. Except when he

drank. Flor had never seen her father consume to excess, and although Pedro had been a serious sort when they'd first met, his time in the United States had loosed his self-discipline. But it was more of an erosion than a complete removal of who he'd been. It was through slow drips of the bottle. And when he'd only been an alcoholic who liked sneaking porn late at night, that'd been horrible, but understandable. He was a man.

A man she handed her check over to weekly, as they'd discussed when they were first married. All money was going toward building a house in DR, a place they could live when they retired, a place where they could die on the soil that had borne them. Week after week, year after year, Flor handed over checks. She'd never thought to check the accounts. Her husband was slowly becoming a drunkard, that was true, but he had never been a thief.

It was not Pastora with her sense of fibs who learned of it. Of all the sisters, it was quiet Matilde, out dancing with her husband one night, who saw him at a club buying round after round at the bar. He'd always been a generous man, but Pedro's excess began to call attention.

She asked to see the deposit stub, one Friday before she gave him her check from the button factory. Work was slowing down, and buttons were being adhered to cloth por allá, far from the warehouses of Queens. She wanted to plan for what might be an inevitable shutdown, and although Flor had a rough figure of how much they had saved, she wanted a more scrupulous calculation.

He balked as if she'd spit on his mother's grave. He sputtered with rage. "What? You don't trust me? I finished accounting school, not you. Qué burla, tú preguntándome a mí to give you an accounting." She knew men had fragile egos. And in that first decade of marriage, she didn't like to give offense where none had been warranted. And a man being generous with his check and with his friends hardly required her to look at the books.

The news at the factory spread the way it often did, hearsay from the manager's office down to the lowly workers in just a few days. The company had lost another major contract. There was button sewing being done faster and more efficiently *and cheaply* elsewhere. Which Flor couldn't even fathom, since her check was hardly enough to cover the transportation to get to work, and a little bit to set aside for groceries and the DR dream house. And still, she'd stretched that little bit. Dreaming of a home back where the pineapple groves were.

She went to the bank in person on a Saturday while Pedro slept off a hangover. She took Ona with her and left the girl to sit in the lobby with one of her books. The account was in both their names, and the clerk she spoke with passed over the stub, his eyebrows high. She remembered how she'd shaken her head. Asked to speak with a manager, who printed out transactions for the last three years. The withdrawals outpaced the deposits five to one.

He'd lost it all. Fifty thousand dollars that they'd saved over the course of twelve years. I mean, Ona had been what, ten at the time when Flor found out? And to add insult to injury, not only had all of their savings vanished, but the damn man had put them in almost an equal amount of credit card debt. Flor could not see through to the other side. She hadn't wanted to tell Ona, who was only a child, why she couldn't visit DR that summer as promised; she certainly hadn't been able to tell her siblings, who would whisper and shake their heads; even Samuel would tsk-tsk the indiscretion and lack of monetary discipline. Flor took on a second job and became the head of the accounts.

———

Which reminded Flor, she'd stopped putting all her money in a savings account years ago. The pictures on the walls could wait; Ona would take care of those. What she needed to do was find the scattered Benjamins she'd secreted in hidey-holes and under the pots and pans.

YADI

answered the door and just managed to stifle a groan. If Tía Flor heard it, she'd take it personally. But Yadi hadn't yet gathered herself from the events of the night before. She kept expecting Ant to come back at any second, to try and talk. And she hadn't yet sifted through her words, picking out the wrinkled ones, discarding them, finding the ones that wouldn't leave her tongue feeling empty. She'd found the picture from her senior class formal on her nightstand. He'd brought it the night before. She could make out the oil of a thumbprint that must have pressed against her pixelated face time and time again. He really had kept it near him.

She needed time to think. Not only had her aunt only given her a month to complete a catering job for over a hundred people, then been up her ass daily changing the menu, then asked her to do her hair *on the day of the event*, but she'd never considered that Yadi might have her own woes to baby. Yadi knew she was being bitchy, but it was only in her head, so fuck it.

Tía smiled as if she could hear her thoughts and was amused by the havoc.

Yadi unwrinkled her forehead. Her aunt was inordinately proud of her hair, and she'd kept it shoulder length for as long as Yadi could remember.

"Oí que Anthony había regresado," Tía said.

Yadi nodded, gesturing to the chair he'd sat in last night. She already had the blow-dryer plugged in. "You saw him?"

"Un pajarito por ahí me contó," Tía said.

Yadi didn't know how to respond. The little birdie could be her mother, could be Ona, could be Tía Flor's own dreams with their omens.

"Y tú, how do you feel?" her aunt asked.

Yadi smirked behind her aunt's head. She sounded just like Ona, always asking how people felt about things. Yadi didn't know. Her body felt things, sick, her hands carried a slight tremble, her mind unable to run the list of "should've's" as pertained to the night before, but none of those factored into feelings.

"Triste," she answered finally. She ran the comb through her aunt's hair. Put that in her aunt's lap. Picked up the big comb.

Her aunt nodded, dislodging a lock of hair Yadi was working on. Yadi started back from the top, making sure to work gingerly. Her tía had never complained, but Yadi knew she was tenderheaded. Her grandmother had once told her how Tía used to cry when getting plaits on Sunday morning.

"It's sad. He had an entire life ahead of him. And still could. But it is sad. All of it." Tía Flor rolled the loose strands that had been choked onto the comb into a little ball.

Yadi released a breath, picked up another clump of hair. Rolled the brush through. Over the loud hum of the blow-dryer, she announced, "We had sex."

Of all her tías, Tía Flor was the prudest, recta to a level where even her own sisters were wary of her censure. The wannabe nun in the family layered a gravitas to even frivolous things; Yadi had not begrudged Ona needing to navigate her mother's strictures. But for some reason, she felt like she needed to confess. Like someone needed to know. Absolution needed to be proffered.

Her aunt pulled away from her hand. Turned to look at her. Yadi turned off the blow-dryer. Waited.

"And . . . how do you feel?"

Yadi laughed, holding the brush up. "I was wondering the same thing before you called me. I have no idea. Were we taught to feel in words?"

Her aunt patted her face, firm with affection. "Ay ya ya."

Yadi nodded. Enough was right. She would not shed tears.

"You were safe?" Tía's question was a quiet one. Yadi nodded.

Now her aunt smiled. "Bueno, probably for the best. You two used to sniff each other like dogs in heat. Who knows what a lifetime of what-ifs would have done to your mind? You know, that kind of stress is bad for your intestines."

It was an inane remark, but said with such sincerity Yadi could only nod. Maybe there was something to be said for having shared what she had with Ant. She turned the blower back on.

She must have let some of her inner conflict lead her hand, because her aunt winced.

"I'm sorry," she said, placing fingers on her aunt's shoulder. "I know your head isn't one for jalones."

Her aunt's laughter raised the funk that'd been blanketing the room. "Me? Este caco is hard as a brick." Her aunt knocked on her skull. "Pull more. The one who used to cry and try to cover her head was your mother. She was always more feral thing than girl. I was reacting to a memory."

Well, that wasn't what Yadi had expected to hear. None of it. Maybe none of them had given Tía Flor enough credit for the ways she had changed in her later years. Maybe Yadi had never fully trusted enough of the older women to ever confide and prove they weren't who she thought them to be. She continued section by section, pulling and curling, and shifting each strand into place.

"There, you look beautiful. Let me just pin the ends." She used her fingers to curl and slide a bobby pin onto the tips of her aunt's hair so it would look just as fresh this evening.

Her aunt patted her hand. "You're a good girl, Yadi. Remember that. You're good."

And then her aunt paused. Took a deep breath. "Can I tell you a story? You've been back home, so you know, you can picture it."

Yadi glanced at her watch. She still needed to get all the food into trays, pack up the chafing dishes, and recount the table linens, but as it was, she'd be scrambling to get herself and the food trays ready in time to get them over to the hall before everyone arrived. The list of things she still had left to do must have nestled onto her brow, or maybe she hesitated too long to respond. Her aunt smiled and stood. As if in concert, a knock sounded on the door. Ant's knock.

"Another time. No te apures. You have a lot to do. And enough to think about! Te veo ahorita, querida."

Yadi made murmurs, trying to encourage her aunt to tell her the story even as she walked her to the door. Her aunt hugged Ant tightly when she saw him. Patted his cheek. Neither Yadi nor Ant made a move as Tía Flor shut the door behind her with a soft snick.

Yadi knew Ant would want to talk. She heard the kitchen chair scrape the floor behind her and then the creak as he settled into it, and she walked to the stove.

"Look, Ant, what happened last night . . ."

She waited for him to jump in. When he didn't, she glanced up. He looked well rested, staring at the fingers he'd steepled onto the table.

She forged ahead. "It shouldn't have. We shouldn't have. It was. I felt, there was just . . ."

Many words could be applied to Yadi, but typically *inarticulate* wasn't one of them. She could hear her heart in her ears. She wiped her hands and grabbed the seat opposite Ant. She was no one's coward.

"I loved you when we were young, in the way first love be. I've loved people since you. I've fucked a lot of people since the days you and I talked about what it would be like. I don't know what last night was. The hang-up I'll need to decompress with my therapist for the next decade?" She tried a laugh. But when Ant still hadn't moved, she said what needed to be said. "It can't be more."

She watched his face closely. Was there hurt there? Disappointment? In the heat of the moment, she hadn't considered whether Ant had ever had sexual relations, if they'd been consensual, what his relationship to physical intimacy was. Then again, was there a level of arrested development she was assuming of him? The implications of the night before were different for them. She just didn't know how wide that difference yawned.

Ant's face didn't change an iota. He stood, nodding. "Got you. Did you still need help taking the trays to the hall?"

Yadi hated the phrase *lump in your throat*. It never felt quite that way to her, like a lump. It often felt more like the tears were trying to rush out and her defensive system quickly threw up a dam, the reservoir of tears preserved for another day when they'd be more necessary, when the deluge would serve an actual purpose. She'd not cried to or for Ant in a long time. And what good would it do to start now?

"Yes. Will you help me pack it all up?"

PASTORA

lifted the rolling gate in front of the store and turned the *Abierto* sign so it faced outward.

She loved working Saturday mornings best. It was always the quietest, as people slept in and strolled into the store after noon. The night before had been riveting enough that she could do with a contemplative morning. Flor had slept in the living room, and Pastora had heard her tossing and turning all night. She'd wanted to soothe her older sister, but she also knew it was best to leave Flor to her sleep; they each had their own process for finding truth. It'd always amazed Pastora she could tell so easily when someone lied to her, but she could lie to herself and nothing in her body even flinched. She'd greeted her sisters that morning, made a delicious mangú, sung in Camila's shower, and acted as if she was just fine, until Flor and Camila eased into the day with the night's tension behind them. But on the inside, she'd been a cluster of nerves. Matilde's husband was not her responsibility, but perhaps she should have held her sister with a gentler hand?

She'd been sitting behind the cash register organizing receipts when there was a jingle over the door. Even before she looked up, she knew it'd be Rafa's other woman. She'd had many things weigh on her heart before, but never the death of a pregnant lady. And she knew this confrontation would come in this life or the next. She searched her heart and found that she was glad the woman had not died.

The woman sat on the same display table she'd sat on the day before. They did not speak. Pastora walked around the register, leaned against the counter so they could see each other, woman to woman. Outside, a bird swooped in and out of the big tree that offered the storefront shade.

"You in good health?" Pastora asked.

The woman gave a sharp nod. "They gave me insulin. The baby, thankfully, is fine. I was dehydrated and something about fake contractions."

"And wearing a jacket that was much too thin. And you hadn't eaten since the evening before, and you were also so excited to rub my face into your belly, so I would run back and tell my sister, that in doing so your heart rate jumped. Dangerously so, apparently," Pastora said this all matter-of-factly.

The girl covered her look of surprise, turning her face into a mask of calm. Her right fist pressed onto her belly, a gavel at rest.

"Where are you from?" Pastora asked.

"La Romana," the young woman said.

Coastal, then. And east.

"And what do you want with a viejo? Pretty thing like you must have your pick." But Pastora already knew.

The young woman had her hair down today. It wasn't perfectly blow-dried; it must have been at least two weeks since it'd been straightened. Pastora could see the oiliness at the roots from where she stood.

"He's special. Took care of everything. *Takes* care of everything," the young woman said.

"Except getting you pregnant, apparently. Unless it was on purpose?" Pastora figured if the girl wanted her to know the dirty details, she would allow it.

Pastora went into the back and opened the employees' fridge. Don Isidro kept his fancy bottled water there. She grabbed two.

The young woman hadn't moved. "I know Rafa is from the capital, but your family isn't, right? I don't hear the airs of Santo Domingo."

Pastora walked over. Handed the woman one of the bottles. "We're country. All of us. From the landlocked center where the pineapple groves grow. Hills and valleys and trees, with birds abundant and colorful. This is a grayscale country."

"We're far from home," the young woman said.

"And closer than you could ever imagine." She opened her bottle of water. "Why are you here?"

"You know, I can hear you calling me a mujerzuela even though you never actually say it."

"*You know*, I've known women like you. Why. Are you. Here?"

"He says you know the truth of things. The other sister sees death. A third can find a remedy for anything. His own wife has nothing."

Pastora shook her head. "You're with a man who has never appreciated the everything of a wonderful woman. It is beyond him. And although it is not my domain, I can assure you, it is a slow death to love a man like that."

"I *do* love him."

Pastora nodded. This was true. She heard it.

"I love my child." The fist softened on the belly. Pastora cocked her head. The girl was not sure of her assertion.

"He's going to leave her. He told me so. I know he will."
Pastora shook her head. Even the girl's heart knew better.

The young woman bowed her head, began to cry in such a
way that the tears created little stains on the fabric taut around
her stomach.

"Is it his?" Pastora asked.

"Of course it is," the other woman answered.

Pastora cocked her head, raised a brow. "You two deserve
each other."

The woman didn't like that. Her right hand cradled her
stomach as she gestured with the water bottle.

"You're a fucking witch. I hope if you have a man, he leaves
your wrinkled and dry chocha for something warmer than you
can ever be." She struggled to stand, and Pastora crossed over,
put a hand at her elbow, which the girl yanked away as soon as
she was upright. She didn't like that Pastora knew, but Pastora
also felt the girl had wanted to confess.

There was a time for logic, and there was a time for peace.
"My husband is the prototype for all of God's molds. I never
doubted who and what I am to him, and, well, it may come as a
surprise, but I am an impossible woman to love. And yet."

Pastora raised a hand in the direction of the exit. "You got
what you came for. Let me walk you to the door."

I kept my eyes on the road as Jeremiah drove. We'd eaten breakfast silently. But with the wake approaching, I sensed a thawing in him. Sometimes it worked like this with us: we needed to push and tug, and give the other person room to organize their thoughts, and once that happened, the high emotions would wane. It didn't fix anything, but it allowed us to file our feelings into the right folders.

"Did your mom say anything about today? How she's feeling?" Jeremiah asked.

I shrugged. "Anytime I asked her about feelings she made this face at me," I said, pinching my lips in the corners as tight as I could.

Jeremiah laughed. "You're hard on her. And you tend to make her harder in your memory than she actually is."

I hated him being right, but I did often add twenty on ten when it came to how I received my mother's critique.

"I can't believe she hasn't said anything. She has to know you worry." Jeremiah rubbed my shoulder, his left hand still on the wheel.

My mother had done many odd things as pertained to her dreams, but this was beyond anything I had ever seen. I just hoped at some point tonight she would give us a date. What was the point of this entire thing if not to give us a heads-up on what was coming?

"She has a form-fitting dress she loves." I don't know why I brought up this fact. Perhaps as an example as to how this truly was a celebratory night? My prim vieja would not wear tight red to anything too morbid. She wasn't going to die right in front of us. I knocked on the little oak tree ornament Jeremiah kept attached to his mirror.

I hadn't understood why my mother needed something so elaborate. Sure, I had been the one to recommend the documentary on living wakes, but only because I perceived my mother as unswayable in her customs, and this was most certainly uncustomary. But Mami had been insistent that no, a dinner party was not enough. And that no, renting the building's basement was not good enough either.

We arrived in the city an hour later than the GPS had anticipated but were still early enough to help set up.

The hall was newly renovated, but cheaply so. That said, the ceilings were high. The purple-tinged chandeliers glittered brightly. It was the kind of place that looked gaudy when the fluorescent lights were on and the chairs stacked, but with the dim settings, the sparkly chandeliers, and the pretty tablecloths that hid the less savory aspects, it became an almost beautiful setting.

Yadi and Tía Mati set the trays of food on the serving table against the back wall. The eggplant fritters and the black beans cooked in coconut milk scented the air. Rolls of sourdough, quinoa and plantains, a plant-based feast for the ages began emerging when Ant brought in more trays from the hall's kitchen.

Jeremiah followed behind me with the huge peacock chair that Mami had ordered. Roses were laced through the wicker. We put that center stage, right between the big speakers.

Although the invite said seven p.m., it was almost eight thirty by the time people started trickling in.

The attire was the most astounding thing. No one knew what to wear to a *living* wake, and the dress code hadn't been specified. A second cousin from Jersey and his entire family rocked all black; his little twins even had tiny somber ties to match. A paternal cousin whose butt job was fresh and fabulous came as a Cardi B doppelganger, her skintight neon jumpsuit looking like it'd split open if she released even the littlest fart. Denim and damask, hair freshly pressed, hair washed-and-go'd, hair pinned into elaborate woven-in ponytails. The seating arrangement was usurped by an elaborate game of musical chairs as people sat according to the bottle of liquor set on the table instead of the name tags we'd spent the last hour arranging and rearranging. Of course the seating arrangement had been a battle royale. The aunties liked to play favorites. And we cousins liked to manage damage control.

Mami arrived at nine p.m. Her eyebrows were plucked prettily. She wore the red. The gown had a tail that swept along the crowded path between tables. She had a prime minister's touch when she kissed cheeks and cooed over babies. The folks who hadn't seen her in years (and had thusly been relegated to the back walls with cheap liquor, no swaps allowed) craned their necks trying to see her. They peered: was her skin sallow, did her bones look frail, what kind of sick was she?

But Mami smiled with her red-painted lips, and greeted those exiled cousins, too, her perfume lingering, as she asked how they were and answered that she, too, was doing well, thank God.

And I couldn't help wondering whether the sharp pain I felt in my gut was a fertilized egg implanting or the first sick realization that my mother might soon be gone.

FLOR

knew one could imagine an event a million times in one's mind, could create a timeline and execute it and still, the final result might leave one wanting.

At her own wake, she did not feel what she'd expected. She sat in her big chair, which was more uncomfortable than baby showers had led her to believe, and looked around the large salon space, taking in:

the nieces, seated closer than sisters, basically in each other's laps as they gossiped about family members

Ona, her beautiful girl, holding hands with her beloved under the table as she took a sip from his tumbler, unknowing that even now she was preparing to grow another heart in her body

her brother, Samuel, sat with his wife and two daughters, both of whom were showing late signs that they had otherworldly inclinations—freshly culled blood from the beyond—but their mother was evangelical in her approach to religion and would not allow any of the aunts to try to guide the women

the flowers were exceptional, Camila was not only good at picking greenery for teas and tinctures, she was also good at setting this spotted petal next to that vibrant one and cutting the stems so that bouquets stood like squat, happy watchmen in the middle of the table, but several blooms dropped, and the arrangements included carnations, which Flor had specifically requested *not* be in any of the bouquets

Ona's DJ cousin from her father's side had been given a playlist, but instead of Flor's old favorites and the songs she'd spent long evenings finding the names of and having Camila Google, the cousin had chosen to treat this like a stranger's gig and kept sneaking in hits from the current era; it seemed a DJ could not resist trying to get people on the dance floor, even if the explicit request was to get Flor prepared for what she had to say

the little ones, the children of the children of second and third cousins, ran through the hall, the sashes at their waists long since untied, the straps holding their dresses up dangling off shoulders, they were encased but freeing themselves in their exuberance

She had not wanted a somber affair. This was what she'd hoped for, she reminded herself. But she'd expected to feel full, to feel light, to be able to walk up to the podium, her dress carving through the crowd, and tell the people who loved her—yes, her family, and also the local priest, the corner store owner, the two neighbors she'd known since she'd first moved to the city, all the people who'd made up the little world she occupied—the truth, the final truth, and she found that as always, she could not do that. She'd wanted the last hurrah before she left to be triumphant. But for the first time, she admitted to herself that she was scared to leave the cacophony of her family's laughter and bickering and the sunlight and moonshine and enveloping darkness of closing her eyes, and the bright green of the first new leaves in the spring, and the pure white of a first snow before her shoe left its imprint, and the big wonder and warmth of love love love love

                                             and yet, we must.
She stood, and the DJ cued the lights.

PASTORA

straightened in her seat when Flor finally stood from her elaborate wicker chair. The sisters had been chortling that Flor thought herself somebody's president the way she sat and waved and was waited on, but then again, Flor hadn't asked for anybody's handout. She'd paid for this whole thing with her own pension monies, and who were they to say anything if what she chose to spend that on was a cushioned seat and a personal server? They said these things although Pastora's left leg hadn't stopped jiggling all night, and Matilde kept playing with the rings on her hands, and Camila had folded and refolded her napkin so that the edges were completely tattered, and they'd yet to even eat.

When Flor got up and walked to the mic, Pastora ignored all the eyes that swung *her* way. Anyone who was in the know looked to her, not to Flor. They watched her face, trying to see the truth of this entire affair. Pastora closed her eyes.

"Thank you all for being here. I know this is rather untraditional," Flor began. "But I appreciate you accompanying me on this night. It is a party, yes, but I hope it is also an opportunity for us to celebrate in the moments we have shared with each other. Some of us see each other daily; some people here I have not seen in decades. I could not gather every single person I have known throughout my life, but I tried my best to bring together on such short notice the ones who have taught me my favorite lessons on being a ser humano.

"A couple of weeks ago, I had a dream."

It was as if someone had flicked a switch wired to all of their lungs; the room's collective breath seemed to stop. What would someone do if Flor fell out right there? Or if she announced the when and how of it? Unease crept into the silence.

"I had a dream that someone died." Flor was struggling through her speech. Pastora knew she'd written and rewritten it this week. Not letting anyone read it but complaining time and again that she was uninspired. But although she held sheets of paper in her hands, she did not glance down at what she wrote. The pause grew long, then it grew awkward. Somewhere a parent hushed a child who wanted to get off their lap and go back to running.

Camila, who was seated next to Pastora, began to cry. Yadi, sitting at the front, clasped Ona's hand. A sob broke into the room.

"I . . . I . . ." Flor's voice choked, the mic so close to her mouth that the sob she attempted to pull back instead echoed into the room, more eerie for being unfinished.

Pastora stood. She walked through the beaming lights to the podium where her sister was and placed a soft hand on her shoulder. Matilde was the next one to make the walk, wrapping her hand around Flor's middle, giving her dancer's strength to her younger sibling. Camila was followed closely by Yadira. They made a pyramid of their bodies, holding her up.

Ona stood last, gesturing at Samuel to sit with his wife, who was attempting to pull him down beside her. He shook her off.

Worked his way to the side of the room. Not with his sisters and nieces, but alongside them, at least.

Ona walked toward her mother, and when she reached the side of the podium, she took Flor's face in her hands. Kissing her softly on each cheek, so close to the sisters who had not let go that Pastora could smell the floral perfume at her neck and the Johnnie Walker on her breath. Ona grabbed her mother's hand, holding it across Matilde's body, which still held on to her sister's waist. They looked out at the crowd, the lights too bright to see anything except for each other in their peripheral view.

The silence in the room set on their skin. Flor cleared her throat. A newfound determination rippled through her.

"I prayed to God. I attempted to barter. It is not the first time I've done so. I've mourned by myself more times than I can count. For people I knew, for people I didn't know well. Their lives and their life's ending revealed. I've learned how to let the grief crash on top of me, how to release myself to the waves.

"I have not learned much. I thought I was getting old despite my heart being young, but when I had this dream, I realized no one is ever old enough. We are here, embodied to experience life, and then we are not. I cannot say what I came here to say. But I am trying to remind myself, you should not be afraid of dying. The Divine does not live in fear, and the godly lives in each one of us. This is one journey, and beyond this there is another. There is no veil between this world and that one. They are the same world, the one before, this one, the one that comes next, a string of pearls, ends tied so tightly you cannot feel the knot that binds.

"Some of you wish for me to tell you the behind the scenes of what I've seen. You want to know of the infinite. But I don't know that part. Only the right-*before* the afterlife. What I know is that the day of my dream will come. And the future will be unknown again. Today we are here. And I did not want this event to be one to mourn. It is a party for a reason. Every end is the stage for a beginning. Thank you, each of you, for making the life I lived feel full."

And then Flor smiled, and as if on cue, all her women let her go. She walked regally to her seat. And the ladies trailed behind her, stopping to kiss her on the cheek before returning to their table. Other family members stood, inspired by the moment, and walked to Flor and kissed her cheek or hand, had their little ones ask for blessings. One by one each guest stood. It was unclear what ceremony they were engaging in. It was not a goodbye, or a thank-you; there were no questions asked, the only sounds introductions of family members who'd not met Flor. It was a ritual of acknowledgment. *We see you, you were here, and when you go . . . we'll remember.*

After the last guest gave Flor a tight hug, she seemed to innately know she'd looked into the face of every person in the room. Flor held up a beringed hand to the DJ, who cued up a salsa song.

The sisters looked to Pastora. "But what does it mean? What does it mean? What did you hear?"

Pastora looked to Ona, who gazed at her mother, Jeremiah's arm tight around her shoulders.

"I do not know what she means," Pastora lied. "Let's eat, and dance, and be alive. That is what she asked us to do, and the crowd will follow the family."

But when the family dispersed to the bar and dance floor, Pastora made her way to Flor. From the pocket of her sequined jumpsuit she took out a little jewelry box, passing it to her sister, who sat like royalty in her chair.

"¿Y esto? San José?" Flor said, lifting up the little saint medallion from where it'd nestled for decades. "El patrón de la familia."

Pastora felt her throat close up but she forced her hand to open. To unclasp the chain and secure it around her sister's neck. "The patron saint of many things, as you well know, querida. And yes, of family too."

YADI

stacked the trays away. Tía Matilde was currently in deep conversation with her husband, so Yadira's mother was the one helping her clean up the serving line. There was not a single grain of rice or quinoa-stuffing crumb left. Yadi had sprinkled lime zest, and juice, and even cut slices that she used for decoration, and people had not only gotten firsts and seconds and thirds, they kept looking sadly in the direction of the hall's kitchen as if more trays of food might be coming. Yadi liked to think that because of her, the ghost of Mamá Silvia had been at the wake too.

"She'll never learn." Her mother's voice was resigned. She looked at her mother, unclear whether as an only child she was missing some profound understanding of sisterhood, but she didn't think so.

"Mami, she's grown. She knows what the deal is, and she chose him. Why are you trying to save someone who is fine where she is?"

Yadi wanted to kick herself for all the words she didn't know in Spanish: *enabler, boundaries, self-worth.* She loved her aunt beyond reason. And many had been the day when she'd wished she was Matilde's kid, but her aunt had a weakness for the man she'd married, and that's not the kind of thing you can loosen from a person. She'd yoked herself time and again despite what she knew. Yadi opined that even if Tía Mati walked in on the man having a threesome with his newly pregnant girlfriend, cameras on as they live streamed to OnlyFans, Tía still might not know how to leave. Removing yourself from someone was a lesson too few of them had learned. And, Yadi wanted to argue, maybe Tía shouldn't. Tía Matilde was comfortable, her man helped with the bills, she never went to a party alone. For sure Tía Matilde was the eldest sister, but she drank green smoothies every day and danced every night, and if anyone was going to make it to their centennial, it was Tía Matilde. She'd need a man who'd defied odds by her side. They'd had this argument often, Yadi and Pastora. The one where Yadi told her mother to mind her business and where Pastora replied that family was not about commerce.

"I want her to love herself more than she loves him. She is cherished everywhere but at home, and it is there she keeps returning." Her mother's voice had fallen a decibel, as if she was reciting a musing she repeated to herself often. Yadi left off stacking a tray and reached out to squeeze her mother's hand.

"Tía Flor just reminded us that even a long life is too short. You miss Papi. You're less entremetida when he's around."

Her mother's laugh was like rehearing her first lullaby, and Yadi smiled in return.

"You're right. I do miss him, and he does keep me almost too busy to be too worried about you all. But it's in me to worry. The world is full of so many lies, especially the ones we tell ourselves." And now her mother was looking straight at her.

The salsa song that came on disrupted their conversation. This was one of the classics, of the variety of songs that the cousins had all been raised listening to, the kind of song that immediately had the aunts declaring where they'd been and what they'd been wearing when they first heard it. The trumpet swept in first, the welcome sign of sound. Then Joe Arroyo's narrative singing, the pause where the trombone replied as if it had thoughts about enslavement too.

Yadi and her mother watched as at their table Rafa put his hand out and Matilde took it. And fuck, fuck him, but the man knew how to dance. Even now at this ripe old age where most men were using VapoRub daily and doing hip stretches, the man swiveled like a well-oiled office chair. And Matilde was transcendent.

"Is that his only redeemable quality?" Yadi asked her mother.

"He's a narcissist. Matilde knows it; she just thinks she can praise him out of it, or outwait his entitlement."

Matilde spun, her eyes landing on Yadi, and she winked. Yadi felt her heart well with all the love her aunt deserved.

"I quit my job today," her mother said. Now that everything was stacked and neatly in bins and bags, she stood at Yadi's elbow.

Yadi took her eyes off Tía Mati. "What? You love your job."

"I love being busy. But I'm tired of trying to sell cheap clothes to sad women. If you ever need help at the making of batidas, I have a free schedule."

"You'd prefer selling mixed fruit and pastelitos to sad men? You'll smell like coconut and frying oil every day. And there's not even a lick of meat at the cafetería."

Her mother smirked. "I'll smell like I put sweat into a dream my daughter built. And I won't have to talk to as many people. Just tell them to point at the menu."

Yadira laughed. Her mother would never not be able to talk to people. But her mother was offering a kind of invitation, and although she didn't reply, she accepted the request.

Her mother patted her on the shoulder and made her way to the bar.

Couples had flooded the dance floor, but although Rafa and Matilde didn't occupy the center, they still owned the spotlight. She twirled, right leg swinging out on the three count. While Rafa took a turn, Matilde shimmied on her own, her hand in his a second later, although Yadi would swear on everything that there'd never even been a moment where his hand had beckoned or hers had had time to respond; the moves were almost telepathic. Slowly the couple moved to the middle, the chandeliers now glittering above them. Rafa always found a way to be the star.

"She's an incredible follower," a voice said at her shoulder. She turned to see Kelvyn.

Yadi smiled at him. "You decided to come. I'll have to introduce you to my aunt. She'll be tickled you were curious about her wake."

"I met your aunt." But he was still looking at Tía Matilde.

A fast twirl on the dance floor grabbed their attention. A couple near Rafa and Matilde had been trying to shimmy while holding their drinks, and one of them had splashed across the bodice of Tía Matilde's green dress.

"Oh shit."

Tío Rafa was berating the young couple, his arms in the air, his wife's honor at the forefront even as his wife was forgotten. Yadi looked around for tissues, but the closest ones were at the bar, which had a legion of people in front of it. It was Kelvyn who grabbed a pack of tissues from his pocket—ancestors preserve a well-prepared man—and was at Matilde's side before any of the family could be. Yadi couldn't see her face, but she took a tissue and patted her chest, returning it to Kelvyn when he held his hand out. The tissues he threw onto a nearby empty table, but then his hand was held out again. He took one step, two steps, three, until they were in the center of the dance floor. Yadi watched as Rafa's tirade sputtered to a stop. Yadi looked for her mother. *I wish she could see you now, Tía!*

If anyone expected Tía Matilde to be shy, they didn't know the whole of her. The thing music did to her blood, because she *was* an incredible follower. Kelvyn barely touched her hip before she was on a fast spin out; his fingers brushed a shoulder and she knew there was going to be a direction change. What he lacked of Rafa's charisma, he made up through the athleticism of a man who'd learned to two-step before he'd learned to walk. They held each other not with the same comfort as Tía and her husband, but still with a familiarity that compelled almost everyone around them to watch. They danced as if they'd been partnered for decades, performing steps that weren't usually done at family parties as they were more of the professional variety: big leg sweeps, and shoulder shimmies that punctuated the big horns echoing in the hall. This was a showcase of ballroom salsa, made for the center stage.

Yadi watched as Rafa began to take umbrage at the fact that his wife was the center of attention, his brows dipped, his chest puffed. A circle of people had surrounded the dancing couple and were watching, clapping. Rafa broke through the circle, headed toward his wife, but Kelvyn was a lead who saw when it was time to change direction, and he spun Matilde out so she could take a solo. Matilde, eyes closed, twirled. She danced on her own, Susie-Qing and sliding a leg through the slit of her skirt. She popped her hips back, her hands styling in ways Yadi had never seen. *She's been holding back all these years.* Her aunt had an entire arsenal of moves she'd known how to make on her own, but had probably never wanted to outshine her husband. But now, she gifted herself the entire dance floor, the air in front and beside her; her hips swung in circles as she took the beat on double time.

And then, because she'd never been a come sola, she opened her eyes and beckoned her sister Flor, who shyly shook her head. But Matilde was not to be deterred, she grabbed her sister by the hand, pulled her from the wicker chair and spun her; she was the lead now. Flor laughed, typically not one to dance, but Matilde knew how to turn her and guide her so her movements were passable. She gave her three more circles before she let her go, grabbing Camila's hand next. They shimmied there, at the edge of the circle, each taking a spin at the exact same time as if they'd practiced that in front of the mirror before, and indeed, Tía Camila told us later, they had often danced together when she'd been a child, Matilde her only companion.

Pastora had left the bar to watch her sisters dance. And although she was smiling, she also seemed hesitant when she caught her sister's eye. As if Tía Matilde wouldn't reach out for her.

Using both hands to beckon her sister to her, Tía Matilde never lost the five, six, seven of her steps. She clasped Pastora's hands in hers, and since Pastora wasn't one to be demure, she strode onto the dance floor. She shook a hip right. She shook a hip left. None of it was particularly on beat. Matilde let go of a laugh that jangled above the music. If one could joke through dance steps, that's what the two sisters did, creating a world of movement unto themselves. When their hands finally joined, the beat had slowed down and their rhythm did too.

And they closed out the dance with Matilde dancing Pastora in intricate figure eights, both laughing at the sheer absurdity of this night, of this life.

Tía Matilde seemed to be made of spun magic. Yadi had of course seen her dance before, and for as long as she'd been alive, Tía had been level expert, but the show she put on tonight was as if she'd been Godtouched to do this very thing.

The music finally stopped, the seven-minute song ending on a long wail from the sax. The sisters clumped together, still laughing, breathing hard.

Tía Flor grabbed a folded napkin and dabbed at her cleavage, leaning over to wipe the sweat off Matilde's brow.

They broke apart when the next song began, Pastora to the dance floor with Junior, Tía Flor in the direction of the restroom. Tía Matilde came to stand next to Yadi, leaving her husband looking bewildered behind her. Kelvyn had grabbed a seat, his eyes never leaving her aunt.

"No dancing for you? The cooking tired you out?" Tía Matilde asked.

Yadi smiled, put her arm through her aunt's. "If I can't dance like you, I don't want to dance at all."

"Well, you need to add some seasoning to your steps, and that only comes with age."

Yadi laughed. But she caught sight of Ant entering the ballroom with his mother on his arm. She turned away quickly, gazing out the windows. Tía set a hand on her arm.

"You don't have to have everything figured out, you know?"

Yadi laughed. "How did you know I'm ready to have a conniption?"

"Your mother has been ready to have a heart attack since she heard he was back. She's worried what it will mean for you. So I can only imagine what you're feeling. Maybe talking to your old therapist might help?"

Yadi nodded. Her therapist had been helpful. To the point that even these women, so shy when talking about mental health, understood that Yadi would always need a professional to anchor her heart to mind.

"You're right. It is a pretty big deal."

Tía patted her on the arm. "Oh, I may not know much about living my own life, but I'm smart for others. And I know the heart is a burial ground for memories that shame and hurt. You can visit and place flowers there and make it a tomb. Or let those things act as fertilizer and pay no homage."

Yadi teared up at the metaphor, so apt for a pair of country girls. "As soon as you said that, all I could think of was the breeze between Mamá's lime trees."

"Maybe that is where you should go do your thinking?" Tía Matilde kissed her on the temple.

"It would feel like running away again. I can't always just leave to DR when things are too hard."

Her aunt shook her head. Guided her to a seat. "My feet are old. Do me the favor and sit with me."

They took chairs at a table scattered with white plastic cups, a baby's clear sippy cup of soda the only one still full. "Would it be running away? Or would it be like those migrating birds, or salmon, who go to where they were born for the season that requires homing? Where better than home to grieve?"

"What do I have to grieve? No one has died."

Matilde nodded. "You've been grieving for a long time. Maybe you need to go home to be finished with grief. Maybe Anthony's return is really an opportunity to close that door."

"The house was sold when Mamá died. Mami told me so."

Tía nodded. "Yes. And as the person who bought out all of my siblings' shares, I am saying you can stay there. It will be yours when I die anyway."

Yadi waited for her aunt to say she was joking. But the woman only continued. "I can run the shop for a while."

They squeezed hands. Yadi did weep then, into her aunt's shoulder, crying for everything she'd lost, and for everything she'd always had.

I

stepped outside onto the hall's terrace after Mami's speech. Music blasted every time the door opened and a couple stumbled out to get some air, but the night was chilly and few people stayed out as long as me. It wasn't much of a view, but I could see straight down Grand Concourse, the line mile of stores and restaurants and flags, an array of color.

The door slid open behind me, and I waited for another cousin or neighbor, but it was Jeremiah's hands that landed on my shoulders.

"You all right, O?"

I turned my head to kiss the knuckles on his right hand. Little spots of crimson dotted the back of his hand from where he'd been spray-painting a backdrop.

"Just thinking about life and death, you know, lighthearted things." I didn't realize how cold I felt until the warmth of his body beckoned.

"Let's just be us." Jeremiah said it quietly, but with the assuredness with which he said most things.

"What do you mean?"

"I can't do anything about the death thing, but about life? What if we put a bit less pressure on a baby? Let's stop trying. Let's stop expecting to expect. For a bit, let's be us. Ona and Jeremiah. For now, do we need more than that?"

I wanted to scream. Yes, yes, we did. Who would take care of us when we grew old? And who would my mother spoil? And what would I do with all the feelings that welled up inside of me every time a chubby-cheeked child showed up on my timeline? How would I watch my cousins and friends have babies and blow raspberries and travel to Disney World and know that I would experience none of it? Where would all the feelings go?

I hadn't realized I'd spoken out loud.

Jeremiah turned me around and took my face in his hands. Kissed my forehead. "*For now*, we'll put all the feelings here between. And we'll organize them, and keep the ones that fuel us, and mourn the ones that don't, and process the ones that maybe we can't let go of yet. I'm not saying we don't have children. I'm saying, your surgery wasn't even a year ago. Maybe there's more healing left for us to do."

"I never thought I'd be this woman, you know? It shames me sometimes. To be so dead set on a kid. It feels selfish to want something so bad. But I do. I do. I can't turn it off like a faucet. It's visceral."

Jeremiah hugged me. Rocked my body gently. "I love you and every form of woman you become and unbecome. I'm not shitting on your wants. I want a family too. I promise I do. And we still have a lot of avenues we can travel to make that happen. I'm just saying, *if* it didn't ever happen, 'us' would be enough for me. When I was a kid, I was loved simply because I existed. And then I came to art and New York, and it's all a world that wants you to prove you're worthy of creating an absolute single thing. With you, I don't feel like I need to accrue accolades or you'll abandon me. I just don't want a kid to feel like a thing I need to check off your list in order for me to be . . . I don't know."

Enough. Loved. I heard it even though he'd stopped speaking.

I didn't know if I could agree with him. Not about loving him, but about whether I would feel full contentment without a child. But I knew the words warmed something even greater than his body heat. As mami has been repeating for the last few weeks, *when* life and death happened was less important than *how* they came to pass.

"Let's go home."

He kissed my neck. "To make a baby?"

I shrugged. "Maybe. Wouldn't that be nice? But mostly, to make love."

"Thank God! Bring that ass! My nostril hairs have been tuned into you all night, and I thought you were going to make me beg."

MATILDE

did not move from the seat when El Pelotero came to sit by her. He looked good in slacks and the tucked-in shirt. And Matilde waited for flutters, but she felt nothing.

"The commute from Connecticut to Manhattan every other day has been brutal."

She did not know why he was saying this to her. "I'm surprised your parents didn't ask you to move in with them. I'm sure your father needs help with more than just his classes."

He nodded. "They did. But I think it's mainly Papi wanting to push his dream onto me. I don't want that."

Matilde tilted her head in understanding. Inheritances were difficult things to say no to. "He's spent years building up his program. And the showcase is right around the corner. I'm sure he doesn't trust anyone else to take over."

"Yes. Which is why I think the person who teaches the class should be someone who has that same passion for it as my father. Someone who has never missed a day. I suggested to him this evening that he let you take over."

Matilde opened her mouth, but El Pelotero stood. "Just think about it. I'm always happy to be your assistant if you have need of me. But who could be better at it than you?" And so, Matilde thought about it. About the direction she would take the showcase. About starting a class for children where she could teach little ones the steps. Of what it would be like to call this man to be her assistant every now and then so she could whirl in his arms. She asked herself if she wanted to do this, especially knowing she might be taking some of Yadi's work at the shop. And inside her, she knew exactly what it was she wanted.

FLOR

walked her daughter to the car. Ona was slightly drunk and listing onto Jeremiah. He gave Flor a conspiratorial wink over Ona's head. She liked Jeremiah; he called her on Wednesdays, he didn't care who gawked at him when he danced his Southern-influenced merengue with all the aunts.

"Nos vemos mañana, Mami," Ona whispered, kissing her on the neck.

Flor leaned into the car window after Jeremiah spilled Ona in. "You two want to come stay with me? I'll make big pan pancakes just like you like." It was the best bribe she could offer her daughter, who might have tried a lot of food in her life, but no pancakes quite like hers.

Ona shook her head. "Jeremiah and I have to get home. But I'll come see you tomorrow?"

Flor smiled, giving her daughter a kiss on her forehead, admiring the lipsticked stain left behind. "Si dios quiere, mi amor."

MATILDE

placed her key into the first lock smoothly. She touched two fingers to the Baby Jesus sticker and let the door slam behind her, her heels kicked off as soon as she got to the kitchen.

She commanded Alexa to play her favorite salsa playlist. It was too late to be playing music so loud, but dammit, she'd lived quietly in this building for years, and she had earned a night to be the one who made noise.

She felt like she could finally breathe.

From the kitchen, she grabbed three big black trash bags. In the bedroom, wearing nothing but her panties, she systematically went through Rafa's drawers. His underwear. His socks and shirts. The pants in the closets, the toiletries. The suits and button-down shirts would have to wait, probably. She went into the living room, taking down framed photo after framed photo. The light spots that had been behind the frames shone bright and new as the day the wall had been painted. The dust and grime that had collected around the pictures hadn't been noticeable before, but now the absence of pictures pointed out that sometimes starting clean meant returning to what was before.

When she was done, she opened the window that faced the street. She would have to do this in big heaves to avoid the fire escape.

Her titties swayed softly as she swung her arm back and forth to build momentum, then she tossed with all her might. The cold air felt good on her skin. The thump when the trash bag landed below her felt better. Any neighbors peeking out their windows would think her una loca encuera, but she didn't mind potentially having a new, less inhibited nickname.

Inside the apartment she locked the first lock, the second, then slid the deadbolt into place. Called to Alexa to raise the volume even higher. Music swelled.

She had half a second where she wondered about where Rafa might be. That she decided she would no longer care.

And when Matilde climbed into bed that night and picked up her phone, she only had one text to send. *Yes.*

YADI

knocked on Doña Reina's door a few minutes before midnight.
She was slightly drunk. Ant opened the door, in boxers and a
tank. He quirked an eyebrow when she held out a tray.

"I have enough for two."

He paused for a second then turned around, the door still
open. Yadi walked into his living room. His mother hadn't
changed a thing since the years when she had visited as a teen.
The couches were the same brown rose pattern. The fish tank
by the heater still had a flurry of tropical fish. For a second she
felt like she'd traveled back in time.

Ant returned from his bedroom in a T-shirt and basketball
shorts.

She heated up the platanos and rice, and they ate in silence.
When they were done, he collected both their plates and walked
to the kitchen. Then he walked back and sat on the couch, playing with the fringes of a cushion.

She sat on his lap. His hands stilled. *What do you want from
me*, she imagined him asking. She was asking herself the same
thing.

"I think I'm leaving. Back to DR. For a bit. There's something I find back home I don't have anywhere else in the world."

She looked at his eyebrows but not his eyes. He tapped her
thigh. "You always said you would."

"I'm sorry. I'm sorry I couldn't just fall back where we left. I'm sorry I didn't visit or write. It was all too much."

Now, the tap turned into a squeeze. "Be easy. Others called. And visited and wrote. I wasn't hoping you'd wait for me."

"You weren't?"

He shook his head. And she believed him. He was hard in his pants. But something else snagged her attention. "A lot of people called and sent letters?"

"Your mom let me know what was happening. My mom came up weekly. And you remember Mileiry, from Morningside Ave? Her brother was locked up with me. We saw each other at visiting once and we started emailing. Then when she visited him . . . she also visited me. She lives in Queens now."

"And you two became friends?"

Ant rocked her back and forth, his chin on her shoulder, his hand back on her thigh. "And we became friends."

"Just friends?"

Ant's smile in response was quick. And the ache in her heart was fast. *There* was the boy. Then his smile was swallowed up by a stoic face. *Here* is the man.

"I mean, we didn't do conjugal visits or nothing. Shit, Yadi! We became friends. And we are supposed to meet up at some point and see how that goes. But . . . I had things I needed to see to first. People I needed to give an opportunity to say goodbye."

And Yadi couldn't help that for the second time that night she wept. Ant cradled her close as she did. And he held her when they made love. And two hours later, when she got the phone call, he held her then too.

FLOR

when she got home, poured herself some mamajuana Camila had made for her years ago. She'd found all the hidden stacks of twenties she could before the wake and had left the envelope near the front door. Ona's name was on it, so it was clear that the three thousand dollars was for her. She'd thought about writing a letter, but what more did she have to say? Ona possessed everything Flor needed to leave behind.

The bath she ran was hot and full of suds. She didn't get in, only hiked up her skirt and put her feet into the water, pretended she was back, back home where the canal ran swiftly and cleaned all that dirtied them. The glass of spiced rum kept clinking against her teeth, and she couldn't prevent the giggle that bubbled up her throat. She turned the shower on too, and turned the showerhead into rain, the droplets like a waterfall.

She eased out of the dress. Pulled her panties down and entered the water naked as the day she'd been born. Water-dappled and glistening and after a while, wrinkled, as a babe being born. Her vision blurred. It was only then that she exited the tub, leaving the water running. She splashed across her floors, leaving wet footprints behind, crawled into bed without toweling off. Her vision dimmed in the corners despite her having left all the apartment lights on. With fingers that trembled she touched the little medallion Pastora had given her. Of course, Flor had done her studies for the nunnery well. In addition to fathers and family, San José was the patron saint of a good death.

Flor closed her eyes, the right side of her body numb. She tried to recite a prayer, the one her mother used to say with her as they kneeled before bed, when she'd been a child and the Divine had felt so close to her fingertips, but her mouth couldn't form the words. She felt a quick lance; already her body was untethering.

Flor gave way to the sleep. The scaled being waited for her.

It was too late to hear the doorbell. She never heard the hard rap on the door: Pastora knocking furiously. The footsteps that rushed away while a spare key was found at Matilde's. The way they rushed in, on quick feet, yelling her name

Flor Flor Flor Flor!

But Flor was already returned.

I

sat in the car, the music turned on loud. Jeremiah held my hand.

I saw Jeremiah looking right and left, driving as if he couldn't wait for our exit.

"Tonight . . . was overwhelming," he said.

I squeezed Jeremiah's hand. The New Jersey skyline beckoned, suddenly beautiful from this particular vantage point.

When we got to the house, I pushed Jeremiah onto the couch.

We got naked quickly. I was on top, Jeremiah's favorite position after doing leg day because he didn't have to strain any muscles. I liked it second-best because it offered a great angle for Jeremiah's hand and my vibrator. Jeremiah hungered for me always. As consistent as his heartbeat.

And this felt so good. His thrusts and my riding reducing my boastful vocabulary to the crudest, and from that most crude language to the first: the Spanish that softly slipped through a stripping away. I spoke Spanish most when I talked to my mother and when I fucked with purpose: distilled to my first tongue by both.

When Jeremiah came, and I had reached the shore of the waves that had carried me, I pressed myself into his neck. Pressing a kiss to the soft skin. He always smelled so damn good.

"I think you got your period."

The overhead fan had been blowing the entire time we were having sex, but the oscillation landed on my back in that particular moment. The warm glow ebbing.

"Huh?"

Jeremiah gave my ass a pat. Both a *there there* and a request for me to shift. I sat up.

"You feel like you do when you have your period. It feels different, more than just wet. I mean, more wet? Closer to watercolors than the usual oils?"

Jeremiah was calm, loose. Eyes still closed. Or he'd have seen the shock of it. The hand I pressed to the scar above my uterus. I was frozen in place, his softened dick wanting to slip out of me, but I bore down.

"Hasn't your period been irregular?"

I slid off of him. Usually I was careful to roll in such a way as to not stain the furniture; peroxide would get the blood out, but I hated the residue of a wet patch. This time, I rolled with abandon. Ran my open hand down Jeremiah's penis. Stood, wiggling all five fingers. There were only a few drops, more pink than deep red.

"My temperature has been all over the place, but it was still high this morning. It would have dropped if this was my period. This doesn't make sense."

Now Jeremiah sat up quickly. "Do you think something is wrong?"

But I held my fingers up to my nose. I'd known my blood's scent, metallic and pungent, since I was thirteen. I knew the cramps that accompanied the blood, the warning I got that let me decide the when of menstruation. The smell of life's possibility undone. But this was not that.

This blood was something different altogether. "I think, I wonder, maybe . . . it's implantation bleeding?"

Jeremiah took my hand in his and stared at my fingers too. "How will we know?"

The body will tell.

ABSTRACT

Collaged from that rumor of silk, that snippet of a poem I found behind your ear. I will have to make up the parts you could not tell me. On how to fortify my own heart, become this kind of monstrous despite—*and for*—those who love me. Collective memory. Here. I collected memory. I used these words to fold placeholders, come feast. This tongue tied like a centerpiece of wild Bayahibe roses. I used this imagination to marble your tombstone. I had to make up the parts you could not tell me. A myth for creation, a myth for death, a myth of a mother, a myth of a clothes hanger I dress with all the things you instilled, and all the things you barred behind your teeth. I teach myself how to forgive you. I make an altar of your name. Genuflect. You taught me: all of us are magic wrapped in skin. And taut with overwrought wonder, for the fleeting time we are beings, we would have to make her up: the woman we require to survive this world.

ACKNOWLEDGMENTS

Listen, two women put in THE WORK to make this novel a thing that others could read: shoutout to my editor, Helen Atsma, and my agent, Alexandra Machinist. Thanks for believing in this grown-folk book! Thank you for trusting my unorthodox process.

To the broader team at HarperCollins, and the team specifically at Ecco, thank you for how you cared; this book enters the world having been touched by so many thoughtful hands.

Kianny Antigua—I know this book is better for having had your eyes and voice to push the mother tongue along. Pa'lante, hermana!

Team Co-Work! Safia Elhillo & Clint Smith, this book would certainly not exist without our dedication to a pandemic writers' group and your close read three years later. There might be a book, but it would not be *this one*, which is richer for having had your hearts and guidance from the very beginning.

Naima Coster, querida. From our retreat, to your echoing support, to your tender read and response, thank you thank you thank you. Mil gracias no es suficiente. I'm so glad I get to write in the same time as you.

Julia Álvarez, Jacqueline Woodson, Angie Cruz, Deesha Philyaw, Kiese Laymon, thank you for agreeing to blurb this book and loving up on me. Y'all are giants. Thank you for shouldering doors open.

To my cousin Limer, I am so thankful for that day we got lunch and you not only coached me on how to make hard choices but then also proceeded to tell me, "I know the next book you need to write . . ." And here it is.

To my cousin Mabel, thank you for your generous read and thorough notes.

Mami Rosa, the stories you told me as a child and that you unfolded for me when I became an adult inspired a need to name the many ways women hold each other across generations. I esteem you beyond words. I hope to have you mother me in any life I am sent to live. For you, all the best emojis: my heart, my rose, my shrugs and hugs.

To my tías, thank you for granting me permission to fictionalize sensitive history and infuse characters with the most difficult and wonderful pieces of you.

Special thanks to Ona Díaz-Santin, who when I told her I was using her name in a book gave me the sweetest kiss on the forehead. My Ona dreams of having your wisdom! And to the librarian in Fort Smith, Arkansas, who in 2019 told me about how she inherited a taste for lemons—I thanked you then for letting me borrow that tidbit in advance, and I thank you now.

Gigi, the vulnerabilities you share with me allow me to tell better stories about the women I love. Thank you.

King, I felt you somersaulting and fist-bumping as I clicked keyboard keys; you are by far the best writing partner I have ever had.

Beloved: We did it, Joe! This book might well be my bravest, and I know I owe that to you. You've believed in my voice before any single thing was ever in print, and what more can I say? Cheers to all that we practice.

Ancestors: you showed up in the season of sorrow and carry me into the season of sweetness/ When I did not know the next word, or passage, or direction of this novel (of this life) you reminded me to return inward / Again / Then again / Praise! for your ever patient and present education / Praise! for how the questions I ask always find answers / I wish you peace and ease / Axé.

FAMILY LORE

ELIZABETH ACEVEDO

A READING GROUP GUIDE

A NOTE FROM THE AUTHOR

Dear Reader,

IS THERE ANY SINGLE ORIGIN STORY TO A NOVEL?
I could pick at so many different threads to explain how I arrived at *Family Lore*, and each one would be true, and each one would be incomplete. Perhaps the best and most unorthodox approach, but the most honest to me and how I write, would be to give some examples of the different streams of thoughts that grounded the novel; the confluence of these inspirational bursts and many more similar moments led to this amalgam of a book.

At some point in 2009, a few weeks before the live performance of my senior honor's thesis, I was walking over a bridge near Townsend Avenue in the Bronx. I thought about my Tía Margarita, whose apartment I was leaving. She'd arrived in the U.S. a few years before, and firecracker of a woman that she is, she wrangled New York into a city that did her bidding. She is tough and joyous, and the woman who acted as my Substitute Mami when I visited the Dominican Republic every summer as a child. She is the kind of woman novels should be written about. But thinking that led me to the fact that my mom is one of nine sisters, and each one of them has attributes, quirks, and contradictions that make them perfect fodder for an unput-downable story. At the time, I was still in undergraduate school, a spoken word poet who performed and had a fear of prose, and I had no idea what my trajectory as a writer would be, but I remember thinking: one day I will write a story in vignettes about my mother's sisters.

Let's drop into September 2019. I sit down at a restaurant with my cousin Limer. We've made it a point to love up on each other and keep each other well informed on family business, since as DC residents, we are the only two living on this side of the Delaware River. She's three years younger than me and decades wiser, and I often turn to her for advice, which on this day I especially needed. But before I could ask about a major career change, with our green curry and pad thai orders placed, Limer turned to me and said, "I know what you should write a book about." I abhor this sentence. Most people don't know what a book should be about—shit, most writers don't know what a book should be about. It's through the writing that the purpose for a story is discovered, not in a tidbit of gossip or random encounter. But, as I mentioned, Limer, like her mother, Tía Margarita, ain't no fool. And she proceeded to hip me to some family history she'd learned through the grapevine. I went home that day and knew I'd found the way into a character, and a moment in time, and a relationship that quickly usurped the anxiety I'd felt when I walked into lunch. I wrote four thousand words in two hours. To be clear, I didn't transcribe the exact scenario Limer had told me, bur while she'd been speaking, I cast an inner eye at the ways families hold secrets, tell one an-other's truths, and protect one another or harm their favorite people. . . . There was a texture I could feel in my cousin's conversation, my writer's mind reading the braille there and noting, *here there be story.*

At some point a few years back, I listened to a lecturer give a presentation on the way that funereal practices are changing. People are turning their ashes into seeds that can be planted to grow a tree, offering a different approach to limiting global warming. Some folks are making their caskets biodegradable. The practice of living wakes has started taking hold in small communities where the ill want a more formal way to say goodbye. In a different life, I would have been an anthropologist. I am moved by how humans create culture and tradition. The rituals and ceremonies that make us unlike other animals, that we pass down, turn away from, or rediscover. I listened to this lecture on the formalities of death without any thought that I'd ever write about it. I love being a student, and all I knew at the time was that human beings who are preparing for death come up with the wildest and most magical ways of dealing with their corporal selves . . . and with their loved ones.

In October 2020, I went to my primary care doctor after some uncommon menstruation patterns. I described my symptoms and lay back on the exam table as she pressed firm fingers into my pelvis and then proceeded to put my feet into stirrups so she could perform a vaginal exam. "Your uterus is heavy," she said. "I know it sounds odd, but it's the only way to describe it. Maybe you're carrying twins." My doctor is very kind to my often anxious self, and in this instance, she knew how hopeful I was at the prospect I might have conceived. "But I want to order an MCAT just to be sure." What I *was* carrying was a fibroid the size of a small orange, which made it difficult for me to sit down and had shifted my uterus into a funny uptilt, and was more than likely the cause for my inability to get pregnant. The surgery to remove the tumor that's implanted into the back of this particular baby-making organ was planned for the top of the following year.

And of course, I'm driven by language. I keep a notebook of words that strike my ear and ring like a boxing match bell. I listen to my mother with one antenna directed toward what she's saying and another perked at the way phrases translate into English or conjugate into double meanings. My mother-in-law and husband speak every day, and they fall into a family cadence that I am privileged to listen to; there's magic in the North Carolina idioms they use, what they say and don't say, and how the space in between speaks a world on its own. It makes me look at conversations with my own family differently, offers another lens with which to make sense of our patterns of disclosure, familiarity, and falsehoods. This too drove the beginnings to the story—the need to encapsulate moments in language where ancestral bonds blossomed or rotted.

There were so many more doorways that led to this book: while on tour, the librarian in Arkansas who told me she developed a love of lemons only after her mother passed; my best friend's creative and gratuitous descriptions of her alpha vagina; the memory of not being allowed to close the bathroom door in my aunt's house because she wanted to check my excrement for parasites. And . . . and . . . and. I wrote scenes and characters out of order, in what many organized folks might deem chaos, but I knew I was building and layering a story with each glinting bit of narrative, each one kick-starting the story anew.

Writing a novel, for me, is like writing this letter to you. I search through the bins of happenstances, vernacular, and human interactions, and I pull at the threads that make me curious, pained, or joyous. *Ah,* I say, *this one has a bold hue of truth that will hurt me to write but will gratify me to capture well. Oh,* I think, *this one is frayed—an old wound that will only heal through being thoroughly thumbed.* And then I weave. And weave. And weave again. I don't worry about what I'm making. I preoccupy myself only with: Is this true? Note, I am not saying "truth." *Family Lore* is not a factual novel or autobiographical fiction, and I was not aiming for either. My true north is only ever what is *true.* What shines emotionally true within this muddled, glittery, and imaginative human experience that I reveal to myself—and to you—through writing and rewriting.

Let's go back to the top. The impetus for *Family Lore* is past, present, and tomorrow; it's beauty, poetry, and our deepest fears. It's my kin—alive and ancestral—and my devotion toward writing my people in a way that is full of tenderness, integrity, and cutting honesty. It's my inclination to ending a chapter with the most precise image or snippet of dialogue, and my project as a writer to allow many points of entry into my work.

And so. I told you how it began. And began again and again. Convergences, like families, real or fictitious, are always messy.

With warmth,
Elizabeth Acevedo

QUESTIONS FOR DISCUSSION

1. Each of the sisters and nieces in *Family Lore* possesses a gift, with Flor's gift at the center of the novel—if she dreams about teeth shattering, has terrible jaw pain, or her own teeth chatter, she knows when someone will die. What lore or gifts have been passed down in your family? What are your thoughts on them?

2. *Family Lore* alternates between the Marte women's six distinct voices throughout the story, with chapters highlighting Matilde, Flor, Pastora, Camila, Ona, and Yadi. What traits about each sister are similar and different, and how does this affect their decision-making throughout the novel?

3. *Family Lore* weaves the past and the present, taking us from Santo Domingo and New York City over the course of three days and also seventy years. What differences do you notice between the first-generation and second-generation women in the text?

4. What roles do family land, herbalism, and natural food and ingredients play in this novel?

5. Each Marte woman has a different relationship with Santo Domingo: Yadi misses home while Pastora was traumatized by home. Discuss each sister's relationship to her ancestral land and how this plays out throughout the story.

6. Discuss the role of matriarchs in the Marte family and compare this to your own family. What similarities and differences do you spot?

7. Now compare the Marte matriarchs to their partners. What roles do these men play in uplifting and also disparaging their spouses?

8. "I was not born with a gift, and I never developed one in the ways of my sisters, whose uncanny senses of the world came from beyond. I cobbled together my own gift. Claimed magic where I'd be told none could exist. That is what dancing was for me. And it is as powerful as any second sight or inclination toward healing." Matilde is said to be the sister who "was not born with a gift" but "cobbled together" her own. Do you feel her dancing could be considered just as much of a gift as the other Marte sisters' gifts?

9. This book uses folk tradition to incorporate magical realism in the text. "My mother's magic . . . is not an orderly system like how fantasy novels can describe the exact structure of where and whence and thusly. The women in my family get struck by an unknown lightning rod." What parts of it felt real to you? All of it? Some of it? Now compare this to your own cultural traditions. Are there similar elements?

10. Soraya encourages Ona to research her own bloodline, yet Ona collects her family stories with no real intention of using them. What do you think Ona's research is motivated by, then? What are some creative ways Ona could turn her family's lore into something shareable? If you were in Ona's profession, how would you showcase your family history?

11. Throughout the text, Ona sprinkles in historical facts about the Latin Kings, Dominicans being descendants of Taíno people, Christopher Columbus, and the 1521 slave rebellion at the sugarcane estate of Diego Colón. Did you learn about this history growing up? If so, where did you learn it? If not, consider using this time to research these events and discuss within your group.

12. This novel shows different forms of self-care—Flor locking herself in the bathroom to lie in the tub and imitate the meditation she saw on television or putting on a mud mask once a week, and Ona going to therapy. How do the boundary and self-care practices and rituals mother and daughter exhibit change across generations, and how do they influence one another?

13. Do you relate to any of the characters? If so, which character best represents you and why?

14. The snake dream is a significant omen in this story. Discuss what it means and its importance.

15. Flor gives a compelling speech about her life at the end of *Family Lore* that raises the question of how we want to spend our lives. What does it mean to live well and die well? What kind of life do you want to live so that you can be okay about coming to terms with your own death?

More from award-winning author
ELIZABETH ACEVEDO

Unforgettable novels brimming with love, hope, and truth.

Quill Tree Books
An Imprint of HarperCollinsPublishers

epicreads.com